PRAISE FOR *LEVEN THUMPS AND THE GATEWAY TO FOO*

—◆—

A Texas Bluebonnet Master List Selection

Book Sense Winter 2006–2007 Children's Picks List

★ "Splendidly unpredictable plot twists. . . . [With] deliciously menacing monsters, equally delicious turns of phrase, and sly riffs on everything from pop music to Harry Potter, the author sends Leven Thumps and company on a long, strange trip, culminating in a literally explosive climax."
—*Kirkus Reviews*, starred review

"Excellent . . . palpable excitement and suspense. Kids and adults will enjoy this charming tale of good and evil."
—*Publishers Weekly*

"This rollicking, suavely told tale should captivate readers."
—*Bulletin of the Center for Children's Books*

ALSO BY OBERT SKYE

LEVEN THUMPS AND THE GATEWAY TO FOO

◆

COMING SOON:

LEVEN THUMPS AND THE EYES OF WANT

LEVEN THUMPS

AND THE WHISPERED SECRET

◆

OBERT SKYE

ILLUSTRATED BY BEN SOWARDS

Aladdin Paperbacks

New York   London   Toronto   Sydney

ALADDIN PAPERBACKS
An imprint of Simon & Schuster Children's Publishing Division
1230 Avenue of the Americas, New York, NY 10020
Text copyright © 2006 by Obert Skye
Illustrations copyright © 2006 by Ben Sowards
All rights reserved, including the right of reproduction in whole
or in part in any form.
ALADDIN PAPERBACKS and related logo are registered trademarks of
Simon & Schuster, Inc.
The text of this book was set in A Garamond.
Manufactured in the United States of America
First Aladdin Paperbacks edition September 2007
2 4 6 8 10 9 7 5 3 1
Library of Congress Cataloging-in-Publication Data
Skye, Obert.
Leven Thumps and the whispered secret / Obert Skye; [illustrations Ben Sowards].
p. cm.
Summary: While Leven, Winter, and sidekicks Geth and Clover battle fantastical
creatures in Foo, contrary forces in Reality plan to reconstruct the destroyed
gateway between the mythical Foo and their own land.
ISBN-13: 978-1-4169-4718-9
ISBN-10: 1-4169-4718-3
[1. Fantasy.] I. Sowards, Ben, ill. II. Title.
PZ7.S62877Lew 2006
[Fic]—dc22
2005035572

To the few who let me fall and then
offered me a way of redeeming myself.
May my words help the cause.

LEVEN THUMPS

AND THE WHISPERED SECRET

CONTENTS

PROLOGUE
TAKING CHARGE xv

CHAPTER ONE
LET 'ER RIP 1

CHAPTER TWO
WEDGIE 20

CHAPTER THREE
THORN IN THEIR SIDE 31

CHAPTER FOUR
CHEW FOR YOUR LIFE 40

CHAPTER FIVE
AND THEN THERE WAS SORROW 53

CHAPTER SIX
THE UNLIKELY COG 61

CHAPTER SEVEN
IT TURNS OUT THERE ARE DUMB QUESTIONS 67

CHAPTER EIGHT
THE RING OF PLAGUE 89

CHAPTER NINE
FRIENDS COME IN ALL SIZES, BUT USUALLY
THEY ARE BIGGER THAN A TOOTHPICK 97

CHAPTER TEN
ROYAL FLUSH 113

CHAPTER ELEVEN
HERE AND FOUL 122

CHAPTER TWELVE
THE WEIGHT OF FATE 128

Contents

CHAPTER THIRTEEN
LOOK BOTH WAYS BEFORE YOU
CROSS THE STREET 146

CHAPTER FOURTEEN
THE SWOLLEN FOREST BEFORE THE TREES 159

CHAPTER FIFTEEN
ICY RECEPTION 165

CHAPTER SIXTEEN
BLACKNESS GATHERS 173

CHAPTER SEVENTEEN
BUGGED 177

CHAPTER EIGHTEEN
THE ONCE-PERFECT BALANCE OF FOO 196

CHAPTER NINETEEN
AISLE SEATS ARE BETTER 204

CHAPTER TWENTY
SEPARATED AT BITE 217

CHAPTER TWENTY-ONE
BE CAREFUL WHERE YOU STEP 228

CHAPTER TWENTY-TWO
THE SPIRITED HITCHHIKER 232

CHAPTER TWENTY-THREE
WASHED AWAY 240

CHAPTER TWENTY-FOUR
I'M ON THE TOP OF THE WHIRLED 248

CHAPTER TWENTY-FIVE
BRIDGE TO NITEON 259

CHAPTER TWENTY-SIX
ENTERING MORFIT 272

Contents

Chapter Twenty-Seven
Snapped 286

Chapter Twenty-Eight
Signs o' the Time 295

Chapter Twenty-Nine
Throwing Fear 305

Chapter Thirty
Egyptian Silk 310

Chapter Thirty-One
Choosing a Path 317

Chapter Thirty-Two
Stolen 349

Chapter Thirty-Three
Echoes of the Blast 357

Chapter Thirty-Four
Door Number One 368

Chapter Thirty-Five
The Fuel of Feelings 385

Chapter Thirty-Six
Opening Your Eyes 389

Chapter Thirty-Seven
The Construction Begins 410

Chapter Thirty-Eight
The Calm 413

Afterword
The Whispered Secret 417

Glossary 423

INVISIBLE VILLAGE
RANT ARMIES
FTÉ
CINDER DEPRESSION
RED GROVE
HIDDEN BORDER
VEIL SEA
THE DEVIL'S SPIRAL
CUSP
THIRTEEN STONES
LITH
WET BORDER

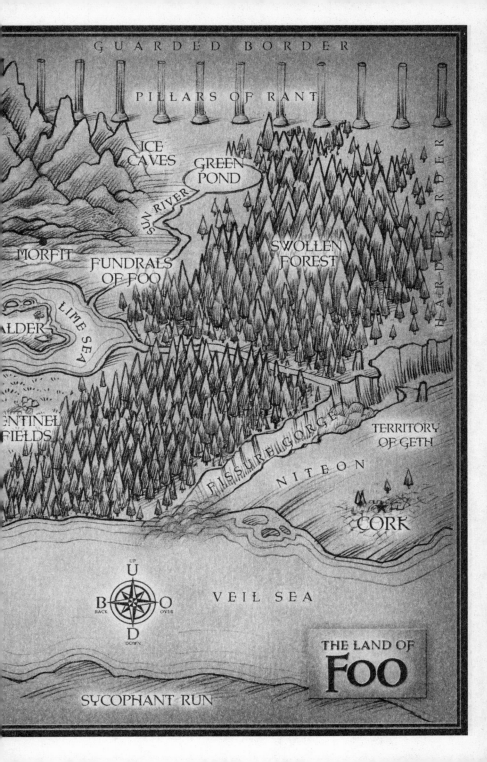

PROLOGUE

Taking Charge

Jamoon stood still, as stiff as a petrified plank in the dead of
winter, the blood in his veins pulsing slowly. The air inside the
cave felt brittle, like paper-thin glass that the slightest movement
would crack and split. He closed his gray right eye and exhaled
slowly, his frosty breath forming a foggy wreath around his robed
head. In his right hand he held a long, wooden kilve, a weapon
that harnessed power from dreams. He looked about but could
see little in the darkness of the rocky cavern.

Still, Jamoon waited. He inhaled deeply, drawing the frozen
fog back into his lungs.

"It's been hours," Jamoon complained. "Many hours."

Sabine and his shadows had left long ago to visit Amelia and
to try to find the gateway. Jamoon had been ordered to remain in

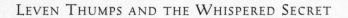
the cave and wait. He shifted from leg to leg and muttered to himself.

"Always second," he grumbled.

A Lore Coil had rippled over Jamoon hours before, filling his head with images and information. The explosion that had destroyed the gateway into Foo had created the Lore Coil—a wave of noise and images that radiated outward, traveling across Foo, feeding bits of information to anything it passed over. When the coil reached the borders of Foo, it would rebound and reverberate back to its epicenter, the clarity of its information weakening with each diminishing wave. Most inhabitants of Foo would not consciously perceive anything after the second pass—except for the Sochemists of Morfit, who spent their days listening for coils and debating the meaning of the information that continued to ripple across Foo.

Jamoon had detected the new Lore Coil on its first pass. He had heard the coil chattering about Leven Thumps, and Jamoon had seen an image of Winter. Jamoon had known Winter from before, and even though she appeared somewhat different in the static waves of the coil, there was no mistaking her green eyes. The coil had also spoken of Amelia Thumps and how she was now harboring Geth. The ripples of the Lore Coil hadn't clearly shown Geth's condition, but they seemed to indicate that he had somehow become small and vulnerable. Jamoon scowled, his half-heart filled with anger and fury. The hatred Sabine had felt for Geth was equally strong with Jamoon.

Jamoon had heard the waves of the Lore Coil exposing

Leven's condition, whispering that Leven and his band of friends had become susceptible to death. Leven had cheated fate by slipping into Foo through the gateway. Because of that, he could be killed.

That was good news. Unlike so many others who couldn't be killed in Foo, Leven, Winter, and Geth were vulnerable and could be eliminated.

"Foolish child," Jamoon said aloud, thinking of Leven.

The Lore Coil had also let Jamoon know that Sabine was still alive. Jamoon was both frightened and relieved by the news. He now stood still, dutifully awaiting his master's return.

Jamoon was a rant and very tall—well over six feet, with the right half of his body in the form of a strong and muscular human. His left side, however, was unstable, continually morphing into the shape of the dreams that someone in Reality might be experiencing. As a rant, Jamoon lacked the ability to resist or shape those dreams, and his constantly changing half was in perpetual conflict with his normal self. At the moment Jamoon's left-hand side had assumed the shape of a Brazilian soccer player, expertly dribbling a ball with that one foot. However, Jamoon's entire form was shrouded in a black robe, and the conflict he was experiencing was visible only in the constant gyrations underneath the thick fabric.

Jamoon was extremely uncomfortable, and as his right and left sides strained against each other, his body creaked in the frigid air. He shivered violently, the cold of the cave having seeped into the marrow of his bones.

His frosty breath ascended to the ceiling of the cave. "Come, Sabine," Jamoon whispered. "Where are you?"

In the distance a mournful howl sounded. It grew louder. Alarmed, Jamoon raised his kilve as if to fight. The noise became clearer, but the darkness kept it a mystery. Jamoon lifted his kilve higher and scratched its tip against the ceiling like a match. The friction made a shrill screech and caused the end of the kilve to glow. Jamoon quickly used the white-hot tip to draw a circle around himself on the floor of the cave for light. The completed arc glowed brightly, illuminating the walls and ceiling of the cave with pale images of old dreams that had been held in the kilve. In the light of the glowing circle Jamoon could see bits of black as they rippled across the ground. The blackness stopped outside the glowing circle, hissing and screaming as though tormented. Jamoon looked on in disbelief and shivered for a whole new reason. At his feet writhed the surviving pieces of Sabine.

"Master?" he questioned.

The black bits did not answer. The explosion of the gateway had blown Sabine apart, leaving nothing but a few hundred tiny specks of him in Foo. Those bits recoiled from the circle of light, back toward the entrance of the cave, compelling Jamoon to follow. Reluctantly, he stepped out of the light and dumbly obeyed, watching as the remains of Sabine snaked through the long, thick neck of the cave, weaving and sliding as though being controlled by some magnet below the soil.

Jamoon followed.

Sabine's dark remains exited the cave and swirled out into the open. The bright, square sun was just beginning to sink in Foo, and in the rapidly diminishing daylight, the surviving bits of Sabine were screeching angrily.

Outside the cave, just twenty feet away from its entrance, stood a fantrum tree whose branches were filled with nihil birds. The ugly fowls were frantically pecking at and devouring specks of old dreams. Those dreams had entered Foo, but upon leaving they had dusted the leaves and the ground surrounding the tree. The nihils were incredibly dirty birds. Black as rot, they did nothing but consume the residue of once-good dreams. They would peck feverishly at trees and soil until the branches were devoid of leaves and the ground was barren. Their call sounded remarkably like a wet cat being wrung out by someone with very large hands. As pestlike and insignificant as they were, this particular gathering of nihils was about to become something much more bothersome and significant.

The leftover bits of Sabine screamed and writhed on the ground, the noise attracting the attention of the nihils. Instantly, every last filthy bird swooped down and began to feast greedily upon the few remaining tidbits of Sabine.

Jamoon gaped in horror at the frenzied sight, his good right eye twitching uncontrollably.

"Foul!" the soccer half of him hollered.

Jamoon stamped at the ground and swung his kilve, but the nihils were not afraid. The birds simply scattered and immediately took to the sky, circling Jamoon in the dusky light of fading day. In a few moments all the nihils had finished eating and were soaring high overhead, their raucous calls creating an ugly din in the gathering darkness.

Jamoon looked to the soil but could see nothing remaining of Sabine. He shivered as the disappearing sun withdrew its warmth and the nihils continued to circle, swooping lower with each pass. Soon the birds were inches above Jamoon, hovering around his robed head. Jamoon looked up as the ugly birds began to falter in their flight, losing control of their wings and fluttering desperately. The birds belched and screamed in pain. Apparently they had eaten something that didn't agree with them.

The Sabine in them was taking a toll.

One by one and ten by ten the nihils plummeted to the ground, landing with dusty thuds. Jamoon covered his head as the flock of dead fowl rained around him. In a couple of minutes every last one of them had collapsed, heaped around Jamoon like a pile of matted fur.

Jamoon brushed one of the soiled carcasses off his head and shoulders. His breathing was heavy, and he could smell the stench of the dead nihils. He looked around.

"Sabine is dead," he whispered, and a thin smile appeared on the right side of his mouth.

The soil beneath the dead nihils hissed.

"Goal!" the left half of Jamoon yelled.

The soil hissed again, and the dead bodies of the nihils began to flutter and twitch. The spastic motion continued for a few moments, after which the dead birds began to rise. The nihils were very much expired, but thanks to their fermenting final meal, their dark bodies were moving.

Slowly at first, then more rapidly, hundreds of dead black birds rose from the ground. They beat their wings and took to the air, screaming and swirling in a dark cloud about Jamoon's head and hovering over him. There was no soul in them, but the final evil traces of Sabine caused their muscles and wings to still burn and react.

Jamoon pointed toward the birds and moved his right hand forward. The nihils moved as instructed. Jamoon lowered his hand, and the dead birds swooped to the ground and began to tear at the soil with their talons, furiously clawing at the earth.

Jamoon raised his hand, and the nihils rose and circled in a large black cloud behind him.

Jamoon liked the feeling of power. His right side smiled. Sabine was dead, but in his dying he had given Jamoon a powerful tool in the fight to merge Foo and Reality. Jamoon had the loyalty of the many armies of rants and those who fought to escape. Jamoon also possessed the secrets and traditions Sabine had instilled in him. He was a rant, but Sabine had shown Jamoon great things. Sabine had trusted him more than he trusted any other, and Foo knew this. Those in dark power would have no trouble aligning themselves with him. Jamoon could continue the battle to mesh his world with Reality, to take the power and gifts of Foo and rule the physical world, a world that wasn't even aware of Foo's existence or of the sacrifices of its inhabitants. Jamoon believed that if Foo and Reality were merged he would finally be whole.

"No longer second," Jamoon breathed.

Jamoon turned back toward the cave, motioning the dead nihils to follow. The hordes of tattered and filthy-looking birds obeyed his will and swirled about him. Their obedience gave Jamoon a feeling of great confidence and power. It was as if he were soaked in the wicked essence of Sabine.

Jamoon moved into the cave and down toward the deeper tunnels and caverns where the roven farms were. He needed to send the rovens to take care of Leven and Winter. He also needed to rally the Ring of Plague to help him find and destroy Geth.

The battle for Foo was far from over.

CHAPTER ONE

LET 'ER RIP

A thin, yellow light trickled through the window, lighting the room like a funeral parlor or like a restaurant wanting to hide its uncleanliness and save on electricity. Framed by the room's only window, a giant cube of sun melted in the purple sky and large, oval-shaped flocks of Tea birds cawed and whistled through the air as they returned to the Swollen Forest. In the distance, Morfit's highest mountain jutted above the horizon, its twin black peaks ringed by thinning patches of marsh-colored hazen, looking like two burnt fingers wrapped in dirty gauze.

Most residents in Foo were settling into their homes and hideaways, preparing to receive the incoming dreams night would bring. The air was quiet and dry, and the last whistle of the Tea birds faded. The trees had folded their branches and tucked their crowns down, like reprimanded soldiers who couldn't bear to look their commanding officer in the eye. As

the landscape dimmed, Foo felt empty, showing no signs of life.

Amelia Thumps stood inside her home, gazing out the window at the darkening view of Foo's sleeping countryside. It was beautiful, and the evening felt as inviting as a warm bed after a long day. But Amelia knew it was not entirely peaceful. She could see there was no one about and nothing happening; still, she could sense something brewing on the horizon. She pushed her thick glasses up on her old, prunelike nose and sighed.

"So silent," she murmured to herself. "So quiet."

Amelia felt certain that if she were to sneeze, it would be heard as far away as Cork.

Amelia looked out the window with purpose. She had experienced enough in her life to know when things were about to change. She shook her head, wishing she could shake off the bits of dread in her heart.

"I'm too old for this," she muttered. "Much too old."

As Amelia stood gazing out the window, Leven was sleeping soundly a few feet away. The room was large, with clean, clay-tiled floors. Heavy, dark beams of wood spanned the ceiling, and the fire in the large stone fireplace was casting dancing shadows onto the walls. In the center of the room was a beautiful table that Hector Thumps had crafted many years before out of the wood of a fantrum tree. Amelia reached out and lovingly ran her hand along the edge of the table.

"Hector," she whispered, the touch of the wood reminding her of the husband she had lost so long ago.

Amelia sighed deeply and bent forward with her shoulders

slumped. Her old bones whined like ancient hinges on a heavy door.

Amelia looked at Leven.

She had always supported the dreams of mankind, but now she was having second thoughts. For the first time in a long while she felt that she had something she could lose.

Winter's soft snoring pulled Amelia from her thoughts. The young, wild-haired girl was sound asleep, lying on a long, feather-covered bench at the opposite end of the room. Amelia glanced again through the window and then turned back into the room, her face solemn and drawn, like a horse that had just learned the world was out of feed. She looked down at the thin sliver of wood lying on the large table. Stepping over, she bent down and poked it with her finger. The sliver awoke, blinked, and smiled up at her.

"A toothpick, huh?" Amelia said. "The great Geth now a needle of wood."

"I was as surprised as you are," Geth yawned. "Fate took me where it would."

Geth sat up and stretched his two thin arms. He flexed the tiny fingers Winter had carved for him and patted his pointed head. He blinked his eyes and looked down at the body and legs fate had given him. He was a toothpick, but he was here.

"It's not going to be easy," Amelia said sternly. "Getting you restored. You know, I hate to say it, but it might not be possible."

"Don't be foolish," Geth responded.

"Reprimand the young," Amelia said, waving him off. "I'll always speak my mind. The truth is, they will hate him like they hate you. The second Leven steps out of here he will have many enemies. The good cower in fear while the selfish move forward with the unraveling of Foo. And you will be sought after by many. Sabine might be gone, but Jamoon will never let you be restored to everything you were."

"We'll make it," Geth insisted. "You know the end. A person as stubborn as you would have nothing to do with this if you did not believe in the end."

Amelia was silent for a moment. Her eyes, looming large through the deep lenses of her heavy glasses, looked pitch black.

"They have been stealing gifts," she finally said.

"What?" Geth said, opening his small eyeholes as wide as he could.

"I have seen many who have had their gifts stolen," she whispered. "Sabine's desire was to transfer the gifts, but I don't think they have that part down yet. Some nits give their gifts up freely for the promise of being left alone."

"I don't believe it," Geth declared, his soul tightening.

"Believe it," Amelia said quietly. "There is talk of Winter having been involved with some of it during her studies with Sabine, years ago."

"Any help she gave Sabine was inadvertent. I know her soul," Geth said. "Look what she's done for Leven."

"I'm just reporting what I hear," Amelia said. "So, does Leven know about his . . . condition?"

"He has no idea," Geth replied.

"He will soon," Amelia said. "I think the destruction of the gateway created a Lore Coil. There is a great silence out there, as if a strong coil has passed over."

"Then we must travel fast," Geth said. "I have to get to the turrets and be restored."

"And Winter?"

Geth looked toward Winter as she slept. "She cannot be restored. Without Antsel, it's impossible."

"I never thought I'd hear you say that word," Amelia smiled. "Your time in Reality seems to have changed you." She looked at Geth closely. "You do seem different."

"I'm just as I was," he insisted mildly. "But I have to tell you . . ." Geth stopped talking and looked carefully around the room. "Clover?" he called softly. "Clover?"

Amelia looked about as well.

"Clover, I know you're here," Geth said, narrowing his eyes.

Clover appeared, red-faced and clinging to Amelia's arm. He was about twelve inches tall with gray hair all over his body except on his elbows, face, and knees. He wore a shimmering robe and a constant expression of mischief. His big blue eyes shone brightly in the dim light, and his leaflike ears fluttered softly. Leven was his burn, and he was a sycophant, one of the most important and magical things about Foo.

"I wasn't listening," Clover promised. "I thought I saw something on her shoulder." Clover brushed Amelia's sweater. "I'm sure it was just a bit of lint or something. I guess you're not big on housekeeping."

Geth and Amelia stared at him.

5

"Oh, all right," Clover admitted. "I heard you mention Antsel, and I couldn't help listening."

Geth smiled, then whispered, "Listen, we've got to get to the fire in the turrets. I must be restored. We can gain the advantage if all that was taken from me can be reclaimed. But if a Lore Coil has communicated our condition, we could be in for a challenge. We can only hope that Jamoon's forces misunderstand or don't receive the message. We cannot—"

Geth was interrupted by a loud wailing noise coming from outside. High above Amelia's home the sky screamed, sounding like every key of an organ being simultaneously pounded. Clover disappeared, and across the room Winter stirred slightly.

Pwwwwump! Skarrrrettt!

Something heavy fell onto the thatched roof, shaking the entire home.

Pwwwummp! Pwwwummp!

There was another thump and another thud and another bang. The noise was followed by the sound of violent scraping and scratching from above. Broken bits and pieces of the ceiling began to rain down. Winter awoke and sat up. The long-sleeved blue shirt and jeans she had on were covered in debris. Winter's green eyes were as wide as lily pads.

"What's that?" she cried, pointing at a huge hole in the ceiling where thick, leathery claws were scratching and ripping their way in. Winter looked at Leven, who remarkably was still sleeping on the couch.

"Lev!" she yelled. "Lev!"

The fire, which had only moments before been singing to Leven, began to echo Winter's scream like a trained parrot. "Lev! Lev! Lev!"

Other giant holes appeared all over the ceiling as numerous claws tore through the wooden roof. Amelia grabbed Geth from off the table.

"Looks like they've heard you're here," she said, shoving the great king behind her right ear. "We can't let them find you." She ran toward Leven, but a giant roven dropped down from the ceiling, landing in front of her and blocking her progress.

The roven was huge and hairy with wide copper wings. It had large, swirling eyes and a thick, hooked beak. Screaming at a decibel level unsafe for most eardrums, it grabbed Amelia's arm with its talons and tossed her aside. She landed in a heap on Leven.

Confused and still half asleep, Leven struggled to sit up as Amelia tried to lift herself off of him.

"What's happening?" Leven asked.

"The rovens are here," was Amelia's only reply.

Leven looked around, not certain if what he was seeing was real or a dream. He was new to Foo and still unsure of what to believe. The white T-shirt he had bought in France and his blue jeans were rumpled from the small amount of sleep he had gotten. He touched Amelia's couch with his hand, trying to convince himself he was awake.

Unfortunately, he was, and it was *raining* rovens.

The large, hairy beasts poured through the holes in the torn-up

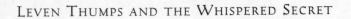

roof and ceiling by the dozens. They had different colors of hair and long, thick, talonlike fingers. They flapped their coppery wings and cawed like a murder of mutated crows. Some were roosting on Amelia's furnishings, while others surrounded Leven and Amelia on the couch, pressing their heavy bodies into them. Winter was on the opposite side of the room, boxed in a corner.

The fire was screaming.

A fine silt of wood and grass from the demolished roof filled the air. Winter counted the rovens and focused her glance as if to work her gift. Unfortunately, fate had other plans. A thick wooden beam dropped from the ceiling, knocking Winter in the back of the head and sending her sprawling onto the floor.

"Winter!" Leven yelled, as a roven seized him by the arm.

Amelia pushed through two big rovens, yelling, "Stop this!"

The rovens cawed menacingly as Amelia knelt down by Winter and checked for life. Winter was breathing, but she was out cold.

Amelia threw a frightened glance at Leven.

A few of the larger rovens leapt back up to the ceiling and began to bite and tear and pull at one of the biggest openings. Moments later they dropped down and backed away.

Leven was looking up at the opening, peering through it at the purple sky, when his view outward was suddenly obscured by the shadow and shape of a giant roven descending into the room. Leven had never seen a roven before, much less a roven of such massive size. The menacing creature was more than twice Leven's height, and its huge, copper wings grew directly from its shoulders

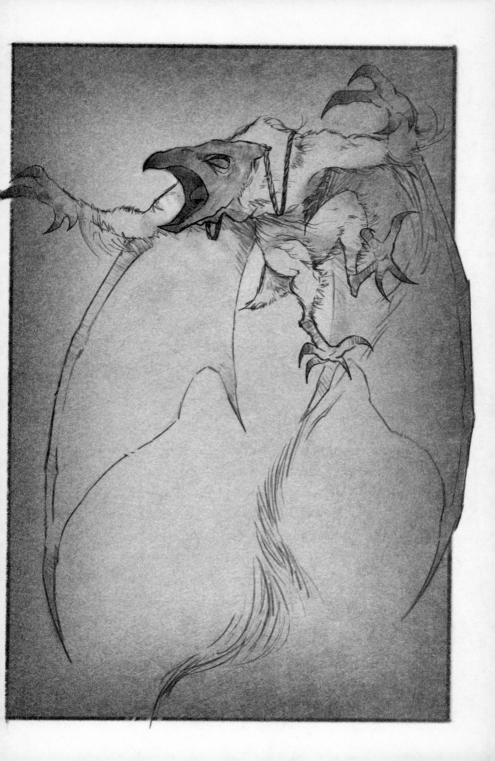

and along its gigantic arms. The wind from its thick wings swept through the room as the roven settled itself. Its entire body was covered with bright orange hair, and a pair of small, hooded, yellow eyes glared out from its fierce-looking face. The hair covering its body was so bright, it was hard to look at it directly. Braided around the roven, like a loose harness, were two thick, leathery bands that crossed in an X in front. The roven's chest was thick and wide like an ape's, but in every other point the creature resembled a mutated raven.

As the giant roven settled heavily onto the floor of the cottage, the other rovens in the room all lowered their heads in deference and spread their wings wide in a bow. The ugly leader opened its beaklike lips and emitted a triumphant bellow, then closed its huge mouth with a resounding clack.

The fire fainted.

Leven was shaking. He had stepped into Foo with the hope that things would be calm and safe. What he was staring at now was anything but.

"Look at my roof," Amelia demanded, talking to the rovens as if they were just a gang of bothersome kids who had cut across her prized lawn. "I'm not fixing that. And what have you done to Winter—"

The orange roven turned on Amelia and roared, distorting the old woman's lips, nostrils, and wrinkled forehead with the force of its cry.

Amelia pulled Winter into her lap.

The lead roven sniffed loudly. It beat its wings and turned to face Leven. It screeched in Leven's face, giving Leven a good whiff of what it had eaten earlier. Judging by the smell, that was something meaty and well past its expiration date.

The roven strutted around in a circle and flapped its wings. It peered under the table and behind furniture, as if searching for something. After a couple of minutes it turned back to Leven, roaring menacingly and covering Leven's face with spit.

Leven was too frightened to even wipe it off.

The orange roven bellowed again and flapped its mighty wings, signaling the rovens around it to move into action. Like robots they arranged themselves into two lines, one along either side of the large room, pushing any furniture out of the way and creating a barrier between Leven on one side and Amelia and Winter on the other. The speed with which they moved and the precision of their formation was amazing, and Leven watched in awe as each found its place and stood at attention. Those rovens who couldn't find a place in the room began to scratch and scream and push out into the open, extending the line outside the house.

Leven dashed from the couch and broke through the line of rovens. The big birds were too occupied with getting into formation to pay any attention to him. Leven knelt down by Amelia, who was sitting on the floor, holding the unconscious Winter in her lap.

"What are they doing?" Leven gasped, his body shaking. "There are so many."

"They're diggers," Amelia spat.

"This could be interesting," Geth whispered, speaking up from behind Amelia's ear.

Once they were all lined up, the rovens began to dig furiously at the ground. There were hundreds of them, and their sharp, leathery talons ripped through the flooring of Amelia's home and into the rich soil as easily as a child spooning a trench in a sandbox. Dirt flew everywhere as the rovens' talons spun violently. The trench they created was long and deep, and in a few moments most of them had dug so far down Leven couldn't see them.

The giant orange roven was still in the room, its yellow eyes trained on Leven and its wide copper wings stretched out as if to hide the chasm the rovens were creating. It glared at Leven, smiling as wickedly as its beaklike mouth would allow.

Leven needed his gift of seeing and manipulating the future to kick in. He tried to clear his mind and get an idea of what was happening. If he could see what was coming, he thought he might be able to manipulate it to his advantage. It was a nice idea, but it was too late. His eyes stayed brown. Besides, the danger was now, not in the future, and there was nothing any of them could do about it.

Finally, the orange roven clamped its wings shut, stepped backward, and dropped down into the trench the others had dug.

All noise faded as the roven disappeared.

Leven looked at Winter. Her eyes were closed, and her breathing was shallow. Her blonde hair hung wildly around her pale face. Leven shook his head; he couldn't seem to focus his thoughts. He had entered Foo with the understanding that it would be a marvelous place filled with endless possibilities. He had thought the main challenge would be to get here. Now, as he looked around, he felt just the slightest bit misinformed.

The air remained still. For all the fuss and fanfare the rovens had made dropping in, it now seemed as though they had simply dug themselves into the earth and vanished.

Leven was amazed at the size of the trench they had created. It was as wide as the room and extended in both directions out either end of the house. Leven could see the large table that had once been in the middle of the room teetering on one edge of the gap.

Leven fell to his stomach and began to inch closer to the large trench the rovens had dug.

"Shouldn't we be running away instead of crawling toward it?" Clover asked, materializing on Leven's back as he crawled.

"I don't—" Leven reached the edge of the trench and stopped talking. Looking down, he groaned deeply.

There was no sign of any rovens, and the trench was so deep and so dark that Leven couldn't see the bottom. Clover jumped off Leven's back to stand beside him, and the two of them peered into the abyss. They looked to the left where the dark void stretched out as far as they could see. They looked to the right and could see no end of the trench in that direction, either. It reminded Leven of a thin, dark, evil version of some huge, un-grand canyon.

"This can't be good," Leven said breathlessly.

Clover leaned forward over the edge, staring into the darkness.

"Dumb birds," he spat. "I have half a mind to jump down there and sink my teeth into them. Who's going to clean up this mess?"

Amelia shifted Winter from her lap and crawled over next to Leven. She peered over the edge with Geth still behind her ear.

"Fascinating," Geth observed.

All of them gazed down into the endless dark.

"Maybe we should . . ." Leven began.

Leven wasn't going to say anything profound or offer up any real solution. He was simply going to suggest something like, "Maybe we should back up," or, "Maybe we should get away from the edge before anyone falls in." But, for all any of the others ever knew, he may have been about to say something that would have been wise and useful, an observation they could have used to buoy their spirits and work toward a hopeful solution and a plan of action.

Either way, it didn't make a difference.

Leven's words were interrupted by the guttural screeching of hundreds of rovens streaming up from the deep, dark crevice they had dug. The large fowls erupted from the darkness like a geyser of colorful, howling demons.

Leven, Clover, Amelia, and Geth didn't even have time to turn away before the rovens were right below them, latching onto the sides of the trench and clinging to the walls.

Leven spotted the huge orange roven. The beast's yellow eyes glowed with hate as it looked directly at Leven and screeched one last time. Then the wings upon the rovens' shoulders and arms began to shift and spin. They whirled together, creating a tremendous fan. Their spinning wings propelled them forward against the sides of the trench they were clinging to. The thrust of their wings was so great that the trench began to expand. It took Leven a moment to realize what they were doing, but before he could inform his friends, Geth hollered, "They're widening the rip!"

The ground groaned as it was being wrenched open, and Amelia's house began to splinter and break apart. Leven felt the soil crumbling beneath him as the walls of the trench collapsed and the ground began to slough off into the chasm. Leven and Amelia each grabbed one of Winter's hands and dragged her through a collapsing doorway into Amelia's small, ivy-covered kitchen.

The kitchen was made of stone, with rock counters and green, mossy growth on all the walls. A large window above a sink showed off the now-darkened landscape of Foo. As the house vibrated, the wooden bowls on the counter rattled to the counter's edge and fell to the floor with a resounding clump, and the kitchen walls began to buckle. Everything was out of focus and jiggling.

The fire in the fireplace regained its strength and began to scream in fear, wrapping itself around any beam or structure it could reach. As it screamed, it emitted fat puffs of smoke.

The large window above the sink blew inward, showering them in a storm of glass. Winter was still out, and the glass littered her hair like diamonds as Leven and Amelia held her up. The floor in the kitchen began to tip and slide toward the rovens' rip.

"We have to get out of here!" Leven yelled, dusting crystals of glass from his forearm and wishing the gateway were still accessible so they could simply return to Reality.

They turned to run, holding Winter's arms, but were stopped by the appearance of more rovens standing in formation behind the lead orange one. As Foo continued to shake, the rovens pushed into the kitchen. Fire lit the scene behind them, and Leven could taste the smoke and dust that hung in the air.

The lead roven looked directly at Leven and screeched.

Behind the rovens and through the kitchen door Leven could see what looked to be the entire landscape sliding violently into the gigantic rip the rovens had created. The fire screamed as part of it was dragged down into the trench.

The noise was deafening. Leven stumbled, trying to find his footing, barely able to stand due to the shaking of the ground.

"They can't kill us, right?" Leven yelled to Geth. "There's no killing in Foo?"

"There are things worse than death," Geth yelled back, offering no comfort whatsoever.

"Some wisdom!" Clover screamed from Leven's right shoulder.

"They're trying to suck us into the chasm they've created," Amelia yelled. "We'll wish we were dead if the gunt gets us."

Leven could think of few things worse than being trapped in the pit the rovens had just torn. And gunt? He didn't even want to know. Leven had spent so little time in Foo that his mind was not yet capable of imagining some of the brilliant and clever and amazing things Foo and its inhabitants could be capable of.

The orange roven threw its head back and flapped its huge

wings. It screeched like a heavy train throwing on all its brakes at once. The rovens beside it did the same. They shook and convulsed in an uneven dance, their wings spinning, their faces puckering in pain. Two seconds later the thick, colorful hair upon their bodies began to fall out in clumps. It dropped to the ground in patches and strips, exposing their white, naked bodies beneath. The hair piled heavily on the ground, surrounding their talons and creating colorful mounds all over the kitchen.

The lead roven continued to glare at Leven. It still seemed powerful, but it looked ashamed of its hairless body. It glanced away and quickly flapped upward through the now-missing ceiling and roof. The other rovens followed its example, pushing off the ground and out into the evening sky. The chasm outside the kitchen was still pulling everything down and under, growing larger every second.

"Watch out for the hair!" Geth warned. "If we're separated, get to the turrets."

Leven wanted to reach for Geth, but the piles of hair the rovens had shed began to swirl and rise, filling the air. Clover materialized, holding a comb. He threw the comb to Leven. Leven looked at the purple comb in his hand and wondered if his life could get any more confusing. He suddenly missed Burnt Culvert, Oklahoma. He missed his school and the normalcy of it. He even missed knowing that, as bad as tomorrow might be, he pretty much knew what was coming and had developed a way of coping with it.

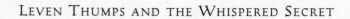
The hair the rovens had shed was swarming now, forming a thick cloud that was swirling toward Leven like a tornado.

"Part it!" Clover screamed, waving his own comb in front of himself. "Part it!"

There was no time for that. The hair was flying through the air and crawling across the floor. Thick handfuls surrounded Leven, smothering his scream, dragging him to the ground, and rolling him toward the edge of the chasm. The cloud of swirling hair pushed up his pant legs and down his shirt, filling his ears and nose. He felt as though he were being rolled up in a giant sheet of hairy sandpaper. Out of his right eye he could see Winter, still helpless, being dragged across the ground by another cloud of hair. He knew that Geth and Amelia were most likely experiencing a similar fate.

Hair filled Leven's mouth and gagged him, smothering his terrified screams. He was powerless to resist. He was going over the edge. He tried to yell again, but it was too late.

The entire house was sliding into the expanding chasm. The fire had gone from screaming to running, grabbing at anything it could hold. A roven got in the way, and the fire twisted itself around its neck, choking the life out of it and setting its wings aflame.

The remaining bits of house gave in. Walls tumbled and folded into the dark void as the rip swallowed everything near its edge. The great chasm was now a mile wide and growing longer and wider with each second.

Leven kicked and screamed, but the hair dragging him was too strong. The funnel cloud of hair carried Leven over the chasm's edge and down into the dark void. The hair then released its grip, flying off into a thousand different directions. Leven grasped at the air with his hands, desperately reaching for anything to halt his fall.

Winter! Geth! Clover! he thought.

It was pointless. There was nothing secure for Leven to grab onto. Everything within his view was being sucked down into the horrific rip the rovens had created.

There was no light. Leven could feel broken sections of Amelia's home and the soil it had stood on tumbling past him as he fell. The dirt tore at him, twisting around his torso. Leven's head bounced off the side of the chasm, and he could feel blood running down his face. As he tumbled downward, his body contorted painfully. Leven could see flashes of fire, and a great rumble filled his ears.

Leven relaxed his body, realizing that there was nothing and no force strong enough to stop him from falling deeper and farther down the chasm. Fate had brought him to Foo, and now fate had tossed him to a very dark end. Leven's head again bounced off the side of the chasm, and his vision began to go black.

He couldn't help feeling incredibly misled.

CHAPTER TWO

WEDGIE

It's not easy starting something new. Few things are more intimidating than walking into a brand-new situation and having to make the best of it. Maybe your parents moved during your ninth-grade year and you had to make new friends in a foreign country where everyone spoke a different language from yours. That's uncomfortable, and, as any well-meaning adult might say, "a character-building experience." But what if you feel like you already have enough character, and you don't want to leave all your friends and go to a foreign country with different money and food and a big school where the other kids ignore you and make you wish you were a treasure chest or a dog bone or anything buried deep beneath the earth and out of sight? What then? Well, you do as your parents tell you, and hope you don't perish from too much character development.

Foo was not new to Geth, and yet here he was in a new situation where he would be fortunate to come out with just a little more character and not something far worse. Sure, he was not one to worry; he was, after all, a lithen who trusted fully in fate.

But something was different now.

Previously, Geth had been a tall, strong, formidable leader, feared and respected by most of the inhabitants of Foo. At present, however, he was a little less strong, a good bit less intimidating, and totally ignored by most people—which was understandable, seeing how no one pays much attention to a toothpick.

As the huge rip opened up, swallowing Amelia's house and everything in it, Geth had somehow managed to get stuck in the side of the crevasse. His frail little toothpick legs were embedded in the wall of the great trench. He closed his mouth and eyes as a torrent of dirt and debris tumbled past him.

He couldn't hear much above the roar of the avalanche of soil, but as the sound died just a bit, he felt the wall in which he was pinned slip and begin to descend in one giant slab.

Fate was having some fun.

Riding the toboggan of soil, Geth slid down into the dark chasm. Finally his descent slowed, and the wall of dirt he was stuck in came to a stop. Geth lay there on his back, looking up at the dim light at the opening of the crevasse, far above him.

A large, dark object was sliding down the wall toward him. For a moment, Geth figured it was a roven whose wings had been clipped in the chaos. But two seconds later, the heavy object landed on him, smothering him. Geth could tell by the smell of lintwood perfume that it was Amelia.

She was out cold and on top of him.

Geth could barely breathe. He would have been fine with waiting for fate to show how clever and wise it was, but he knew that what he most needed now was to get out from under Amelia and find Leven and Winter. He wriggled his arms and did his best to poke Amelia as she lay on top of him. It took a little effort, but on the fourth try he was able to give her a pretty good jab.

Amelia moaned.

Two more jabs, and she was fully conscious and moaning in complete sentences.

"That'd better be you, Geth," she warned. "And if it is, stop poking me!"

Amelia rolled off of Geth and felt carefully around on the dark ledge. Her right hand found the edge of the shelf while her left hand located Geth. She pinched him extra hard as she pulled on him and popped his legs out of the dirt.

"I suppose I deserved that," Geth said.

Amelia brushed him off the best she could in the dark.

"I think I have an amber stick," she remembered. Reaching into her pocket, she pulled out a wooden stick about three inches long. It was rough on the ends and smooth in the middle. She slid her fingers along the smooth center of it, massaging a small bit of oil from the wood onto the thumb and middle finger of her right hand. Then she snapped her fingers near one end of the stick and it lit up, crackling and spitting. She snapped her fingers at the other end, and it too burned. The light gradually drew into the center of the stick, causing the entire thing to glow while remaining cool to the touch. She held the stick out over the chasm and peered downward.

"Wow," she whispered.

The rip the rovens had created was gigantic, and things were still settling. Of course Geth and Amelia had no way of determining just how long it stretched or how deep it went, but they could detect a low, buzzing sound way up above them.

"Do you hear that?" Geth asked.

"Locusts," Amelia answered. "Jamoon is probably using them to inform the whole of Foo that he's after you."

"We've got to get out of here," Geth said.

"How?" Amelia complained. "We're trapped."

The ledge they had landed on was thin at one end, but there was room to move around on the other end. Amelia moved to the wider part and snuffed out the amber stick. Geth worked his way up to her right shoulder and patted her gently on her large, wrinkled earlobe. He was glad it was dark.

"I've never known you to give up," Geth said.

"Give up?" Amelia sniffled. "People give up when they have choices. We have no choice. The gunt will be here soon."

"Fate has fixed worse. Let's hope the message the locusts are delivering falls upon more friends than enemies," was Geth's only reply.

Amelia was a bit dumbfounded. "You've changed, Geth," she said softly. "Where's the fire you used to have? Where's your anger?"

"I don't know what you mean," Geth answered.

"The Geth that Antsel took from Foo all those years ago was considerably more hotheaded. Sabine took your life and your city and all you had worked for. Where's your resentment, your anger?"

Geth was silent; if he had had a brow it would have been furrowed. Amelia's words seemed to impact him. He couldn't see himself very well, but he looked at his arms and legs and wondered at what he had become.

Geth thought back to Reality. He remembered being a tree and the restraint he had used to contain himself. There had been many days when he had wanted badly to wrap a root around the necks of Leven's sort-of parents, Terry and Addy, and strangle them for being so cruel to Leven. He recalled too how he used to flex and thrust his roots violently under the soil for miles just to let off steam.

And he thought back to his life in Foo before any of this had begun. He could remember his mission and his hatred and disgust for Sabine and for what Sabine wanted to do to Foo. He could still remember Sabine capturing him, and the pain he felt as his soul was extracted and put into a seed. He had felt nothing but hate. But Geth felt none of that now. He had been reduced. His desire to stop what was happening was as strong as ever, but there was no anger in his heart—no hatred.

"Interesting," Geth whispered to himself. "I hadn't thought about it."

His thoughts were interrupted by a faint voice yelling in the distance. Geth jumped off Amelia's shoulder and inched to the lip of the ledge. Amelia was still sniffling.

"Shhh," Geth said gently. "I think I hear Winter."

Amelia caught her breath.

"Geth! Leven!" the voice sounded.

"You've got a bigger voice," Geth said with excitement to Amelia. "Yell out."

Amelia moved cautiously to the edge of the ledge and peered down into the darkness. "Winter?" she called.

Winter was somewhere below them. They couldn't see her, but her voice was just loud enough for them to make out what she was saying.

"Are you there?" she yelled from down below.

"We're here!" Amelia replied.

"And Leven?"

Amelia looked at Geth, wondering what to say.

"Tell her the truth, of course," Geth insisted.

"He's not here!" Amelia hollered.

"He must have fallen farther down," Winter called back. "I'm going after him."

"No!" Geth and Amelia shouted simultaneously.

Amelia relit her amber stick and peered over the edge. She still couldn't see Winter.

"I can see your light," Winter yelled. "I'm on a ledge below you."

Amelia dropped the amber stick off the ledge, and it drifted down like a falling star about three hundred feet and then stopped.

"Thank you," Winter called, picking up the glowing stick. She held it up and peered through the darkness at her surroundings. Although far below Geth and Amelia, she still was nowhere near the bottom of the chasm.

Glancing downward, Winter noticed a shaft of light rising from the darkness and shooting toward her. Winter was startled. The light was white and cylindrical and filled with floating circles of color and waves of blue. When it reached Winter, it stopped and leaned toward her. Winter stood still and speechless, waiting for it to touch her. She shivered with excitement.

It had been over thirteen years since Winter had enhanced a dream.

The shaft of light touched her under her chin and quickly spread through her, illuminating her entire being. All at once she was alive in the dream of someone in Reality. It felt so warm and safe and normal that Winter wanted to cry.

The dream belonged to a young girl in Africa—a young girl without a father, who had just lost her cat. Winter took the dream and amplified it by opening her mind. She moved the images around and took away any uncertainty and made it familiar for the young mind dreaming it. She gave the scenes within the dream an unusual hue and pushed the edges out to fit greater amounts of hope and imagination.

Winter felt so alive.

Peering over their ledge, Geth and Amelia could see the dream touch Winter. They watched Winter as she manipulated the light. The bright glow radiating from her body lit up the chasm and revealed a thin ridge that connected the ledge Geth and Amelia were on with Winter's platform below. Amelia didn't waste any time. She shoved Geth behind her ear and jumped down the ridge, sliding clumsily toward Winter, digging her heels in the dirt to keep her from plummeting all the way down. Small strings of soil reached out at her, slowing her down as she slid.

Winter manipulated the dream until it began to fade. Then she pushed the light out of her palms and sent what was left of the dream back into Reality.

As her mind was clearing, Winter felt some clods of dirt tumbling down from above. She lifted her amber stick up to see Amelia sliding toward her. More dirt rained down on Winter. Two seconds later, Amelia landed with a thud on the shelf of dirt next to Winter.

"Are you okay?" Winter asked, helping Amelia to her feet.

"Fine," Geth insisted, peering out from behind Amelia's lumpy ear. "But we'd better find a way out of here. The gunt will be coming soon."

"Gunt?" Winter asked, having no recollection of what that was.

"To fill the rip," Geth answered. "There are borders to Foo. The gunt makes it impossible to dig yourself out. And the last place you want to get stuck is in its path. Many souls have been caught in the glue and trapped forever."

"Then let's hurry," Winter said nervously.

"Hurry how?" Amelia asked, rubbing her sore backside.

"We need to get to the bottom," Geth replied. "Once we hit the floor, we can run until we reach the end of this rip."

"What if there is no end?" Winter asked.

"We'll let fate figure that out," Geth said.

Amelia took Winter's hand and scooted to the edge of the shelf. She sat down, wiggling her rear in the soil and tying up her skirt between her legs. Grateful she was wearing jeans, Winter sat next to Amelia, and Geth hopped up onto Winter and made his way to the front pocket of her shirt. It was a position he was very familiar with.

"So we just slide?" Winter asked, holding the glowing amber stick out in front of them and staring off into the darkness.

"The wall looks sloped," Geth said.

"The wall looks sloped," Amelia growled. "That's easy for you to say—it's not your rear you're riding on."

A mournful cry sounded from behind them, dull, but audible.

"The gunt is coming!" Geth said loudly.

Amelia pushed off the shelf and began sliding down the narrow ledge. Winter followed her lead. The ledge, made of clay, was wet from the many streams of water running up the sides, and Amelia and Winter quickly began to pick up speed on the slick surface. Long, fingerlike strands of dirt reached out from the wall of the chasm, attempting to slow them down as they raced. Amelia and Winter were moving too fast for the dirt to have much effect. It was a wild, uncontrollable ride that ended when Amelia's dress snagged on a protruding root, pulling her to a sudden stop. Winter slammed into Amelia's broad back.

The dull sound of gunt was no longer dull, but thundering

and crashing. Winter looked up behind them and could see thousands of white, froggish blobs showering down. The mushy white blobs meshed together and swelled, beginning to fill the chasm.

"Let's go!" Geth hollered. "It's coming."

"What do you think I'm trying to do?" Amelia shouted, tugging to free herself from the root.

She pulled at her dress, but it wouldn't give.

The gunt showered closer.

Amelia bent forward and with her old teeth tore at the cloth and bit herself free. Then she grasped Winter's ankles and pulled her with her as they began to slide again.

The gunt was upon them, racing after them so swiftly it created a tremendous wind, which whipped at Winter's hair.

"Go!" Geth yelled.

They weren't fast enough. A huge, sticky frog glob flew into Winter and pushed her from the ledge. Winter would have fallen all the way to the bottom, but the gunt caught her by the ankles, and she hung there upside down on the wall like a fly in a sticky trap. A two-foot-thick waterflight was running up the side of the chasm, making the area where Winter hung a muddy mess. Amelia reached out to try to free Winter.

That was a mistake. As soon as Amelia touched Winter's ankles, her hands were instantly caught in the white, sticky gunt. She had no choice but to hang onto Winter as millions of gunt balls continued to fill the entire rip in the soil. Gunt was also rising from the floor of the chasm and getting closer.

"This is not good!" Winter screamed, still dangling upside

down against the wall, water and mud washing over her and Amelia.

Straining to keep from falling out of Winter's upside-down pocket, Geth gazed out at the cascading wall of gunt. "I hope Leven's okay," he said.

"What?" Amelia panicked, glaring at the toothpick as if he were crazy. "We've got to do something! I didn't wait all these years to be buried by a pile of gunt."

"It's in the hands of fate," Geth said nonchalantly.

Amelia was dumbfounded. She too was a believer in the power of fate, but she knew something was not right with Geth. He was not the person he had been when he was first captured. Then he had been the lead token of the Council of Wonder, motivated by his hatred for anything that sought to destroy Foo. Now here he was rolling over, instead of actively willing fate to work for him.

But none of that mattered at the moment.

The gunt was at hand.

Packed together, like thick globs of egg white, billions of frog-shaped blobs of gunt advanced, pressed together, creating a river of sticky ooze that poured down the walls of the rip, rapidly expanding to fill the void.

Winter watched as a wall of gunt taller than any building or mountain she had ever seen inched steadily toward them.

She looked up at the thick stream of water flowing up the wall. She glanced at Amelia, who was still stuck to her ankles.

Then Winter closed her eyes and triggered her gift.

CHAPTER THREE

THORN IN THEIR SIDE

Tatum Manufacturing was a big, diversified company. Its managers had their figurative hands and literal money in hundreds of products and ideas. Chances were that in a week's time most people in North America had either sat on, eaten off, or passed by some product that Tatum had helped manufacture.

Geth, of course, was the result of their wood division. It was Tatum that had taken the chunk of him that had contained his heart and turned him into the toothpick he was now.

Geth was appropriately grateful.

The shape he had been shaved down into had made him easy for Leven and Winter to transport, and it had kept him small and out of the direct sight of Sabine.

Yes, Tatum had helped fate well. If questioned, Geth would have nothing but positive things to say about the company that had carved up his heart and spit him out looking like the sliver he was now. But Geth might have felt differently if he had known what else Tatum had done. You see, when the large chunk of tree that contained Geth's heart had been tossed into the blades and cut down in size, fate had kindly preserved enough of the great king's heart intact to keep him alive and enable him to guide Leven to Foo. But the monstrous blades of Tatum's wood division were not quite as skilled and precise as, say, the hands of a well-trained surgeon. In fact, they were less precise than the fins of a poorly trained circus seal. What those imprecise blades had done was put the majority of Geth into one toothpick. But those machines had also trimmed a tiny part of Geth and put it into a separate toothpick. That toothpick had been packaged and shipped from Burnt Culvert, Oklahoma, to North Carolina, while the toothpick known as Geth had stayed in Oklahoma.

And whereas Geth was a traditional-looking toothpick, the small piece of heart shaved from him ended up in a less conservative, specialty toothpick. That specialty toothpick was then packed into a box labeled "Ezra and Son's Extra Fancy Party Toothpicks." The marketing line on the label read: "Perfect for picking at even the most prestigious parties." The toothpicks in those packages were extra long, with fringed plastic purple tops.

Well, no sooner had that package of Ezra and Son's Extra Fancy Party Toothpicks been trucked across the country and delivered to a large grocery store in North Carolina than Charlie Pork had purchased the pack of toothpicks and carried them to the small sandwich shop he and his uncle Telly ran just off Interstate 40.

It was in that box of toothpicks that this small portion of Geth now lay. Of course, it was no longer Geth. Like a kidney that you might give to a friend in need, this vital part of Geth had been removed and now belonged to a toothpick all its own. And whereas the Geth we all know was a noble being whose every desire was for Foo and fate, this toothpick was different. This toothpick had received the dark part of Geth, and it harbored nothing but anger and hatred.

And confusion.

It was as confused and dark as any toothpick had ever been. Of course, it wasn't hard to be king of that heap, seeing that there are so few toothpicks who feel anything at all. But as it lay there in that box, the world dark, with thoughts of anger racing through its wooden head, it grew more and more hateful and anxious.

Thanks to a ding, or an imperfection, in the side of its top, the toothpick could hear. His hearing was a bit muffled due to his purple plastic top, but on more than one occasion he heard the name *Ezra.*

"Throw me that box of Ezra's," Charlie Pork yelled.

"This box of Ezra's?" the help yelled back.

"Them Ezra's."

The dark, angry, and confused toothpick had a name.

Ezra was taken out of the box along with a number of lifeless toothpicks and laid in a small tray near the soda fountain. He couldn't see this, but deduced it when he heard Charlie Pork say, "Put them toothpicks in that small tray next to the soda fountain."

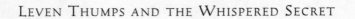

Every once in a while Ezra would feel a hand reach into the tray, fumble around, and withdraw one of the toothpicks surrounding him.

Ezra knew his time would come. He would be picked, and when he was, he knew what he must do. That part of him that had been taken from him must pay for the horror he now had to suffer. Geth had forced Terry to chop down their tree. Now, thanks to Geth's thoughtless act, Ezra was incomplete and felt nothing but misery. He was being tortured and had been left with the bad end of the toothpick. Ezra knew of no one to blame besides the one who had gotten the good part of the deal—the one who had taken everything else and left him with nothing but anger. He would find that one and finish him off in a way that would clearly express just how upset and wronged Ezra was. Ezra had only one purpose, one desire—and whereas on a shopping list one item might mean a quick in and out at the grocery store, Ezra's one item was going to take some time and some very bad fate.

Geth must die.

ii

Tim Tuttle sat silently at his dining-room table. His body was still, but his mind was racing.

Tim was about as average as a person could be. Stick him in a photo with a thousand other people his age, and he would be the last one to stand out or be spotted. He did have two larger-than-usual ears, and his chin looked a bit like a turtle whose head

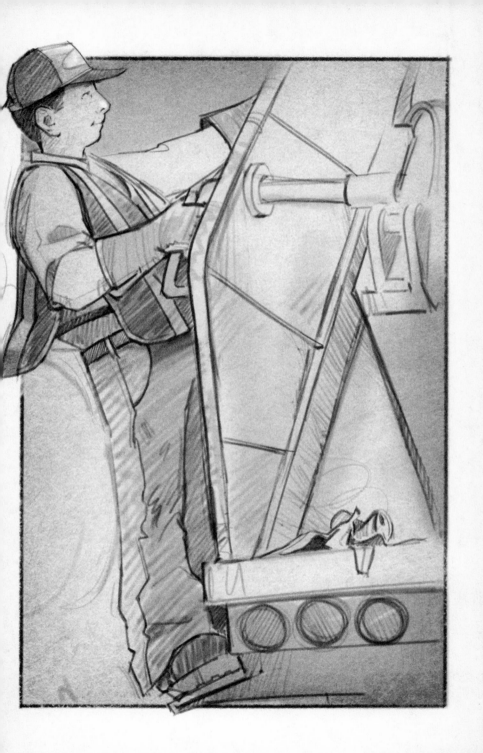

was constantly retracted, but those were his two most distin-
guishing features. Aside from that, his five-foot-ten stature,
brown eyes, white teeth, regular nose, and all the other bits and
pieces that make up a fairly normal thirty-nine-year-old man
were unremarkable.

Tim Tuttle—an average man with an average job.

Tim had been a garbage man for over twenty years. Some
might argue that he wasn't living up to his potential, but those
arguing that should know that Tim loved his work. Why?
Because it gave him the opportunity to think. He had all the
time in the world to ponder. And, while collecting cans and
dumping trash, Tim was always thinking. He had in fact
thought of many great and marvelous things and had fabricated
countless machines and toys from the discarded trash of others.
But he had also pondered the meaning of life as he hoisted rotting vegetables into the bins, had formulated the answers to the
world's most difficult riddles as he piled old newspapers into the
trucks, and had found inner peace while hosing four-week-old
egg salad off the curb.

Others, if they thought of him at all, might have thought him
to be simply a garbage man with a sad life. In reality, Tim was
more content and fulfilled than many of those who generated
even the nicest trash. Tim had a beautiful wife, two great children, a comfortable home, *and* he had time to think.

But at the moment, Tim's thoughts were far from comfortable. His mind was completely focused on Winter Frore. It had
been over a week since he or his wife, Wendy, had last seen

Winter, and Tim was more than worried—he was scared something horrific had happened to her. Winter was not their daughter, but they had loved her as though she were. She had been a part of their family, and the Tuttles had tried hard to make up for the horrible life Winter had at home with her mother, Janet Frore. The Tuttles lived a few houses down from the Frores, and they had always kept an eye on Winter.

It's not terribly unusual for a kind neighbor to be aware and watchful toward someone in need on their street. And the Tuttles were about as kind and solicitous as anyone. But there was a reason beyond the obvious for Tim's concern for Winter—a reason even Tim and his wonderful mind hadn't completely sorted out.

It had been almost thirteen years since an old woman had shown up on the Tuttles' doorstep and whispered a secret. Tim could still remember her face—wrinkled and lumpy. She wore a brown hood over her head and had a pair of horn-rimmed, thick glasses perched on her bulbous nose. She was slightly agitated, but determined in her whispering. At first Tim had not understood her, her speaking was so soft, but she had pulled him closer and whispered fiercely.

He had never forgotten what she said, nor had he repeated it.

When Winter was ten years old the old woman had once again shown up at his door. Tim had been stepping out to go to work, and there she was. Just as before, she had leaned in, whispered the secret, and forbidden Tim to tell another soul. And now Winter was missing.

"Are you okay?" Tim's wife, Wendy, asked, sitting down next

to him. "You look like you have the weight of the world on your shoulders."

Tim's heart began beating faster. Something wasn't right. His meal sat untouched upon the dining-room table in front of him. Steam rose softly from the sugared ham and the small, roasted red potatoes that circled it. There was salad and bread softer than most pillows. A long, thin bowl sat filled with dark gravy, and in two separate spots on the table there were dishes of butter and jam, waiting to be spread onto bread and consumed.

Tim's two sons, Darcy and Rochester, were sitting on the opposite side of the table. They both had dark blond hair, round noses, and very sad eyes.

"You're thinking of Winter, aren't you?" Wendy asked.

"She wouldn't just leave," Tim insisted. "I know she wouldn't. She's not that kind of child."

"If it meant she could get away from . . . that Janet woman, she might," Wendy said.

"She would tell us," Darcy cried. "She would tell us and say good-bye."

Tim looked at the faces of his two young boys and at Wendy.

"Maybe you should talk to Janet," Wendy suggested. "She's her mother. Find out what she knows."

"I don't think she'll talk to me," Tim said.

"You have to at least try," Wendy begged.

"You have to try, Dad," Darcy chimed in. "Winter's like our sister."

"She might be in trouble," Rochester added.

"I'm sure she's fine," Tim said, trying to comfort them. "But I'll tell you what." He stuck out his weak chin and tried to smile. "If it makes you feel better, I'll talk to her mother and to the police."

It was as if Tim Tuttle had just announced that there would be four Christmases this year. The other three faces lit up with hopeful smiles.

"And if they don't know anything, I'll try to find her myself," Tim threw in, knowing that Winter was too important to simply forget about. "But we have to believe that she is okay. We have to hope for the best. After all, she's a remarkable girl."

"I'll say she's remarkable," Rochester said. "She froze her whole class."

"Froze her class?" Tim asked in confusion.

Rochester's cheeks reddened and he glanced at his own knees.

"Froze her class?" Tim pressed.

"I don't know if it's true," Rochester finally admitted. "But some older kids were talking about how she froze her class—she turned them all into ice."

"Don't be silly," Wendy said, picking up her fork and stabbing a thin slice of meat. "They weren't speaking literally. How could someone freeze her class?"

Rochester shrugged and looked at Darcy.

"Last I heard it was impossible to freeze people," Tim tried to joke, his heart still racing. "Now, let's eat before this *meal* is frozen."

All of them ate with Winter on their minds.

CHAPTER FOUR

CHEW FOR YOUR LIFE

Leven opened his eyes to find nothing but darkness. The slide to the bottom of the chasm had not been easy, and his head let him know it. It was throbbing. If not for the cold ground beneath his back, he would have had no idea which way was up. He closed his eyes, hoping that they would adjust to the darkness and that he would be able to make out something.

Nope.

He sat up and held his right hand in front of his face—he couldn't see any of it. The air was still and cool and smelled of damp dirt and mold. The sound of a few remaining dirt clods raining down from above made the darkness even more threatening.

"Boo!" Clover said from behind him.

Leven jumped three inches.

"Boy, someone's jumpy," Clover remarked casually. "That was some fall. You're lucky we slid the way we did. The soft, needy dirt kept picking at you, trying to slow down your fall. It helped some, but we're a long way from where we fell in. You probably would have even enjoyed the ride if you'd been conscious," Clover rambled on. "I wonder how deep we are now. We're obviously on the bottom, and my wrist is flaring up." Clover tisked. "I think it's swollen."

"So, what happened?" Leven asked, still in shock.

"It's an old injury, actually," Clover said. "I glued a lobb ball to my hand and threw it. I was trying to see if I could—"

"Not to your wrist," Leven said. "What happened up there?"

"Oh," Clover sniffed. "Well, those were rovens, and now we're miles below the surface of Foo."

"What are rovens?"

"I think they come from the medieval dreams period," Clover said. "Useless—they can't even manipulate dreams. Plus, they can be killed, and they let their hair do their dirty work for them. Don't mess with them, though—their talons are sharp as razors and can dig through anything. When they shed their feet or hands, or when they're killed, their talons are used as weapons."

Leven could feel Clover walking on the top of his head. He reached up and pulled him down. He wished Clover could see his eyes and in doing so realize how seriously confused he was.

"Where's Winter? And Geth?"

"Well, that's a good question." Clover cleared his throat. "I'll be honest with you. I have no idea. We slid a long way over. We could be miles away from them."

Leven stood and patted his arms and forehead, checking to

see if he was all there. Even though he had a cut on his head, a scrape on his right side, and a swollen ankle, he seemed otherwise okay. At least he was alive.

Well, sort of.

It's hard to feel alive when you find yourself in a place that only weeks before you didn't even know existed, miles below the surface, in a space so dark that death seems almost attractive if it brings with it the possibility of a little light.

"We've got to find Winter," Leven said, feeling lost without her. "Which way is out?"

"Up," Clover said, "but I think that might be a bit difficult. So our choices are that way," Clover turned Leven's head to look right, "or the opposite way."

Leven held his hands against the wall and walked sideways, feeling for any opening. There was no light, no gray, no contrast, only blackness.

Leven heard the sound of chewing, followed by the noise of blowing. Suddenly from out of nowhere there was light. Leven spun to find the source and spotted Clover standing on the ground with what looked like a glowing lightbulb sticking out of his mouth.

"What are—"

Before Leven could ask what Clover was doing, the lightbulb burst, and it was dark again.

"Holm on a sec," Clover chewed. He worked his mouth for a moment, then blew another bubble. As it grew it glowed, illuminating the area around him.

The light didn't do much to comfort Leven; it actually revealed in an awesome way just how dark and desperate a situation he was in.

"Wow," Leven whispered, looking around him. "We're in trouble."

The chasm was gigantic. Leven could see nothing but black dirt and darkness in all directions. Both walls of the chasm towered up beyond the light and seemed to extend forever. There was no sign of an opening. Leven could still hear the sound of dirt settling and water running up and down the walls in spots. The dirt in Foo vibrated, looking like great walls of staticky soil.

Clover's bubble burst, and they were plunged into darkness again.

"What is that stuff?" Leven asked, referring to the gum.

"Bubble bulbs," Clover chewed, his speech slurred. "I neva chew it 'cause it only comes in lemon flavor." Clover blew a big bubble and once again lit up the chasm. He handed Leven a piece of the gum. "Only one piece left after this."

Despite all the burns he had experienced at the hands of Clover's candies, Leven didn't hesitate; he put the piece in his mouth and began to chew. Clover was right: It was bitter, without even a hint of sweet. Leven grimaced. The gum was tough and tasted like the rind of an old lemon. Leven chewed for a bit more and then blew a bubble about the size of Clover's head.

It glowed brightly.

He turned, shining the light on everything around them. He could see bits of grass and deep gashes in the steep walls of the canyon. There were also roots and rocks sticking out of certain portions of the chasm walls and floor. In spots, water ran like thin ribbons up the walls. Leven put his right foot in front of his left and began walking along the floor of the chasm into the darkness, hoping there was a way out at the end.

Leven popped his bubble with his tongue. "So you think this will lead us somewhere?" he chewed.

Clover snapped. "Seems like a logical guess."

Leven blew. The new bubble was big but not quite as bright.

"Eventually the glow runs out," Clover lamented.

Leven's bubble burst.

"I'm not sure I made the right choice following you into Foo," Leven said. "Some paradise."

"Isn't it nice?" Clover replied, ignoring the sarcasm. "Wait till spring, everything is so much greener."

Leven wanted to point out the fact that they might not make it to spring, but he chose instead to light up the way. Clover glowed alongside him, two dimming bubbles making their way down the dark crevasse.

After a few minutes Leven stopped to check his swollen ankle and the cut on his head. The blood was dry, and there was no sign of new bleeding. Both the bubbles he and Clover were currently sporting popped.

"Looks like you'll live," Clover chewed supportively.

"I have to live," Leven said seriously. "Seeing how there's no killing in Foo. I might not understand everything here, but I'm pretty sure those rovens were trying to kill me."

"Phooey," Clover scoffed. "They didn't push you over the edge, it was their hair."

"So hair can kill?" Leven asked, dumbfounded.

"It can help," Clover replied. Both were still covered in darkness, having chosen not to blow. "Besides," Clover whispered, "you *can* be killed. Fate didn't bring you here, you snuck in."

"I was pushed in."

"Pushed, snuck, what's the difference?"

"So, I could have died falling into this?"

"Shhh. That's not something you want everyone to know."

"How do you know I can die?" Leven said, suddenly in shock.

"Your grandfather was killed," Clover said seriously. "He cheated fate and snuck back in, and it was sort of a surprise to everyone when it was discovered that he could be killed."

"Geth said my grandfather died, but not that he was *killed*," Leven said desperately.

"You know Geth," Clover sighed. "He's always trying to rainbow up things. Here Geth is dying himself, and he's still trying to act like everything's great."

"Geth is dying?" Leven questioned, the surprise in his voice echoing off the chasm walls. "Where did you hear that?"

"He just told Amelia," Clover said. "Said unless he's taken to the flame in the turrets he won't last more than a couple of days."

"Am I the same way?" Leven panicked.

"No," Clover waved. "You're not a toothpick."

"We've got to get to the turrets," Leven said, ignoring Clover. "Geth will know what to do."

"Of course," Clover insisted. "If Geth isn't restored, then the battle to save Foo will be almost impossible. And as for you, you might be able to die, but I'm sure you'll live a long and full life."

"This is crazy. How am I even alive now?" Leven asked incredulously. "We fell such a long way."

"Like I said, you were lucky you slid down the side just right."

"So I'm the only one in Foo who can be killed?"

"There are a few other exceptions—Winter, Amelia, Geth, the rovens, siids, some rants, most vegetation, sheep—but aside from them, pretty much everybody else is indestructible. Of course, Sabine had creative ways to make accidents happen."

"I heard Amelia telling Geth how some here in Foo would hate me because I destroyed the gateway."

"Yeah, about that," Clover sniffed, "I wouldn't run for any sort of office at the moment. The votes might not be in your favor."

"Unbelievable," Leven sighed.

"Life," Clover sighed softly in return. "I think we'll look back on this—"

A gigantic sloshing noise sounded out from far behind them. The sloshing quickly became a gurgle, sounding as if the ground itself were gargling. Leven turned toward the sound and blew a bubble as fast as he could. There was nothing but black as far as he could see. The noise sounded again, this time louder.

"What is it?" Leven asked, suddenly shaking.

"Well, I'm not certain, but usually when the rovens rip the soil, gunt follows," Clover explained. "Normally they don't begin sealing the thing up so soon, but this is a big rip."

Clover did not sound like his usual fearless self.

Leven blew another bubble. It was large, but it was dim. The noise was getting closer, but Leven didn't turn to run. He needed to see to believe. He could feel a rising wind blowing on his face. Then in the far distance Leven saw a white glob smack the ground. Another large glob hit the wall, then another hit the opposite wall, splashing against the dirt like snowballs. There was one up high and two down low and three new ones at eye level. One smacked against the wall not too far from Leven; it looked less like a snowball and more like an albino frog. The gunt belched and then oozed into the wall, waiting for another of its kind to smack up against it and begin to seal the wound the rovens had created.

"We have to go," Clover insisted.

Leven's bubble wilted.

It was completely dark, but the sound of gunt smacking into the walls and floor of the chasm was almost deafening now. As the growing glob drew closer it was creating a terrific wind. The air pushed past Leven, blowing his hair and clothes. Leven quickly blew another bubble into the wind.

He half-wished he hadn't. The gunt blobs were everywhere, up the sides and piling up at the bottom of the rip. The large, white, froglike balls were wiggling and hissing and meshing together, creating a huge, undulating, sticky-looking mass that was filling up the bottom of the chasm and sticking to the walls. The mass was racing like a wave toward Leven and Clover.

The strong air popped Leven's bubble and pushed it back into his face. Leven turned and began running. He blew another bubble; the weak light lit up only ten paces in front of him. Clover blew too, but his gum was also wearing out.

Leven jumped over a huge hole in the floor of the rip. His gum popped, and he blew another bubble as quickly as he could, hoping he would be able to keep his footing as he ran. The guttural sound of the wall of gunt mounding up behind and rolling toward him was deafening. Like the sound of an approaching tornado.

Smlooooosh!

Leven felt something glom onto the heel of his right foot. It instantly stuck like cement, and Leven's forward motion wrenched his foot out of his shoe. He didn't stop to try to grab it, understanding for the first time just how sticky the white gunt was and how stuck he would be if it got hold of him entirely.

Both bubbles burst.

"We're not going to make it!" Leven screamed. "We don't even know where we're going!"

"Just blow!" Clover screamed.

Continuing to run, Clover and Leven blew as quickly as they could. The puny gum bulbs lit just two feet in front of them. The chasm took a turn, and Leven and Clover barely missed running into the wall. A large wad of gunt smacked into the back of Leven's left shoulder, throwing him off balance and up against the side of the chasm, pinning him to the dirt. Leven frantically tore at his shirt until he was able to rip away from the wall.

Leven kept running, but his bubble was out, and Clover's was wilting.

"Wasn't there another piece of this gum?" Leven yelled.

Clover was one step ahead of him, fishing in his void for the last piece of bubble bulb. "Here it is."

Leven felt Clover shove something in his mouth as he ran. It was a bigger piece than the last.

"I thought you said it only came in lemon!" Leven yelled, running and chewing as fast as he could. "This tastes like cheese."

Clover didn't say a word as he quickly checked his void. He pulled out the last piece of bubble bulb.

"Uh-oh," Clover replied.

Leven lurched forward two more steps. His stomach began to rumble and boil, generating huge bubbles of hot air that raced through his veins and into his hands and fingers and feet and toes. Clover stuck the last piece of bubble bulb into his own mouth and got a good look at what was happening.

Leven was quickly turning into an inflated, giant wad of goo.

Leven raised his hands to his forehead to feel what was going on. Both hands stuck to his head. As he tried to pull them away, they stretched like a piece of warm taffy. He tried to lift his feet from the ground, but they too stretched, stuck to the ground like a wad of chewed gum. Leven groaned and teetered as his body bent completely out of shape. He could feel his insides sticking together and swirling. He cast a wild, desperate look at Clover.

Clover's bubble wilted. "Sorry," Leven heard him say. "I thought I had thrown that candy away. They haven't made 'You

Be the Gum' in years. Ever since . . . well, I don't want to bother you with details, so let's just leave it at that."

Leven might have enjoyed the exchange he and Clover were having if, say, they had been back in Reality, sitting on a porch on a warm afternoon, watching the sprinklers and sipping a cool soda. But Leven was not sipping soda on a warm day. He was miles below the surface of Foo in a chasm ripped by rovens, being chased by roaring, gluelike frogs, and turning into a large piece of gum.

Leven's eyes burned gold. He was startled. His gift had seemed completely gone ever since he had entered Foo. But now he was feeling a sudden sense of relief and new strength, knowing that it was not gone. He could see the ocean of gunt closing in on them. He could see the fate they would suffer if caught in the seal. He could see the powerful wind the wave of gunt was creating in front of it as it undulated ever closer.

He could see exactly what he needed to do.

"Hold on," was what Leven wanted to yell to Clover. But his mouth stretched and sprang back like thick gum. He stretched his mouth again and through a tiny hole he hollered something that sounded like, "Muds pon!"

Luckily, Clover spoke gum, and he jumped onto Leven's shoulder.

Leven relaxed, and his torso began to expand like a giant gum bubble, growing and stretching to the size of a parachute. His cheeks filled out as well, giving him even more buoyancy. The wind created by the approaching mound of gunt blew him forward and helped him gain speed as he began to ascend.

The walls of the chasm were racing by them as if they were on a supersonic elevator. Leven could see some light now. The gunt was everywhere below them, rapidly filling in the rip. Luckily for Leven, his previous experience navigating across the ocean in Reality had given him a little practice with manipulating wind, and he was able to help fate push him faster up out of the canyon and toward the surface.

Leven couldn't see Clover, but he could hear him yelling, "Wheeeeeeee!"

They rose out of the chasm and were suddenly floating like a blimp over the ground. Below them, Leven could see the gunt continuing to pile up in the giant rip, and he developed a sudden urge to belch. As he did so, the air rushed out of him and he drifted to the ground.

Actually, "drifted" really isn't the most accurate word to use.

Leven's deflating body was propelled backward, swooping and diving, as if he were a balloon with all the air rushing out of it, and he ended up slamming into a large fantrum tree, where his gooey body stuck to the branches.

He was a complete mess—drooping and stretched in every direction. The condition was extremely painful and caused Leven's gumball eyes to see starlike bubbles. Clover wasn't helping the situation. He was horribly tangled in Leven's right arm and couldn't seem to get free. Leven tried to yell at him and help

Clover understand that even though the "You Be the Gum" had saved them, he still wasn't happy about his current state.

A weak "Waupsa donta" was all Leven could get out.

"You're welcome," Clover replied, not as fluent in gum as Leven had first thought.

Leven closed his eyes and passed out.

CHAPTER FIVE

AND THEN THERE WAS SORROW

W inter had experienced a number of uncomfortable things in her life. Like the time when she was ten and she was out playing in the woods with her sister, Autumn, and Autumn had dared her to swim in the river that ran behind their house. Winter didn't usually go for dares, but she felt her sister needed some show-ing up. So Winter jumped into the water and easily reached the other side. After she pulled herself up onto the bank, she looked back across the river and stuck her tongue out triumphantly.

Autumn yelled for Winter to swim back across, but Winter decided to mess with Autumn's mind a little more and ran off into the woods. She crossed the old train bridge and then fol-lowed an overgrown road at the bottom of a gully. Winter stopped where the road met up with a wide dirt lane. She was standing above the gap between the two paths where they didn't quite match up when she looked up. The temperature was a

warm ninety-one degrees, and there in the early summer sky was a brilliant shooting star.

You can probably guess what happened next.

Winter was taken into Foo, snatched from her family and normal life at the young age of ten.

That had been an uncomfortable and confusing time for Winter.

Right now, however, Winter was every bit as uncomfortable as that, and then some. At the moment she could remember nothing of her previous lives. All she knew was that she was buried in gunt and was being smothered. The white stuff had oozed over and around them and hardened quickly, trapping Amelia, Winter, and Geth. The new gunt gave off a faint white glow, allowing them to see shapes and shadows.

Amelia had held her scarf over her face to create some breathing room, and Winter had pulled her shirt up over her head to do the same. Geth was pinned inside Winter's pocket, where he was also uncomfortable but not overly concerned. He merely wondered what fate would do next.

Their only hope was that at the very last second, Winter had frozen the stream of water flowing up the side of the chasm. The little waterflight was a couple of feet wide and about thirty inches thick. The gunt had been forced to form and harden around the shaft of ice.

The only problem was that Winter couldn't reach the ice to touch it and restore it to water. Well, that wasn't the only problem, but it was a big one.

Winter's voice was muffled under the layer of gunt. "If I can thaw the water, then we can try to climb up the shaft it created," she explained. "I just can't reach the water."

"Push your foot," Amelia hollered. "The gunt is thin there. If you can push through it, you should be able to reach the ice with your bare foot."

Winter pushed as hard as she could, and the coating of gunt cracked. Her right foot touched the ice and it instantly thawed.

Sure, Winter had achieved what she wanted, but she had actually made the situation much more urgent. Thawed water began to flow up into their space, fighting to steal every inch of air. Winter scrambled up into the tunnel the frozen water had created. She dug her fingers into the mud and pulled herself up through the rising water. The hole was like a flooded, crooked chimney with no light at the top. Winter held on to the sides of the shaft as a stream of mud and water cascaded up over her.

She looked down and reached for Amelia.

Amelia stretched her right hand up toward Winter, and Winter reached down as far as she could, but she could not quite touch Amelia's fingers.

"Reach!" Winter yelled desperately. "Reach!"

Amelia groaned and stretched her wrinkled hand upward.

"A little more!" Winter cried. "Just a little more!"

Amelia blinked her eyes, and as she opened them up she looked at Winter and curled her fingers inward and away.

"Amelia!" Winter yelled.

The water began to fill in even more, rising around Amelia

like a coiling snake. Winter could feel the gunt softening. Soon it would seal off the shaft the frozen water had created.

"Give me your hand!" Winter demanded.

"Do as she says," Geth ordered Amelia. "Grab her hand!"

Amelia's fingers opened just a bit and then closed to make a tight fist. Winter and Geth stared at her in despair.

"Go," Amelia said weakly. "Go. Climb before the gunt seals up this shaft."

"No!" Winter shouted. "Take my hand; I'll pull you up behind me."

Amelia blinked sadly.

"I won't leave you!" Winter cried, still desperately trying to reach down and grab Amelia. "We need you! Leven needs you!"

Winter watched Amelia's eyes briefly light up with the mention of Leven, but the happiness was quickly gone as the liquid rose up and around her neck. The old woman's thick glasses magnified the sadness in her eyes.

"Please go," Amelia pleaded with Winter. "Please. Find Leven and save Foo."

Geth jumped from Winter to Amelia and began pulling at the neck of the old woman's dress. "Come on," he demanded. "We need you. *Foo* needs you."

Amelia could only blink as the rising water covered her mouth and nose.

"No!" Winter cried out. "Stop her, Geth."

Amelia blinked her large, magnified eyes. She closed them and held her breath as water rose above her eyebrows.

"Help her, Geth!" Winter screamed. "Help her!"

Geth looked up at Winter. He was a toothpick, but it was apparent from his small eye holes knitted together that he knew hope was gone. Geth let go of the neck of Amelia's dress as the water floated him upward. "We have to climb before the gunt fills in," he declared.

"No," Winter sobbed. "We can't leave her."

But even as Winter whispered the words, she also knew it was too late. She looked down at Amelia, who was now completely submerged in the rising water. The last bit of air escaped from her nose and mouth, sending bubbles up. Despite the dire straits, Amelia looked almost peaceful.

Winter was sobbing, and Geth was bobbing in the rushing water. Never one to turn his back on fate, Geth jumped into a large bubble and rode it upward. As Geth rose, Amelia sank farther into the water. It looked as if she were encased in glass—a wrinkly old sleeping beauty that only a blind and desperate prince might kiss.

Winter could only cry. She hurt inside for herself, but even more, she hurt for Leven. Amelia was his only true family, and now she was gone. Winter wanted to curl up into a ball and let the gunt smother her, but instinct wouldn't let her. She began desperately clawing at the sides of the wet, muddy shaft, crying bitterly and inching her way to the top as the water pushed her up.

Her hands were bleeding and sore and she could no longer see much, due to the mud and tears filling her eyes and face. Sometimes clean water would clear her vision, but moments later her eyes would be packed with mud again. Her shoeless right foot was numb, and the gunt lining the shaft was growing sticky and making her progress almost impossible.

Just as she thought she could climb no farther, her hand reached the top of the chasm. Using her last bit of strength, she hauled herself out of the muddy shaft and over the lip of the chasm where she collapsed on the ground, crying.

Water sprayed up around her.

Geth was there waiting. He had tried to help pull her out, but being a toothpick, he wasn't much aid.

The gunt groaned and slurped as it wrapped its sticky self around Winter's remaining shoe and pulled it off. Winter jerked her leg away from the gooey mess and watched as her shoe became permanently enshrined in the gunt, the small, froglike bodies molding themselves into a continuous thick slab, their expressions and individual forms disappearing as they solidified.

The water stopped spraying.

Winter's shoe stuck partway out of the gunt, becoming a pathetic tombstone for Amelia.

Winter was a mess for more reasons than one. Her blonde hair, which had never been very manageable or neat, looked like a tangled nest of seaweed. She was wet and muddy, and both her shoes were gone. Her hands were raw and bloody and looked like a couple of cut-up beets.

Winter rolled over onto her back and cried some more. Amelia was gone. Leven was lost, and Foo was in turmoil. A wave of homesickness washed over her as she remembered Reality and what she and Leven had been through over the past few days. A couple of Winter's Foo memories also returned, but there were still some big gaps of gray forgetfulness in her brain.

She didn't know who she was.

Geth had the smarts to remain quiet and let Winter mourn.

The night was dark, with the purple sky pulsating. Stars rolled across the canopy like marbles on an invisible track. Occasionally two stars would collide, click, spark, and roll off in separate directions. It would have been soothing were it not for the situation they were in. Foo was beautiful, but even the landscape was wise enough to recognize this as a moment of mourning.

Finally, Winter rolled over onto her knees and crawled to the now sealed-off stream that had helped save their lives. She thrust her raw hands into the still water and rinsed them thoroughly, then splashed water onto her crying eyes. She was covered with mud. She worked on her hair and then her face and arms. She picked up Geth, dunked him in the water, and held him in the palm of her hand.

"I can't just leave her," Winter whimpered.

"She is with Hector," Geth said softly. "We can't let what she fought for fail."

"Is there even hope anymore?" Winter asked sadly. "Are we doing the right thing?"

"There is always hope," Geth answered. "We have secured that. Now it's up to us to make it stick. We must find Leven, and we must do it fast."

Geth had not told Winter about his condition, but he could feel himself hardening. He figured that at best he had two days before he would be nothing but a tiny piece of inanimate wood. His small body couldn't hold his soul much longer.

Winter tried to smile. She looked at Geth in her palm and could see traces of mud still on his head.

"Hold on," she said.

She dipped him back into the water and washed him off, then gazed for a moment at the reflection of the moon in the dark pool. She could see much more than just the moon.

Winter quickly turned around and saw twelve beings and twelve pairs of new eyes staring directly at her.

And, for the record, none of the eyes were smiling.

CHAPTER SIX

THE UNLIKELY COG

Dennis Wood slouched in his chair and sighed. The diner was empty except for him and an older couple quietly eating soup two booths down. Dennis was wearing a white, short-sleeved, button-up shirt and tan polyester slacks that required no ironing whatsoever. If for some odd reason you wanted to, you could take his pants, crumple them up, stomp all over them, and they would still shake right out, wrinkle free. Of course, what his pants possessed in ease of care, they lacked in style. Strung through the belt loops of those pants was a thin brown belt closed at the same hole that had closed it for the last ten years. Dennis had gained a pound three years before and lost one since then. He had on brown loafers with a wide Velcro closure above the tongue and was wearing a pair of his usual white socks. His digital watch showed thirteen hundred hours. It was set at military time because it made Dennis feel militaryish and

a part of something he really wasn't nor would ever be.

Dennis had a big, white head. His light blond hair was thin and almost the same color as his skin. His hazel eyes were small and fuzzy, the pupils looking more like smashed raisins than perfect circles. He also had a pug nose and a tight mouth that opened only when food was coming in or when he had to reluctantly communicate with someone.

"What can I get you?" a middle-aged waitress asked as she

stepped up to the table and forced him into a small conversation.

Dennis tried to smile, but his expression more nearly resembled a grimace. Instead of speaking, he pointed to the item he wanted on the menu.

"Turkey sandwich?" the waitress asked.

"No mustard or onions," Dennis said apologetically.

"Right. And to drink?"

Dennis pointed to the word *milk* on the menu.

The waitress looked at him as if he were the sole reason she would never date again, took the menu from him, and walked away.

Dennis glanced around the cafe. He was seated next to a window, and through the glass he could see the building he had worked in for the last ten years. He could see the gold plaque attached to the corner of the building near the door. Dennis was too far away to make out the letters on the plaque, but he knew exactly what they said:

Snooker and Woe, Attorneys at Law.

Of course, Dennis was neither Snooker nor Woe, just Wood, Dennis O Wood, the janitor. The "O" didn't stand for anything. It was just an "O." His parents had felt he needed a middle initial, but lacked the creativity to come up with anything besides "O."

For ten years Dennis had cleaned the toilets and mopped the floors in the Snooker and Woe building. He had removed chewed gum from the outside sidewalk and cleaned every surface at least a thousand times. He had also emptied trash cans and ashtrays and passed many people in the halls, always without speaking to them.

For ten years.

And yet, just this morning, after Dennis had changed the toner in the copy machine, Jack Mortley, the man who had hired Dennis, the man who signed Dennis's checks, the man who had known him for ten years, had had to ask him his name before telling him there was a spill in the break room.

Ten years, and Jack still didn't know his name.

Dennis smoothed down the blond hairs covering his white head. He worked the knuckles of his hands into his eyes and rubbed. When he dropped his hands to the table, he was disappointed, but not at all surprised, to still be right where he was—having a late lunch, in a cheap diner, all by himself.

The waitress returned to his table and dropped off the sandwich and the milk.

"Enjoy," she said with little sincerity.

Dennis sniffed. He rotated the plate a half-turn and picked up the sandwich. It was limp at the sides, held together by a long toothpick with purple plastic fringe at the top. Dennis sighed and pulled the toothpick out of his sandwich. He would have simply set the toothpick aside and taken a bite—but, for some reason, as he held the toothpick between his fingers, he experienced a peculiar feeling.

He felt good.

And bad.

Dennis rolled the toothpick between his thumb and middle finger and watched the plastic purple fringe spin in circles. Then he set the toothpick down and took a bite of his sandwich.

The toothpick did what toothpicks do—it just lay there.

Dennis took another bite and looked through the window toward his workplace. He took a sip of milk, watching the toothpick out of the corner of his eye. There was something about it.

He set his glass down and picked the toothpick up again. He rolled it between his fingers. He switched hands and rolled it with the other. He scratched his pug nose and blinked.

He couldn't understand it.

He couldn't understand what he was feeling or if he was even feeling anything. He wondered if there might be a gas leak in the diner or if he was finally going loony from all the cleaning supplies and bleach he had breathed over the years.

The toothpick vibrated in Dennis's fingers.

Startled, Dennis dropped the toothpick into his glass. As he reached in to retrieve it, he tipped the glass over, and milk spilled out onto the table and ran off onto his easy-care tan pants.

Dennis didn't care. His pants were invincible.

He lifted the toothpick out of the puddle of milk, then stared at it as if it were a diamond ring or a gold coin he had spent years searching for. The old couple two booths down were caught up in their own conversation and as indifferent to the rest of the milk dripping down into his lap as Dennis was.

"Hey, hey," the waitress scolded, walking quickly up to the

table with a rag. "You could've used those napkins to stop it."

Dennis said nothing.

"If you stand up, I'll wipe the bench," she directed.

Dennis wriggled out of the booth and stood up, still holding the toothpick in his hand. He leaned over and reached for the handle of his briefcase. He didn't actually need a briefcase, but he thought it gave others the impression that he was more important than he actually was. He fished a ten-dollar bill out of his brief-case and put it down on a dry part of the table, dropped the tooth-pick into the case, snapped it shut, and walked out of the restaurant.Outside, Dennis hurriedly turned and headed toward the building with the gold plaque.

CHAPTER SEVEN

IT TURNS OUT THERE ARE DUMB QUESTIONS

Leven had transformed from a large, sticky wad of gum, plastered in the branches of a tree, back to his normal self. But there were still bits of leaf and twig stuck to his clothes, up his nose, between his fingers and toes, and matted in his dark hair. A thin green twig was sticking out of the white streak in his hair, making it look like a misshapen dove carrying a tiny branch.

Clover busied himself helping Leven remove the larger pieces.

As he was pulling bits of debris off his clothes, Leven looked toward the chasm they had just blown out of. It was now completely filled with gunt and resembled a broad stripe of snow running through the landscape, with the deep purple sky giving it a kind of milky texture. In time, after the gunt had settled and lost its stickiness, some of it would be harvested like blubber and burned or used as cooking fuel. But most of the dense, spongy material would become covered with vegetation, providing nutrients for what was growing out of it.

"That was way too close," Leven said, referring to their escape from the flowing gunt.

Clover was earnestly chewing gum and didn't say anything.

"Are you still chewing that awful lightbulb stuff?"

Clover's hairless cheeks reddened, and he cleared his throat.

"What?" Leven asked. "Is that . . . wait, where did you get that gum?" Leven looked around himself.

"Well . . . I . . . I . . ." Clover stammered.

"Is that from me?" Leven panicked.

"I just wanted to see what flavor you were," Clover explained.

"What flavor?" Leven gasped, still frantically looking himself up and down for a missing chunk.

"It's not from you," Clover waved. "It was your shoe. I took a bite before you changed back."

Leven looked at the one shoe he was wearing. There was a large bite missing from the heel. Leven picked a speck of tree from his nose.

"So, who makes all this candy you have, anyway?" Leven asked. "I haven't seen a structure in Foo besides Amelia's place."

"I know," Clover complained. "Amelia really lived in the sticks. It's not good for people to be so isolated. I bet that's why she's so chatty."

"She seems okay," Leven said. "Now, about the candy, where do you get it?"

"The Eggmen," Clover said.

"The Eggmen?" Leven asked skeptically, brushing a large leaf out of his hair.

"They're pathetic warriors," Clover sighed. "Pathetic. I mean, talk about messy casualties. But they make terrific candy."

"And they use magic?" Leven asked, knowing of no other way to create candy that can turn its chewer into gum.

"No," Clover laughed. "Magic's not real. They use dreams. They live beneath the Devil's Spiral, and as the water from the Veil Sea runs through the massive canyon, it mixes with the dreams. It's quite a process. I'll take you there sometime."

"Devil's Spiral?"

"It's one of my favorite sites in Foo," Clover said. "The spiral eventually forces the water thousands of feet high and keeps the city of Cusp wet."

Clover began to sniff the air. "Do you smell that?" he asked.

"Smell what?" Leven asked.

"It smells like the tharms."

"Tharms? What are—" Leven stopped talking and put his hand to his right ear.

Something was moving nearby. Clover turned invisible.

"You're a great person to have around when things get tough," Leven whispered mockingly.

Leven looked behind himself. He could see nothing but darkness. The sound of chirping bugs filled the air. Leven turned back, and right in front of him was a grown man about Leven's height. Leven jumped. The man stood there scowling. He wore an orange robe and had long gray hair that hung down, partially covering his faded gray eyes. He was breathing like an angry bull and had his weathered hands on his hips.

"Leven?" he asked, in a deep, forced voice.

Leven nodded and backed up a step. "How do you know me?"

"The Lore Coil."

"What's—?"

"Where's Geth!" the personage demanded.

"We were separated," Leven answered.

"Perfect," the old man said sarcastically. "We . . . *I* need Geth."

Leven stood tall. "Who are you?"

"I'm . . . far . . . oh . . . ," he sniffed, scratching his head as if confused.

"Farrow?" Leven helped.

"That's it," the being said, relieved. "You need to follow us . . . me. You need to follow I, me. You lost Geth, but we'll find him. I think I know where he may be."

"Where?"

Farrow looked at Leven and wrinkled his brow. "Do all things from Reality ask so many boring questions?"

"Things?" Leven asked.

"*There's* a surprise," Farrow mocked. "Another question."

"Well, I'd like to know where we're headed."

"How 'bout I show you where we're going when we get there?" Farrow smiled unevenly.

"Last time I saw Geth, we were falling down a giant chasm. Do you think he might have escaped the gunt?" Leven asked.

Total Money Makeover

Dave Ramsey

"Too many questions. It would be best if you simply didn't talk," Farrow declared. He turned from Leven, using his bony hands to sweep his long gray bangs back behind his ears. "I said I, me, we'll find Geth. You're not a runner, are you?"

"I almost made the school track team a year ago," Leven answered naively, still picking bits of tree from off his arms.

Farrow growled. "No, is your *gift* running?"

"I don't think so," Leven replied.

"Good," Farrow said. "I hate trying to keep up."

Farrow twisted and began walking away. After ten steps, he turned to look back at Leven. "Aren't you coming?" he barked. "We'll have to walk and hope we find Geth before anyone . . . well, let's just hope we find Geth in time."

Leven looked to the sky as if there might be an answer written in stars. A huge yellow moon shifted, passing in front of a much smaller blue orb and hiding it. A ribbon of green light danced across the horizon.

"I only have one shoe," Leven hollered after the old man.

Farrow just kept walking.

Clover appeared and pulled a used shoe from his void. "I've been saving all the ones you grew out of," he whispered. "I can't believe you guys in Reality just throw these away."

Leven recognized his old shoe. It was from a year ago and had been well worn.

"Thanks," Leven said, taking the shoe. Hopping on one leg, he crammed his foot into it, then leaned down to lace it up. Shod, Leven took a few giant strides to catch up to Farrow. As he came up beside the grizzled old man, Farrow glanced at Leven and shook his head.

"Leven Thumps," he sneered, the tone of his voice turning cold. "'Look at me, I lived in Reality.' Then Geth abandons Foo and brings you back. His stone has been vacant far too long, if you ask us."

"Us?"

"Another boring question."

"Well, what do you mean by *his stone*?" Leven asked.

"That's not a question you should be asking," Farrow snapped, wobbling as he did so. "Try to remember who you are and who you are talking to."

"I was just curious because—"

Farrow wheeled to face Leven. His old gray eyes were swirling—and not the good kind of swirling like when you twist chocolate syrup into a dish of ice cream. No, the swirling in Farrow's eyes was more like the maddening kind of dizziness and confusion you feel right before you throw up or lose control of your emotions.

Farrow grabbed Leven by the neck of his shirt and steadied himself. His hands were old and rough and smelled rank.

"Curious?" Farrow rumbled, sounding like a different person than he had been moments before. "Curious gets you trapped in a seed and sent to Reality to wait while everyone else is left here to suffer and fight a losing battle."

"But I thought—" Leven tried to explain.

"You *thought*," Farrow spat. "I wish I had a medal to give you. Listen, Leven Thumps, the sooner you realize that you understand nothing, the better off you will be. Nothing is the same here as in Reality. All that you have known is now different. The air you are breathing is different. You think the sun will rise tomorrow?" Farrow challenged.

Leven nodded cautiously.

"Ha!" Farrow scoffed, letting go of Leven's shirt. He wobbled and grabbed onto Leven's sleeve. "The sun might rise tomorrow, and it might not. Maybe you'll grow older, and maybe not. Either way, you would be better off to forget what you know."

Leven's face burned red with frustration. "I know Geth would never—"

"Don't say Geth!" Farrow ordered. "He might be the heir, but he has done more to disrupt Foo than help. In my opinion this is no longer his battle. He should step down and leave the future to Morfit. I will help you find . . . Geth. But on the day that your need is met, I will feel nothing but pleasure as I turn and walk the opposite direction."

Farrow shook his head, let go of Leven, and flung the hood of his orange robe up. He twisted awkwardly again and began walking quickly down the path they were on.

"That guy should write greeting cards," Clover whispered softly into Leven's ear.

A low buzzing filled the air as bit bugs began moving into the night air from the branches of trees where they spent their days. Leven waved them away, irritated by their swarming. The bit bugs were ugly little things, nothing more than small bits of actual bugs that had escaped from dreams. Some were just legs, or antennae, or body segments, and they flew about erratically. Leven began walking again and after a few moments he had caught back up to Farrow.

"So we're heading to where Geth might be?" Leven asked.

Farrow stopped and looked at Leven with a scowl. "Who cuts your hair?" he snapped.

"What?" Leven questioned.

"Whoever did it, they did a bad job," Farrow said, starting to walk again.

Leven ran his fingers through his hair.

"Nice guy," Leven whispered to Clover. "This is ridiculous. We'd better be heading toward Geth. What time do you think it is, anyway?"

"What does that matter?" Clover asked. "Time is different here. No one ever really knows for sure."

"You don't keep track of time here?"

"Well, not like in Reality," Clover replied. "It's a bit more relaxed in Foo. Say you're enjoying a beautiful sunset, and you want it to last longer. Or it's three more days to Winsnicker Day, and you just can't wait, so you need time to speed up."

"Winsnicker Day?"

"One of my favorite days," Clover said happily. "There's a lot of skipping and decorations and singing about Professor Philip Winsnicker and his heroics."

"So when is Winsnicker Day?" Leven asked.

"It comes at a different time and day each year. I wish I had my schoolbook with the schedule. I hope I didn't lose it."

Leven shook his head, totally confused by his surroundings and the order of things in Foo. It was like nothing he had experienced in Reality, and he wondered if he might not be dreaming. But he still felt an urgency to find Geth.

"Well, even if time is working for us, we should be going faster," Leven said. "Do they have cars or airplanes here?"

Clover laughed. "Airplanes? Those big metal things that used to fly over your house in Oklahoma?"

Leven nodded.

"There are none of those things here," Clover said, as if surprised that Leven would even suggest such a thing. "No cars or airplanes, or anything made out of metal."

"You don't have metal here?" Leven asked.

"We do, but it's . . . well, sacred."

"Metal is sacred?" Leven laughed.

"That might not be the perfect word," Clover admitted, "but metal is something only those who occupy the Thirteen Stones are permitted to possess. It used to be that everyone used metal, but then there were abuses and trouble with it. All the great wars have been fought over metal."

"How does a realm with no killing have wars?" Leven asked.

"They fight blindfolded," Clover answered, as though it were the most natural thing that could be imagined.

"Seriously?"

"Both sides cover their eyes so that any strong blow is an accident."

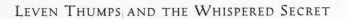

"That's ridiculous," Leven scoffed. "You said Foo was a place of possibilities. But I keep hearing about more and more restrictions."

"The wonder and beauty are what we are fighting to restore," Clover explained. "The privilege of working with metal is not a restriction. It's an art that belongs only to the Council of Wonder."

Leven drew in a deep breath, wondering at what he was learning. He scanned the landscape and took a good look at where he was.

Despite its strangeness, Foo was absolutely beautiful. The green-tinted moon was smearing itself down toward the horizon and radiating long strands of light that wiggled like wet noodles up into the purple sky. Under that light, the white streak in Leven's hair had a phosphoric glow to it.

The trail Farrow was leading them down was dark and paved with narrow, rectangular stones. It looked like a billion sticks of multicolored gum had been used to lay it out.

Leven took everything in and breathed deeply again. Despite the surrounding beauty, Leven felt like he didn't belong here. He was scared to death and wished the gateway still existed. He wished that Winter and Geth and Amelia were back by his side—that they had not been separated. He wished he had more faith in fate and knew more clearly what part he was supposed to play.

Farrow had made no effort to shorten his stride, and he was now well ahead of them. Leven wasn't sure that Farrow had the answers, but he began trotting to catch up to the crotchety old man again.

"So what's this stone of Geth's?" Leven asked Clover, who had gone invisible again.

"His stone is part of the Thirteen Stones. He . . . actually, it might just be easier to show you." Clover suddenly appeared in front of Leven's face. He had his feet planted on the sides of Leven's neck and his hands were clutching Leven's ears. Clover had materialized many different times and many different ways, but he had never gotten into Leven's face before like he was now.

"What are you doing?" Leven asked, drawing his head back.

"Hold on," Clover said. "Watch my eyes."

"Can't you just—"

"Watch," Clover insisted.

Leven obeyed, and Clover closed his eyes. After a moment, wisps of gray fog began seeping out from the corners of his eyelids, and when Clover opened his eyes, a large cloud of fog drifted out and up. As the fog cleared, Clover's blue eyes glowed bright and then darkened. Patterns of dancing, colored light moved from Clover's right eye to his left, then disappeared.

In the blackness of the eyeballs, a map materialized with a legend that said Foo. Leven studied it. He could see that the land of Foo was all one mass. As he watched, a succession of brightly lit scenes burned up through the surface of the map. There were vivid images of people behaving strangely, fantastic landscapes, animals such as Leven had never imagined, and lots of colors and motion. Each little episode would appear for a moment, then dissolve as another took its place.

Leven could hear Clover's voice explaining: "What you're seeing are dreams as they enter Foo."

Clover closed both eyes, and when he opened them again,
Leven could see the towns and villages that were scattered across
Foo. Clover blinked, and another image appeared. "These are
scenes from Foo's past," he said.

Through a fine mist, Leven could see crowds of people coming out of their dwellings, gathering, then moving in waves
toward the town of Cork. While he watched, one by one, large
chunks of land broke off from the bottom of Foo and began
drifting out into the Veil Sea toward the Wet Border. The images
leapt from Clover's right eye to his left, and a moment later Leven
could see a series of islands forming off the shore of Foo, located
in the Veil Sea, near the Hidden Border. There were thirteen of
them, and each had its own distinctive shape. As Leven watched,
a large, hand-shaped section of Foo reached out toward the
islands.

Leven pushed his right hand through his hair and rubbed his
own eyes.

Clover began to speak, "Those thirteen islands have great
control over what happens in Foo. The land reaching toward
them is controlled by the collective will of the dreams of Reality
and the desires of the inhabitants of Foo."

Clover blinked again, and Leven saw in Clover's eyes the
image of an old man with a long beard, wearing a dark cloak. The
man was breathing heavily, kneeling down, bent over, seeming to
stare not just *at* but *into* the ground. As the man pulled a seed

from his robe, Clover suddenly sneezed, and the image instantly faded. The little sycophant shook his head, and his eyes were back to normal.

"Excuse me," he said.

"Amazing," Leven whispered. "Is there anything you can't do?"

"Well, I can't juggle. And according to my fourth-grade teacher, I can't write poetry," Clover said disgustedly, letting go of Leven's ears. "What an elitist. So the word *buddy* doesn't exactly rhyme with *pretty*. I was expressing myself. I wish she could have—"

Leven cleared his throat. "Who was that old man, and what happens when he looks into the dirt?"

Clover didn't answer immediately. Instead he cleared his throat. When he did speak, he sounded choked up. "That was Antsel," he explained. "He could look into the ground and see everything, as if he were standing on a bluff and looking out into the open sky. A real soil seer can see much farther underground than anyone can see above. Antsel could see across the world, or most of Foo."

"What good does that do?" Leven asked.

"You'd be surprised," Clover said. "He saw where to plant Geth, and his gifts were such that he could see dreams even before they reached the surface of Foo."

Leven closed and opened his brown eyes slowly, revealing a small band of gold around his pupils. The band of gold flared and then cooled, blending into the brown.

"I haven't seen a dream yet," Leven admitted as though he were confessing a dark secret.

"That's not unusual," Clover said, jumping up onto Leven's left shoulder and patting him on the top of his head. "Some people never see them. For most, it takes a few weeks for the first ones to appear. And usually the first dreams that nits pick up on are ones coming in from relatives. But since you don't have any relatives, it might take you a bit longer. It will happen. One day you'll be walking and suddenly you'll see a shaft of light split through the soil. If you're close enough, it will attach to you and you'll begin to enhance it."

"Attach to me?"

"Through the soles of your feet or the underside of your chin—maybe up through your palms," Clover explained. "Don't worry, it won't hurt. It's quite remarkable."

"I'm not sure I believe that," Leven said. "More than a few of your stories have been wrong."

Leven tried to walk faster, but Farrow was still hundreds of feet ahead of him.

"So, where's the battle?" Leven asked Clover. "I've seen a number of odd things, but I see no war. Where's the great fight Geth talked about?"

"You'll see," Clover said. "The day will come when each of your questions will be answered. That day's just not now. Not everyone can be the Want."

"The Want?" Leven questioned.

"He occupies the thirteenth stone and is pretty important— big house, all kinds of power. He can see every dream that enters Foo. Some say it's made him a bit . . . well, eccentric."

"Every dream?" Leven scoffed.

"Every dream," Clover confirmed. "He alone possesses the power of the gifts. Some say he's mad from all the images he sees, but he's still the Want, and his power holds Foo together."

"So he's more powerful than Geth?"

"Of course," Clover laughed. "But Geth has been in his presence. That's not something most here could handle. I'm not really supposed to be telling you these things. I took a few liberties in Reality, but here sycophants are supposed to know their place and stay in it. So, it might be wise for you not to mention all this to Geth. The Thirteen Stones control everything here. Each member of the Council of Wonder occupies one of them. The largest is home to the Want. He used to visit other parts of Foo, but now he just remains there, watching and shifting dreams."

A giant, birdlike snake flithered overhead and hissed before settling into a thick patch of fantrum trees. Foo was unbelievable; Leven just wished he understood it better.

By now, Farrow had moved out of sight, and Leven jogged up the path looking for him. The fuzzy light from the moon dripped down, throwing dark shadows across the path from the fantrum trees that lined the way.

"Farrow?" Leven called, still not able to see him. "Farrow?"

There was no answer. A wind began to blow, rustling the leaves of the trees, softly at first but rapidly increasing in force. Soon the limbs were roaring with air and thrashing about wildly.

"Clover," Leven said. "Something feels wrong."

There was no answer.

"Clover?" Leven said a bit louder.

There was no sound but the howling of the wind in the trees.

"Farrow!" Leven shouted.

The moon shifted color from green to white, sizzling like a big Alka-Seltzer tablet. It glowed bright and then began to hiss and dim, and the wind suddenly quit blowing. Everything grew still and silent.

"Come on, Clover," Leven said nervously. "You have to be here."

"He's not," a voice said.

Leven turned to find Farrow standing only a couple of feet away. The old man stood with his arms crossed in front of him, the hood of his orange robe pulled up over his head. His eyes glowed a pale red.

"Where'd you—?" Leven began.

"Quiet!" Farrow ordered, his eyes pulsating.

Farrow uncrossed his arms and inserted two fingers of his right hand into his mouth. He created a high-pitched whistle that sounded out into the surrounding forest. Something began to rustle in the trees.

Leven looked around nervously. He glanced down at the trail in front of him and for a moment thought he saw Clover standing there, looking at him.

"Clover, thank—hey, you're not Clover."

Whatever it was, it was a few inches taller than Clover's twelve inches. The creature had stubby ears that resembled swollen corks, and where its tail should have been there was a third arm with a hand that it was using to scratch its forehead vigorously. Its face was square with a round, wrinkly nose and narrow eyes. It opened its tiny mouth and cooed at Leven. The creature rocked and bounced back and forth like a monkey.

Leven stepped back. Farrow whistled again, and a second creature slipped out from the trees and stood behind the other. It too scratched its forehead and began to rock. Soon they were cooing and bouncing in harmony. Two of them were far less cute than one. A third appeared at the side of the trail and also cooed, erasing any trace of cuteness.

"Clover," Leven whispered, "what are they?"

A fourth emerged from the dirt while a fifth and a sixth shimmied down a tree and stood behind Leven—all staring at him and cooing loudly.

"Seriously, Clover!" Leven said desperately. "Where are you?"

Three more dropped from the trees onto the path. Seven rolled in from behind. A dozen emerged from the forest—all of them cooing, their combined sound growing. Fifty of them pushed up from the side of the trail and joined the gathering. Some of them began to stand on the others' shoulders. Leven began to panic. Clover had clearly abandoned him, and the growing crowd was quickly closing in. The ugly creatures gave off a dirty, rank odor.

Leven closed his eyes and willed his gift to kick in.

Nothing.

"Farrow," Leven pleaded.

"Where is Geth?" Farrow barked.

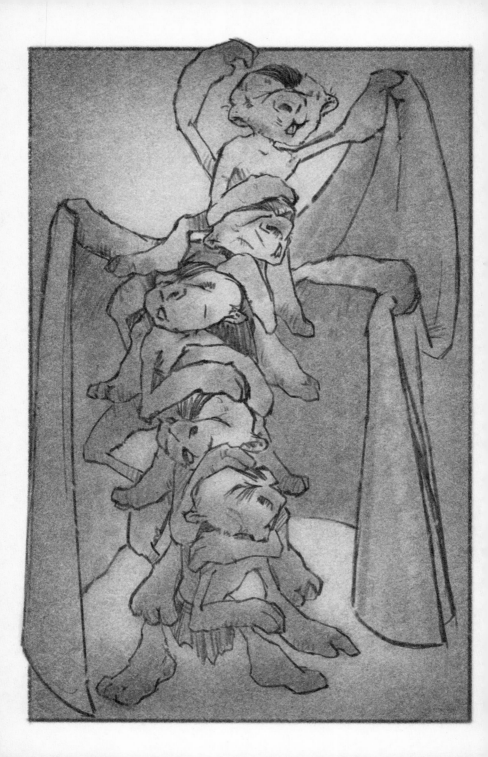

"I have no idea. You said—"

"What does he look like? What form is he in?" Farrow pressed.

"What?" Leven answered, confused.

"The Lore Coil was short on description," Farrow growled. "The locusts the Sochemists sent out only described him as being small."

"He's not small," Leven lied. "And he will be here any moment."

Farrow looked around nervously and then stamped his feet in a rage. The hundreds of creatures surrounding Leven tightened their circle. And when a loud whistle sounded in the distance, Farrow smiled and whistled back.

"Tell me where Geth is!" Farrow raged.

"He's coming," Leven insisted, holding his chin out and staring Farrow down with his eyes. "You won't stop him."

"I brought you here to give you a chance," Farrow seethed. "But I can see now you are no good to us. You know nothing and should be buried."

Farrow began to tremble and shake. His lower half darkened and cracked, exposing the fake that he was. Like a cover being pulled off to expose a statue, Farrow, as Leven had known him, vanished. In his place were five of the little creatures stacked on top of each other like a totem pole. They squealed with delight, and the top one spoke.

"It's a first-impersonation quilt," he said, nodding down to the cloak they had been hiding under. "We tharms need them to

disguise ourselves so we can make better first impressions. Our smell and shape seem to turn people off."

The five tharms that had once been Farrow hopped off each other and joined the hundreds of others pressing in on Leven.

"You should have given up Geth," they cooed in unison.

Another whistle sounded, and all the tharms jumped at once toward Leven. Instinctively, Leven sprang forward into the thickest gathering of them. He knocked over a half dozen before he was dragged to a stop by all of their tiny hands grabbing and holding him. Their third arms were particularly strong.

When Leven tried to scream, a couple of dozen little hands crammed his mouth into silence, and he was lifted off his feet. Hordes of the cooing creatures piled in under him, their tiny hands pinching and hoisting him higher. Then they took off running, holding Leven above them. Moving with surprising swiftness, they raced into the forest. Suspended on his back, Leven could see tree limbs flying over him, inches from his head and body. The pack of tharms pushed up a steep mountain not slowing in the least; in fact, they were gaining speed with each step, cooing madly like a million psychotic pigeons.

They crested a rocky mountain cap that was covered with a white, spongy fungus and rocketed down the backside, flying across the landscape. Leven was being held by a thousand hands, but he still bounced up and down with each movement and step. Leven's mind flashed back to his life in Oklahoma. He remembered the afternoons when he had tried to get home from school without the neighborhood ruffians Brick and Glen throwing rocks at him or running him over with their bikes. Leven had always run to get away, but now he was beginning to feel different. He could see the value in fighting for himself. As the tharms held him in their hands, running, Leven wanted desperately to act instead of being acted upon.

Leven's legs and arms burned as if they had fallen asleep and now blood was racing back into them like pins and needles.

Suddenly the creatures flipped him like a gangly pancake onto his stomach, so that he was being carried facedown and backwards. A great swarm of bit bugs hovered over the racing horde of tharms, their mass glowing brightly. The light from the bugs combined with the glowing bark of fantrum trees and a dim moon to give Leven more than enough light to see what was happening.

After a time, the strange escorts slowed, and Leven could see hundreds of other tharms standing in a circle around a large, dark hole in the ground. Each had all three of its arms raised above its head, fists full of soil.

The sight wasn't exactly comforting.

"Clover!" Leven screamed. "Winter! Geth! Anyone!"

It was no use. Nobody was going to help Leven. As they approached the hole, the tharms cooed in a great chorus, and the ones surrounding the hole parted to let the others through. The tharms carrying Leven stopped abruptly. They drew their arms back in sync and heaved Leven into the air over the hole.

Leven yelled, frantically grabbing for something to prevent his fall, then dropped like a rock into the hole. It was about seven

feet deep, and in an instant he landed painfully in the bottom.

Immediately, the tharms began throwing handfuls of dirt in on top of him, pelting his whole body and quickly pinning him down. The clumps of soil clutched at Leven. Leven tried to stand, but the weight of the dirt was too much. He was being buried alive.

Leven's eyes burned gold. He tried to picture fate in a saving manner, but all he could see was the little bit of air around him in his hole—the same hole that was quickly filling up with dirt. Leven wanted to fight. He could see soft wind blowing through the trees of the forest. Leven manipulated the wind to snake through the dirt like a bionic worm and create a bubble of air around his body. The wind drew in and enveloped Leven like a bubble-wrapped mummy. Dirt continued to rain down. In a few moments Leven was entombed seven feet beneath the surface of the Swollen Forest, wrapped in thick, soft air.

Leven concentrated his thoughts to keep the air intact around him. The tharms were working like mad to fill in the hole, and the weight of the dirt piling up on top of it was overwhelming.

The air he had worked in began to heat up, and sweat poured into Leven's eyes. He trembled violently, fighting the very soil as it settled and acted upon him.

CHAPTER EIGHT

THE RING OF PLAGUE

Jamoon stood towering over Winter. There were eleven red-robed beings behind him. Winter had seen their eyes reflecting back at her from the puddle water she had been cleaning herself in after climbing up out of the gunt.

She stood to look directly at Jamoon.

Jamoon's thick black robe obscured all but his right eye, which was glaring. A bright red ring was embroidered on the cuff of both his sleeves, indicating Jamoon's status. Winter quickly pushed Geth up her sleeve as her heart rose to her throat.

A warm wind blew against her wet hair.

Jamoon's robe billowed, giving him a greater form than he already possessed. Winter would have been terrified just seeing Jamoon, but it was the robed figures with him that bothered her most. Eleven beings stood tall behind Jamoon—six on one side and five on the other. Each of them wore a scarlet cloak with a black band running around his lower sleeves. From a former memory, Winter knew who and what they were.

The whole of Foo knew who they were.

One of Sabine's most effective weapons of war had been his establishment of the two great Rings of Plague. Each Ring consisted of twelve nits, each possessing a different gift. Nits were people who were snatched from Reality by fate and brought to Foo, where each was given two things: a sycophant to help them cope with the shock, and a unique gift that they were expected to use in the work of enhancing dreams.

The gifts didn't come in nice red boxes with yellow bows. They were abilities that developed slowly and over time, based on the nits' needs and personalities. The gifts were ultimately bestowed by one of the Thirteen Stones in the Veil Sea.

Within each Ring of Plague Sabine had organized there was a complete assortment of powers: one to fight with ice, one to see through the soil, one to throw lightning, one to fly, one to fade, one to shrink, one to breathe fire, one to run like the wind, one to burrow, one to see through rock, one to levitate objects, and one to push and bind dreams.

Possessing all these gifts, the Rings could not be easily defeated. There was almost nothing they couldn't do or fend off. Under Sabine's direction, these Rings of Plague traveled across Foo, capturing any who would not join them in their quest to fuse Foo with Reality, and causing accidents to those who opposed them. A third of the inhabitants of Foo resisted Sabine's leadership, but most of those beings lived in Cusp or the beautiful, well-protected, and prosperous city of Cork. Now, the members of the Ring of Plague were looking to find a way to infiltrate these last few strongholds of resistance.

They had no mercy, only a quest.

And that quest was to achieve the ability to move freely between Foo and Reality. Having been originally snatched from Reality, the members of the Ring knew what they were missing and desired to go back, taking with them the gifts they now had. Like Sabine, they believed it was possible.

For all its power and determination, the Ring of Plague was not an invincible foe, however. With the help of Winter and others, Geth had defeated the first one years before. Using his ability to travel by fate, Geth had succeeded in capturing the twelve angry nits and now had those devoted followers of Sabine held captive in secret places throughout Foo. Only Geth and Antsel knew where they were being detained, but of course Antsel was now gone, which left the secret to Geth alone.

Enraged by Geth's disruption of the first Ring of Plague, Sabine was driven by an insatiable hatred of Geth, who as the head token of the Council of Wonder was the legitimate heir to the throne of Foo. Many years before, Sabine and his shadows had succeeded in capturing Geth and forcing his soul into the seed of a fantrum tree. But the rightful king of Foo had somehow escaped, and in some disguise was now back in Foo. If it was Geth's aim to pick off the members of the second Ring of Plague, Jamoon was determined to prevent it.

Winter was now confronted by Jamoon and eleven ominous

members of the second Ring of Plague. As a rant—an ungifted offspring of a nit and a cog—Jamoon was a being of such weak determination that he couldn't ever just manipulate a dream and move on. As with all rants, his left half was in a state of constant change, continually reflecting dreams coming into Foo from Reality. Even so, Jamoon had somehow risen to be Sabine's first in command and exercised some control over the members of the Ring.

Winter counted those there and realized that the Ring wasn't complete. She wondered what gift they were missing. Had she realized that the absent member was Sabine and his gift of freezing, she might have simply frozen them all and fled. Unfortunately, because of her fear and confusion, that fact didn't register.

Jamoon cleared his throat. "Hello, Winter," he said calmly, suppressing all surprise. "You have returned. I would not have recognized you were it not for your eyes."

Winter looked directly at him with her green eyes, fearing him, but having no clear understanding of who he really was.

"Where's Leven?" Jamoon asked.

Winter was silent.

"Where's Leven?" the eleven Ring members echoed in an ugly chorus, inching closer to the wild-haired girl.

Winter's skin crawled.

"How should I know?" she shouted, getting to her feet and trying to act brave. "Those stupid rovens knocked me out and split us up."

"And Geth?" Jamoon asked, as if he had only a casual interest. "Where is Geth?"

"Gone," Winter snapped, hoping they wouldn't search her.
She pointed. "Look at the size of that chasm. He could be
trapped anywhere in there."

The gunt had completely filled in the rip, but that didn't
make the size any less spectacular. As far as anyone could see there
was nothing but the dull shine off the gigantic river of gunt. It
looked like a massive glacier that ran for miles.

"The rovens did an above-average job," Jamoon smiled. "And
Geth was in there, you say?"

"I'm sure he was," Winter said sadly.

Jamoon and the members of the Ring hovering behind him
began to hiss and shake, but whether they were registering frustration or joy, Winter couldn't tell.

"And the old woman?" Jamoon asked.

Winter's green eyes burned with hatred. She made a tight fist
with each hand and could feel her fingernails digging into her
palms, but she forced herself to take a deep breath and then
release it. Gradually, the hatred in her eyes was replaced with
sadness.

"She was trapped in the gunt," Winter answered defiantly.

"Then she is dead," Jamoon said sharply.

Winter was surprised by what Jamoon knew, but she forced
herself to remain stone-faced and passive.

"Your eyes always could hide mountains," Jamoon sniffed.
"But I can see that the Lore Coil did not sweep over you—

perhaps when it echoes back . . . For now, take comfort knowing that all of Foo knows of your mortal state. The Coil has been spotty on many things, but it spoke clearly about this. You are capable of dying. Reality, it seems, has made you vulnerable."

Winter's mind was racing, filled with impulses and synapses, frantically searching for some memory of what a Lore Coil was. The thought of everyone knowing that she and Leven could die was as frightening as any thought she had ever had.

As Winter was searching her mind, Jamoon tilted his head back slightly and clucked his tongue. Then he raised his arms, and the bottom half of his robe began to billow and sway.

Winter stared as bits of black seeped out from under his robe and rose into the air, where they separated, screaming and spitting and filling the sky. In just seconds, Jamoon and the Ring were surrounded by black, dead, yellow-eyed fowls. Jamoon motioned his arms forward, and the entire gathering of decaying nihils swooped toward Winter.

Winter froze them, but it didn't slow the dead birds in the least. Frozen they screamed even louder, hurling toward her like an aggressive ice storm. The nihils swirled about her like a frigid twister, violently whipping her hair, the beating of their wings sucking the air from her lungs. A single nihil landed on her shoulder, clinging to her with its ice-pick talons. The nihil pecked Winter sharply on the neck.

Winter felt the sharp beak penetrate her skin, sending frozen waves of dark emotion and fear throughout her body. Winter swatted and yelled, fighting the hundreds of other birds away. It

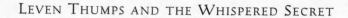

was useless. Her vision pulsated like a dying star. She felt her knees buckling, and her mind and body were filled with thousands of dark and troubling thoughts.

As Winter sank to the ground, Jamoon lifted his arms and the nihils gathered into a cloud, then swooped down and disappeared up under his robe, as though they had been vacuumed up. As they did so, their hissing and screaming ceased, and silence descended over the scene.

In the darkness, Winter lay on the ground, her body twitching and shivering.

"Bring her," Jamoon ordered. "We will see what she remembers."

Two members of the Ring of Plague picked Winter up. Geth pushed up against Winter's wrist and scooted farther up her sleeve, hoping to remain undetected.

CHAPTER NINE

Friends Come in All Sizes, but Usually They Are Bigger Than a Toothpick

Dennis Wood didn't have his own office at Snooker and Woe, but he had discovered and claimed for his own a small, unused utility room—a closet, really—with a little window overlooking the street. Two years before, when the firm was throwing out some old furniture, Dennis had snuck a desk and a banged-up metal filing cabinet for himself and set them up in the closet. On the top of his desk was a cheap metal holder with a plastic strip embossed with the word *Janitor* on it. The name holder was the one thing he had been given by his boss. Dennis didn't view it as a gift; he viewed it as one more way for his employers to make sure he knew exactly what he was.

Dennis kept his cleaning supplies in one of the drawers of the filing cabinet and tools for building model toys in his desk drawers. He spent a lot of time at that desk pretending to think, assembling model planes, tanks, and cars. Sometimes he could waste an entire day just sitting there. It was a good day when nobody came looking for him to clean something or empty something else.

Of course, his time was never completely wasted. Dennis loved assembling his plastic or balsa-wood models—the more intricate, the better—and he would spend hours lost in the act of building. He wanted desperately to own a plane that could fly him away or a tank that could bust him out of where he was. But Dennis knew that would never happen, so instead he spent his money and time building what most of the world would call expensive toys.

Dennis wasn't building today.

For the last two hours Dennis had been sitting at his desk, staring at the toothpick he had come across during lunch. The toothpick felt warm and seemed to vibrate just a bit when he held it.

Dennis studied the sliver carefully, holding it underneath the thick magnifying glass he used for building models.

It was a long toothpick with a dark grain of wood running up and down one side. Just beneath the purple fringe top there looked to be the tiniest round knot, and above that to the side was a slight notch in the wood. The knot was no bigger than the tip of a dull pencil. Dennis reached for one of the X-Acto knives he kept in an empty mayonnaise jar on his desk and picked up the toothpick.

Dennis carefully poked the knot with the tip of the knife.

As he did so, the blade and the toothpick buzzed, causing

Dennis to jump and toss both to the ground. The X-Acto blade clanked loudly against the linoleum floor, while the toothpick bounced and rolled under the desk.

"I'm losing it," Dennis said to himself. "Losing it. My father was right."

Dennis's father, Chuck, had always been worried that his son, like him, would someday lose his mind, run away from his family, hide out in an abandoned building for a year, and eventually be committed to an asylum.

"A toothpick," Dennis muttered. "I got a sandwich and there was a toothpick in it. Lots of people get lots of sandwiches with toothpicks in them."

He tried to take his mind off the little sliver of wood lying beneath his desk, but it was nearly impossible.

"There's a toothpick on the floor," he mumbled. "So what?" A slight red crept into his cheeks, making his white head look like parts of it had been laundered in a load filled with red socks.

Dennis glanced at the small digital clock on his desk. The glowing numbers changed up one.

Dennis couldn't take it any longer.

Frantically, he pushed his chair back and fell to his knees, feeling under the desk for the toothpick. He found a washer, a paper clip, and an old fortune cookie slip. It read: "Dare to dream." Dennis remembered the day he had tossed that down. Not only was it not technically a true fortune, it was a painful reminder of his dreamless life. He tossed it aside again and pushed the desk back so as to be able to reach farther under.

He didn't know why, but he was desperate to find that toothpick. He groped around under the desk until his fingers brushed against the toothpick's purple top and he took hold of it and pulled it out. As he got up from the floor and settled onto his chair, he laid the toothpick on the blotter on his desk and studied the little stick.

The toothpick vibrated.

"What the . . . ?" Dennis muttered, furrowing his brow. Two seconds later the toothpick vibrated once more and rolled to the side just a bit.

Dennis rubbed his eyes. He glanced around the little room, then fumbled through his top drawer and pulled out an even thinner X-Acto knife. Holding the toothpick beneath the magnifying glass, he used the point of the knife to touch the tiny knot on the toothpick just below where the purple plastic top was attached.

The knife buzzed.

The hair on the back of Dennis's neck stood like the quills of a threatened porcupine. Dennis pushed the tip of the knife just slightly into the wood, and, like a miniscule cork being fired from a pent-up bottle of champagne, the tiny knot of wood popped out and shot up. It ricocheted off the magnifying lens and desk and into Dennis's right eye.

Screaming, Dennis dropped the knife and reached for his eye. But his concern for himself was short-lived as a much higher-pitched and more alarming scream sounded. Dennis let go of the toothpick to cover his ears. He looked around frantically. The noise seemed to be growing. He glanced at the tooth-pick, realizing that the tiny hole he had just opened was the source of the screaming. He pushed his index finger over the opening to shut it up.

The toothpick bit him.

Dennis drew back his hand and leaped up off the chair. The toothpick was still wailing. Panicking, Dennis reached for a broken stapler and slammed it down on the toothpick.

"Ahhhhhhhhhh!" it wailed, much louder than one would expect something so small to do.

Someone outside the closet began banging on the door.

Dennis moved the stapler off the toothpick. He tore off a piece of Scotch tape from a dispenser on his desk and stuck it over the hole he had made, taping the toothpick to the desk and putting an abrupt end to the screaming. But beneath the tape, the toothpick was still vibrating madly.

The banging on the door stopped and someone yelled, "What's going on in there?" The door handle jiggled as whoever it was tried to make his way in. Dennis, of course, always made sure the door was locked. He had been interrupted too many times straightening staples or sorting pencils.

"Are you all right?" the voice asked with more disdain than sympathy.

"Fine," Dennis lied, noticing for the first time that the spot where the toothpick had bit him was bleeding. "I'm fine. The toner in the copy machine was leaking," he lied again. "There was a leak in the toner," he repeated, as if saying it twice would make it true.

Dennis tore off another piece of tape and secured the bottom half of the gyrating toothpick. The stapler he had hammered it with had done some damage. One end of the toothpick was slightly bent, and the tip had been split, creating what looked like tiny legs with a short, striped tail hanging down between them.

The vibrating ceased. Dennis just stared. He was trying desperately to make sense of what was happening but had no answers. He thought for a moment that he was simply dreaming, but that didn't seem likely because Dennis never dreamed. According to his father, this inability to dream was a family trait; the men in the Wood family didn't dream. When they closed their eyes at night they saw nothing but gray. Dennis had always wanted to doze off and see things in a way his sad life didn't offer, but it never happened. So he built models and pretended that he was someone else doing something altogether different from his actual activities.

Now, however, here he was, gaping at a toothpick taped to his desk and wondering if he really wanted to experience something different from what his days had always offered.

He decided he might.

After a few moments, Dennis peeled the tape off the top end of the toothpick to see if it would scream again.

Silence.

Dennis touched the purple, hairlike fringe and pulled back.

"Happy?" the toothpick whispered fiercely. "Captured Ezra, have you? Well, you've got me, now finish me off, coward!"

"What?" Dennis asked, confused.

"End it!" Ezra snarled. "But before you do, I want to see you. I want to see who cheated fate and did Ezra in. Slice me an eye."

"E . . . e . . . excuse me?" Dennis asked nervously, more than just a little unsettled by what was happening.

"An eye, you fool!"

"I can't cut you—"

"I demand to see!" Ezra screamed.

Dennis picked his X-Acto knife back up. He looked at the blade reflecting under the glow of the humming fluorescent light. There was perspiration on his forehead, and the palms of his hands were moist and cold.

"Do it!" Ezra yelled. "Slice me an eye!"

Dennis put the tip of the sharp blade against the toothpick. He had no real idea of what constituted proper feature arrangement for a toothpick, so he skimmed the edge of the knife across the base of the purple fringe and above the hole he was getting yelled at through. It was only a light cut, but it did the trick. The single horizontal cut opened just a bit and then fluttered due to the brightness of the light. The eye closed and the mouth sighed.

Dennis felt his own forehead to see if he was ill. "It's happened," he moaned. "I've lost my mind."

Dennis stood up and began pacing the small space. He grabbed a blue paper towel from a metal shelf and wiped his forehead and hair.

"Sit down," Ezra ordered.

Dennis sat.

"Listen," Ezra whispered, causing Dennis to lean in closer.

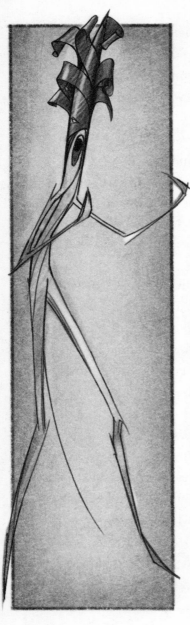

"All I want to be able to do . . ."

Ezra pushed himself up and out of the tape and sprang from the desk directly onto Dennis's forehead, where he bit down hard. Dennis screamed, swatting at Ezra as if he were a pesky fly. The blow knocked Ezra loose, and he landed on Dennis's left shoulder.

"Ahhhhhahhahh!" Ezra screamed just before sinking his mouth into Dennis's neck.

Dennis slapped his neck, trying to stop Ezra, but he was too slow. Ezra was now on top of his head, violently jumping up and down.

The banging on the door started again.

"What's going on in there?" a voice demanded. "Should we call someone?"

"I'm fine," Dennis yelled back, looking frantically around for Ezra.

"You're not fine!" Ezra screamed, diving from off a high metal shelf. "I will finish you!"

Dennis spun, accidentally

knocking over a large, open jar of rubber cement. The dark bottle rolled to the edge of the desk and dropped to the floor with an impressive *splack*. Rubber cement oozed out over the floor as Dennis batted the air like a six-year-old girl who has just seen a big, scary bumblebee.

Ezra dug into Dennis's right hand with his pointed tail, and Dennis pushed away, sending Ezra to the ground and into the spreading splotch of rubber cement. Ezra lay trapped on his back, more angry than ever, growling maniacally. He writhed in the sticky goo, screaming for Dennis's head.

"What's going on in there?" Dennis's coworkers outside the door yelled. "Open up right now!"

"Please stop screaming," Dennis whispered fiercely to Ezra. "I'll get you out, just stop screaming!"

Ezra closed his mouth hole for a second and stared Dennis down with his one eye. He opened his mouth and blew.

"You have thirty seconds," Ezra hissed.

"How do I know you won't just start biting me again?" Dennis asked.

"It's a chance you're going to—"

Ezra's threat was cut short by the sound of people slamming up against the door. Dennis's coworkers had lost all patience. They were working the doorknob with a screwdriver, trying to pop it open and find out what was happening inside Dennis's closet.

If this scene were in a comic book, you would have been able to see a tiny wooden lightbulb go on above Ezra's head. But this was not a comic book, so all Dennis saw was a slight mischievous smile from Ezra's mouth.

"You hate it here," Ezra said, giving voice to a secret that Dennis for years had been too afraid to admit.

Dennis nodded warily.

"You would do just about anything to get away from this place, wouldn't you?"

Again Dennis nodded, this time with more surety.

Ezra looked closely at Dennis. Ezra wasn't exactly coming from a position of strength. He was, after all, a party toothpick stuck to the floor with rubber cement. But he was exuding enough anger and rage to seem like a four-story-tall giant.

"Pull me out, and I'll take you with me," Ezra offered wickedly.

Dennis looked at Ezra like a fish that had been held from water for hours and was now being offered an entire lake.

"Take me where?" Dennis whispered.

"Foo," Ezra spat.

Dennis had no idea where Foo was, but he was fairly certain it wasn't located in the building he now cleaned, or in the city he had resided in for the last twenty-eight years.

Dennis reached for Ezra just as the door to the closet was finally forced open. He closed his hand around the toothpick and stood up to face those who had so rudely barged in.

"What is going on?" a short woman with big teeth and skinny legs demanded.

"Who were you screaming at?" asked Randall, the firm's newest partner.

"I'm sick," was all Dennis said.

He squeezed out the door, pushed into the hall, and ran toward the elevator. He rode twenty floors down to the lobby, where he walked quickly across the tile floor and out the front revolving door. It wasn't until he was three blocks away that he finally opened his fist and looked at the sticky toothpick in his hand.

Ezra growled.

"I'm sorry," Dennis apologized. "I didn't want anyone to see you."

"You have the spine of a used tissue," Ezra said meanly. "We could have taken them."

"You were stuck in glue," Dennis reasoned.

Ezra spat.

"You're a toothpick," Dennis added.

Ezra didn't like that. "Pig!" he shouted, jumping from Dennis's hand onto his forearm. He began rubbing himself against the hairy skin, giving Dennis one terrific burn.

Dennis blinked to stop himself from crying. On the basis of a promise from a very hostile toothpick, he had just walked out on the only job he had ever had, and now he had a wicked burn to go with the bite marks on his forehead.

Ezra scrambled up Dennis's arm and stopped on top of his shoulder. He was breathing as heavily as a toothpick could.

"Sorry," Dennis offered.

"Boy, I'll say," Ezra replied coldly. "If you're going to come with me, you have got to watch what you say. I might be what you see before you, but I will not always be."

That was too deep for Dennis.

"I need arms," Ezra insisted. "I'm not waiting for fate to mold me."

Dennis stared dumbly at him.

"Bite me," Ezra instructed.

Dennis felt like crying again. It's not easy, after all, to be insulted by anyone. It's even worse when you're being insulted by a small piece of wood that was once holding your sandwich together. Before Dennis could begin crying, however, Ezra worked himself up Dennis's face and forced his way into his mouth. It wasn't too hard, seeing as how Dennis was already in the process of dropping his jaw. After getting inside, Ezra stretched out across Dennis's front bottom teeth. He eyed the top teeth up above and then scooted over just a bit.

"Do it."

"Do uht?" Dennis asked, his mouth still hanging open.

"Bite me!" Ezra insisted.

Dennis gingerly closed his mouth.

Ezra hollered, "That's the worst biting I've ever seen. Bite, you baby!"

Dennis opened his mouth and chomped down hard.

This time Ezra screamed for an entirely different reason.

Dennis released, and Ezra called him a coward. Somewhat irritated by Ezra's bad attitude, Dennis ground his front teeth together. He could feel Ezra beginning to split in two. After grinding for a few moments, Dennis spat Ezra out onto the sidewalk.

Ezra bounced a couple of times and came to a stop. Glaring at Dennis with his single eye, he spat and growled. Dennis knelt down and instantly began to apologize.

"You are an emotional toddler," Ezra declared.

Dennis had never felt more confused in his life. And it is somewhat important to point out that Dennis had been plenty confused in his life. Like the time his mother told him she needed to go out for just a moment and then never came back. That was confusing. Or all the times his father would say he loved him and then would leave him for weeks to fend for himself. That was confusing too.

Now a toothpick had called him "an emotional toddler." That was also confusing.

Dennis reached to pick up Ezra but stopped when the toothpick ordered him to leave it alone. Dennis stared at the poor little thing as it writhed and moaned on the ground. Ezra's torso was wet and bent, thanks to the biting he had just endured. Ezra wriggled and yelled and took advantage of his soggy, chewed condition by painfully ripping a small strand of wood away from his side and forming an arm. The pain didn't slow him. He gasped as he struggled to rip a second appendage away from his body.

He succeeded, but the pain was too much. The tiny toothpick, which now had two arms, closed his only eye and passed out.

Dennis sat down on the curb and tenderly picked Ezra up. He laid the beat-up toothpick on his knee and folded a bit of his trousers over him. Ezra's damp purple-fringed top looked like an odd bug resting on his leg. Dennis shifted his position and leaned

his back up against a huge Dumpster. As he looked at the battered little toothpick, Dennis couldn't help it. He began to cry.
This time in earnest.

ii

The tiny chair just outside the classroom door was considerably less than comfortable. Tim Tuttle shifted in the seat and
thought about just how he would phrase the questions he wanted
to ask Winter's teacher. He wadded and tugged at the blue baseball cap he held in his hands. His heart was beating loudly.

After keeping Tim waiting another fifteen minutes, Mr.
Bentwonder came to the door. He looked down the hall in both
directions and let his eyes settle on Tim. Mr. Bentwonder sighed
heavily, as if he had just solved every problem in the world and
nobody had taken the time to thank him. He then blew his nose
into a dirty handkerchief, shoved it into his pocket, and
announced that he would see Tim now.

After they were seated in Mr. Bentwonder's office, Tim said,
"Thank you so much for meeting with me."

"A teacher's time is a precious thing," Mr. Bentwonder
breathed, his fat, mushy face jiggling as he spoke. "Now, how
may I enlighten you?"

"I have a question about one of your students."

"You may have heard wonders about my intellect, but I'm
afraid I can't read your mind," Mr. Bentwonder said, feigning
modesty. "To which pupil are you referring?"

"I'm sorry," Tim said. "Her name is Winter. Winter Frore."

Mr. Bentwonder's face went from pink to pale in two seconds flat. He began to stammer and cough. He pulled his dirty handkerchief back out to cover his mouth, but that did nothing but leave his nose open to spray. He coughed so violently that Tim stood and started patting him on the back in support.

"Are you okay?" Tim asked.

Mr. Bentwonder brushed him away and tried to compose himself. He closed his eyes and patted his fat cheeks. "What about her?" he asked defensively. "She is no longer my pupil."

"What happened to her?" Tim asked.

"I've already told the police," Mr. Bentwonder sniffed. "It was the worst experience of my professional life."

"So she was expelled?"

"She would be if she walked in that door again," he said like a spoiled baby. "She put a spell on all of us."

"A spell?"

"On the entire class." He shook his head in disbelief. "One moment I'm filling their brains with information that might very well propel them to greatness, and the next thing I know the entire classroom is . . . frozen."

"Frozen?" Tim asked in disbelief and with a slight smirk.

"I know what you're thinking," Mr. Bentwonder said, shaking a finger at Tim. "Trust me, I understand science. I could have taught any number of subjects."

"I'm sure you could have."

"It *seemed* as though the room had turned to ice, but I'm

certain it was some sort of illusion. That witch," he growled. "Regardless, when I awoke from her trance, my tie had been cut in half, the principal was locked in a hall closet, and that brat was nowhere to be seen."

"Brat?" Tim asked. "And no one went after her?"

"Why should we?"

"Don't you have a responsibility to—?"

"I don't like your tone," Mr. Bentwonder said. "Who did you say you were, anyway?"

"I'm Winter's neighbor."

"Well, then, what business is this of yours?" Mr. Bentwonder asked testily.

"Don't you think—?"

"No, I don't think," Mr. Bentwonder interrupted. "And I will ask you to leave before I am compelled to use force."

"No need for that," Tim said, standing. "Thanks for your time."

Mr. Bentwonder blew his nose in response.

Tim Tuttle stepped into the hall and walked out the front door of the school. Nothing seemed to make sense.

"A frozen classroom," he said to himself. "How is it possible for a teacher to be hypnotized by a thirteen-year-old girl?"

Tim Tuttle pulled his baseball hat from his back pocket and put it on. He was more determined than ever to find Winter. He was also more curious than ever to find out exactly what had happened.

He stepped off the curb and headed to the Frore home.

CHAPTER TEN

ROYAL FLUSH

W ake up, Winter," Geth whispered. "Wake up."

Winter could faintly hear his voice, but her head felt like a thick wad of throbbing clay.

"Are you okay?" Geth whispered. "You must wake up."

Winter had no idea where she was or if she would ever be able to open her eyes again. She was lying on something cold, and her hands were tied behind her and bound tightly to her body. A heavy shroud covered her from head to foot, and she was completely unable to move.

She moaned, her head full of cold, empty thoughts.

"Good girl," Geth said kindly. "Push the blackness out of your mind."

"But I can't open my eyes," Winter managed to mumble.

Geth smiled. "That's all right, there's nothing to see. Just relax."

"Where are we?" she groaned, licking at her dry lips.

"I'm not certain," Geth replied. "Something bit you, and Jamoon transported you here on the back of a roven."

Winter struggled against her bonds. "My wrists hurt," she complained.

"Of course," Geth said, patting her on the shoulder as she lay there. "They don't want you touching anything."

"Why don't they want me touching things?" Winter asked. "I don't need to touch things to freeze them," she added. "I only need to touch things to—"

It suddenly made sense—the cold against her back, her trapped and covered hands. Winter used everything inside of herself to force open her eyes.

She gasped.

She could barely see out of the slits in the mask, but she could tell that the entire room was solid ice and smaller than her height in all directions. The low ceiling was frozen, and crystals of ice drifted down from above, illuminated by a pulsating white light. Winter rolled her head from side to side. There were no windows or doors. The walls were solid sheets of ice, glistening in the dull light the crystals on the ceiling provided. In the corner was what looked to be a block of ice about the size of a bucket. There was a shallow basin on the top of the block and a small hole in the center of the basin.

"Sorry, but that's the rest room," Geth blushed.

"I don't know what good it will do me. With my hands

bound I can't use it anyway," Winter moaned. "How long till they take us out of here?"

"Well . . ." Geth cleared his wood hole. "They bring people here for one reason only. This place was Sabine's creation. He knew he couldn't kill, so he built this sadistic waiting room. He would keep his enemies here until they were weak enough for him to steal their souls and put them into an endless dark dream, or perhaps cram them into a fantrum seed."

"This is where he kept you?" Winter asked, feeling herself come awake even more.

"Yes," Geth answered. "It was three months before I was weak enough for him to extract my soul. You, however, are different." Geth closed his eyes as if overcome by thought.

"I understand. It's not a great feeling realizing the whole of Foo knows we're expendable," Winter lamented. "So a Lore Coil gave us away?"

"Yes, and it will probably drift back and forth for years, weakening with each pass. Some coils take hundreds of years to vanish completely. Even now, the air is filled with bits and pieces of conversations and events that have long since expired. Of course, most can't hear anything carried by the Lore Coil after a second or third pass. The Sochemists of Morfit can, but even they fight over what they think they've heard. There appears, however, to be no argument about our mortality."

"What about Lev?" Winter said quietly.

"Fate will tend him as it will us," Geth whispered.

"Hopefully he is well and headed for the turrets."

"So what'll we do?" Winter asked. "I can't even stretch out in here."

"Well, I hate to be the one to suggest it because then I've no one to blame but myself. But I could always find out where that toilet leads."

Winter turned her head as far as she could and looked toward the frozen stump.

"I would never have suggested that," she insisted, trying to smile.

"Fate's not always pretty," Geth sighed. "I'll get out and restore myself in the fire of the turrets. Then I can free you and alleviate your condition."

"My condition?" Winter tried to smile. "Oh, yeah, dying."

"Death is just a condition fate is forced to use at times," Geth said seriously.

"You're making me feel a lot better," Winter lied.

"Sorry," Geth said as nicely as he could. "You need to stay alive. Save your energy, because I don't remember this place serving meals."

"I'm already thirsty," Winter complained.

"Think of the bright side," Geth smiled. "There'll be less reason for you to use the facilities." And with that Geth took off running toward the block of ice in the corner. He flew across the floor, leaped into the air, and dove into the small hole, using the facilities in his own special way.

* * * *

ii

Major amusement parks would do well to study the pipes and drainage system of the caves that Geth was traveling down. It would make quite a ride—the Toilet of Terror. He first entered a long, steep pipe where he gained terrific speed before hurtling headlong into a succession of multiple bends and wickedly sharp turns that would have left a normal person breathless. After what seemed like hours, Geth shot out of a hole in the mountainside and into the Sun River. The river pulled Geth along for about a mile before he was able to work his way over to the bank and crawl out onto dry land.

Geth struggled for a time to catch his breath. Finally he stood and took a look around, surprised at how confused he was. He recognized the Sun River, but he wasn't sure at which point he had ended up. More of a concern, however, was that he had absolutely no idea where he had just come from. He would never be able to backtrack to find Winter. Geth knew Foo pretty well. He knew the places of breathtaking beauty and the places best avoided for fear of capture or danger. But he had no idea of the location of Sabine's ice caves. When he had first been captured and taken there, he had been in a drugged state. And when he had arrived with Winter a few hours ago, he had been tucked in the hem of her sleeve and so had seen nothing. Now, thanks to his wild ride through the pipes, Geth couldn't even begin to guess what direction he had just come from.

"Perfect," Geth said to himself. "Nothing like a challenge."

Geth dove back into the Sun River and swam quickly downstream. He paddled evenly and calmly. Stroke by stroke he raced through the water toward the Lime Sea, the strong current carrying him along at great speed.

By early afternoon, Geth was in the Lime Sea, paddling his way to shore. He hid in the water underneath the forest docks, waiting for someone or something traveling on through the Swollen Forest. Large, bloated mons swam in the water around him. Mons were disgustingly fat, fishlike creatures with large, wrinkled, pruny eyes and cellulite-coated bodies. They populated the Lime Sea and were considered a delicacy by the Waves of the Lime Sea. The mons would eat algae and weeds until they were so big they would explode; the Waves would then harvest and enjoy the carnage left behind. Everyone else in Foo found their remains to be too fatty, too tough, and too much like blown-up fish remnants to be at all appetizing. The mons sniffed at Geth, realized he was tasteless, and swam away.

Geth bobbed up and down, surprised at the level of concern he was feeling. After all, he was a lithen of the highest order, and it was completely out of character for him to be worried about *anything*.

His worry wasn't for Winter and her suffering and possible starvation, even though it didn't exactly bring him joy to think of her weakening in that coffin of ice.

He wasn't worried about Leven, either, even though the boy was a crucial player in what would happen in the battle to preserve Foo and completely restore the dreams of mankind.

He wasn't even worried about Clover. The little sycophant was amazingly resourceful and could no doubt take care of himself.

No, Geth's worry was for *himself.* As neat and compact and woody as a toothpick is, one's soul and heart can give it life for only so long. Geth had already beaten the odds by surviving the blades that had chewed him up as a chunk of tree. He had tempted fate by slipping from Foo and back. He suspected that his small body simply couldn't last too much longer, and Geth was beginning to experience worry—something no lithen had ever done. Geth suspected that if he were not restored to his former self within a couple of days, his heart would give out, and he would become nothing but a useless sliver of wood, good only for picking teeth and spearing cocktail weenies.

It was not a pleasant prospect.

Geth reached down and rubbed his left foot. Already he could feel the wood at his southernmost tip hardening.

"Interesting," he said, continually in awe of fate's working.

From beneath the docks he spotted a band of palehi, their faces reflecting the trauma of the many frightening things they had seen. The palehi were lean and short, with long, white hair pulled back in leather bands. They were usually shirtless, their arms marked in red stripes, each stripe representing a time they had successfully made it through the Swollen Forest. The palehi wore loose skirts that allowed their legs full range of motion, and their feet were wrapped with gunt-lined leather that was tied tightly at their ankles. They lived in the edges of the forest, and perpetual fear had bleached their skin a pale white.

Like the lithens, the palehi had been in Foo since the creation. But unlike the lithens, the palehi had never become a positive force in Foo. Following the wars, the palehi resisted ever taking sides again. However, for a price, the timid beings would escort anything that wished to travel through the Swollen Forest. They didn't guarantee they could safely get you where you were going, but they were as effective a way through as any.

Geth watched as a group of palehi tentatively circled a tall nit who was looking to traverse the forest. The nit had a fat sycophant on his right shoulder and was counting the red stripes on the arms of the palehi.

"You get me through the forest, and I'll make it worth your while, yes indeed, yes indeed. I'm very important, mind you," the nit said.

"I'm sure you are," one of the palehi responded. "Now, keep up and we should have no problem. Your name?"

"I like the name Francis, but unfortunately mine's Albert. Albert Welch," the nit replied. "I hold a position of great importance in Niteon."

The palehi looked unimpressed. One even smirked.

"I'm Simon," the lead palehi said to Albert. "Your sycophant's name?"

"Delph," Albert replied.

"We prefer not to see him," Simon said. "Sycophants only complicate things."

"Well," Delphinium huffed, "I know when I'm not wanted."

"That would be now," Simon said. "The last thing we need is some sycophant making things messier. If we don't see you, you can't interfere."

Delphinium glared and then disappeared.

Their white faces showing only fear, the palehi formed a circle around Albert. The tall nit straightened the felt hat on his head and buttoned his vest.

"Run quickly," Simon said to Albert. "We'll keep you circled."

Geth climbed out from beneath the docks as Simon was talking and ran as fast as his small legs would carry him. He scrambled onto the road, breathing hard in a dash to reach them. The palehi were beginning to move into the forest, and Geth's short legs made it almost impossible for him to catch up. Fortunately, *impossible* was a concept Geth had some trouble grasping. Geth lunged forward and snagged the right cuff of Albert's pants. He pulled himself up over the hem and into the cuff and settled in as Albert and the circle of palehi took off running into the forest.

CHAPTER ELEVEN

HERE AND FOUL

Clover hated the tharms. He had once had a run-in with them, when he was in his early fifties. It had been a dark night, and they had ambushed him, stealing him from off Antsel's shoulder and binding him in a silver dream sack that he couldn't work his way out of. Eventually Antsel had ransomed his release, and Clover had been set loose with a new love of freedom and a new dislike for the three-armed, foul-smelling, cork-eared miscreants.

Clover had hoped that single incident would be his one and only, but his hopes had now been dashed. He had just been sitting there, minding his own business, when suddenly and without warning he had been netted off Leven's head and whisked away with such speed that there was no way Leven could have known what had happened. And even though Clover was bound in a dream sack and hidden deep within a tharm's tunnel, he didn't fear the creatures or the place where they held him. What he feared was Leven thinking he had abandoned him.

Sycophants don't do well with feelings of having let their burns down.

The tunnel was dank, and the only light came from two burning torches, which were spaced about twenty feet from each other and stapled to the tunnel walls with thick, yellow rib bones of rovens. The torches illuminated a part of the tunnel that had been dug out to create a sort of room. That cavern had thirty or so silvery bags hanging from roots sticking down through the ceiling. All the bags hung still at the moment except for one that was rocking and twisting.

"Hello!" Clover hollered out from the bag. "Hello?" He knew from his previous experience that he was probably being held captive with other sycophants.

"No one's going to answer you," a voice yelled back.

"Good to know," Clover replied. "Where are we?"

"Who knows?" the voice answered. "Dirty tharms. They don't even give you a chance—snatching you when your back's turned."

"So where's your burn?" Clover asked.

"I've no idea," the voice said, breaking up a bit. "We had just come out of the Swollen Forest alive and were celebrating our success when I was snatched from off my burn's head. Poor Steven. I don't know what he'll do without me."

"They'll probably bury your burn," another sycophant said. "They've taken to burying nits these days."

Clover began to thrash around in his bag. If Leven was buried, the boy would suffocate. Clover had no time to hang around.

"I have to get out of here," Clover cried.

"How?" a few sycophants answered back, sounding confused.

"There has to be a way," Clover said, racking his brain.

All the other sycophants were dumbfounded. Sycophants did as their burns required. They were carefree, completely motivated by someone other than themselves telling them how to live their lives. For generations, sycophants had been snatched by the tharms and held captive until someone ransomed them. That was just how things were. "But—" one tried to argue.

"Stay if you want," Clover said. "But I'm in the mood for helping fate. Does anyone here have any matches?"

"This cannot be good," a high-pitched sycophant voice wailed.

"Matches or an amber stick," Clover clarified.

There was no answer, only the sound of some whimpering from the other bags.

"Fine," Clover shrugged.

He fished around in his void until he found a tin of I-Chews. He rubbed his finger over the wrapper, and the words on the label glowed. He read it out loud: "One piece will gently inflate your ego. Two pieces will cause excessive swelling. Three pieces or more, and you're asking for trouble."

Clover pried the lid off and poured every last piece into his mouth. The candy tasted like lint, and he could hardly chew, there were so many pieces. But as he chomped on it, the candy gradually liquefied and ran down his throat like syrup. He coughed and sputtered as he continued to chew.

"What are you doing?" a thin-voiced sycophant asked. "Are you all right?"

"I—" Clover would have answered, but he suddenly felt too self-important to address such common sycophants. His head began to swell, and the swelling was accompanied by a rapturous feeling of superiority that expanded as Clover's perfect body and ego continued to grow.

Clover looked at his arms as they rapidly enlarged. He smiled. They were, after all, such nice arms. The candy had him thinking of no one but himself.

"I am a rather gorgeous-looking sycophant," he observed smugly.

The swelling continued. Clover's eyes turned into puffy slits as his face bulged, making it difficult for him to see clearly. Clover felt some sadness over not being able to better look at himself. His body expanded, growing ever larger and filling up every inch of the dream sack he was hanging in.

His head was reaching beanbag-chair proportions.

His feet had grown to the size of watermelons.

The dream sack Clover was in was stretched to capacity, and it began to creak under the stress. Clover's ego was too big to hold. The sound of the dream sack stretching alarmed the other sycophants, and they yelped and moaned as they thrashed about in their sacks.

Clover swaggered in his bag. "Any football team would be pleased to have me," he bragged aloud.

Suddenly, there was a loud pop as Clover's dream sack burst, dropping him to the floor of the cavern. He bounced like a giant rubber ball. Freed from the sack, his ego and body continued to swell until he formed an almost perfect sphere.

"I must look quite spectacular," Clover said as he rocked back and forth. "Pity you're not able to see me," he yelled to the other bags still hanging.

"Get us out," the other sycophants yelled.

Clover would have replied, but a number of tharms who had been up on the surface had heard the popping of the sack. They now stood in the tunnel, staring with slack jaws, vigorously scratching their foreheads with the fingers on their third hands.

There was no time to lose. Clover rocked until he began rolling down the tunnel.

"Look at me!" he cheered for himself.

He bowled over three tharms and bounced and rolled down a side tunnel that had a steep decline.

Clover was finally able to pick up some real speed.

Tharms popped out from side tunnels and small caves along the way, all of them trying desperately to stop Clover. Their efforts were in vain. Clover plowed over all of them until he came to a long straightaway that leveled out, leading to a light at the end of the tunnel.

Clover smirked arrogantly as he shot out of the opening and rolled into the Swollen Forest. Hundreds of tharms burst from the tunnel behind him like an explosion of gangly rats hot on his tail. Despite wanting to allow everyone the pleasure of looking at him, Clover turned invisible. Thankfully there was still a little humble voice inside him that had its wits about it. Even though he was invisible, it was not hard for the tharms to follow the mangled trail of growth Clover was creating.

Gradually, the I-Chews began to wear off. After a few more positive thoughts and a number of spectacular tumbles, Clover's feet were back to normal. Moments later he was thin enough to maneuver easily through the thick growth of trees.

A few tharms were still pursuing him, but most had given up. Glancing behind him, Clover quickly pulled himself up into a fantrum tree and held his breath as those tharms still following ran right underneath him.

Clover congratulated himself as his body continued to contract. He wanted to rest and catch his breath, but he knew there was no time. If Leven had been buried, there wouldn't be a moment to spare.

Even so, with the effects of the candy still lingering, Clover had an urge to pull a mirror out of his void and admire himself.

"No," Clover said, fighting off his inner ego.

He dropped out of the tree and began running.

Leven was not far. He could feel it.

CHAPTER TWELVE

The Weight of Fate

Sometimes it isn't easy to know what to think. Sometimes people experience or see things, and they have no idea what to make of them. Your friend tells you that you have to see a movie because it is the greatest thing ever filmed. So you get dragged to the theater, and it turns out to be a story about a girl who writes things in a journal and the journal becomes her friend. And there is even a scene where the actress dances with the journal, and the journal sings back. And when you walk out of the theater you not only doubt your friend's taste in movies, but you are beginning to doubt your choice of friends.

Sometimes it just isn't easy to know what to think.

Leven was experiencing one of those moments.

He was lying on his back, buried in the dark hole dug for him by the tharms, fighting desperately to manipulate fate enough to keep a protective suit of wind around him and maintain some breathing room. But the weight of the soil above him was growing too great, and the dirt was becoming increasingly aggressive. Particles of soil were pushing into the air bubble he had formed and filling his eyes and mouth. Even more concerning were the tree roots he could feel wrapping themselves around the outside of the bubble, acting as if they were preparing to get a grip and squeeze.

Leven rolled over inside the protective air and lay on his stomach. Sweat sprang from his skin and burst like tiny, wet fireworks in the confined space. The weight of the dirt at his feet had him pinned down and was compressing the air up toward his thighs, kneading and pinching his legs. Leven pushed up onto his elbows and focused his vision, concentrating his thoughts, straining to manipulate the wind he had drawn in.

More dirt closed in around his waist.

Leven didn't know how deep he was, but he strained upward. Each time he moved, more dirt filled in behind him, causing the wind wrapped around him to shrink and compress. Leven thought of Reality and the smothering he had often felt living with Addy and Terry. There had been more times than he could count when he had felt he was going to suffocate from their cruelty and neglect. Now, however, Addy and Terry were nowhere near, and Leven's fate was up to him. He took a deep breath, using up a big chunk of the precious wind. Leven refused to give up, tired of being acted upon. He pushed up with his palms. What little air remained was hot and stifling. It reminded him of being in the giant dirt snake that had swallowed him and Winter in Oklahoma.

By straining as hard as he could, he moved up slightly, but

more dirt beat down on his back. His head was pounding from the strain of manipulating the air around him and trying to resist the weight of the dirt holding him down.

Leven gritted his teeth and pushed up again, but it was no use. The weight of the soil was too much. The only air remaining was just that around his head and face.

Sweat was pouring off his forehead into his eyes. The air was diminishing, and his chest ached from trying to breathe. He could see no solution in his eyes, and his lungs were on fire. His thoughts began to go fuzzy, and resisting the blackness seemed pointless.

It's too hard, he thought to himself. *It would be easier to just go to sleep.*

Visions from his recent life flickered through his mind: Geth. Winter. Sabine. Amelia. Clover. Then his throat constricted as he felt his lungs begin to burst.

ii

Clover's heart was thumping so hard that it hurt his chest. He searched around frantically. There was no sign of Leven, but the little sycophant felt that he was in the right spot.

He looked down. The ground beneath him was dark and soft, as though it had been recently tilled, and there was a tall fantrum tree bedded in the loose soil. Clover could see the tops of its roots wriggling.

Clover knelt down and began digging. He thrust his tiny hands into the dirt and threw handfuls back over his head. He could sense

Leven beneath, and the fear he felt caused him to dig even faster. Despite feelings of confidence left over from the I-Chews, Clover knew that he alone was not enough to get Leven out.

He looked around, desperate for some help. There was nothing but trees and darkness. Clover dug some more, but the tharms had dug too deep a hole. Clover sighed, wiped his brow, and did the one thing he could think of.

He began whistling.

Sycophants have remarkable powers and the skills to do many things. They are loyal beyond measure, and their ability to make themselves invisible is as coveted as any gift in Foo.

On top of all that, the sycophants occupy the only uncharted bit of land in Foo—Sycophant Run—a place so mysterious and unknown that no one other than sycophants has ever been there. If an individual or creature were to attempt to reach Sycophant Run, they would be bombarded by the sycophant pawns, who guard its location zealously. Many have tried to reach their lands and learn of their ways and mysteries, but in a realm otherwise full of endless possibilities, invading Sycophant Run remains impossible.

But for all the wonderful and fantastical things that sycophants can do, there is one thing sycophants are sorry at.

They can't whistle.

Oh, they can make a whistling sound, but it is not pleasing in any way. Something about the lips they are blessed with produces a most horrible and discordant screech whenever they pucker up and blow.

Clover knew this and was counting on his whistle being more awful than ever before. As he blew through his lips forcefully, he rotated his head so as to throw the sound all around him, and the forest was filled with the awful screech and echo of Clover's whistling wail. It sounded like the desperate call of some poor creature suffering a violent death.

Clover's plan began to work almost immediately. As he whistled, he spotted a pair of tiny eyes flashing in the darkness between two distant trees. The eyes were filled with a look of concern.

Clover whistled louder.

More eyes, more concern.

Clover blew as though Leven's life depended on it. All around him more eyes appeared. The eyes moved tentatively toward Clover, curious about the suffering they were hearing.

There are a lot of mysterious and scary things about the Swollen Forest; it is not, for instance, a great place to picnic. But as in all of Foo, there are some wonderful things there as well. And some of the nicest things about the Swollen Forest are the Sympathetic Twill who live there. The timid creatures hide all day, but at night they busy themselves cleaning up leaves and mending tree branches that travelers might have broken. They also free sheep or animals caught in tall brush or thick bushes. The whole while they sniffle softly and reassure each other, patting one another sympathetically on the back. They are about knee-high and have large, lumpy heads and oversized feet. Their big heads are covered with wild, silver hair and house familiar faces with deep eyes and thick smile lines.

They aren't particularly brave, so they avoid threatening creatures, but the sound of a lone sycophant suffering by himself in an open field was impossible for them to ignore.

Dozens of sad-faced Twill shuffled out of the trees and cautiously surrounded Clover. One with an orange, knitted vest patted Clover lightly on the back and looked at him with great empathy. Another rubbed Clover's knee.

Clover pretended to cry. "My friend," he sniffled, pointing to the ground.

As if they understood, the Sympathetic Twill all began to dig. They plunged their hands deep into the writhing dirt, and in a matter of moments had excavated a good two feet.

Clover hopped down into the cleared area and continued digging. Dozens of hands made light work, and in a couple of minutes Clover's hands struck a small root. He pulled at it to clear the dirt away.

The root wiggled.

Clover stopped digging and clapped with excitement. All of the Sympathetic Twill began to sing for joy. It was only a finger, but Clover had a pretty good idea who was on the other end of it.

The finger moved slightly as Clover and the Twill continued to work. In a few seconds Leven's entire right arm was uncovered. Knowing that Leven desperately needed air, Clover dug as one possessed, hurling dirt out of the hole, heedless of the Sympathetic Twill he was peppering with soil. As Clover worked to clear the top of Leven's head, Leven used his own free arm to help.

"Don't die," Clover pleaded.

There was a muffled reply that became more audible as Clover uncovered Leven's face. As he cleared the dirt away, Clover could see Leven blinking his eyes.

Bawling with relief, Clover continued digging.

iii

Leven had felt the tug on his finger and figured it was some dead relative on the other side, trying to pull him into the next life. The thought made even more sense as a small circle of light began to show through. As the light became greater, Leven saw a face, and he had a different thought—either angels were hairy, or Clover was here to save him.

Leven's lungs burned so horribly he couldn't properly register what was going on. He blinked as the world opened back up to him. His head was now completely exposed in the round hole Clover and the Twill had dug. He instinctively gasped, desperately sucking in a breath of air. Leven scratched at the dirt with his free hand and was able to pull his other arm out and use it to help as well. Dozens of short, worried-looking Twill were digging like mad. Clover would dig with his hands and feet for a few moments, jump onto Leven's head, pat Leven, and then jump down and dig some more. A couple of Sympathetic Twill began to comb and smooth Leven's hair.

In a few minutes Leven was able to twist his waist. He threw his hands forward and tried to pull himself out of the hole. Everyone tugged and cheered him on.

"Almost there!" Clover yelled.

Leven pulled one more time and freed his lower body. For those looking on, it appeared that the soil was giving birth. Leven crawled out of the hole to level ground and collapsed on the soil. Clover let him cough and moan for about twelve seconds.

"Are you okay?" Clover asked, jumping on Leven's back.

"I think so," Leven spat, looking around. "Who are these guys?"

"Sympathetic Twill," Clover answered. "I couldn't dig you out fast enough, and they came to your rescue."

The Twill were gathered around Leven and Clover. Some were crying joyfully, and a few had their hands clasped above their hearts. All of them looked concerned but happy. A thin one with few teeth offered Leven a warm mug of what tasted like thick chocolate and two hot, buttery rolls dripping with jam.

"Thank you," Leven said, wiping dirt away from his mouth.

Leven ate every wonderful crumb and drank every delicious drop of chocolate. He handed the mug back and thanked them again.

The Sympathetic Twill all lined up, and one by one they hugged Leven or kissed him on the cheek. Then they slipped off into the woods and out of view.

"Where are they going?" Leven asked after the last one had patted his knee.

"Back into hiding," Clover answered.

Leven continued to breathe deeply, still trying to take in enough air to regain his strength.

"We really should go," Clover said, pulling on Leven's arm. "We have a goal to achieve."

"Just one second," Leven gasped, his chest still heaving. "I was buried. Remember?"

"You humans and the past," Clover said. "We need to keep moving."

Leven brushed his face, feeling the dirt on his skin. He knew that it was different from the dirt in Reality and that he was a long way from any home he had ever known, but he was alive.

"Where'd you disappear to?" Leven asked.

"The tharms bagged me. But I got away," Clover said, as if Leven might not have noticed. "It looks like I arrived just in time."

"I was working my way up," Leven said, brushing dirt from his hair.

"If you breathed through your fingers like the Waves you might have had a chance."

"Waves?"

"Of the Lime Sea," Clover answered. "But that's not important. The important thing is that I saved you, and you are lucky to know me."

The effects of the I-Chews hadn't completely worn off.

Leven smiled at Clover. "That's true. Are you okay?"

"I ate too much candy," Clover admitted.

Leven got to his feet, then reached down and scratched Clover on the head. He took another deep breath. "So where are we?"

"This is the Swollen Forest," Clover answered. "We were entering here when the tharms got you."

Leven looked around at the forest. "The trees are all bent," he said. "They almost seem angry."

The trees grew in odd directions. Some grew straight, but an equal number grew sideways or diagonally. Some were twisted into spirals, and some were bent into shapes or had grown into large knots. Most had branches that grew low on their trunks and stuck out like warped, greedy little hands and arms. Their bark was thick and deeply furrowed, and the tops grew together, the leaves forming a thick canopy that blocked out most of the light, shrouding the floor of the forest in even greater darkness.

The gnarled trees made Leven uneasy. He had always liked trees. Geth as a tree had been one of Leven's few comforts in life. But these trees were different—almost menacing.

"Why is it called the Swollen Forest?" Leven asked.

"The trees are constantly swelling and shifting," Clover explained. "At the heart of the forest, the trees are as big around as a building. I've seen one swell so big it burst. It's a lot more disgusting than you might think. All that sap and tree ligaments and . . . well, it's not pretty. As they swell, those around shift to give them more room. The forest reaches from the Guarded Border down to the Veil Sea."

Clover bent over and brushed some dirt out of the hair on

his ankles. As he straightened, his ears twitched. "It's an exciting place," he added. "Most people avoid it, but I've always liked it."

"What do you mean by that?"

"Well, for starters, there are many secrets buried in here. So don't go digging up things that you don't know what they are. I let out a secret years ago, and it's still haunting me. Luckily, it never really recognized me, and I've been able to keep it confused. I'll bet my trip to Reality really messed it up."

"You can bury secrets?"

"Of course," Clover answered. "People try to bury secrets in Reality, but here the secrets are literally buried. Weird things happen under the crust of our surface. There are also some amazing animals here."

"Animals?" Leven asked.

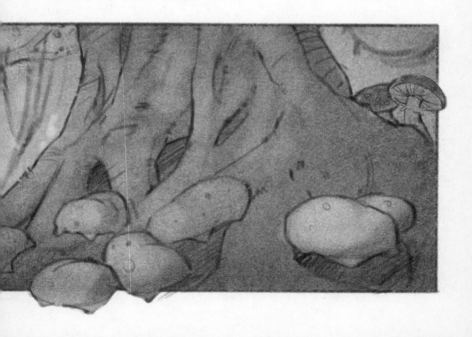

"They're not your soft, fluffy kinds of animals. The animals here are mostly dream mangled."

"What does that mean?"

"They're escaped bits and pieces of odd dreams. Have you ever dreamed you had a pony and then in that same dream your pony turned out to be a pig?" Clover looked to Leven as if for an answer.

"No," Leven said.

"Oh," Clover said, sounding a bit hurt. "Well, if you had, and if you had woken up before you should have, that pig-pony might very well have escaped your dream and been driven into the Swollen Forest."

Leven was silent.

"By *driven,* I don't mean that someone actually rode it here," Clover tried to clarify and fill the dead air simultaneously. "It was more figurative. Like the people of Cork chased it here because they didn't—"

"I understand the concept of driven."

"Good," Clover replied, as if he were a parent who had just escaped explaining something embarrassing to a child.

"So we are in a forest that is getting ready to burst, sitting on top of buried secrets, surrounded by mangled pigs?"

"And outlaws, and the sarus, and at least one siid," Clover added.

"Of course."

"This is one of the best places for them all to hide."

"So, can we get out of here?" Leven asked.

"If you want to," Clover said, looking around.

"Are all sycophants as helpful as you?" Leven asked sarcastically.

"I told you before, I'm not the best sycophant." Clover cleared his throat. "In fact, I'm probably one of the worst." The candy had completely worn off.

"I don't believe that for a second," Leven said honestly. "When I saw your face digging me out I was so relieved. Now, we need to do as Geth said and get to the turrets as fast as possible."

"Be careful," Clover warned, holding his finger in front of his mouth.

"About what?" Leven asked.

"Speaking a plan out loud can bring about thousands of difficulties," Clover whispered. "There are many in Foo who fight only to destroy the plans of any who dare to dream in ways contrary to their own. If they hear of yours, you could be in for it."

"Who would hear it out here?" Leven asked. "There's nothing but trees and dirt—"

Leven's thoughts were cut short as he tripped over a wriggling tree root that was slithering across the ground in front of him. Leven flew forward, sprawling with his right shoulder into a decaying, fallen tree trunk.

"Are you okay?" Clover asked.

"Fine," Leven said, embarrassed. He leaned against the tree as he tried to right himself, and the rotten tree moved. As it did so, a soft hissing sound came from the loose ground around its base.

"Can you hear that?" Leven asked.

"Yes," Clover said.

Leven pushed against the fallen tree a little harder, and the hissing grew louder.

"We should probably walk away," Clover cautioned.

Curious, Leven ignored Clover and leaned on the rotting tree even harder. It toppled over, exposing a large, flat, dirt-covered stone beneath its roots. Leven knelt down and brushed some of the dirt away. As he did so, the hissing increased.

Leven brushed some more dirt away, uncovering a row of large purple rings running across the top of the stone. The surface of the rock was warm, like the outside of an electric clothes dryer after it has been running for a while. Leven looked closely at the rock. Something was pulling him toward it.

When he touched one of the purple rings with his finger, the rock hummed.

"Leave it alone," Clover whispered. "It's probably hiding a secret."

"How do you know? What if it's someone? We can't just leave someone buried," Leven argued, remembering the fear and suffocation he had experienced when trapped underground.

"It's probably not a *someone*, it's a *something*. Now leave it alone," Clover said, beginning to panic and tugging on Leven's leg.

Leven ran his finger over the top of the boulder. His fingers snagged one of the purple rings. When he pulled on it, the boulder shifted slightly and the ground below it released a small, silvery wisp of steam. Leven pulled harder on the ring. The stone groaned and shook and then popped out from where it was lodged. Steam hissed up from where the stone had rested. Leven studied the indentation.

The dirt was packed, and there were tree roots running through it. And in the center of the depression was what looked like a round cap to some container.

"Just great," Clover moaned. "We need to get out of here."

Leven didn't listen. Instead, he leaned down and touched the cap with his fingers. It was solid and had a raised ridge across the top of it. He gripped it. He couldn't pull it out, but it turned easily.

"Don't!" Clover pleaded.

All Leven could think about was the suffocation he had felt. He couldn't let that happen to someone else. He turned the cap twice more and then lifted it from the ground. A burst of steam escaped from the wooden jar it covered. Leven peered into the jar and shivered, his brown eyes darkening.

"We should go," Clover begged.

The uneasiness was so strong Leven would have obeyed, but he was distracted by a golden glow he could see at the bottom of the jar. Leven reached for it and wrapped his hand around it. It was a metal handle of some sort. Leven turned it, and there was a loud clicking noise. When he tugged on it, the handle came loose, and he pulled it out of the jar. It wasn't gold, but it was a metal key, about the size of a pocketknife. The teeth of the key were ornate and the bottom of it was shaped in a swirling circular pattern. It was heavy and tarnished, but something inside Leven sensed that it was more important than it looked.

"What is that?" Clover asked.

"Nothing," Leven answered, closing his right hand around it.

"So, you're hiding nothing in your hand?" Clover asked.

"I think it's a key, but we should—"

Leven would have said more, but he was distracted by a reddish glow coming from the small hole the key's absence had created.

"Don't look at it," Clover commanded.

It was too late. Leven stared at the glow, hypnotized by its color. As he did so, the glow began to take shape and ooze up out of the lock.

Two fiery arms pushed out, squeezed from the lock like glowing putty. The arms were followed by a brilliant swatch of fire. Leven leaned back and then in. Around the edges of the flame were dozens of tiny sparks. As Leven watched, the sparks snapped and danced, morphing into a dozen glowing beings that cavorted around the edges of the larger body of fire continuing to rise out of the ground. It came up with a swoosh and towered over Leven, crackling and spitting tongues of flame.

"Get out of here!" Clover screamed. "Move!"

"What is—"

"Run!" Clover insisted. "You've released a secret and a bunch of decoys."

"What?"

"Run before any of them recognize you!" Clover screamed. "If they discover who you are, they will follow you the rest of your life."

"But shouldn't I—"

"Run!" Clover demanded. "I told you not to touch the dirt."

Leven shook his head, trying to pull himself out of the trance the fiery specter had cast.

"Run!" Clover ordered again.

Leven felt something on his face. He looked, cross-eyed, and there sitting on the bridge of his nose was a small, burning silhouette. The tiny being looked into Leven's eyes and glowed bright.

"I ate the last of the dub-rubble pie and blamed it on the neighbor boy," the small secret whispered. It smiled, looking greatly relieved, and then jumped from Leven's nose and dashed off into the forest.

"What was—?"

"Oh, you must have unearthed one huge secret," Clover moaned, his voice quavering. "When big secrets get buried, they generate a bunch of decoys in case someone unearths them one day. The little ones are trying to make you think it's no big deal to listen. We have got to get out of here!"

A wave of fear suddenly washed over Leven, so strong he felt as though he might throw up.

"Run!" Clover insisted.

Leven stood there, frozen in the light of the fiery secret. Clover grabbed a sharp stick from the ground and jabbed it as hard as he could into Leven's right thigh.

That did the trick.

"Ouch!" Leven blurted, grabbing his leg.

"Run!"

Leven took off running just as the liberated secret pulled itself erect, tilted back its head, and screamed.

CHAPTER THIRTEEN

Look Both Ways Before You Cross the Street

Dennis looked at his trembling hands. As hard as he tried, he could not get them to stop shaking. He ran one through his thin hair and then sat on both of them, hoping that would keep them from twitching.

It didn't—now his whole body was shaking.

There was a faint banging coming from the inside of his filing cabinet, where Dennis's briefcase, wrapped in pillows and duct tape, was holding one very angry toothpick. Dennis's small, sad, dreamless life was being turned upside down, and he didn't know if he should scream for help or hide somewhere until it all went away.

Like a trained seal, Dennis had returned to the only place he knew—his work. Here in his closet he was safe for a moment. Sure, he had run out the day before, but nobody here had even given that a second thought. They figured it was just the way of the janitor. Now he was back, locked in his closet, and trying to understand what was happening and what to do next.

The muffled banging from inside the metal drawer continued.

Dennis took a quick assessment of his life. He had no family. No wife. No children. He had an apartment, but the window leaked, and the people upstairs were world-famous cloggers who would dance in their wooden shoes all night long. Once, Dennis had worked up the nerve to go and ask them if they could dance without their shoes. It had been a bad idea. The father had brought one of his wood-covered feet down onto Dennis's big right toe while yelling something about Dennis being a tyrant and trying to suppress art.

After that, the dancing intensified.

Dennis did have a little savings—a few hard-earned dollars he had put away. But he had no friends or future to spend it on. In fact, all Dennis had was a pillow-wrapped briefcase with a mani- acal toothpick in it. He knew if he asked for help or understand- ing from his coworkers, they would simply have him locked up for mental instability and then go on about their business.

Dennis felt doomed. He glanced up at the single, small win- dow in his "office" and could see only one solution. He climbed onto a folding chair and pushed open the base of the window. Noise from the city drifted up from the street and burst into the closet—the sounds of taxis honking and traffic flowing. It was twenty stories down to the street, but the sound of someone yelling at someone else could clearly be heard. Dennis stuck his head out the window. He was afraid of heights, and it made him dizzy just to look down. He quickly pulled his head back in and went to his filing cabinet, opened the drawer, and took out the pillow-wrapped briefcase.

For the moment, Ezra was quiet inside, and Dennis wondered if the toothpick knew what was coming. He ripped off the duct tape, unwrapped the pillow, and stared at the briefcase. He thought back to when he had purchased it. It had been his five-year anniversary at Snooker and Woe. He had heard and seen all the other associates there having parties and giving gifts to each other as each celebrated his or her fifth year of service.

But there had been nothing for Dennis.

So he had taken some money from his savings and walked down to the luggage store. There he had bought the third-least-expensive briefcase as a gift to himself. He had imagined someone asking him where he had gotten it, and him answering, "It was a gift for my fifth year."

But in all the years since, not a single person had shown even the slightest interest in Dennis or in the briefcase he always carried. The closest he had gotten to anyone saying anything was once in an overcrowded elevator when a woman told him to move his stupid briefcase because it was digging into her backside.

Dennis stared at the leather case one last time. He rubbed the smooth outside and sighed. Then he climbed back onto the chair and flung the briefcase out the window as hard as he could.

He watched it sail through the air and eventually come crashing down on the edge of a vacant lot, twenty floors below. The briefcase burst under the impact, sending bits and pieces flying everywhere over the empty block.

Dennis didn't know whether to sob or cheer. Fortunately for him, that was one more decision he didn't have to make, seeing how his thoughts were interrupted by a voice on his shoulder.

"Wow," Ezra growled appreciatively. "I didn't know you had that in you."

Startled, Dennis jumped, and as he came back down his right foot slipped off the folding chair and he toppled to the floor, slamming into his desk and banging his right cheek against the metal lamp. Blood shot out of his cheek like ketchup squeezed from a bottle. Dennis put his hand over the wound and struggled to his feet. Ezra hopped from his shoulder, where he had been standing, but Dennis couldn't see him.

"How'd you get out?" Dennis asked, scanning the room for the insolent toothpick.

"I worked my way through the latch," Ezra said, his voice coming from the direction of the highest shelf. "From there, pushing through the pillow was no problem. Looks like I got out just in time."

Dennis glanced toward the window.

"I . . . I didn't . . ." Dennis tried to explain.

"Don't explain yourself," Ezra commanded. "I'm proud of you, and for the first time."

Dennis was shocked. "Proud? I tried to kill you."

"You showed some backbone," Ezra growled again. "Sit down."

Dennis did as he was told.

Ezra jumped from the shelf onto the desk. He walked as close to Dennis as he could and looked him in the eyes.

"Listen," he whispered fiercely. "I might have been wrong. I mean, the way I've gone about this, but I need your help."

"My help?" Dennis questioned.

"There's someone I must find," Ezra spat. "I need you to take me there."

"Where? Who? Foo?" Dennis asked, still shaking and thinking back to what Ezra had told him earlier.

"Does it matter?" Ezra laughed scornfully. "What will you be leaving behind?"

"I can't just walk away from my job," Dennis reasoned.

"Fine," Ezra snorted. "Throw me out that window. I'll find someone else. I'll leave you here to your *cleaning*," he sneered. "I'd hate to take you away from *this*."

As uneasy as the toothpick made him, Dennis was smart enough to realize that Ezra was making a rather solid point. It would be no more pathetic to follow a toothpick somewhere than it would be to stay right where he was and wish for nothing more.

"Is it a certain city we're going to?" Dennis asked.

"We're?" Ezra growled.

"Do I need different clothes?"

"Do you *have* different clothes?" Ezra asked.

"Well, no."

"Listen," Ezra said irritably, hopping onto Dennis's shoulder. "We're going somewhere important. We are going to find the one who did this to me, and we are going to help him understand what he did. We are going to a place no map here knows of."

"Like Asia?" Dennis asked without thinking.

"Is Asia on maps?" Ezra howled.

"Well, I—"

"Hello! Are you in or not?"

"Will we ever be back?" Dennis questioned.

"No."

"I'll never see this again?" Dennis asked, motioning to his surroundings.

"Why would you want to?"

"Will it be dangerous?"

"Ahh, yes," Ezra smiled. "Very."

A feeling unlike any he had ever experienced washed over Dennis—a warm, thick, smothering feeling. The sensation swirled around and tugged at his soul with a strong emotional undertow. He bobbed a bit where he stood, letting the sensation soak him entirely.

"Do you know what you're doing? What if—" Dennis began to ask.

Ezra screamed at him. "What-ifs are worthless!" He threw his short, toothpick arms in the air. "You have no idea of what lies around you—this Reality and its lack of imagination! My world has already begun to seep in, thanks to those who have traveled back and forth to Foo."

Ezra touched the wall and smiled an evil, cold smile.

Dennis might have wondered what the smile was for, but his

wonder was interrupted by the building beginning to shake and wobble. Dennis could hear screams coming from outside his closet as the world jiggled. Cleaning supplies crashed in their metal drawer, exploding. Dennis could hear screaming through the window from the street down below. There was also a symphony of cars honking and careening into each other.

As the building continued to sway, Dennis looked out the window and saw the scenery moving. It was such an odd sensation that he had to hold onto his desk to remain standing.

The building of Snooker and Woe was moving—all twenty-four floors of it.

Its corners shifted in sync as the building literally "walked" across the street, blocking traffic and causing anyone within a mile's radius to stare in wonder. The entire city seemed to shake and wobble. Pipes beneath the building stretched and burst. Water and sparks shot everywhere, making the scene wet and smoky. Most people ran for their lives while a few fainted and a few others drew closer to take pictures. The building hoisted itself over the curb and up into the empty lot where the briefcase had landed earlier. Once cleared of the street, the building stopped moving.

As it settled it let out a gigantic, "Ahhhhh!"

Everyone inside the building and out screamed and hollered as they tried to comprehend what had just happened. What it looked like was that one of their city's skyscrapers had stood up, walked across the street, and sat down in a new spot.

"What happened?" Dennis asked breathlessly, backing up against the wall. "Did you do that?"

"You pathetic people and your lack of imaginations," Ezra scowled. "Thanks to the gateway, there are traces of Foo everywhere. Now, are you in?"

Dennis looked out the window at his new view. He heard things still trying to settle, and he could see the world from a different angle. It made him hungry to see even more.

"Where to first?" Dennis asked.

"The gateway," Ezra barked. "And hurry, you've already wasted too much time."

"The gateway?" Dennis questioned.

"Just get us to the train station," Ezra yelled. "I'll fill you in on the way."

Dennis stepped over the puddles of cleaning fluid that had leaked out onto the floor and moved into the hallway outside his closet.

"You might want to take the stairs," Ezra commanded. "I'm not sure the elevator's in the best shape."

Dennis took the stairs, four at a time.

ii

"Twelve thousand, four hundred and sixty-two dollars," the teller said. She was a pretty woman, with dark brown hair pulled tight up onto the top of her head and light green eyes that looked two-dimensional under the warm bank lights. "That's a lot of money," she smiled. "Good for you," she added, patting Dennis's hand.

"I've been saving for a while," Dennis blushed.

"Would you like an escort out?" she asked. "It's bank procedure to offer extra security to anyone making a large cash withdrawal."

"I . . . well . . ."

"No," Ezra whispered in his ear.

Ezra was tucked up behind the right side of the dark sunglasses Dennis was wearing.

"No," Dennis said loudly.

"Okay," she smiled. "Well, then, thank you for banking with Bindle County Bank." The pretty teller reached across the counter and pressed a sticker onto Dennis's chest. The sticker read: "I save a bundle banking at Bindle."

Dennis smoothed the sticker as if it were a precious gift given to him by a treasured friend. "Thanks," he said, feeling a little light-headed.

Ezra growled behind his ear. "Come on, lover boy. We don't have all day."

Dennis took his money and stuffed it into a small, red fanny pack he had purchased before coming into the bank.

"Outside," Ezra ordered.

Dennis zipped the fanny pack and walked outside. For a man with twelve thousand dollars in his hands, he seemed to have extremely low self-esteem. He walked more like a man with empty pockets and a fistful of debt.

"Where now?" Dennis asked.

"We need to get to Germany."

The thought was so absurd that Dennis hardly registered it. He stopped and scrunched his eyes and twitched his nose in an effort to compute what Ezra had just said.

"We need what?" he asked.

"We need to get to Germany," Ezra huffed. "And fast. There's a chance they haven't arrived there yet."

"Where? They?"

"Germany, you twit," Ezra spit in a rage. "And by *they*, I mean the ones who put me in this condition."

"Germany's across the world," Dennis whined. "And I don't have a passport."

"Well, then," Ezra said soothingly. "Why don't we just lie down here on the sidewalk and give up?" There was no soothing left in his voice. "I suppose the only people that ever go to Germany have passports."

"It's the law," Dennis pointed out.

"There's a new law," Ezra snapped. "Mine. What's the fastest way to get there?"

"Plane, I suppose," Dennis answered. "We could fly to the coast, but we'll need a passport to get across the ocean."

"There are other ways," Ezra insisted. "When you build one of your toy . . ."

"Models," Dennis corrected.

Ezra rolled his one eye. "Whatever," he grunted. "When you're missing a piece, what do you do, give up?"

Dennis was silent.

"You give up?" Ezra asked with disgust. "Well, this is not one of your toys. We will make it to Germany despite how many times fate tries to stop us."

"Fate?" Dennis asked.

If Ezra had had a tongue he would have stuck it out. "The power of Foo," he mocked. "Well, I think it's about time that I showed Geth what fate can do when placed in the right hands."

Dennis did not have a good feeling about things. "We're going to need some help," he pointed out. "I mean, a toothpick and me?"

"Help!" Ezra yelled. "Now, who in this sorry realm would be able to help someone like us?"

Dennis didn't answer.

iii

"And what business is that of yours?" Janet Frore asked Tim Tuttle, her eyes red from too much sleep and her skin white and pasty from too little sun. She was sitting on her ratty couch, wearing a nappy velvet red robe that was pulled together with a green rope of frayed material. Next to the couch was a large refrigerator that Janet had moved there shortly after she had lost her job at the post office. The refrigerator hummed softly as Tim shifted in the rough wicker chair Janet had reluctantly allowed him to have a seat in.

"We're just concerned," Tim said politely.

"You should waste your concern elsewhere," Janet insisted. "The child is not right."

"Excuse me?" Tim asked.

"Don't you collect trash?" Janet asked.

"I work for the waste management—"

"And don't you have your own kids?" she interrupted.

"Two boys, but I—"

"I'll tell you what . . . ," Janet slurred, smacking her dry lips. She interrupted her interruption to take a drink from the garden hose she had pulled in from the outside through a window. Water was cheaper than soda, and the hose allowed her to not have to move to quench her thirst.

Tim stared at her in disbelief as she shot water into her face. She looked like a bloated red fountain, water spraying in and out of her mouth.

Things got more than a little wet.

Tim jumped up and wiped some stray water from his face.

Janet kinked the hose. "Sit down!" she ordered.

Tim remained standing. He had had enough; besides, the seat he had been occupying was drenched. He thrust out his weak chin as far as possible to make it clear how determined he was.

"I'll tell you what," Janet continued. "Go raise those little boys of yours to be future trash collectors so that I can sleep comfortably, knowing my garbage will always be removed. And then, stay out of my business," she barked.

Tim's face burned red, not from embarrassment but from disgust. "Excuse me?" he said. "That is no way to talk."

"Oh," Janet jeered, "a man of principle."

Tim had no idea what she meant by that.

"Listen," Tim insisted, his mind racing. "I think the authorities need to get involved."

There was a flash of panic in Janet's eyes. The last thing she wanted was for more policemen to come snooping around, asking questions. Besides, Janet wanted to keep reaping the welfare benefits she received as a single mother.

"Hold on a moment," she snapped. "There's no reason for you to trouble yourself over the girl."

"Winter," Tim added, feeling that her name needed to be spoken.

"Whatever," Janet waved. "Don't get all panicked on me. She'll show up. The only friends she had were you and that nosey wife of yours. Where's she got to go?"

"My point exactly," Tim said. "She could be in trouble."

Janet snickered. "She's not in trouble. She always promised she'd run away. She's just keeping her word."

Janet Frore was a gigantic horse's behind. Sorry. It is unquestionably bad manners to talk poorly of others, but people like Janet make it hard to keep your words kind.

"I know she hoarded money," Janet added, opening the refrigerator near her and hauling out a long stick of pepperoni. Janet gnawed off a big bite and did Tim the great disservice of talking with her mouth full. "She'll come around when the money runs out," she splattered. "Now, if you don't mind, your large forehead is distracting."

Tim could take a hint.

CHAPTER FOURTEEN

THE SWOLLEN FOREST
BEFORE THE TREES

The Swollen Forest was growing rapidly. Every day its borders expanded closer to the Sun River and the shores of the Veil Sea. If not for the Fissure Gorge blocking its way, it would have already overtaken Cork.

As big and beautiful as it could be, however, the Swollen Forest was not a good place. It was home to no cute elves or motherless deer that ran around smelling flowers with their rabbit friends. Likewise, you would never find a house made of candy there, or a young, naive, red-hooded girl skipping around with a basket. It was a dark, foreboding place, as unpleasant as a blind dentist informing you that all your fillings need to be dug out with a dull butter knife.

The Swollen Forest was home only to those who wished to stay hidden. Many a soul had wandered in and never wandered back out. The safest thing would be never to venture there, but if you did have to traverse it, your best strategy would be to travel fast. Travel through the Swollen Forest was best done with lighted torches and in company with a large group—or, better yet, encircled by a ring of palehi.

One of the things that made the journey so perilous was the dreams coming in from Reality. A dream would swoop in and latch onto any creature it could find. In that vulnerable moment, while frantically trying to manipulate and enhance the dream, the inhabitant of Foo might be pounced upon by any number of creatures, to be dragged off to be buried or sold or cleverly hidden for hundreds of years.

Albert had gone to Morfit as an agent of Cork. The tall nit operated one of the gatehouses on the edge of the land of Niteon and was concerned about the state of Foo and the conflicts that were raging. When the Lore Coil communicated that the gateway had been destroyed, it did not expressly say what had happened to Sabine or to Leven Thumps, the destroyer of the gateway. In an effort to learn the truth, Albert had gone to visit Morfit and was now on his way back to Niteon. To get there, he had to pass through the Swollen Forest, and he was understandably nervous. All he wanted was to get home and let someone else worry about Morfit's problems.

Albert and his escorts were now about halfway through the dark forest. The palehi were running swiftly, and as he struggled to keep up, Albert was totally unaware that there was a living toothpick riding in the cuff of his pants.

They were all breathing hard, and their legs were tired. The palehi's straggly hair was drenched with sweat and hung down over their eyes, making it hard for them to see clearly. So far the band of runners had successfully managed to avoid any incoming dreams, but fear of what might happen if they stopped kept them moving quickly.

Albert was especially short on breath, and he was gasping as he asked the lead palehi, "How much farther, Simon?"

"We are closing in on halfway," Simon replied.

"Has the forest been quiet lately?" Albert asked.

Simon stared at Albert as if he were crazy.

"What I mean is, have there been any new . . . problems?" Albert clarified, his lungs burning. "Those Lore Coils can wreak havoc on normalcy."

Simon didn't answer immediately, but finally he said a single word: "Jamoon."

"Jamoon?" Albert asked.

"He has new power."

"Power?" Albert gasped, stumbling over a large boulder and struggling to keep up. "What kind of power?"

Simon wasn't exactly a great communicator, and Albert had difficulty making sense of his reply.

"Shadowy nihils surround him, and their bite can rot the mind. He is searching for those who slipped through, and his birds have a powerful effect on those who do not have the right answers. Some of his victims have been found wandering without purpose, looking for shade dark enough to hide them forever."

"I say," Albert panted, wiping sweat from his eyes.

"The Lore Coil spoke of Sabine," Simon added.

Albert shivered. Hanging on to keep from being bounced out of Albert's pant cuff, Geth put his small hand to his ear.

"You think Sabine has something to do with this?" Albert asked.

"Perhaps with the nihils. But Jamoon, they say, is acting under the influence of something unknown, much as Sabine was. Regardless, Jamoon will find Geth or destroy Foo trying," Simon said. "Everything up is down. The poison of Jamoon and Morfit is too strong to ignore."

Simon shivered, turned his head from Albert, and picked up the pace. Albert struggled to keep up, while Geth strained to hear over the sound of running feet on the forest floor.

"Morfit is gigantic," Albert said. "There are more regrets than ever. And all sorts of beings walking around with silly looks and concerns upon their faces."

"Go back to Niteon and forget," Simon said. "Cork is blessed not to know how tainted the rest of Foo has become."

Running at a smooth, even pace, Simon was still talking in riddles. "I'll tell you this," he said, "the Children of the Sewn can't frame the darkness fast enough. Their walls are filled with dark images—so much gray. Many in Foo won't step out of their homes for fear the Ring of Plague will steal their gifts."

Albert's ears burned at the mention of stolen gifts. Simon also had Geth's attention.

"Stealing gifts?" Albert sputtered, his breathing and stride both uneven. "Impossible."

"Believe as you will," Simon said indifferently.

"But what about—" Albert started to say.

"Watch out!" Simon yelled, throwing out an arm to stop Albert.

Simon's warning was too late. A thick, yellow dream rose up through the floor of the forest and trapped Albert, flowing up around him like a glass tube. Albert looked out at Simon, but the lead palehi was unable to help him. All that he and the rest of the palehi could do was surround Albert and the dream he was caught in and wait.

Albert frantically worked with the vision. It was a long, detailed dream that belonged to a math professor back in Reality. The professor was consumed with a certain complex problem and was dreaming about a possible solution. Albert tried to manipulate the details of the dream to resolve the man's frustration so that he could simply take a deep breath and awake refreshed, but the dream was too intense and long.

In the darkness of the surrounding forest a low moaning and clicking noise sounded. Absorbed in the dream, Albert couldn't hear it, but the palehi could, and they glanced about wildly.

The sound grew louder.

"Sarus!" one of the palehi yelled. "Sarus!"

The palehi began to tremble and run in place.

"Stay!" Simon commanded. "He will pay. He will pay!"

"Payment means nothing if we are suffering in a gaze!" another palehi yelled, bolting off into the trees. His departure was like a bullet from a starting pistol at a marathon. Except for Simon, all the palehi raced after him. Only Simon remained, standing there staring at Albert stuck in the dream.

Albert could see the palehi fleeing, but the dream he was working in would not end. He began manipulating things in such a way that the professor having the dream would be confused and wake up. Albert threw in a vision of a clown, a little red wagon, the professor's first-grade teacher, and a scene played by garbage men. In Reality, the professor tossed and turned as the unrelated and implausible images filled his mind. But he was tenacious and didn't give up.

The moaning and clicking grew louder. Now, even Simon was panicked. He turned toward the moaning sound, then back at Albert.

"Sorry," he mouthed. "I can't take sides."

Simon turned and ran as fast as he could in the opposite direction, leaving Albert on his own.

Of course, Albert wasn't completely alone. Geth stood tall in the cuff of Albert's pants, peering out, curious what the outcome of this would be. He could feel Albert thrashing about, frantically trying to put to bed the dream he was working on. Geth could also clearly hear the sound of what was coming in the woods. He knew the noise, and he knew the sarus were at hand. He wasn't at all surprised that the palehi had fled.

The thunderous clicking was deafening now, and Albert was sweating, madly moving things around in the dream. In desperation, he threw in a vision of the professor's ex-wife, and the terrified professor awoke instantly, ending the dream.

Albert was free, but it was too late.

CHAPTER FIFTEEN

ICY RECEPTION

There are lots of wonderful places that most of us might like to visit someday. The beaches of Costa del Sol seem like a good place to go. Maybe you'd like to see the Grand Canyon or the pyramids of Egypt or the world's biggest ball of yarn.

Then, there are the places you would rather not go—a tax collectors' convention, a sewage treatment plant, or maybe the home of someone who keeps spiders as pets and insists on taking them out of their cages and making you hold them.

You could also add the ice caves in the Mediania Mountains of Foo to that list of undesirable destinations.

At the moment, those ice caves were home to Winter Frore, who was being held captive there, encased in an icy coffin. After Geth had escaped, the room had gradually grown smaller until Winter was lying on her back, not even able to lie entirely flat, and her whole body was screaming out in pain.

Winter's stomach growled. Her throat was parched, and her body was running out of energy. She had no idea how long Geth had been gone or if it was morning or night. She missed Leven and Clover and Amelia and Geth. She wanted desperately for Leven to appear and tell her everything was going to be all right.

Winter didn't know how much longer she could last. In her cramped condition, she felt like a seed that desperately wanted to grow but was wrapped in cellophane.

She was also confused. When she had stepped back into Foo, her head had begun to fill with memories and images of the life she had known before going to Reality. Now, however, those memories were beginning to fade. They were like a wave that had pushed onto shore, but the ocean was now receding. All she could clearly remember was her life in Reality. She also remembered Leven, but what they were fighting for was fuzzy. If they had some cause, she could not remember what it was.

"Hello?" she hollered out in a panic, as if she might forget who she was if she didn't act quickly. "Hello!"

Through the narrow slits in her mask, she stared at the icy ceiling above her.

"Please, Jamoon," she yelled. "I'm ready to talk."

There was no reply.

"Please!"

A loud click sounded, followed by the creaking of breaking ice. The ceiling and walls began to slowly move outward.

Winter's heart beat with hope.

After a few moments, Winter actually had enough room to

stretch out. Her legs and back and neck rejoiced in the movement. There was some ferocious tingling as her blood rushed back into veins and muscles, but the pain was almost glorious.

The ice continued to groan and creak, and in a few minutes the room was back to the size it had once been.

A tall, narrow door opened, revealing a short rant standing in the doorway. He wore a dark blue cloak and a hood that covered everything but his right eye. Winter could tell from his height that he was not Jamoon. She couldn't see all of him at once because of her mask, but she could see from his stance that his left side was that of a model. Somewhere in Reality some young girl was dreaming of becoming a runway model.

"If you freeze me, we will draw the walls in even tighter," the rant warned her.

"I won't freeze you," Winter promised.

"Follow me," he commanded. "But remember there are eyes watching."

Winter tried to roll over and stand, but the shroud held her down, and she was too weak.

"I can't get up," she said. "My legs . . ."

The rant grunted irritably. He stepped into the room and lifted the shroud off Winter but left the hood in place and her hands tied. He took hold of her left shoulder with his right hand in a grip so strong that Winter feared he might break her collarbone. But despite the pain, she kept quiet, not willing to acknowledge his strength.

He yanked her to her feet, and she wobbled like a newborn

colt. Her right leg was okay, but her left one gave out, and she found herself back on the floor.

"Is this a trick?" the rant barked.

"I can't walk," Winter insisted. "My legs have been cramped up."

The rant seized her by the shoulder again and hauled her up. "Prisoners like you are more trouble than they're worth," he growled.

"I'm . . ."

"Sorry," he finished for her. "Very sorry, indeed. I know all about you, nit. And a weak apology is not going to make right all the trouble you've caused. Jamoon will finish Sabine's work, and you will be nothing but a memory a few misguided souls will be forced to recall."

Winter held her tongue. She was not used to rants talking so boldly to her. Despite her loss of memory, she knew that in the social order of Foo, rants certainly had no place talking down to nits. Rants were of less importance than cogs, and cogs were looked down upon by most nits. The only reason rants were so loyal to Sabine was that they were weak and easy to control. It always baffled Winter that not a single rant could see the truth— the truth being that a merger of Foo with Reality would be an end to every rant. In Reality their dream-halves would die and they would cease to exist. Sabine had filled their heads with the lie that their bodies would be restored.

"What's my motivation for this photo shoot?" the model half of the rant asked. "Be quiet," its other side ordered.

It was difficult, but Winter followed the rant down an icy hallway. The hood obscured her vision, and she felt pain with each step. But there was also a better range of motion and movement for her legs and arms, and as they went along, she tried to see and memorize as much as she could of the layout of the caves.

There were portraits on the frozen walls—some beautiful, some ugly—all of them coated with patterns of frost. They passed a picture of a man standing over something, a jagged metal sword in his hand. Winter looked away. The floor was also frozen, and there were no windows anywhere.

The hallway made a turn, and Winter slipped on the uneven floor. With her hands still bound, she had no way to stop herself from falling.

"Get up," the rant ordered.

Winter tried to stand but lost her footing again.

"I think I hurt my shoulder when—"

The rant grabbed her by the sore shoulder and pulled her up with one quick jerk. Winter saw stars.

"In here," the rant directed, pushing Winter through a low doorway into a warm room.

Through the slits of her mask, Winter could see Jamoon seated behind a large wooden desk at the far end of the room. There was a fire humming in the fireplace behind him, and the floor was covered with thick, furry animal hides.

Jamoon looked up, his right eye glaring at Winter.

"She said she wants to talk," the rant informed Jamoon.

"Good," Jamoon replied, laying aside a thick scroll he had

been looking at. "It doesn't take long for the ice rooms to break a soul."

Winter commanded her mind to stop being so jumpy and confused, but it only halfway obeyed. The rant pushed her farther into the room, hurting her sore shoulder again.

Winter winced and couldn't help whimpering.

"The lighting in here is awful," the model half of the rant complained. "If I come off looking pale . . ."

"Leave us!" Jamoon ordered, annoyed.

The rant bowed and backed out of the room, his model half whining about the shoes she was forced to wear.

Jamoon stepped over to Winter and lifted his hand toward her.

"Get away from me," Winter demanded, shrinking from his touch.

Jamoon ignored her and unhooked her hood, pulling it off to expose Winter's head.

Winter looked around. The room was filled with heavy pieces of furniture, and its walls were mossy. The fireplace and mantel were large and ornate, and thick patches of black nihils clung to the ceiling, fluttering like bats.

"Why am I here?" Winter challenged. A long strand of her blonde hair stuck to her lip, and she spat it out.

"Winter," Jamoon said, walking around her. "You don't look like the Winter I used to know. Do you remember me?"

"I know you're Jamoon," Winter answered.

"And?"

"That's all I can remember," Winter replied honestly. "My

visions of Foo are fading. I can only remember Reality."

Winter felt odd being so truthful, but she couldn't see any advantage in creating lies. She had lived such a solitary existence in Reality—few friends and only the coldest communication from her fake mother, Janet.

Jamoon stepped closer to Winter and leaned down so that his mouth was only inches away from her face. She could smell the bad breath coming from whoever was currently occupying his left side.

"You remember nothing of the . . . plan?" he whispered, withdrawing just a bit.

The dead nihils on the ceiling screeched.

"Plan?" Winter whispered back, feeling as if discretion were needed.

She could see only Jamoon's right eye, but he used that eye to stare deeply into both of hers. He was looking for something, but Winter's green eyes were too hard to read.

"Morfit holds the answer for you," Jamoon growled softly.

Jamoon straightened. His right side was under control, but the left side of his body flailed about wildly. Somewhere in Reality, someone was beginning a new dream. There was a sucking noise, like a big wad of wet clay being expelled from a glass tube. The noise was followed by deep breathing, and Jamoon's left side collapsed beneath his robe. He now looked like half a person standing on just one leg with a deflated left half. He hopped over and sat down behind his wooden desk.

Winter tried hard not to stare.

There was a faint croaking sound, and Winter made the assumption that half of Jamoon was a frog at the moment. She was glad he was robed; the uneven matchup would have been almost impossible not to laugh at.

Jamoon leaned back in his furry chair, trying hard to balance his unequal self. He now smelled wet and mossy. On his desk was a mug of hot liquid. He picked it up and took a sip.

"What of Morfit?" Winter asked.

"Morfit was necessary to the plan," Jamoon said hoarsely.

"And I was a part of it?" Winter asked. "How could that be?"

"You don't understand," Jamoon snapped. He paused and lifted his right hand, pulling the hood of his cloak even tighter. Only his right eye showed. "We were in this together. You implemented it. Don't you remember?"

The pain in Winter's shoulder was mild compared to the sock in the gut she felt on hearing Jamoon's words. "In this together?" she whispered. "How could that be? Who am I?"

There was a sharp knock on the door, and Jamoon quickly stood. The wide wooden door opened, and a hooded messenger announced, "The Sochemists have sent word."

Jamoon glanced at Winter. With his right hand he quickly pulled her mask back over her head and sealed it.

"I have a few things I need to take care of in Morfit," he said. "You'll be returned to your cell."

Winter stared as Jamoon left the room. "Who *am* I?" she whispered again.

CHAPTER SIXTEEN

BLACKNESS GATHERS

Berchtesgaden is a beautiful little German village filled with interesting locals whom tourists enjoy watching. There are quaint cobblestone streets lined with Alpine-style houses that, with their black exterior beams and white walls, look like life-sized cuckoo clocks. And as with cuckoo clocks, every so often a door or window opens and a German maiden steps out and waters blindingly red flowers in a flower box or enjoys a smoke from her pipe.

The buildings alone are a visual treasure, but add a lake of magical beauty right next to the village, and surround those uniquely green waters with an emerald forest towered over by spectacular, snowcapped mountains, and, well . . . there are not words to describe it. Poets have tried, but all have come short of capturing its true enchantment. The village of Berchtesgaden and the nearby lake called Konigsee are two of the greatest photo

opportunities Mother Nature has ever put together.

But Mother Nature had to be a little concerned about what had been happening lately in the picturesque setting. It had begun a couple of days before, when the locals had awakened to find hundreds of fish floating on the green surface of the Konigsee. The fish appeared to be dead, but when the townsfolk began to scoop them up, they realized that they were still alive. They were just limp and listless.

The lake water was tested, but there was no indication of conditions that would cause fish to suddenly give up swimming and decide to float on the surface. Besides, there were still plenty of fish swimming in normal fashion in the lake. The locals cleared the lake of those floating on top and continued on as if nothing were the matter.

But, the next morning, there were more floating fish.

The residents of the Konigsee area were baffled.

What they didn't understand was that the mysterious underwater explosion that most of them hadn't seen or heard had blasted Sabine into hundreds of bits. A lot of those bits had perished; others, still stunned from the blast, were alive but too sluggish to escape the mouths of hungry fish swimming by. To the fish, the residue of Sabine looked like nice little treats. But after ingesting particles of Sabine, the poor fish became despondent—so much so that they simply stopped swimming and floated to the top to await their deaths.

As those listless fish were being hoisted on board the boats, bits of Sabine oozed out of their mouths and slipped away.

All day and night long, tiny flecks of black worked their way out of the water and oozed on shore. Some attached themselves to boats and rode up to the docks. Some clung to the outsides of fish being hauled out, and a few grabbed hold of any tourist who had the nerve to stick a finger in the water to see how cold it was. Each of the surviving bits migrated to a spot behind a weathered shed. There they waited until all had gathered.

When the gathering was complete, the bits merged into a mass the size of a soccer ball. Moaning softly, it lay on the ground like a giant, black, pulsating amoeba.

Sabine was not finished.

He could feel his incompleteness. He was aware that the best of him—or, more appropriately, the worst of him—had been destroyed. But he sensed that a part of him had survived, not only in Reality but also in Foo. His plan to mesh the two realms had not been completely thwarted—not yet, anyway.

He would need some help. He could feel that somewhere in Reality there was something else from Foo—something or someone who had made it out of the gateway. Sabine willed his residue to form a shape that the wind and the elements could manipulate more easily, flattening out into a thin, black sail. He was but a shadow of his former self: His edges were tattered, his two thin arms were hard to control, and his face was nothing but a couple of eyes above a white, oozing slit, but it was a start.

Sabine moaned, and the wind scattered in fear. He hissed, and the ground trembled.

He was exultant. His dream was not yet over. There was an ocean to cross and someone he desperately needed to find.

He billowed, letting the wind lift him up and away toward the west. Riding a strong current, he sped along, hissing like a black bullet through the sky, heading directly toward America.

CHAPTER SEVENTEEN

BUGGED

L even maneuvered between two exceptionally thick fantrum trees and jumped over a hole the size of his old twin bed. His breathing was hard and labored. Clover clung to his neck screaming about how much better the immediate situation would be had Leven actually listened to him and left the humming dirt alone. Now a handful of confusing secrets were tracking him.

"Sorry," Leven said as he ran. "Do you think they're still following us?"

"If any saw you, they are," Clover replied sternly. "Secrets don't give up."

Leven scrambled up a small hill and ducked behind a pink bush that was shaped sort of like a squatty camel.

"I can't run any farther," Leven wheezed. "Let me catch my breath."

Clover materialized on Leven's head. He was shading his eyes with his hand, peering over the bush for any sign of what Leven had just dug up.

"You might be lucky," Clover said, turning invisible again. "I'm not sure the big secret saw you."

"I hope you're—"

Leven stopped talking. There on his nose was another small burning secret. Before Leven knew what was happening, the secret made eye contact.

"I didn't wash my hands before making that bread you're eating," the small secret admitted. The secret laughed joyfully and wiped its brow, looking relieved after having confessed. It then dimmed and took off running away from Leven and Clover.

Leven ducked farther behind the bush, hoping no other secrets could see him.

"What do we do?" he asked Clover.

"Stay hidden."

"The secrets don't seem very dangerous," Leven pointed out.

"That's exactly what they want you to think," Clover explained. "They're trying to lull you into a false sense of security so that when the real secret catches up to you, you won't run away."

"How many little ones are—?"

The bush they were behind began to shake. Leven stared at it. The bush then spit, hunched its back, and walked off, looking more like a camel, and leaving Leven and Clover crouching there exposed.

"I thought that was a bush," Leven said, moving to hide behind some trees.

"It is," Clover said. "Our bushes, like our clouds, have a

tendency to become what you imagine them to be. You must have thought that looked like a camel."

"I did."

"Well, then, it's your fault it walked off," Clover said. "It's probably looking for water."

A loud, deep scream pierced the sky from behind them. Leven turned to face the noise.

"I don't think I like this forest," Leven complained.

"Shhhh," Clover whispered.

The screaming sounded again.

"What is it?" Leven asked.

Clover let just his hands become visible. Both hands opened and spread.

"I have no idea, but I think it's wise to run from screaming things. It could just be a tree or rock, trying to trick us into helping. Then when we get there, whack." Clover smacked both his hands together.

There was another long scream, followed by the sound of moaning and a clicking noise. Leven could think of few things he would enjoy more than turning and getting away from the sound, but he couldn't just leave someone in danger. Despite what he knew was right, he was still a little surprised to find himself actually running toward the noise.

"I hope you know what you're doing," Clover said, hanging onto Leven's neck.

"So do I," Leven replied.

The screams sounded desperate. There were hollow pockets

of noise around each, like feedback from a hot microphone.

Leven plowed through a patch of shrubs, searching for the source of the cries. In the distance he saw a man hovering a few inches above the ground, seemingly caught in a large shaft of light. Surrounding the shaft of light was a thick swarm of millions of flying bugs. The bugs surrounded the man like a gigantic cloud of dirty exhaust. Several palehi were shrieking and running in various directions off into the woods.

"That's Albert Welch," Clover hollered into Leven's ear. "I know his mother's sycophant quite well. We used to go—"

"That's great," Leven interrupted. "What's he doing?"

"A dream has him," Clover yelled. "When the dream fades, the sarus will take him captive."

Leven had no idea what was happening, but he found himself unable to stand still. He picked up a large, dead tree limb. As he gripped the end of it, the bark seemed to mold around his fist.

"What are you doing?" Clover asked.

"I'm not sure," Leven answered.

Leven held the stick above his head and ran toward the shaft of light and the circling cloud of insects. Before he could reach the man, the dream apparently ended and the shaft of light dissolved, leaving Albert free to be attacked.

Being a nit, Albert was blessed with the gift to be able to see below the surface. He fell to his knees and pressed his face into the soil, looking for any cave or underground spot where he could hide and be protected. His gift did him little good. The sarus swarmed beneath him and began to lift him off the ground.

Leven hollered and shouted. He waved his stick and swatted at the cloud of sarus. The sarus dropped Albert and turned all their attention to Leven.

The sarus clicked and moaned even louder as they turned. Leven waved his stick at them and tumbled onto his back. The tiny, buglike animals buzzed in chaotic victory. They poured down upon Leven like a thick wave of fleshy pebbles, clicking and moaning.

Flapping their dusty wings in unison, the bugs crawled up under Leven's shirt and penetrated his nose and ears. Leven was instantly unrecognizable. In only a moment, the swarming sarus covered him completely and were piling on top of each other, causing Leven to look like a lumpy green mummy.

Then the biting began.

The sarus bit down on any spot they could find. Their dull teeth pinched Leven like tightly wired clothespins. When Leven screamed, the sarus entered his mouth, muffled his cry, and streamed like beads down Leven's throat and into his lungs.

He began retching and choking, spitting out sarus by the hundreds. He could feel their tiny mouths clamping down on his hair and his clothes and on any exposed skin. The pain was intense, but Leven didn't dare open his mouth to holler again.

With a hold on him, the sarus began to lift Leven from the ground. Their wings beating in a whir, the sarus climbed into the air, carrying Leven back toward the shelter of the forest. Leven kicked and struggled, but the sarus had him and were not about to let go.

ii

Albert quickly got to his feet and hid himself behind a bush that looked like a large rock. As he peered over the top of the bush, Albert felt something sharp jab him in the ankle. The stabbing sensation then moved up his right arm, and before he could swat away whatever it was, Albert saw a toothpick standing on his shoulder.

The toothpick cried, "Hold on, Leven!" and jumped from Albert's shoulder, running after the swarm of sarus.

Albert rubbed his eyes. He bent over and picked up a handful of stones. From behind the bush, Albert began throwing the stones at the sarus. His sycophant, Delphinium, reappeared.

"What are you doing?" Delphinium screamed.

"Helping," Albert argued.

"Well, knock it off," Delphinium insisted. "How am I to keep you safe if you keep trying to help people?"

"Good point," Albert said, dropping his stones and running for safety. "I'm far too important for this."

iii

Geth followed the swarm as fast as he could. He gasped at the number of sarus covering Leven—there were millions. He knew fate would not be as kind to Leven here in Foo as it had been in Reality, but fate *had* helped Geth find Leven again. That had to be a good sign.

What wasn't a good sign was that Geth could feel his feet and legs hardening, and the hardening was making it difficult to run.

Geth hopped onto a tree stump and gazed into the distance toward where Leven was now being levitated by the sarus higher and farther away. Geth whistled, just as a large single sarus was flying past him. The sarus immediately turned and attacked Geth, knocking him from the stump. The two of them rolled across the ground, Geth administering blows with his small sliver arms, and the sarus trying desperately to take a bite out of Geth. Finally, the sarus used its pincers to grab Geth's toothpick head. The agitated bug then shot up into the air holding Geth. Geth twisted and tried to pull free, but the sarus wouldn't have it, flying even faster and higher. Geth thrust the top of his sharpened head into the belly of the sarus, and the bug exploded in a puff of dust, leaving Geth alone in the sky.

Screaming like a teakettle venting its frustration, Geth tucked his arms in and dove directly toward Leven. He aimed for a fistful of sarus covering Leven's right shoulder. Geth's sharp head skewered three of them perfectly, and they were pulverized, evaporating in a puff of dust that drifted toward the ground. The sarus could be caught, or smashed, or stabbed, but they would always just turn to dust, which pollinated the other sarus and kept their kind multiplying by the hundreds.

Geth threw out his right arm and grabbed hold of Leven's left shoulder. The sarus swarmed, and Geth began going at them with his legs and arms. They squealed like tiny winged pigs as he punctured one after another, each victim turning to dust.

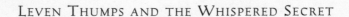

Leven was struggling as hard as he could, swinging and kicking as he was lifted higher into the air. The sarus continued to fill
his mouth. Gasping for breath, Leven retched and bucked wildly
in the air.

A thick, dirty sarus buzzed in as Geth lost his grip and fell to
the ground. Geth stood quickly and tilted his head toward the
flapping menace. The sarus flew into the tip of Geth, cutting its
wing and slapping down against the ground like a hand against
water. Ten more flew down into Geth. He fought them off with
the tip of his head and twisted, throwing himself onto the back
of a particularly large one. The sarus he was straddling rocked
and twisted upside down in an attempt to throw Geth. But Geth
grabbed hold of the two thick strands of hair that grew out of the
sarus's head like antennas. Gripping them tightly, he was able to
control the sarus he was now riding. He pulled the hairs back,
and the sarus raced straight toward Leven. Hundreds of other
sarus saw what was happening and swooped in to knock Geth off
the back of their comrade. Geth wouldn't have it, and by pulling
and pushing the two hairs he maneuvered brilliantly around all
the incoming sarus and back to Leven.

Geth flew around Leven's head, down the length of his body,
and beneath him as Leven floated in midair. There were very few
exposed spots on Leven. The sarus had their mouths clamped
down on his skin and clothing and were lifting and flying Leven
as a team.

A huge sarus flew directly into Geth's path, causing a miniature head-on collision. Geth flew off the back of the sarus he was

on and shot down the length of Leven and up against Leven's ankle, where he blew through some biting sarus and scratched up against the skin. The tip of his head twisted just a bit, and Geth became caught in Leven's sock.

The sarus didn't notice. They just shifted and continued to bite down on Leven, their wings beating, lifting him higher and higher.

The swarm finally began to descend into the forest and beneath the trees. There the sarus on Leven thinned just a bit, and he could see out of his right eye again. The air was dark and smelled of wet, musty wood.

As they descended farther, Leven was suddenly plunged into water. The swarm was lowering him into a huge vat that had been fashioned from the hollowed-out trunk of a very large tree. The water pushed up past his waist and chest. The sarus who had been biting onto his lower half released their hold and spread across the top of the water like a thick oil slick. It was nice to have them off him, but being lowered down into water was not exactly something that Leven liked. He was not a strong swimmer, as he had proven when it came time to dive to the gateway.

As Leven's chin hit the water, the remaining sarus on him released their mouths. Leven bobbed almost softly in the sarus-covered water; he spat a few stray sarus from his mouth and wiped his brown eyes with his hands while dog-paddling to stay afloat. The entire watery surface was covered in millions of moss-looking sarus, dipping themselves in the water and washing the taste of Leven from their mouths.

Leven didn't feel sorry for them in the least.

The vat was round and about twenty feet in diameter. Leven had no idea how deep it was, but he couldn't feel the bottom. All around the vat were gigantic trees with thick trunks, many as big around as the vat he was in.

Very little light fell from above, due to the canopy of trees, but the rim of the vat glowed as if painted fluorescent. The glow was strong and lit up everything in the area. Leven had no idea what the sarus wanted from him or what he should do. He could see over the rim of the vat and into the trees. In front of a few trees were tall piles of thin sticks, stacked like teepees without material covering them.

Something poked Leven on the ankle, and he kicked frantically to defend himself. As he flailed in the water, the sarus moved back, creating a clear circle around him. Leven was making so much noise that he barely heard Geth whisper into his ear.

"Don't say anything, but I'm right here."

"G——" Leven stopped himself from saying Geth's name, but nothing could have prevented his smile or held back the wave of relief Leven felt just knowing Geth was around. "How did you——?"

"Don't let them know I'm here," Geth whispered. "They have excellent hearing. You need to talk to them."

"To the bugs?"

"Shhh," Geth warned.

Leven could feel Geth slide back behind his right ear.

"Talk to them?" Leven said to himself, looking at the thick, fuzzy patches of sarus that covered every bit of water except for the small circle around him.

Leven cleared his throat.

"Hello?" he called out.

The sarus seemed to collectively shiver in the water.

"Who are you?" Leven asked.

They were silent. In fact, the entire forest seemed silent. Leven had not seen too terribly much of Foo, but so far what he had seen had either been deathly still or deathly loud. Leven wasn't sure which he preferred.

"Where am I?"

The sarus vibrated, making the water shimmy. It took a second, but Leven began to realize that the vibration was actually sounding something out.

"We have you, Leven," the water vibrated, sounding like a shaky train whistle with a deep echo. "The water has you."

"Who's we? And how do you know my name?" Leven asked.

"The sarus," they vibrated. "We have you. That is enough."

The vibration stopped, and in a couple of moments it was completely quiet again. Leven turned himself in the water. His head bobbed just a bit and water entered his mouth and nose. Leven blew out and looked over the rim of the vat and into the forest.

"What now?" Leven whispered to Geth. "Are they going to just leave me here?"

"Who are you talking to?" the sarus vibrated.

"No one," Leven lied. "I was just thinking."

"Thinking?" the sarus questioned. "You have nothing to think about. We have you, and you will remain here forever."

"Forever?" Leven asked, slightly panicked.

"Not forever," the water vibrated. "Eventually, the seed will swell and you will die."

"Seed?" Leven asked.

"Your death will have purpose beyond the reward," was their only reply, and as far as replies go it wasn't terribly comforting.

"I don't understand," Leven said, scared.

"You are Leven?"

"Yes," Leven answered hesitantly.

"Then Jamoon will reward us for your demise," the sarus vibrated. "And this seed shall grow strong from your gifts."

Leven's legs and arms were growing tired from treading water. His thighs burned so badly he was surprised to look down and see that they weren't actually on fire.

"I can't swim forever," Leven complained. "Can't you just let me lie on the ground forever? I'll hold the seed or whatever."

The water vibrated madly. "We know what you nits are capable of if you lie on the ground."

Leven thought of his Grandfather Hector. He had lain on the ground of Foo and eventually, thanks to his brain chemistry and his willpower, had convinced himself to disbelieve in Foo and return to Reality.

"The water is a constant reminder that you are still here," the sarus buzzed. "No more questions."

The sarus vibrated and began to lift off the water's surface.

They swarmed and moved out from over the water and above the piles of dry sticks stacked in front of the trees. They dropped onto the sticks, buzzing around them. The sticks began to click and rise, the sarus swarming on each piece of wood. Leven could see that the piles of wood were actually pieces hooked together. The sarus perched and clustered on the wood, standing it up and creating what looked to be a disjointed stick man that stood about five feet high. They walked stiffly toward the vat, clicking and spitting.

A fist-sized cluster of sarus zoomed through the air and swooped to the ground. They picked up a small object and flew over Leven's head. They dropped the object, and Leven heard the tiny splash.

The sarus stick man bent over and picked up a long pole.

He . . . it . . . they . . . whatever . . . lifted the stick up above the vat and brought it down, whacking Leven on the head. It was so sudden and unexpected that Leven didn't have time to react.

Leven saw stars swirling around his head, and his eyes were white with pain. He reached to the top of his head and felt the gigantic goose egg that was already beginning to grow.

"What was that?" Leven said loudly.

"They can't answer you," Geth whispered back, still behind Leven's right ear. "They can only speak with the water. They probably didn't mean to hit you; they're just incredibly clumsy on their sticks."

Geth was right. The stick came down toward Leven two more times, but it looked more like they were trying to knock something other than Leven with it. Eventually, after Leven had been smacked two more times and the sarus had thrown the pole down at least two dozen times, the stick connected with a notch in the rim of the vat. The second it connected there was a great whooshing sound as a massive, circular wood cover clamped shut over the top of the vat.

Leven and Geth were trapped.

With the cover closed, the vat resembled a giant wooden egg. The sarus danced clumsily around the container, hitting it with sticks. The sticks caused the water inside to swish and splash around.

"What do we do?" Leven asked Geth, swimming from the center of the vat to one of its sides.

Though the vat was closed, there was still enough fluorescent green light to make it perfectly clear just how doomed they were.

"This is interesting," Geth said, sounding a bit less optimistic than he usually did.

"What'll they do to us?" Leven asked.

"Nothing," Geth answered. "We're in a gaze. The sarus use them to nourish fantrum seeds. That was a seed they dropped in here. Eventually it will swell so large it will crush you and use your body and soul as nutrients. With your gifts you could help create a gigantic tree. When the seed cracks the gaze, it then drops down into the hole beneath, and a tree grows." Geth moved from Leven's right ear over to his left.

"Of course, we won't last more than a couple of days in here," he went on. "You'll drown, and I'll harden to the point of death long before the seed swells. It's only a matter of days before I'm done."

"If we do get out, do we have time to get you to the turrets?"

Geth was silent.

Leven wouldn't have it. He found a small ridge where the top and bottom halves of the gaze met. It was enough of a ridge that he could hold on and not have to keep treading. Water continued to slosh as the sarus outside pounded the gaze.

"What are they doing?" Leven asked.

"Keeping the water moving," Geth answered. "They don't want you to forget you are experiencing this. They'll stop in a moment, but they'll come back and beat it at least once a day for as long as you live."

"We have to find a way out," Leven said with determination. "Where's Winter?"

Geth considered telling Leven she was just fine, but he knew they needed to deal in truth, not lies. "They've captured her."

"What?" Leven asked, losing his grip and splashing in the water. He grabbed the ridge again and steadied himself. "Who captured her?"

"Jamoon," Geth said solemnly.

"And you just left her?" Leven accused Geth.

"I am no good to anyone if I don't get to the turrets," Geth explained softly.

"Clover!" Leven said, remembering his sycophant. "Clover can help get us out of here. Clover!" His voice sounded hollow in the closed vat.

There was no answer.

"Was he with you near the trail?" Geth asked.

Leven nodded, and Geth wiggled with the movement of his head.

"He would have known to stay quiet and get out," Geth said, still trying to sound hopeful. "I'm sure he's working from the outside right now, trying to get to us."

The beating of the sticks against the gaze stopped. The sarus were done for the day. After the echoes of the beating faded it was shockingly quiet once again.

Leven began to search the gaze for any possible way out.

iv

There were a few things about Reality that Clover was beginning to miss—the casual pace of life being one of the biggest. It just seemed as if he'd had so much more free time in Reality. Leven's entire life had been slow, and Clover had needed to do very little to keep up with him. But ever since the day Clover had revealed himself to Leven, it had been almost nonstop running and rescuing.

Clover missed his "me time."

It used to be that he could watch Leven fall asleep and then spend the night out in Burnt Culvert, looking for rocks or interesting trash. He would always know that when he returned to the porch, Leven would still be there asleep. Now, however, it seemed that every time they turned around, something huge happened.

Clover didn't mind the adventure, but he was looking forward to the day when things would settle down a bit.

Today, unfortunately, was not that day.

Clover had tried to warn Leven against helping Albert, but Leven had too much hero in him to let Albert just stand there and be captured by the sarus. Now, thanks to Leven's big heart, the sarus had him instead of Albert.

Clover shivered, clinging to a tree branch high above the gaze Leven was imprisoned in. He watched the sarus dance around the gaze, beating it with their sticks, making sure Leven was fully aware of the elements around him.

As the sarus stopped their beating and retreated from the gaze, they moved directly below Clover and began to abandon the sticks they were controlling. The sarus would vibrate, and the stick skeletons they were clinging to would rattle, slide out from under them, and click up against the ground in a pile. The thousands of sarus who had controlled each stick would then fly off into the forest to find other victims to keep in other gazes.

Clover watched quietly.

In a matter of minutes the sarus were all gone, and Clover was alone in the tree, looking at the still gaze below him.

He shivered again.

Clover was not a big fan of the sarus. Years before, when Antsel had been working his way through the forest to rescue a lithen who had been buried here, he had stumbled into a cloud of sarus. They had attacked Antsel, and Clover had tried to help fight them off. It was a silly thing for Clover to even try, seeing

how Antsel's gifts made him amply able to take care of himself.
The sarus had swarmed Clover and forced their way into his
mouth and nose and even into the void he had on the front of his
robe. Fortunately, Antsel and Clover eventually got away. Clover
was able to spit and blow the sarus from his mouth and nose, but
it took him years to get all of them out of his void. In fact, the
last one he had pulled out had been in Reality.

Clover shivered a third time.

He was not about to show himself to the little pests. They
would certainly cram and hide themselves in his void so that
every time he reached in to get something he would be attacked.
So he stayed invisible and hidden until the time was right for him
to rescue Leven.

The time now looked right.

Clover jumped down from the tree and onto the gaze. The
giant vat swayed just a bit under his weight. Remaining invisible,
he yelled, "Leven!"

There was no answer. Clover banged on the top of the gaze,
but he couldn't hear anything from inside. The gaze was too thick.

Clover crawled around on the rounded lid, looking for something that would open the vat. He had watched the sarus beat it
closed, but now he couldn't find a single notch or lever or crack
to open the thing up.

"My little yolk," Clover said sadly, knowing that Leven would
not approve of the nickname, but using it anyway because he
knew Leven couldn't hear. "Hold on. I'll get you out."

Leven didn't reply because Leven didn't hear.

Something whispered from the nearby woods. Clover looked around nervously. The noise was thin and garbled, but it seemed to penetrate Clover's skin, wrap around his bones, and shake him.

It was not a good feeling.

The whisper rustled again, and Clover knew that the secret Leven had accidentally let loose in the woods was still searching for them.

It was not a good secret. Clover could feel that in his bones.

Clover leapt from off the gaze and back up into the trees. He dug his feet into the bark of a tree and sprang through the air to a tree farther down the way. Then he stopped for a second to think.

"Yes," he said to himself, having thought of a possible solution. "Of course, it could be dangerous." Clover shrugged, as if the danger were something for someone else to worry about. He pushed off a branch and ran in great leaps toward the center of the Swollen Forest.

He had a burn to rescue, and a secret to save him from, and he could think of only one creature that might be able to help on both accounts.

"Why not?" Clover clicked. "He owes me."

CHAPTER EIGHTEEN

THE ONCE-PERFECT BALANCE OF FOO

C lover found a particularly thick grove of fantrum trees. He climbed to the top of the tallest one and rested on its leafy crown. His ears fluttered. He reached into his void and pulled out what looked to be a small rock. That small rock was actually a duft, a unique object that came in very handy for locating something lost. The duft was white with a ring of red running around it. In the center of it was a small black smudge. Clover pressed one of his fingers into the smudge.

The duft began to purr. Clover used his finger and thumb to spread the small smudge around. Like clay, it moved and spread easily. Unlike clay, it purred and shivered.

Clover twisted the duft with both hands, and the duft quickly expanded to the size of a large dinner plate. Then Clover spat on the duft and rubbed the spit around with the hem of his robe. In a few moments the surface of the duft began to shine. Clover lifted it up so that it faced the square sun.

The purring intensified.

The duft began to glow and pulsate with what sounded like a strong heartbeat. Clover smiled, pulled it down into his lap, and looked at its glowing surface. With one of his fingers he began to draw on the shiny duft. He drew thick, bumpy horns on a long, bloated body. He drew large teeth and a gigantic, split, tongue-like tail. He drew deep, swirling eyes and stony, hoofed feet. Clover even sketched two little creatures hanging off the beast's ears. When he was done drawing, the duft was still glowing slightly. Clover looked at the likeness and smiled again.

"Not bad," he said to himself.

Clover folded the edges of the duft back into itself, covering the drawing he had just created and bringing the duft closer to its original form. Clover worked and massaged it until it was a ball again.

The purring died down, and slowly a thin, red line curled around the circumference of the duft, until it looked almost exactly how it had appeared when Clover had first pulled it out.

"Perfect," Clover said. "Well, almost, just one last thing."

He took his fingernail and scraped out the initials "C.E." on the bottom of the duft. Holding the duft in his hand, Clover lifted his arm to the sky, swirled his wrist around a few times, and then threw the duft as hard as he could in an upward direction.

The duft whizzed through the air, flying up. It arched and

began to turn back and over. For a moment it appeared as if it were losing speed, but suddenly it shot off over the Swollen Forest like a bullet.

Clover took off after it, jumping from tree to tree like a lemur trying to outrun a forest fire. The duft was traveling too fast to follow closely, but each time Clover thought he had lost it, the duft would circle back, show itself, and turn in a different direction.

Clover threw himself up against the crown of a thin, pink fantrum tree. The top of the tree bent forward under Clover's weight, snapped back, and then violently sprang forward, catapulting Clover in the direction of the duft.

The purple sky lightened, causing the duft to be almost invisible. It would have been impossible to spot if not for the glowing red band spinning around it.

"Slow down," Clover screamed as he hurtled through the air, the wind and his speed causing his cheeks to ripple. "Sloooow dooooown!!"

Thick flocks of Tea birds lofted up, under, and around Clover. Screeching, they scattered about him, bothered by someone other than themselves flying through the air. A few pecked at Clover as he flew by. Clover covered his eyes and tucked himself into a ball. He bowled through the birds, the force from the tree that had flung him propelling him farther still.

Clover was closing in on the duft. He stretched his fingers and reached out to grab hold of it. His grip didn't slow the duft in the least. It simply dragged Clover up and through the air.

Clover screamed.

The duft changed course, pitching and spinning to the ground like a one-winged bird and taking Clover with it.

Clover let go and clutched a tree branch. He pushed off down toward the direction the duft had taken. The duft zipped out of sight, screaming as it neared its target.

Clover aimed for the noise.

Clover tore through the thick upper branches of tightly packed fantrum trees. He skidded down and around the trunks. He tried to grip anything that would slow him down, but his hands kept slipping off the bark. Clover slammed suddenly into the ground and rolled to a stop near a moss-covered boulder.

Clover shook his head and brushed the dirt out of the hair on his arms and legs. As usual, he wished someone other than himself had been there to witness what he had just been through.

The noise of wood snapping sounded from behind.

Clover disappeared, letting his eyes alone materialize. He glanced toward the noise.

"Hello?" Clover whispered.

Another branch snapped.

Clover backed up and scanned the area for the duft. The forest was dark, thanks to the thick trees. The only light came from the heavy blanket of kindle moss that covered most of the forest ground. It glowed lightly, giving the space beneath the tree canopy a cavelike feel. Clover spotted the small band of red shining a few yards away.

"There you are," he said happily, forgetting the noise he had just heard. "I know you only work once," Clover continued, moving toward the duft, "but I'd like to keep you for my scrapbook."

Clover reached the duft just as the red band dimmed to nothing. He bent down and touched the duft.

It was warm.

"So where is he?" Clover asked.

The duft just sat there on the ground. With only his eyes showing, Clover looked around, wondering if the duft hadn't worked.

"You were supposed to lead me to a siid," Clover sighed. "It's pretty unprofessional of you not to do your job." Clover leaned over and picked up the duft. "How can I be expected to—"

Something snorted right in front of Clover, startling him and spraying him with a coating of sticky goo. He couldn't see the source of the snort, but he had his suspicions—a siid.

Clover could still remember Antsel's eighth-grade oral report on the mysterious siids. Antsel had stood near the Education Trough in the classroom, dispensing words that filled the trough out of which the younger, less-educated students fed. Clover could see Antsel clearly in his head. He could see the words tumbling out of his mouth and into the trough:

"The siids were created to balance the weight of Foo," Antsel had begun. "There were seven originally, all of them spread out over the entire realm of Foo. The siids also possess the power to kill, overriding the usual invulnerability of the inhabitants of Foo. Most of the time they remain hidden, happy to be ignored, but as their stomachs become empty, they are forced to leave their hiding places and devour, say, half a village, or an entire class of school students who are too engrossed in their studies to simply look up, scream, and run for their lives."

Clover smiled, remembering how Antsel had paused at that point to create a greater dramatic effect. Antsel then continued:

"After years of siid problems, the citizens of Cusp decided they were tired of living in fear, so they captured a siid in an effort to restore peace. They bound the siid and imprisoned it on the edge of Cusp above the Veil Sea. Their thought was that other siids would see what they were capable of and leave them alone. What they didn't understand, however, was that since the siids possessed the power to kill, they also had the power to die. They fed on villagers and other creatures because they needed to live. They also needed to be a certain size because their weight stabilized Foo.

"After being put on display, the siid they had captured eventually died of starvation, and its rotting body was dumped into the Veil Sea. The people of Cusp were amazed and empowered by what they had done. They had destroyed a siid.

"The other six siids were then sought for game. Two more were killed, and the remaining four went into hiding. Two are rumored to be living in the Swollen Forest, and the other two are thought to be somewhere in the mountains above Fté. Together they help Foo maintain some balance. It's not unusual to feel Foo move when one of the siids is up and wandering about."

Clover was still proud of the A grade Antsel had gotten on his report.

Another snort sounded. It drew Clover out of his thoughts about Antsel. The snort also showered Clover with another wave of sticky spit. He stepped back a few inches and made his eyes disappear. He felt it was better to be heard and not seen.

"Easy," Clover nervously said to the dark. "If you're what I think you are, then I need you."

Another snort. Another torrential wave of goo.

"A warning would be nice," Clover tisked, wiping thick saliva from his face. "Or perhaps you could turn your head when you do that."

Another snort.

The space was dark, without kindle moss or light of any kind. And then the siid opened its glowing eyes.

Clover half wished for the dark again. The beast stepped out of the gloom, looking very much like a gigantic version of the drawing Clover had sketched. The siid lunged at Clover, its heavy hooves tearing at the ground and sending a shower of dirt flying. Clover was invisible, but the siid could smell him. The beast opened its gigantic mouth and clamped its jaw shut over Clover, trapping him inside its mouth.

Clover relaxed and, acting on instinct, began to rub himself against the siid's rough tongue, giving the siid a good taste of what it had inside. Clover knew that the siids learned by licking; he only hoped the beast would remember him. Or at least recognize that he was a sycophant and not digestible.

The giant siid flung its head and rolled Clover around in its mouth. The creature then drew its snout in like an accordion and thrust it back out, shooting Clover from its mouth to roll into the dirt.

The siid roared.

Clover stood and became visible again. He wiped at some of the wet slime on his fur and looked up at the siid.

"I'm glad you remember me," Clover said.

The siid roared again, communicating with Clover its unhappiness at being disturbed. Two small creatures dangled from the siid's ears. They were called waxels; all the siids had them. The waxels hung off the siids' ears, cleaning the beasts and arguing with one another. At the moment the two waxels were arguing about how impolite and disgusting Tea birds could be.

Clover ignored the waxels; he had come for the siid. He also knew that the siids liked motion.

"Sorry to bother you," Clover said, swaying to make his point. "But I have some friends who are dying, and you seemed like the only hope to save them."

To appease the beast further, Clover shook his right leg and shimmied a bit.

The siid roared a third time, giving Clover the go-ahead to climb aboard, and the little sycophant didn't hesitate.

CHAPTER NINETEEN

AISLE SEATS ARE BETTER

Desperate times call for desperate measures. That's a saying, or a bit of advice, or a catchphrase, or a string of words used to confuse people less intelligent than you. In any case, it means: Life is tough, so you'd better fight hard—or something like that.

Dennis Wood had never been more confused in his entire life, and he had no idea how to fight hard. At the moment he could barely breathe. He was thirty-two thousand feet above the earth, flying toward New York. The plane ticket had cost him six hundred and twenty-five dollars.

Dennis had never flown before. He had built thousands of toy planes and had often imagined himself swooping through the air, shooting enemies and destroying anything in his path. But playing with model airplanes was a far cry from riding in the real thing.

Ezra was hiding out in Dennis's fanny pack. It was hard for the aggressive toothpick to remain quiet. It was not in Ezra's personality to stay hidden away. He had bitten Dennis's fingers each time Dennis had unzipped the pocket to check on him. Ezra was a pain, but considering that what he really wanted was to scream at the passengers and poke the pilots, he was actually behaving halfway decently.

Dennis looked out the window and took stock of his life. He could see nothing but the top of the airplane's right wing surrounded by white clouds, and he wondered what had caused him to do something so out of character. He had withdrawn his life savings, quit his job, and here he was traveling across the world—all under the direction of a toothpick he had found in his sandwich.

When he thought about it that way, he felt even more thick-headed than usual, and he was suddenly glad his father and mother had died years before. He knew they would have been beyond disappointed with what he had become and what he was doing now.

Dennis glanced out the window again and gasped. He rubbed his eyes in astonishment. Emerging from the white clouds and keeping pace with the plane was an inky-black shadow that in some strange way looked like a man. The billowing form had long, thin arms and a pair of white eyes that were turned on Dennis, staring at him intently. At first the shadow was floating on the wind, but then it settled on top of the wing, spreading itself out like a puddle of black paint.

Dennis blinked and pressed his face to the window. When the blackness suddenly rippled up against the window, Dennis gasped and reared back, leaning into the man sitting next to him. The man had previously been drinking and was now sound asleep.

"Excuse me," Dennis said, shaking the man's shoulder.

The man grunted and opened his eyes.

"Do you see that?" Dennis asked, wide-eyed, pointing at the window.

Sleepily, the man leaned across Dennis to look where he was pointing. Just then the black form swirled into a ball and pressed its white eyes up against Dennis's window. The large man shrieked in terror and recoiled, attracting the attention of all the other passengers.

A flight attendant came quickly to his seat. "Sir," she said sternly, "you will need to calm—"

"Look!" he slurred, gesturing toward the window.

The flight attendant looked, but there was nothing but white clouds.

"What is it?" she asked.

"There was something black," he spit. "This guy saw it too."

Dennis just sat there like a post, staring straight ahead. He didn't shake his head or nod in any fashion.

"Listen," the flight attendant reprimanded the agitated man, "you are making the other passengers uneasy. Any more outbursts from you, and you will be arrested at landing."

"But . . ."

She let her eyes show him how serious she was. His hand trembling, the large man reached for what was left of his drink and finished it off in one swallow, then laid his head back on his seat, eyes wide open, and breathed heavily.

Nervously, Dennis glanced back out the window. There was nothing but the top of the wing and clouds.

ii

Sabine moved along the bottom of the wing, fighting the slipstream of air, searching for an opening to get in. He could feel that whatever had been touched by Foo was inside this plane. He hissed, the sound mingling with the rush of air under the wing. "In," he whispered violently. "In."

On the back edge of the wings there was a tiny seam between the wing and one of its flaps. Sabine arranged himself into a long, black thread. He pushed through the small seam and, like fishing line being reeled in, coiled up into the plane. He threaded himself through the wing. He found a pinpoint of room next to some wires leading into the fuselage of the plane and moved himself into the inner body of the 747.

"In," he whispered. "I'm in."

Sabine slipped in under the service quarter door and traced the lighting track that ran along the carpeted aisle of the plane. The front end of him glowed white with two small eyes. The rest of him was as black and thin as the devil's dental floss. Sabine hated that he was no longer the person he had once been, but his ability to change shape to suit his need was a half-decent consolation prize.

He inched across the floor, letting himself feel where to go.

He still didn't know exactly who he was after, but he could sense that what he was looking for was here. Someone on the plane had been touched by Foo.

Sabine twisted around the ankles of a tall, skinny woman with short hair. She was not it. He swirled around the ankles of the man next to her. Not only was he not it, but he needed to change his socks.

One by one, Sabine made his way around the ankles of everyone there.

Nothing.

Nothing.

Nothing.

Something.

Sabine wrapped himself around the ankles of a pale man with ugly shoes in row seventeen. It was clear that this man had not been to Foo, but he possessed something that had.

Sabine's whole stringlike being crackled, causing at least two passengers to glance around as if they had heard something. Sabine slithered up Dennis's leg and along the tightly buckled seat belt. Dennis, still looking intently out the window, was unaware of what was happening right in his lap.

Sabine pulled the toggle back with his tiny mouth and slithered into the fanny pack. To anyone looking on it would appear that there was simply a very long black string hanging out of Dennis's fanny pack. Sabine could see Ezra lying there on a big wad of money. Ezra turned.

As quickly as a snake's tongue, Sabine shot out and around

Ezra, wrapping himself tightly around the toothpick. Ezra tried to fight back, but Sabine had him sewn up. He cautiously pulled at Ezra, slipping him out of the fanny pack and pulling him down the carpeted aisle. Ezra clawed at the carpet and tried to fight back. It was no use; Sabine carefully dragged him all the way to the rear of the plane. There he pulled Ezra under the service door and into the service area. Sabine drew in his long string to create a more sinister and ghostlike shape. He hissed, staring intently at Ezra as he clenched him in his thin, shadowy hands.

"You've been to Foo," Sabine moaned.

Ezra couldn't answer due to Sabine's grip over his mouth.

"You," Sabine hissed. "You." He moved his shadowy fingers away from the top of Ezra.

"You're a real brain," Ezra spat. "You? You who?"

"Geth," Sabine whispered in fear.

"Geth?" Ezra whispered back. "I'm not Geth," he growled. "We are no longer one. He betrayed me."

"Be still," Sabine commanded, relaxing his grip just a bit.

The purple plastic fringe on Ezra's top rippled. He blinked his one eye and then jumped up and began to stab Sabine. Sabine reached out, trying to get hold of Ezra, but the tiny toothpick was too quick. Ezra bounced off the walls of the plane, screaming threats about what he would do to Sabine. The purple fringe on top of Ezra was flailing wildly and created a zipping noise as he whizzed around the cabin. Sabine was too slow to catch Ezra. He thinned into a string again and shot toward the vent he had slipped through earlier.

"No, you don't!" Ezra screamed.

He grabbed the end of Sabine as he tried to slip away. Sabine pulled and wiggled out of the service area and into the innards of the plane. He pushed out into the wing again and slithered out the same seam he had entered. Ezra was still holding tightly to the end of Sabine back in the plane.

The air outside the plane was violent and tore at Sabine, whipping him around like the loose string he was. The open air expanded Sabine's form into a thick rope. Sabine flapped up against the wing, while inside, Ezra held onto the tail end of him, refusing to let go. Ezra was as angry as any toothpick had ever been, furious over the thin string of Sabine trying to get away.

iii

Dennis looked out of the window for the hundredth time. There was nothing but white clouds.

"You did see that?" he asked the drunken man, referencing the sight they had seen earlier.

"I see a lot of things," he replied. "I don't trust my eyes anymore."

Dennis turned from the man and remembered Ezra. Surprised to find the pack unzipped, he reached in, half expecting his fingers to be bitten and half disappointed when it didn't happen. Dennis sorted through the few objects in the fanny pack, searching for a spot of purple.

There was none.

Dennis leaned forward and looked down at his feet. No purple. He glanced around the plane, wondering where Ezra could be and if he should be nervous about his absence.

As he turned to look out the window, he saw something flapping around like a long black rope, the end of it glowing white.

Dennis screamed. He couldn't help it. He had been holding it in, and like a bad bit of air it had popped out of his throat at the most inopportune time. His scream caused Mr. Drunk to scream, and Mr. Drunk's scream set off the rest of the passengers as one by one they looked out the windows and realized that something quite concerning and out of the ordinary was going on.

Little did they know Sabine was just getting started.

Dennis wished he had taken a train.

iv

Tim Tuttle stared at Terry Graph in awe, but not in the good kind of awe. This was not like when you are fortunate enough to witness a huge meteor racing across the sky and slamming into the ground. Nor was this the kind of awe that hits when you are driving across the country and there on the side of the road you spot a restaurant in the shape of a hot dog. This was the kind of awe you feel when you realize you have the great misfortune of standing there right in front of the ugliest, most stubborn, most cold-hearted person on earth.

"So you don't know where he is?" Tim asked.

"He's not even my blood."

"But—"

"But yourself," Terry snipped. "That boy was forced upon us. He was lucky we had the generous spirit to put up with him for so long."

As I mentioned, Tim was in awe.

"Addy," Terry yelled back into the apartment. "Come tell this fool what that dumb boy did."

Addy made her way to the door while Terry receded into the interior of the apartment.

Tim had been fortunate enough to pick up on the trail of Winter. After he had left Janet Frore's house, he had considered all the possibilities of where Winter could have gone and had concluded that she had most likely traveled by bus. Besides hitch-hiking, there was really no other way out of town.

Tim knew that if Winter had stayed around, she would have hidden out with him and his wife. They would have been happy to hide her. So, figuring that she must have fled the area, the bus seemed like the most likely mode of travel. Unfortunately, no one at the bus station was much help. One ticket lady seemed to remember selling a ticket to a minor, but she couldn't remember where that ticket had been to. Tim had been discouraged until a couple who were getting off a bus overheard him asking questions and told him they remembered meeting a nice girl with blonde hair when they were leaving the week before. It was entirely fortuitous. The couple debated with each other for a moment before they agreed on the fact that she had been heading to Oklahoma to visit her grandmother.

"Sure it wasn't Texas to see her grandfather?" the man said.

"Certain," the woman answered.

Tim took the first bus he could get to Oklahoma. After asking a dozen bus station employees and four taxi drivers, Tim had been fortunate enough to find a cabdriver who remembered dropping Winter off at a school in Burnt Culvert, Oklahoma.

"Home of the Fighting Ashes," he had said.

That same taxi driver took Tim to Sterling Thoughts Middle School. There Tim found hundreds of kids who were willing to tell him all about the strange girl who had come to their school and frozen its two biggest bullies. The children had even pointed out Brick and Glen, who now spent their lunch breaks standing against the wall, shaking like nervous Todd. The students then added a new depth to Tim's search by informing him that Winter had run off with a strange kid with a white streak in his hair, a boy named Leven Thumps.

At the public library, Tim had not found a single Thumps in the phone book, but he did find a Thumps in the newspaper. It seemed that not too many days before, the home of one Terry and Addy Graph and their adopted son, Leven Thumps, had been frozen and destroyed, lifted into the air and dropped to the ground. It wasn't too hard from there to find where Addy and Terry were now living.

Tim half wished he had never found them. They were awful people and reminded Tim a great deal of Janet Frore.

"Addy, tell him about that brat," Terry demanded. They had never invited Tim in, so he just stood there on their doorstep.

Addy Graph stepped up. She was a large woman with a big forehead and messy hair. The apartment Terry and she were living in was a disaster. Tim couldn't see the whole thing from the door, but what he could see was awful. It looked like something a trash dump might throw up if things like trash dumps were capable of having the flu. There were dishes and litter all over. Leven had always been the one to do the cleaning; in his absence, Addy and Terry did nothing.

"I'll tell you what that selfish boy did," Addy spat. "He picked up our house and smashed it into a million—"

"Billion!" Terry yelled from inside.

" . . . a billion pieces," Addy said. "My sister dies in childbirth and leaves me a burden like that? What's this world coming to?"

"This isn't the America my father fought for!" Terry yelled.

"So do you know where he went?" Tim asked.

"How would I know?" Addy barked. "If I knew where he was, I'd have him over my knee administering the punishment he has due."

"I need to find him," Tim added.

"Why's that?" Terry asked, stepping back up to the door.

"I think he could be in trouble."

"Trouble?" Terry snarled. "Trouble?"

Terry was beside himself. Not literally. This story would be that much more painful if there were two Terrys, able to stand next to each other and simultaneously curse Leven.

But Terry felt he had been cursed since the day Leven had been brought home from the hospital and he and his wife had been forced to take care of the kid. Leven had made Terry's life miserable. Leven was always hanging around, eating their food, sitting on their furniture, and talking without being asked to. Life with Leven had been hard for Terry.

So imagine how surprised Terry had been to discover that with Leven gone, things were even worse.

Shortly after Leven had walked out, things had gotten weird. Addy had thrown a fit and insisted that Terry find work. She had also stolen Terry's drinking money. And, as if a dry throat and the prospect of having to find a job weren't bad enough, the tree outside had snuck up on Terry through the toilet.

Those now seemed like the good old days, seeing as how Terry had subsequently lost his entire house. It had been lifted up by the roots of the dead tree he had hacked down, frozen, and then dropped. The house had shattered against the earth, sounding like a million ceramic golf balls being dumped off the Empire State Building. In the end there was no chunk bigger than a stick of kindling left. That night Terry had stood there dumbfounded, confused, and scared. Sure, it wasn't far from his normal state of dumbfounded, confused, and *angry*, but the fear sparked something in him. It twisted and turned until the fear was more of a burning *hatred* for the kid he had been forced to take in all those years before.

That trailer home had been all that Terry had. Yes, there was Addy, but Addy's value was depreciating faster than the mobile home had been. Now Terry had nothing. The house had not even been insured.

The hatred grew.

As the hard, dark thoughts filled his head, Terry began to realize something. It was almost as if for the first time in his life he could see something he needed to accomplish. He could feel and think and spit nothing but hatred for Leven. The kid had to be *somewhere*. An ungrateful fourteen-year-old boy with no money can't just disappear off the face of the earth.

That would be impossible.

"Last we heard, some church in Maine claims to have spotted the boy," Terry spat. "I was going to call them, but I lost the number."

"Maine?" Tim asked excitedly.

"It's in Canada someplace," Terry snipped.

Tim didn't correct him. "Thanks," he said. "If I find him, I'll let you know."

"Oh, goody," Terry slurred. "Did you hear that, Addy? He'll let us know. Well, you better. I got a score to settle with that brat."

Terry slammed the door, ending the conversation.

CHAPTER TWENTY

SEPARATED AT BITE

It was so silent. Leven could hear himself breathing, but nothing else. He repositioned his hold on the narrow rim inside the vat. He and Geth had been soaking in the gaze for hours, and Leven had little or no doubt that his body could now outwrinkle any raisin around. His entire being felt like a massive bruise.

"We've got to get out," Leven urged.

"Only the seed can set us free," Geth said solemnly. "They build each gaze as an intricate puzzle. A series of blows with wood in certain spots closes the gaze. And only the growth of the seed opens it back up."

"So this is it?" Leven asked. "We're done for?"

"We'll see what fate has in mind," Geth said.

"Maybe Winter will come for us," Leven suggested, more to himself than anyone else.

"Actually," Geth said, "Winter has her own problems. By the time she might find us it will be too late."

"What about Amelia?"

Geth was silent.

"She's trapped too?" Leven asked.

Geth was still silent. "I'm afraid she was caught in the gunt," he finally answered, knowing Leven deserved to know. "Winter tried to save her, but it was no use."

"She's dead?" Leven asked sadly.

His eyes burned momentarily and then cooled.

"Are you sure?" Leven added.

"I'm sorry."

Leven had barely known his Grandmother Amelia, but she had been his only real family. He had nobody else, and the knowledge that he was the single remaining Thumps was as painful as learning of Amelia's passing.

"She was so kind," Leven whispered.

"And important to Foo," Geth added.

Leven hated the rovens. He hated everything that was happening. He hated the selfish and dark dreams of Reality that had helped give beings like Sabine power. Leven wiped water from his eyes.

Geth patted Leven on the shoulder.

"I want to get out and see where she died," Leven insisted.

"Then we must hope that fate has us favorably in its sight."

"Amelia wouldn't want us to give up," Leven said. "At least Clover is out there; he can help. That's something."

"That's true," Geth replied. "But it will take more than a single sycophant to save us from this gaze."

"You don't know Clover," Leven said. "He won't stop until we're free."

"We'll see what fate has in mind," Geth agreed with excitement, even as his tiny body was hardening further. "This is always my—"

Geth was interrupted by a terrific screech that pierced the air. Leven shook, and Geth grabbed onto a lock of Leven's hair right below the white patch. The screech continued, and in the faint glow Leven could see rows of pointed, white objects piercing the sides of the gaze. The container began to vibrate, and Leven lost his grip and floated toward the center of the vat. The agitated water splashed into his eyes and up his nose. He sputtered and wiped his face and could see the dots growing larger and beginning to look like white wedges pushing through the wood.

"What's happening?" Leven yelled.

"I have no idea," Geth yelled back, water sloshing everywhere. "But I think those are teeth!"

Leven looked closely and realized Geth was right. The small white mountains were huge teeth, penetrating the gaze. From the pattern of the teeth it was obvious something gigantic was biting down.

There was a horrific wrenching noise as the gaze was lifted. It began to shake violently, rattling Leven and Geth around like beans in a child's toy. Water sloshed up Leven's nose. His head

banged against the walls of the gaze. Then, like lightning striking, his gift kicked in.

Leven's eyes burned gold. His mind reeled as streaks of blinding light flashed through his head, popping like the flashbulbs from a thousand cameras. Leven could see himself in the water as the powerful jaws of the beast holding them finally came together and bit off the entire top of the gaze. Leven could also see himself caught in the teeth of the beast.

He couldn't let that happen.

Leven shook off his thoughts and glanced around as he was being sloshed about in the water. The light from his eyes lit the inside of the gaze in a brilliant manner.

"What do you see?" Geth yelled.

"We're about to be eaten," Leven yelled, "unless we duck!"

As much as he hated the water, Leven dove below the surface. Fighting to stay submerged, he opened his eyelids and looked up. His eyes shone, and he could see Geth a few feet above him, floating on top of the water. Leven reached up with his right hand. Just as his fingers were about to close around Geth, the beast's bite cracked the shell of the gaze, and his mighty teeth clamped together like a tightly wound bear trap. Leven closed his hand, whipping it back just as the creature's jaw closed. Water rushed into Leven's mouth and nose. He gagged and swallowed huge fists of liquid as he struggled to breathe. The bottom half of the gaze broke away and the vat tipped onto its side, pouring Leven and the water out in one humongous wave.

The beast screamed.

Leven tried to catch his breath as his chest burned and heaved. He spit and moaned, gasping for air.

The beast screamed again.

Leven scrambled from the broken gaze and opened his fist to set Geth free, but Geth was not there. Frantically, Leven patted his body, searching for Geth. He could feel nothing but the key still in his pocket.

The beast screamed even louder, as if bothered by Leven's ignoring him. Leven looked up to get his first real glimpse of his assailant.

It would not be lying to say that Leven suddenly longed for the peace and quiet of being trapped in the gaze forever. Towering over Leven was one of the seven siids—the fifth one, to be exact.

A hundred avalands would have been less threatening.

The siid stood on four thick, meaty legs, each capped off with a hoof the size of a small hill. Its legs were wrapped in twisted vines and strands of old rope that looked to grow from the belly of the beast. The siid's body was long and wide, like that of a bloated whale. The creature's skin was pockmarked and scarred. There were spikes sticking out of its back and circling down under its body and around its hind side. The head of the beast was round, with a square mouth and long, twisted ears that looked like fleshy braids. Clinging to the end of each ear was a small, monkeylike waxel. One was red, the other yellow.

The siid's green-burning eyes were as large as its bottomless nostrils. On its shoulders were two mushy humps, and behind those humps were two long, leathery arms that were tearing at the ground with pointed claws, scooping up water with flat thumbs and carrying it up into the creature's mouth. At the far end of the beast was a thick tail split down the middle like a forked tongue. Both bits of tail whipped at the air, slapping and cracking in a circular motion.

Leven tried to catch his breath, but the sight before him stole every ounce of air his lungs had held. His throat burned painfully as air rushed out of his mouth. Leven closed his eyes and tried to calm himself—and to control his gift.

There was nothing but fear.

The siid lifted its head and breathed in, sucking broken tree limbs and loose dirt up from the ground. They stuck to the siid's nose as if it were a vacuum, and when the beast blew out, debris and saliva flew everywhere.

Leven could feel his knees weakening as he tried to decide what to do.

The beast opened its gigantic mouth and roared, sending noise and wind circling madly, like a small tornado. Caught in the wind, Leven stood there shaking, easy prey for the siid. The beast moved forward and with one swoop picked up Leven in its gigantic mouth.

Leven could feel the monster's mouth clamped tight against him. He half expected to hear the sound of himself being crushed but couldn't feel any teeth tearing into him. The siid reached into its own mouth and took hold of Leven's head with one arm and Leven's feet with the other. It turned Leven in its mouth, licking him with its thick, beanbag-looking tongue. Leven felt like a buttery ear of corn. He wanted to scream, but he also longed to keep his mouth shut so as to prevent a better taste of tongue.

After rotating Leven a few more times, the beast let him roll out of its mouth onto the ground. Leven lay there spitting and coughing. He felt his arms and legs and realized that he was still intact.

The siid stood right above him and snorted.

Leven looked around at the night. There was no one in sight. No sarus, no Geth, just the broken gaze and a creature as big as a mountain.

Leven was astonished to hear someone talking to him.

"Did I come through or what?" Clover asked, invisible but nearby.

"Clover?" Leven looked around in disbelief.

"How many times am I going to have to save your life?" Clover asked proudly.

"You did *that*?" Leven asked, looking up at the siid.

"It was no big deal," Clover said, blushing so strongly that his two red cheeks materialized momentarily and then disappeared. "He owed me. Plus, I promised him a fresh fantrum seed and gaze water. Siids prefer water that's been sitting around."

Leven got to his feet, his legs as wobbly as wet noodles. He could feel Clover helping to steady him.

"Thanks," Leven said honestly, still not comfortable standing so close to the siid.

Clover whistled and materialized. The siid quickly whipped its tail around and picked up Leven with one half of the fork and Clover with the other.

"Don't worry," Clover said. "It'll get us out of the forest."

"I can't leave without Geth," Leven insisted, struggling in the fleshy fork of the siid's tail. He broke free and began feeling the ground around him, calling, "Geth!"

Clover bounced around doing the same.

"Where was he last?" Clover asked, smiling.

"He was in the gaze," Leven lamented. "I tried to grab him, but he got away. We have to find him."

"He's not here," said Clover, pointing out the obvious. "He was probably caught in the runoff. I'm sure he's in the Waz River by now. He'll float to Fissure Gorge."

"Geth!" Leven yelled, his chest burning with pain for his misplaced friend.

The forest began to moan. The sarus were returning.

"We need to get out of here," Clover said urgently. "Geth is a master at making it back. Besides, he told us if we were split up to get to the turrets."

"Geth!" Leven yelled one last time.

In the trees there was a sweeping whisper. As Leven turned his head, a small, burning secret burst from the trees and sprang onto the bridge of his nose.

Clover spotted it and yelled, "Don't look at it!"

Leven shut his eyes and tried to bat the secret off his nose. The secret wouldn't have it. It pushed up on Leven's eyelids, forcing Leven to open his eyes. Leven had no choice. He looked at the secret, and it smiled.

"I embezzled from my boss," the secret whispered. Then it clapped its tiny, fiery hands and dashed away.

"The secrets are getting more serious," Clover said. "We have to get out of here."

"But Geth . . ."

Clover wasn't listening. He gave his pathetic imitation of a whistle, and the siid picked Leven and him up again with its tail. Clover semi-whistled a second time, and the huge beast began to step quickly. Foo rocked as the siid pushed forward. The scales on its body clicked and rubbed in an awkward rhythm as the two monkeylike creatures hanging on its ears continued to argue with one another. Apparently the red one really felt it was the yellow one's turn to clean the siid. Their high-pitched screaming cut through the air and reminded Leven of brakes squealing on a car.

"This is the way to travel," Clover said, excited. "We should make up some time."

Leven could think of little besides Amelia and Geth and the time they didn't have.

"Now's probably not a good time to complain about you not ever really thanking me for bringing you here, is it?" Clover asked.

"I don't think so," Leven answered sullenly.

"That's okay," Clover said. "We can talk about it later."

Leven closed his eyes and tried to see the future—nothing.

"Come on, Geth," he whispered. "Come on."

The siid ran.

Leven didn't feel so well.

CHAPTER TWENTY-ONE

BE CAREFUL WHERE YOU STEP

J anet Frore wasn't comfortable. Ever since the dumb man with the dumb forehead and dumb hair had come by, Janet had been bothered.

"What business does he have worrying about the girl?" Janet whined. "Besides, I did everything I could for Winter, and if she runs off it's no concern of mine," she tried to convince herself. "I should add up how much that child has cost me. I'm sure the total would be astounding."

Janet didn't stand much. She stood up for things like moving from the couch to the bed, going to the rest room, walking out to get the mail, or driving to the grocery store. Other than that, she sat on the couch, eating and thinking nasty things about everyone she knew, had known, or would someday meet.

Today, however, was mail day, and Janet was in for some standing.

Janet liked to let the mail build up for a few days and then gather it all in a plastic sack. Normally she would venture out in midafternoon, but thanks to a terribly engaging soap opera, Janet had been unable to pull herself away from the TV and get the mail at an earlier hour.

So, here it was, eight o'clock at night, and Janet was suddenly feeling an unusual burst of energy. She decided to use that energy to go for the mail.

Janet hefted herself from the couch, rising like a fat wad of dough in a hot oven. She pushed up and onto her two poor legs. She gave her lower limbs a few moments to adjust to the shock, then began to shuffle out of the room.

Janet stopped at the front door to catch her breath. She had decided to shed her robe and was now wearing a yellow house-coat with a row of red flowers stitched around the bottom hem and along the sleeves and neck. Of course the flowers didn't stand out half as much as all the food stains she had dribbled down the front. Janet cleared her throat and choked a bit on some food that was still sitting in there. She ran her puffy fingers through her long, thinning hair and reached for the doorknob.

She pulled, and the world around her came leaking in.

Janet could see the night sky. She could see the lights on in the neighbors' homes. She listened to the streetlights buzzing and took in the sound of a softball game being played down the way. It had been so long since Janet had stepped out at night that she had almost forgotten how it was.

She looked down at the walkway. It was littered with rolled-up newspapers that she had never taken the time to come out and collect.

She stepped onto the walkway and began to journey down toward the mailbox. A light wind blew through her hair and around her body. The smell of fresh-cut grass filled her nostrils.

Janet stopped in her tracks. There was something about being there, covered in night and a veil of stars. There was a celebration in the wind and a sense of nature in the sounds around her. For a brief and fleeting moment, Janet almost regretted how much of life she was missing.

"Dumb nature," she muttered, shaking the feeling off.

Three young boys appeared, riding down the street on their bikes, their laughter and talk filling the air. They pedaled near Janet's house; upon spotting her, the tallest one yelled out, "Hey, look at that whale in a dress!"

They all laughed and continued on past.

Without even thinking about it, Janet reached down and grabbed one of the rolled-up newspapers she had been too lazy to gather up. She flung it as hard as she could, knocking the tallest boy in the back of the head. His bike wobbled, and he crashed into the curb. He rolled over and looked back at Janet.

"Serves you right," she barked as she stood on the edge of her walkway where it haphazardly met up with the city's sidewalk. "You need to—"

Janet stopped talking due to the appearance of a shooting star streaking across the black, fuzzy sky. She looked up at the celestial miracle and watched it fade in the distance. The temperature was a perfect sixty-three degrees. She wasn't standing directly over the mismatched sidewalk, but there was a bit of her hanging over the line, a bit that might not have been there had she spent the last few months of her life doing something besides sitting and eating. Fate snatched a wisp of her, and although she had no understanding of what had transpired, she could feel that something about her had changed.

"I need to stop getting up," she complained, shaking her head.

Janet collected her mail, shuffled back inside, slammed the door, and locked it tight.

CHAPTER TWENTY-TWO

The Spirited Hitchhiker

To Leven, the Swollen Forest was nothing but a confusing maze of trees and terror. Noises he had never heard and could not identify seemed to sound at every turn and from every patch of darkness.

It didn't exactly help that he was racing through the place twisted into the tail of the fifth siid, with a whispering secret stalking him. Or that he was beginning to feel ill.

"How do we know he's not just taking us somewhere to eat us?" Leven yelled to Clover.

"I guess we really don't," Clover yelled back. "He promised he would take us to the far bridge, but I've heard stories about what a hard time the siids have keeping their promises."

"That's great," Leven complained. "So you talked to him?"

"Well, it wasn't so much talking as it was—"

"Telepathy?" Leven guessed, thinking about a movie he

had seen once where a bear talked to a horse with its mind.

"No," Clover answered. "It was more like swaying."

"You talked to him by *swaying*?" Leven asked.

"I hope that's what we were doing," Clover said, suddenly embarrassed. "Let's just consider it a good sign that he hasn't eaten us yet."

"Perfect," Leven said sarcastically.

The siid moaned. A round, furry creature with big ears and a number of legs ran in front of it. With one smooth motion the siid dipped its head and scooped up the poor creature. The beast chewed and crunched on its victim as it continued running. The sound was a bit distressing.

"This is not good," Leven hollered. "I don't feel well."

Crunch!

"What else can we do?" Clover hollered back. "It's a jarring ride, but we'll get there."

There was a sickening squishing sound as the siid swallowed. The squishing sound was followed by a soft popping noise coming from across a distant field. That noise was followed by a long, drawn-out scream. Leven quickly turned his head. Up ahead, a middle-aged man was standing there next to some trees, screaming.

"What's he doing?" Leven yelled to Clover.

"It looks like fate just brought him here," Clover replied.

"You mean he just stepped into Foo?"

"I think," Clover said. "If the sycophants come then we'll know for sure."

No sooner had Clover said it than dozens of little Clover-like creatures began to appear on and around the man. Some were red and some were black as well as gray and yellow. Some were fat, but most were thin, and all of them were wearing small, shimmering robes. Sycophants dropped in from above and sprang up and out of the trees, all of them complimenting and yelling flattering things at the poor soul who had just stepped in. There were so many they muffled his screaming. The man swatted and screamed with even greater force as the sycophants kicked and scratched at one another, fighting over who would get to claim the new recruit as their burn.

"Pick me, pick me!"

"He's mine!"

"I burn for him!"

The conflicts became increasingly violent, and hundreds of sycophants backed off, letting only the most determined fight it out. In a few moments one sycophant stood triumphant on top of the screaming man's head.

The man batted and swung at the larger sycophant as the rest of the sycophants booed and hissed. Those who had lost began to disappear or slunk off dejectedly. The winner instantly started to console and comfort the screaming man.

"You're okay. I've got you now. You've entered Foo, that's all."

It was an awkward thing for Leven to watch. He turned his head away from the scene as the siid continued to lumber through the forest.

"What an awful jolt that must be. I feel sorry for that poor guy," Leven said after they were far away from him.

"What do you mean?" Clover asked naively. "He got a sycophant."

"And an entirely new life."

"He'll get used—"

"Where will his sycophant take him?" Leven asked.

"Probably to Cusp, or, if he's lucky, to Cork," Clover said. "He'll be safe and happy there. It is the most wonderful—"

"Why doesn't Winter have a sycophant?" Leven interrupted.

Clover was silent.

"Does she?" Leven asked.

Clover shivered.

"Well?"

"Lilly," Clover whispered.

"Lilly?" Leven questioned. "She has a sycophant named Lilly?"

"She did," Clover answered. "She had to let her go when she returned to Reality as a baby. It was the Want's decision."

"Can't she get her back?"

"No right-minded sycophant would ever take back a burn who had let it go," Clover said passionately. "Especially Lilly. When Winter was first snatched into Foo, she was immediately assailed and piled on by dozens of sycophants, just like that guy. All the sycophants were arguing and fighting over who would claim her as their burn. In the end a white sycophant named Lilly won."

Clover sort of sighed.

"Lilly was an exceptional sycophant," he went on. "She

worked patiently with Winter, trying to make her feel at home and safe. She told her the things she needed to know and helped Winter recognize and cultivate her nit gift of being able to freeze things. Lilly was as devoted to Winter as any sycophant has ever been. She loved Winter, and under Lilly's guidance, Winter became one of the most outspoken and truest defenders of Foo. When Antsel proposed the idea of Winter returning to Reality as an infant to help Foo, Winter agreed. But it meant giving up Lilly."

The siid groaned and picked up speed.

"Lilly took the separation very hard. She was completely crushed. To her, saving Foo wasn't half as important as being with Winter. When Winter cut Lilly loose and stopped being her burn, Lilly wailed and mourned and lost all sense of who she was or why she would even want to live."

"So does Lilly have another burn now?"

"I don't know," Clover said. "I suppose . . ." Clover stopped talking as the siid came to a jarring halt, the ground pushing up in front of them like a huge wave as the beast settled.

"What's happening?" Leven asked.

"Either we're here, or we're in trouble."

The siid unwound its tail and with a gentle lob tossed Leven and Clover to the ground. It turned, breathed in, and blew gunk all over them and then turned back into the forest, leaving Leven and Clover alone. The ground rumbled as the great beast moved away.

Clover smiled and said sheepishly, "That's actually the third time it's helped me. It has the worst memory, and keeps on forgetting we're already even."

"You'd better hope it never remembers," Leven said.

"It'll never remember," Clover waved. "Now, the waxels on its ears might."

"So, where are we?" Leven asked, changing the subject and wiping the last bit of spit from his eyes.

"Right where the siid swayed it would set us," Clover answered. "The first bridge is just over that ridge. It will lead us to the turret trailhead."

"Let's go," Leven urged, holding his hands to his queasy stomach.

Leven squeezed between two large bushes that reminded him of a gate. He then began running between the trees, searching for the best direction to go and feeling like a kid looking for a hiding place during a competitive game of hide-and-seek.

Leven stopped at the edge of a purple stream. The large rocks in the water were shifting and moving about like stone turtles. Just across the stream, behind the trees, someone or something was crying.

"What's that?" Leven asked.

"It could be a trap," Clover said casually. "Sometimes unburied secrets will trick their victims into coming to them."

"I don't think this is that," Leven said. "It sounds almost human."

The sobbing did sound human—and scared. Leven had never cried quite like that, but there had been many times in his life when he had wanted nothing but to wail like the voice he could now hear.

A cloud of shimmering orange bugs flew across Leven's view. Leven waved them away and looked to the distance. He was somewhere he had never known existed, and the haunting sound of someone in pain was too much for him to turn away from.

"I can't ignore that," Leven whispered.

"It's your future," Clover shrugged, turning invisible and hopping up on Leven's head.

Leven waded through the water toward a dark patch of trees where the noise was coming from.

"Hello?" Leven called out.

The crying stopped.

"Are you all right?"

"Who are you?" a strong, suspicious female voice shouted back.

"It doesn't matter," Leven insisted. "But if I can help . . ."

"Where am I?" the voice cried.

"In the forest," Leven answered, still unable to see who was speaking.

"These trees aren't normal," the voice said. "I've never seen the things I'm seeing now. I'm not right." There was a long pause followed by another, "Where am I?"

"In Foo," Leven answered.

There was more sobbing and then silence.

"I can help," Leven added. "There's a bridge just over there."

Leven's assurance did little good, seeing how she couldn't really see him or where he was pointing.

"I don't belong here," she cried. "I'm not whole."

"Come with me," Leven said forcefully, surprised to find strength in his voice.

There was silence for a few moments. Then a whisp in the form of Janet Frore emerged from the forest like a ghost.

"We can help," Leven offered.

Janet simply cried.

Neither Leven nor Janet had any idea who the other was.

CHAPTER TWENTY-THREE

WASHED AWAY

I t's not hard to doubt yourself. Many people have encountered miraculous things, only to talk themselves out of believing what they have seen. Millions who have witnessed unusual events and actions have later allowed others to convince them that they didn't see what they actually saw.

Sometimes our minds are out to get us.

Winter was in just such a state. She was back in her icy chamber, lying on her back, covered again by the mask and shroud, with her hands tied behind her body. Her wrists and hands ached from being tied so tightly, and her brain buzzed with the knowledge that as long as her hands were covered she couldn't touch her surroundings and thaw anything.

She also had absolutely no idea what to believe. She thought she knew who she was, but Jamoon had messed with her thinking. She wanted so desperately to see Leven. She knew that he would know what to do. She wished for Clover to suddenly appear, or for Geth to yell out that he was back and that he would take care of things.

Winter was worried about her mind. It felt as if someone had stuck a hand into her head and was now peeling away her thoughts and recollections. Winter couldn't remember anything about who Jamoon was. She had no idea whose side he was on or if she was on that side along with him. She shouldn't have been surprised. When she had been reverted to a baby so as to return to Reality and help Leven, she had known that she was probably giving up all her other memories.

Under her shroud, she thought about the small, makeshift toilet that Geth had escaped through and realized how next to impossible it was that he could somehow rescue her.

Still, she had to have hope.

Winter's brow furrowed, her long, white-blonde hair hanging down under her mask and covering her right eye. She blew out, trying to move her hair from in front of her face, but the mask made it useless. She got painfully to her feet and twisted her body, trying to see her bound hands. She couldn't see them at all. She moved to the corner, away from where the door opening was, and stood so that she could see her hands in the reflection of the icy wall. With the mask over her head, it wasn't a perfect glimpse, but Winter could see what was binding them.

"What fools," she whispered. "Why did I not think of that before?" Winter smiled as her stomach growled and her mind prepared a course of action.

She moved to the far wall and stood with her head down and her shoulders slumped.

"I need to speak to Jamoon," Winter pleaded to the walls.

"It's late," a voice echoed back. "Jamoon is in Morfit."

"I have no idea of time," Winter replied. "And if Jamoon is not here, let me speak with that sickly rant. I know he'll want to hear what I have to say."

There was a long, pregnant pause as the guard digested what she was saying. She could almost hear him imagining the reward Jamoon would give him if he were to deliver a talking prisoner. Of course, Jamoon would be equally unhappy if she had nothing to offer and the guard had interrupted him for no reason.

"Well?" Winter said impatiently.

There was the noise of cracking ice followed by a slit of light that shone through the wall, exposing the exit. The crack in the ice expanded, and there stood a single rant. He was wearing the traditional black robe. He was tall on his right side and lumpy on his left. Winter couldn't even guess what the left half of him was at the moment. In his right hand he held a long, wooden kilve.

"If you—"

One could argue for days about what the guard had intended to say. Perhaps he was going to say, "If you want, I'll carry you." Or maybe he was going to say, "If you find a pair of prescription reading glasses, they're mine." Of course, both of those possibilities seem unlikely, seeing how he was a rather aggressive rant who didn't like to do extra work and had perfect vision.

What he was about to say will most likely never be known

because as he began to speak, Winter froze his right side while simultaneously freezing the covering on her hands. She hurled herself against the icy wall, shattering the frozen rope and cloth that had been keeping her hands bound.

With her hands free, Winter touched and thawed the rant's kilve. She snatched the staff from the guard as she stepped around him and began running down the icy hall. The kilve was long and wooden and painted with the ashes of dark dreams. The pointed end was sharp, with its edges so finely sanded they could have slit the throat of a roven. The other end was as blunt as a steel fist. Kilves were an effective weapon for beating your enemy or for utterly destroying incoming dreams. Winter could feel the evil this particular kilve had been a part of.

She shuddered and kept running.

Looking out through the slits of the mask, Winter tried to remember the little bit she knew of the place, but everything was ice and there seemed to be hundreds of hallways heading hundreds of directions. Most of the ice was smooth and reflective. Winter felt as if she were in a house of mirrors, with her reflection looking back at her from all angles.

Winter raced down a wide corridor, shaking her arms to get the blood flowing back in her wrists and hands. Her shoulder hurt from the beating it had previously taken. An angry shout behind her rang out.

They were coming.

Two large rants appeared in front of her, running toward her as if they knew of nothing else worthwhile in life. Winter thought of them as ice. Their dreamlike sides writhed and complained, trying to support the weight of their now-frozen right halves. Winter dashed between them and pushed them to the side.

The footsteps and shouts behind her grew louder.

Winter ran as fast as she could, her heart and head pounding like wet shoes tumbling in an electric clothes dryer.

"Stop her!" a thunderous voice screamed.

Winter touched the wall with her right hand as she ran. Instantly the structure thawed, turning into a wall of water, which collapsed in a terrific wave. She threw the kilve to her other hand and touched the wall on her left as she ran. It too became a gigantic wave of water. Winter could see the entire fortress behind her beginning to thaw, the water rising, picking her up, and carrying her down the hallways as it melted. She put her arms out in front of her and let the giant wave hurl her away from her pursuers. She could hear their screams fading behind her.

Winter raced with the wall of water down a steep set of stairs, out into and across a brick courtyard, and into another hallway. Ahead of her she could see a gigantic stained-glass window. The image was of the Want working with metal. It was a beautiful piece of art, but Winter knew it was her or the window. She extended her arms and held the blunt end of the kilve out in front of her.

The kilve shattered the glass with the water following right behind to wash the bits away. The room behind the window was huge, and as the water dispersed and ran off in a thousand directions, Winter settled to the floor and gently washed up against the brick fireplace.

She pulled herself up onto her hands and knees, her hair hanging down inside her mask like a bunch of wet spaghetti noodles. Winter had had enough. She jabbed the pointed end of the kilve into the seal of the mask and ripped it open. Winter threw off the mask.

She frantically looked up and back.

It appeared that no one had made it as far as she had. Winter worked herself out of the loose bodysuit she had been shrouded in, exposing the outfit she had been wearing when she had stepped back into Foo. Winter knelt and bit at the wrist of her right sleeve. There was already a small opening in the cuff thanks to Geth having hidden there. Winter pulled out a small length of elastic. She bit at her other sleeve and pulled out another small piece. She flipped her hair back and grabbed a handful on the right side. She twisted the elastic around it, creating a long, wet pigtail, then did the same to her left side.

Winter sighed. It was heaven to have her hair out of her eyes at last.

She was searching around for an exit when a voice spoke out, startling her.

"You look much younger than the Winter Jamoon spoke of."

Winter jumped in shock and took a defensive stance with the kilve. Hidden in the shadows near the edge of the fireplace was the small, disgusting rant. He stepped closer and coughed. As the light hit him, she could clearly see his red right eye.

"I told Jamoon you would try to escape," he said knowingly. "Jamoon is too slow to listen to me."

"Well, now that we both understand what I'm doing, I'll be going," Winter said with determination.

"Wait," the rant said, coughing and waving his right hand impatiently. "You still don't remember your part? Jamoon said you would remember and help us."

"I don't know what you're talking about," Winter said, her own soul wriggling uncomfortably.

The rant's right eye burned.

"Just let me leave," Winter bargained. "When I remember what you're talking about, you'll be the first to know."

"I can't let that happen," he growled. "You will die before you get—" He stopped talking due to his left half beginning to bubble and hiss.

As much as Winter wanted to know what the rant had to say about Jamoon, she knew she needed to act fast. Rants were weakest when they were shifting. It was a dirty play, but she was not about to lose the opportunity.

Winter drew back and swung the kilve with as much strength as she had. The stick struck the sickly rant in the right shoulder, and he collapsed like a pile of stacked cards, screaming as he hit the ground.

"Stop!" he cried, his body still adjusting.

Winter was out the door and into the mountains before the rant could say another thing.

CHAPTER TWENTY-FOUR

I'm on the Top of the Whirled

S ome people like to fly. You may have met such a person. Perhaps he was a tall guy in a red hat who sat next to you. And maybe he went on and on about what a miraculous thing flying is, and how it's the second safest form of travel, elevators being the first. But even a person like that would have a hard time finding the joy in flying in a plane that had thin, sinister black strands whipping around the wings and slapping against the windows.

Let's just say the passengers of flight 7229 were concerned— meaning they were screaming and fanning themselves and making deals with their Maker for him to save their lives.

Dennis Wood was still buckled in his seat, nervously watching the long, black cords of Sabine whipping around the plane. Dennis had never really thought about dying, but he began to wonder if this wasn't his time. He looked around at all the crying and screaming people and thought, *At least I'm not alone.*

Outside the plane, the string of Sabine fought valiantly, try-ing to pull away from Ezra and regain a position of strength. Neither Sabine nor Ezra was making much headway. It was hard for Ezra to destroy someone who was really already dead. And in turn it was fairly difficult for Sabine to get away from such a determined toothpick.

"Let me go," Sabine hissed from both ends.

"Never!" Ezra yelled, still holding on to the tail end inside the plane.

Sabine whispered to himself. "The clouds," he spat. "The hazen."

In Foo the clouds were called hazen and took their shapes from the imaginations of the inhabitants. Sabine felt it was time to wake up the clouds of Reality. With the end of him outside of the plane, Sabine twisted himself into a loop, stretched up, and lassoed the clouds. He tightened his loop, and all at once the clouds turned a burning orange color. As the clouds changed color, lightning began to strike.

Once.

Twice.

Fifty times.

The clouds were no longer just clouds, they were hazen, and they were desperate to prove their difference. Sabine imagined them as violent beasts.

The plane bumped up and down like a jerking seesaw.

The captain came on the intercom. He sounded as if he couldn't decide whether to cry or scream. He nervously announced that they would be climbing higher to find smoother, safer air. Most passengers wished he had announced that they would be flying lower to find safer *ground*. The announcement failed to comfort any of them, seeing how the very clouds around them were beginning to take shape and attack the plane.

Dennis was sweating. The thick clouds were gaining color and form. Like gigantic marshmallows they brushed up against the plane. They smeared across the windows and left a pale, glue-like residue.

Seven passengers and one flight attendant passed out, which caused the rest to begin pulling their hair and rocking violently. A short man, who looked like a lima bean in a suit thanks to his green face and squat body, began tearing at his seat, searching frantically for a parachute.

Dennis pressed his face to his window. It looked like the earth was coming apart, the unraveling beginning in the air. A few of the clouds had thick, burning faces and long, billowing arms that were anything but cute. Dennis remembered as a child lying in a park looking up at the clouds. Back then he had seen the shapes of toy boats and horses. Now, however, the clouds looked horrible, huge and evil.

The plane rocked and twisted as the clouds grabbed hold of it. The four engines struggled and whined as one very large hazen pushed against the plane going forward.

The captain flipped desperately through his book trying to find any sort of instruction for handling rabid clouds.

"Anything?" the copilot yelled.

"No," the captain yelled back frantically. "But there is a section for taking notes."

A sinister hazen moved in front of the plane. Its eyes looked like pieces of white-hot charcoal, and its mouth looked like a meteor crater. It opened its mouth wider, and the plane flew right into it. All the lights in the aircraft flickered and dimmed as the plane turned upside down. Those who had long ago given up obeying the seat-belt sign dropped to the ceiling and then back to their seats as the plane turned back over. Four thick clouds wrapped themselves around the wings and pushed the plane forward and down.

Dennis wiped his forehead and bit his tongue. It felt as if they were traveling just over the speed of life.

"Ezra!" Dennis yelled.

Ezra didn't hear Dennis, but if he had he would have been angry about him even asking for help when Ezra had his own troubles to deal with.

As the plane rocketed toward the ground, all the passengers gave up hope of ever living through such an ordeal. A number of people sat back in their seats and let their lives flash before their eyes, while others screamed until their lungs were raw, then collapsed in fear and exhaustion.

Dennis unbuckled his seat belt and stood. He looked down at the bank sticker on his shirt and at his unwrinkled pants. For some reason that seemed to comfort him. His outfit felt like a uniform, like he was a part of something. The plane rocked to the north, and Dennis flew into a young lady whose face was the color of a honeydew melon.

"Sorry!" Dennis screamed.

She looked at him as if he were crazy.

The plane tilted forward even further. Three of the overhead bins popped open, and bags exploded and rained down on passengers.

Outside, the hazen were fighting over the plane. Dennis's stomach lurched. He needed a bathroom, and he held onto the seats as he worked his way toward the rear of the plane. He leaned over far enough to look out a window. Despite all the clouds wrapped around the plane, there were a few holes where he could see the ground.

It wasn't far away. At the speed they were traveling, they would hit the ground in a few minutes.

The plane suddenly flew sideways, and Dennis lost his footing. He fell to his knees and began clawing his way toward the bathroom. Passengers and luggage burst into the aisle. When he reached the rear of the plane he could hear a high-pitched screaming. He stepped away from the bathroom door and pushed open the service door. Still feeling sick, he moved into the very back of the plane. There, up near the ceiling, was Ezra, twisted into and holding onto a thin strand of something black.

"Help me pull!" Ezra screamed, his small voice barely audible over the screams of the passengers and the roar of the engines.

"Let go!" Dennis screamed back. "The plane's going to crash!"

The black cord Ezra was clinging to sizzled and hissed.

"Let go!" Dennis shouted, grabbing onto Ezra and trying to pull him off Sabine. "Please!" Dennis begged. "Please."

Ezra swore, made a rather harsh remark about Dennis not

being a man, and let go. Sabine slithered out.

Almost instantly the hazen stopped pounding, and the plane began to level out. Dennis could hear a more hopeful chorus of screams from out front.

"You fool! He's from Foo," Ezra screamed at Dennis. "I shouldn't have let him go. He can get us back."

Ezra's purple top was writhing and swirling.

"Only if we're alive," Dennis reasoned.

Dennis grabbed Ezra and shoved him into the fanny pack. He walked back out front. Everyone was still screaming, seeing how the plane was still moving rapidly toward the ground. Dennis looked out and hoped that he was right about letting go of the black string and keeping them alive.

The thick, orange hazen began to cluster under the plane, pushing upward as the plane hurled toward the earth. Dennis could see trees and mountains rising up. The clouds pushed some more, and the plane slowed. Several wet hazen wadded themselves up and crawled into the engines. The engines coughed and stopped, allowing the hazen to slow the plane to a complete stop about fifty feet above the ground.

It is quite a sensation to be sitting in a huge metal plane, hovering above a busy freeway being held up by a ring of clouds. The cars below came to a screeching stop, frantically trying to get or stay out from beneath the hovering plane.

Then, as if to make a point, the hazen flipped the floating plane one last time and set it down gently on its top in the middle of Interstate 40.

ii

Tim Tuttle looked at his surroundings and wondered exactly what year it was. The home he was sitting in looked as though it had not been touched or updated since 1952. A large portrait of a young girl holding a bundle of wheat hung over a small fireplace that was fronted with a rock facade. The carpet underfoot was yellow shag, with wide wear patterns that ran the entire length of the room. In one corner there was a birdcage with a single tiny, sickly sounding, orange bird in it. Every couple of seconds it would try to chirp, but the sound was more like a wet cough. In the other corner, two small desks faced a green chalkboard. Written on the chalkboard was a list of difficult-looking spelling words. The desks were occupied at the moment—one by a girl with a blonde bob who looked about ten and the other one by a boy with a buzzed head who looked around twelve.

Tim was sitting on a short couch with a huge rose pattern print. He was in the home of John and Margo Hunch. Thanks to Terry's tip about Maine, Tim had made the trip out there to see if he could get one step closer to finding Winter and the boy named Leven with whom she was said to be traveling.

Tim had spent the morning at the public library looking for information.

Luckily for him, it had not been very long since Winter and Leven had been through Maine, and the story of a boy and girl driving a car off into the ocean was not hard to find. Most of the stories talked about Cape Porpoise, and most mentioned a woman by the name of Margo Hunch as the last person to talk to the boy, at a church barbecue. Leven and Winter had run off after Margo had asked too many questions about who they were. A number of people had chased after them but, according to the story, the two kids had stolen a car and driven it off a wharf into the Atlantic Ocean.

Tim had come to the Hunch home hoping to find some answers. Margo had welcomed him in and then run off to get him something to drink. She came back into the room and handed Tim a teacup filled with lemon-flavored water. Tim took a sip and set the cup down.

"Delicious," he lied. "So, Margo, you talked to these children?"

"Mrs. Hunch," she corrected. "And just the boy. The lemon helps with the digestive tract," she added, pointing to the cup of water she had served up, and settling into her own seat.

"Oh," Tim said, confused. "Thank you. Well, what did they say?"

"Not much. I didn't recognize them so I walked up to the boy. I thought, *New faces, let's welcome them in.* Anyhow, I . . ."

Her daughter, sitting at her desk, raised her hand.

"Yes, Florence?" Mrs. Hunch said.

"What's the capital of Norway?" Florence asked.

"If I told you, that'd be cheating," Mrs. Hunch sang. "But I'll give you a hint: Norway is often referred to as the Land of the Midnight Sun."

Florence didn't look all that grateful for the help.

"So," Mrs. Hunch continued, "I was fascinated with a white streak of hair the boy had. I was only showing interest in him, and I think he got offended. But I had seen a report on him on TV about how he supposedly ruined his parents' house."

Her son's hand went up.

"Yes, George."

"Can I use the bathroom?"

Mrs. Hunch was silent.

"*May* I use the bathroom?" George corrected himself.

Mrs. Hunch picked up a small egg timer that was sitting on the end table near her. She flipped it over, and the sand began to run down. "Be back before the last grain," she said, giving permission.

George raced off to the bathroom.

"You've got quite a system here," Tim said, referring to her home-schooled children.

Mrs. Hunch sighed. "It's not always easy. But if you knew what goes on in some public schools."

The last grain of sand dropped in the egg timer just as the sound of the toilet flushing was heard. George came racing back into the room and frantically slid into his desk. He looked at the egg timer and sighed.

"Two paragraphs on why soil erosion is less of a problem than the government says it is," Mrs. Hunch said, handing out George's punishment for taking too long.

"But—" George tried to argue.

"Three paragraphs," Mrs. Hunch said.

George slumped in his seat.

"Well, I can see you're busy," Tim said, standing. "I won't take any more of your time. Just one last question, though."

Mrs. Hunch looked perplexed by the thought of a question being asked without a hand being raised first.

"The newspapers all say that the children drove the car right off into the ocean," Tim said.

"That's actually not a question," she pointed out, "but from what I hear, that's what happened."

"And the car just sank?"

"It hit some ice, or rocks," she said. "It was very cloudy, so nobody got a perfect look at where they fell in."

"Have they found it? The car," Tim clarified.

"Not that I've heard," she said sadly. "What a terrible tragedy. Those poor little hoodlums. I'll try to make their lives count by using them as an example in my teaching."

Tim just looked at her.

"A bad example," she specified.

Florence raised her hand and asked her mother if she could build a working volcano for her science project. Mrs. Hunch nixed the idea and suggested instead that she paint the back porch.

As Tim stepped out the front door he asked, "How far is it to the spot where they drove into the ocean?"

"Two miles that way," she pointed. "There's a small flower shop just before the turnoff."

Tim thanked her and made his way to his rented car.

iii

The ocean looked gigantic. The sky was clear and blue. Tim had driven past the flower shop to the end of the wharf. He had then gotten out and searched for signs of a car flying off. At the end of the dock he found the exact spot where the car had gone into the water. The skid marks from the police car that had been chasing Leven and Winter were thick and dark.

"Where are you?" Tim asked the air.

The newspapers had all reported about how the authorities had searched the ocean for the sunken car but found no sign of it. Some speculated that it may have floated for a few moments and then been pushed farther out to sea by an especially strong current. None of that made sense. Tim knew there had to be more to the story.

He knew that Winter was still alive.

Tim kept thinking back to the old woman who had twice stood on his doorstep so many years before. He thought about what she had told him and wondered if what was happening now had anything to do with the secret she had shared.

Regardless, Tim knew he couldn't give up. Winter was somewhere, and even if the trail had grown cold here at the edge of the Atlantic Ocean, he couldn't stop looking. He turned and headed toward town and back to the public library, his heart practically bursting in his chest.

CHAPTER TWENTY-FIVE

BRIDGE TO NITEON

L even had never seen a whisp before. Of course, he had never seen rovens or sarus or siids or tharms or Foo either. But there was something about the whisp that was sadder than all the things he had seen so far. A whisp was a person, but it was an incomplete person. Sometimes those in Reality are not properly lined up on a mismatched sidewalk or lane, so fate snatches only a wisp of them into Foo. Such an occurrence leaves the person in Reality feeling as if he or she is missing something or not all there, and it creates a whisp in Foo—an incomplete being that can't touch or feel and has no physical capacities.

A great sorrow radiated from the whisp Leven was looking at. It was clear she knew she was not whole and seemed to understand that she never would be again.

"Where am I?" Janet asked.

"Foo," Leven answered.

She was a large woman with a wrinkled face and dirty, unkempt hair. She looked like a pale prune in tight slippers and a yellow housedress.

"What's the matter with me?" she cried.

"You're a whisp," Clover said, materializing on top of Leven's head.

Janet jumped back three feet and put her hand to her mouth. She had been startled by Clover, but she was terrified by the fact that when she threw her hand to her mouth, it went right through her head.

"I'm a ghost," she whimpered, looking closely at her hands.

Clover laughed. "Ghosts aren't real. You must not have been lined up right for Foo to snatch you completely. So, it took a little of your essence and left you mostly whole in Reality."

Janet reached out and tried to touch Leven. Her hand went right through his shoulder. In the last green light of dusk Leven could see tears streaking down her face.

"Am I dead?" she asked.

"No," Leven said, trying to calm her and wondering how he could explain a place he still didn't fully understand. "This is Foo. We'll get you some help, but we need to hurry."

Janet just cried, but she followed behind as Leven began to walk. Clover pointed out the direction, and Leven made his way around some thick, knotty trees and through a patch of gigantic, oval-shaped boulders.

The trees behind them whispered. The whispering sounded confused, as if searching for a direction.

"This place is creepy. Let's get out of here," Leven said, walking faster.

The trees opened up, and there was the entry to the first bridge. The bridge spanned Fissure Gorge, which was enormous. The far side looked miles away. As wide as the gorge was, it was over twice as deep, and its depths were pitch black, except for a thin line of orange running along the very bottom. The orange ribbon glowed and pulsated, sending up currents of warm air.

The whispering of the trees could still be heard, hissing throughout the forest like a snake in search of food.

"The secret's not going to give up, is it?" Leven said in a hushed voice.

"Let's hope that it stays in the trees and doesn't cross the gorge," Clover said, his voice indicating that he was holding onto Leven's right leg. "Most secrets don't dare expose themselves in the open like that. And it will never enter Cork."

Leven reached the opening of the bridge. There was a large brick arch spanning the entrance. On the left side of the arch was a small stone building with a crooked chimney jutting out of its thatched roof. A door opened in the guardhouse, and a gigantic bird stepped out. The bird was as tall as Leven and wore a blue jacket and glasses. His feet looked white under the moonlight.

"You wish to cross?" he asked.

"We're on our way to Niteon," Leven said.

"Is that whisp yours?" he chirped.

Leven turned and looked at Janet. "She was lost in the forest," he said. "After we get to the turrets, we'll take her to Cork."

"Are you aware of the war?" the bird asked suspiciously, walking around Leven.

"I am," Leven answered, begrudging the time they were wasting standing there, "if you are talking about the war Sabine started."

The bird nodded and stepped back. "I wish you well," it said.

Leven nodded back and moved toward the bridge. He was stopped by the excited clamor of the bird.

"What are you doing?" the bird squawked.

"I was going to cross," Leven said, confused.

"Without flattering it?"

"Excuse me?"

"The bridge," the bird said with disgust. "Have you never crossed before?"

"No . . ." Leven began.

The bird sighed, which actually sounded like a very long whistle. "See those rocks over there?" The bird pointed to a number of rocks jutting out from the near side of the gorge.

Leven could see the rocks. He could also see numerous other rocks sticking out into the gorge. Some actually extended out over the gorge a number of feet. Some were only a few inches long.

"Those are young bridges," the bird explained. "The stones on this side get curious to know what it's like on the other side. So they shift and stretch and grow until they either give up or connect with another bunch of curious stones reaching to get here from the other side."

"You *grow* your bridges?" Leven asked in disbelief.

"They grow themselves," the bird chirped. "It is a miraculous thing when they actually meet and a new bridge is created. Of course, once the two sides meet, they realize there really is nothing great on the other side, and they become indifferent. They sit there until someone tries to cross. Then they simply fall apart and drop into the gorge."

"So if we cross, they'll fall?" Leven asked incredulously.

"If you don't flatter them, they will," the bird replied in a tone that suggested Leven was far from brilliant.

"Flatter them?"

"Tell them they're doing a good job. You know," the bird said. "We must preserve the bridge."

"So I talk to the bridge?" Leven laughed.

"And you'd better be convincing. Otherwise the bridge is destroyed and you're caught in the air of the gorge or you drop to burn forever in the glow." The sentinel bird stopped talking to dig under his right wing with his beak. "Sorry," he apologized, "I'm trying to kick the bird in me, be a bit more dignified. But let me say this, even if you did make it back out of the gorge after you fell, there would be so many angry about the loss of another bridge that you would wish you were dead."

Leven glanced at the bridge, then looked again at the gorge. It seemed deeper than any sky Leven had ever gazed up into.

"I'm doing this for Foo," he said to himself, only just beginning to feel the power and purpose such a place as Foo really held.

"So, I just . . . *flatter* it?" he asked.

"Yes, and you'd better sound sincere," the bird whispered.

Leven stepped up to the very edge of the bridge and cleared his throat. His stomach was even more uneasy. He looked out over the gorge. It was so wide he couldn't clearly see the other side. By now the night was fully upon them and the moon shone bright. The moon's light was like white syrup being drizzled slowly over the entire scene. The light was so dense that bits dripped from the sides of the bridge and dropped in zigzag lines into Fissure Gorge.

"How come the moonlight doesn't drip straight down?" Leven asked Clover.

"The gorge is filled with soft and hard air that makes up a maze of sorts," Clover answered. "If you were to fall off into it you might just as easily fall to the side or diagonally, or down, or even up. The air never stays the same. The heat at the bottom belches, and as the warm air rises, the composition of air within the gorge changes. Things that fall into the gorge can sometimes be suspended in the air for years and never reach the bottom. I had a friend who threw a pout in there years ago, and last I heard it was still screaming and falling in one direction or another. People and animals have fallen in and eventually died of old age, trapped in the air, their decaying bodies floating around until they're gone."

"That's pleasant," Leven said.

"I know." Clover pointed. "See how the moonlight slides and drops so beautifully?"

"So if we fall in, the air will catch us before we hit the bottom?"

"More like *trap* you," Clover said. "There are things worse than 'splat.'"

Leven looked into the gorge and watched streaks of moon-light sliding back and forth and up and down like erratic shooting stars.

"We'd better hurry," Clover reminded him.

Leven cleared his throat again and began talking to the bridge.

"Hello."

He waited a moment for the red in his cheeks to subside.

"We would very much like to travel across such a fine-looking bridge," Leven continued, glancing at the sentinel bird for approval. The bird nodded as if impressed.

"I've been on other bridges," Leven said, more earnestly, "but none were as impressive or beautiful."

The bridge seemed to shiver.

"I really would enjoy the journey across you," Leven said. "I can't wait to reach the other side and tell everyone what an out-standing job you do."

The bridge really shivered, and the bird practically beamed.

"I think that will do it," the bird whispered, nodding happily.

Leven glanced at Janet and then down at his feet. He touched the edge of the bridge with his toe and quickly pulled his foot back. He shrugged his shoulders, closed his eyes, and took a tentative step out. He had no desire to fall into the gorge, but he would have no way of knowing if his flattery had worked until he started across.

The bridge was still shivering.

Leven took another hesitant step. The bridge was holding up. Leven looked back at the bird and waved.

"Good-bye! I am off to enjoy the beauty and strength of this marvelous bridge," Leven said loudly for good measure.

The bridge liked that.

Leven walked cautiously but with purpose, deliberately placing each step. He wanted to run, but he had no idea how the bridge would respond to that. He also made the mistake of looking down. It was a long drop. The thin, iridescent ribbon of light at the bottom looked miles away and glowed like molten lava. Leven proceeded carefully.

After about thirty feet Janet spoke up.

"How come you're whole?" she asked as she floated behind him. It sounded like a question she had been longing to ask for some time.

"Whole?"

"Not like me," she said.

"You're a whisp," Leven answered, not fully understanding things himself. "Most of you is still in Reality. Just a tiny, wisp-like part of you is here."

"So is it because I lived a horrible life?" Janet asked. "Is this what happens to bad people?"

"What?"

"I know I was a hard person," she said defiantly. "My mother always said I wouldn't make it to heaven. Now look at me. I am nothing but air. I didn't even love my own child, and now she's gone."

"I'm sure she's okay," Leven said indifferently, concentrating on getting across the bridge.

"She left me," Janet said, "because of who I was."

"Life's a long time," Leven said, walking as quickly as he could and wondering if he was making any sense. "I never thought I'd be here because I didn't know here existed. Now I'm racing against time to save a toothpick just to be able to live in a place where I'm still not convinced I belong. It's the same for you, except you're still who you were in Reality as well."

Janet's eyes began to leak again. "That frightens me almost as much as being here," she said. "Few people get to step away from themselves to look at who they really are."

Leven didn't answer. Moonlight poured over him and ran down his left side. He could feel the sensation of it and marveled at the complexity and beauty of Foo. Two stars streaking across the sky crashed into each other and sent sparks flying everywhere. Leven thought he heard the moon sigh.

A small, burning secret raced up from behind Leven and drifted up his leg. Before Leven noticed, it was perched on his nose and staring him in the eyes.

"I had a lifelong crush on Sally Teon," the secret giggled as it danced on Leven's nose.

Leven swatted it away. The small secret happily flew off into the night.

"I thought you said it wouldn't follow us," Leven whispered.

"That was just another decoy secret," Clover replied from on top of Leven's head, still invisible. "The big one won't expose itself."

"What are you talking about?" Janet asked, not having seen the tiny secret.

"Nothing," Leven said, looking in the direction the secret had run.

"So, can I affect what I'm like in Reality?" Janet asked. "I mean, can I help change myself in the condition I'm in?"

"I don't know," Leven answered. "But it's probably not too late to try."

For a second Janet's eyes showed hope, but that hope was quickly drowned by more tears. Clover materialized and offered Janet a tissue from his void. She reached for it, and they were both reminded of her limitations.

"Sorry," Clover said, feeling bad about offering it. "When I see a person crying, I just naturally . . . and, well, I forgot you weren't really a person but a . . . I mean, people come in all shapes and sizes and well . . . I wonder what it would feel like to be invisible right now."

Clover disappeared hastily while Janet continued to cry and drift along behind Leven. He walked steadily across the gorge, his feet kicking up the moonlight wherever he stepped. Light flashed like sparks around his shoes.

After a time, Clover reappeared on the top of Leven's head. The sycophant commented on how much he preferred being carried to walking himself. Leven smiled and reached up and scratched him behind his ear.

Leven could clearly see the other side now. He slowed and looked around him. For the thousandth time in so few days he was amazed at where he was. The bridge across the gorge reminded him a little of the ice highway that he and Winter had driven on while crossing the Atlantic Ocean.

The glow at the bottom of Fissure Gorge belched, and warm air raced up, sending the streaks of moonlight shooting back into the sky.

"Why are we slowing?" Janet asked.

"Yeah," Clover added, "I don't want this bridge to change its mind about holding together."

"It really is beautiful here," Leven said. "I can't wait to see Cork and the other parts."

Leven kicked up a puddle of moonlight as he picked up his pace. He waved the moonlight away as if it were a batch of bubbles.

"Beautiful?" Janet scoffed. "Don't be stupid. I think you have—" She stopped herself, realizing that she needed help, not more enemies. "I suppose if you squint it's not awful," she tried.

Clover squinted and looked at Janet as if she were daft. There was a light wind, and Janet drifted over just a bit. She tried to grab Leven's arm for support, but she had that pesky lack-of-substance problem still going on.

"Just let the wind go through you," Clover advised.

Trying to do so, Janet drifted back a few feet and then began moving forward again.

Sitting on Leven's shoulder, Clover spoke softly into Leven's ear. "So, now that we're out here, why don't you show me what you dug up?"

"What?" Leven replied, playing innocent but knowing perfectly well that Clover was referring to the metal key he had found when he was digging up the secret.

"I saw that key," Clover explained. "You pulled it out before the secret."

Leven wanted to show Clover the key, but he didn't want anyone to take it away before he understood what it was.

"If it's made of metal, it needs to be reported," Clover warned.

"Really?" Leven asked. He thought back to when he had been ten and had attended a baseball game in Oklahoma. Terry had won two free tickets in a radio contest. Terry didn't want to take Leven, but Addy had screamed and yelled at him about how important it was that Leven have a positive male role model so that he didn't grow up and come back and steal from them.

The afternoon had been nice—the weather had been warm, the game exciting, and Terry had sat two sections away from Leven. Then, in the sixth inning, as a soda vendor was walking up the stairs near Leven, a foul ball flew up and hit the vendor in the back of the head.

The poor guy collapsed, his drinks bouncing and rolling all over. One can of soda fell into Leven's lap, and he quickly slipped it under his seat. The vendor was dazed, but after he shook it off he began collecting his sodas. He wasn't sure, because of the blow to his head, but he thought he was missing three. Leven's face burned red as he nudged the cold soda beneath his seat with his toe. He wanted to give it back, but he had only tasted soda a couple of times in his life, and he was so thirsty. After the vendor asked four more times, however, Leven sheepishly pulled out the soda and pretended that he had just found it.

His hope was that the vendor would let him keep it. The vendor didn't. In fact, he didn't even say thanks. The imagined taste of what Leven had missed was still strong in his mouth.

Now he was afraid that if he showed Clover the key, Clover might make him give it up. Clover smiled and held out his hand.

Leven sighed. He reached into his pocket and pulled out the key. It was a golden color, and as a bit of moonlight touched it, the key glistened. Reluctantly, Leven set it in Clover's palm.

"Beautiful," Clover whispered. "It's definitely metal."

Leven held out his hand, and Clover hesitantly gave him the key back.

"Hold on," Clover said, reaching into his void. He pulled out a thin string of leather. "Put the key on this," Clover explained. "Then you can keep it around your neck and you won't lose it."

Leven took the leather string and threaded it through the key. He tied a square knot and slipped the key and band over his head. Leven pulled on the neck of his shirt, and the key slipped down, hidden beneath.

"What was that?" Janet demanded. "What are you doing?"

"Nothing," Clover insisted. "Drift over there."

Janet did as she was told. Clover disappeared, and Leven touched his T-shirt to make sure the key was still there.

"Be careful who you tell," Clover whispered.

"I will," Leven said, rubbing his chest.

"Are you okay?" Clover asked.

Leven didn't answer, but something wasn't right.

CHAPTER TWENTY-SIX

ENTERING MORFIT

It was considerably warmer than Winter usually preferred it. She was also much hungrier than she had been in a long time. Winter half wished for the filler crisp Clover had given her at sea. Her stomach felt like an empty cavern filled with nothing but wind.

Jamoon had not fed her in captivity, and the only food she had been able to find in the hours since she had escaped were some young bickerwicks growing at the base of a sweaty fantrum tree. Not all fantrum trees are created equal, mind you. Some thrive well in the cold, others do better in the blistering heat, and some do all right in either. Unfortunately for the trees, however, they usually don't get to choose where they're planted. So, those poor fantrum trees who are stuck in a hot place when they prefer the cold will sweat a lot. And wherever there is fantrum sweat, there are bickerwicks.

Bickerwicks grow in clusters around the base of sweaty trees, and as they grow and begin to crawl they emit a chilling zap that keeps the trees cold. Bickerwicks are small, orange, and egg-shaped. They are spongy and have a marshmallow taste, but they are also cranky and make such a fuss as you chew that a person can tolerate only a few of them at a time. In her state of hunger, however, Winter had eaten more than just a few.

She was now regretting it.

Gulping them down as fast as she had, she had failed to chew them thoroughly. Winter could still hear them yelling and fighting with each other from inside her stomach. She willed her digestive system to hurry up and digest them.

Her stomach rumbled.

Winter skirted past a flock of mud-covered little men who were building a large wooden vat, and through a prairie filled with temperamental holes that kept opening and then snapping shut at her. Without the bodysuit she had been shrouded in, her feet were bare. Winter found a couple of thick fantrum leaves and, using strips of kindle moss for laces, fashioned herself a pair of makeshift shoes.

They were far from fashionable, but they fit.

Winter had no clear idea where she had been held captive, so she simply headed downhill.

After about an hour she spotted the top of Morfit in the far distance. The peaks were covered by a large, lazy gathering of thick, orange hazen.

"Morfit," Winter whispered in awe. From what Jamoon had

said, perhaps that was where she would find the pieces of the puzzle that would show her who she really was.

Winter proceeded with caution, having no idea who she would encounter or who was on her side. In fact, she wasn't sure what side she was on any longer. She wished she could just find Leven and Geth and have them help her sort things out. Winter kept her eye on the top of Morfit and pressed forward, hoping to find a clue there.

Two hours later, Winter could see the base of Morfit at the end of the road she was on. As always, beings from all over Foo were walking toward Morfit, carrying boulders that represented their guilt or sorrow or sin. After arriving, they would set their rocks in place and walk away without their burdens.

Winter couldn't believe how huge Morfit was. Her memory of it was vague, but she couldn't recall it being nearly this humongous. It sat there like an entire mountain range, its base thick and as wide as a large lake. It was different shades of black, causing it to look as if it were covered in bruises of varied intensity. There were smaller mounds in front of larger mounds and larger mounds circling a massive center peak higher than the rest. At the top of the peak was a lone tower that looked tiny and millions of miles away. All over Morfit there were holes and caves and archways—thousands of openings in the great black mountain. The size and darkness of the place were overwhelming.

"We have to be losing," she whispered to herself. "Unless I'm on the bad side," she amended, "in which case it looks like we're doing okay."

A high, crumbling brick wall surrounded Morfit. It wrapped around the entire mountain, resembling a fat, decaying worm with moldy growth between its segments. There were four entrances—one on each side of the towering mountain. Outside the wall were round lumps of earth, houses to rants and cogs who had not yet proven their loyalty to the point of Morfit granting them a place to live.

Winter emerged from the woods, breaking from the forest near the entrance at the back of Morfit. Two huge rants stood near the gate. Both held thick kilves and were carefully checking those passing through the gate. Winter watched one of the rant guards stop a traveler and pull back the traveler's hood to look at his face. They appeared to be searching for someone. The thought made Winter happy, knowing that if they were still looking, Geth and Leven were probably still free.

"I need in," she whispered to herself.

Winter looked at the ends of her hair and at her arms.

"This won't do," she said. "They'll spot me instantly." She slipped back into the forest, looking for a wen nest. Winter's memory was filled with holes, but she had recollections of many small bits of Foo and the people and creatures who occupied the realm. Wens were common birds who laid eggs that were good for only one thing—throwing. So many dreams coming into Foo involved people throwing or smashing things, and the wens were a result of that. They laid eggs that were filled with nothing but color, perfect for young kids to steal and throw at things.

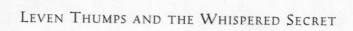

Winter, however, had another use in mind. She climbed seven trees before she found one. A large wen with a pink puffy face, a green pointed beak, and no feathers except on her behind, was sitting in the nest. The wen saw Winter and sighed. She mumbled and then grudgingly moved her plush behind to reveal a nest full of white eggs covered in black diamonds.

"Perfect," Winter said.

Winter rubbed each egg with her palm, and as she did so the black diamonds changed color. Winter pulled out the three eggs that had shown red diamonds.

The wen, who had been watching, sighed again.

"Work all day just so you can throw things," the wen complained.

"Excuse me?" Winter asked.

"I didn't say anything," the wen lied.

Winter didn't feel the least bit bad stealing eggs from the wen. She knew the strange birds didn't lay eggs to create other birds. Most wen eggs were used to torture and vandalize the Children of the Sewn who lived in the roots of the Red Grove. Winter was simply taking the eggs for a more dignified use.

Winter jumped from the tree and crouched back behind a boulder. She smashed the first egg against the top of her head.

Deep red dye bled down her hair.

She pushed the thick dye back from her forehead and smoothed it into the two pigtails she had created. Then Winter cracked the other two eggs on the sides of her head and massaged the red dye deep into her white-blonde hair. It was messy, but it was working. In a few minutes, Winter had brilliantly red hair.

It still wasn't enough of a disguise.

Winter washed her hands off in a small stream and worked herself back out to the trail. A couple of people passed her, each carrying rocks to drop off. Behind them a single cog in a black cloak was making his way down the path, carrying a rock in his cold blue hands. He was mumbling something about how he would never lie to his wife again once he set that rock down.

Winter stepped out in front of him, holding her kilve in her right hand.

"Ah!" the cog screamed, his orange forehead wrinkling.

"Heading to Morfit?" Winter asked.

"Yes," he said.

"Drop your burden and cover it with your cloak," Winter insisted, waving the kilve.

"But I need—"

"The rules have changed," she snapped. "Drop it here!"

"But—"

Winter didn't want to, but she swung her kilve and struck the cog behind his right knee. His leg buckled, and he fell to the ground, dropping his rock. He struggled to get to his feet. Winter thrust her kilve down, pinning the back of his robe to the ground. The poor cog pulled and screamed his way out of his cloak, then took off running as fast as he could, yelling something about his wife and waving his blue hands in the air.

"It's so much easier when they just obey," Winter said, wondering where she had learned to use a kilve like that.

She slipped the cloak on and pulled the hood up over her head. Then she picked up the rock, held it in front of her, and began to shuffle toward Morfit, moaning. A small shadow passed over her. Winter looked up. Way overhead she saw the sickly rant she had left in the ice cave. He was riding on the back of a large roven. The roven screamed and swooped toward Morfit.

Winter pulled her hood even tighter around her head, hoping not to be spotted.

Near the gate she met up with two other travelers and tried to make it look as if she were moving with them. One was carrying a rock; the other had a bundle of fabric. Winter could clearly see the rants that were guarding the door—both were as tall as the actual gate. One rant stopped the nit carrying the fabric.

"Business, or the result of pleasure?" the rant questioned, bending down.

"I'm to see the Council of Whisps," the nit said.

The rant laughed. "The Council is gone."

"Gone?" the nit panicked. "My cause was up for review. I've brought them fabric. When will they be back?"

"Never," the other rant growled.

The poor nit just stood there, looking as though his life was over. "What's happening?" Winter heard him whisper to himself as she shuffled past.

"Stop!" the taller rant commanded Winter.

"Business, or the result of pleasure?" he demanded.

"Business," Winter said. "I have dreams to trade."

"Where did you get that?" he asked, referring to the kilve she carried.

"It was given to me by a rant much bigger than you," she said with authority. "Now, may I pass? Or would you like to explain to him why I was held up?"

Rants were not great under pressure.

"On your way," he waved.

Winter walked through the gate. Her heart felt like it was in her throat, as if with one good cough she could expel it. She moved farther into Morfit and stopped to compose herself.

Winter knew she shouldn't be here; if Jamoon spotted her, there would be more trouble. But she wanted to know what Morfit held for her and what Jamoon meant by her knowing the plan. She needed to see if she could discover who she really was. She tossed aside the rock she was carrying and listened to it hiss and groan as it became part of the mountain.

Winter worked her way through the lower slums of Morfit where those who were frightened by light lived.

"Hello, pretty," someone yelled out to Winter.

She kept going as if she hadn't heard. He moved toward her to better make his point, and Winter pictured him in ice.

She climbed up a long, dark, twisted spiral of stone stairs. From heights all over Morfit water fell in thick streams and misty veils, the water originating in the many springs Morfit had been built around. At the top of the stairs was a round pit filled with the bones of sheep. The bones rattled as a large rat scurried through them, searching for some small scrap of leftover meat. The rat hissed at Winter and called her a spy.

Winter moved on.

She made her way along a narrow, jagged ledge that led to an archway opening up into the grand chambers. All around her were the sounds of laughter and fighting. Winter couldn't remember Morfit being this dirty or this dark.

Above the base of Morfit was a large, roofed courtyard, ringed by small rock caves and burning torches. Gathered in that chamber were hundreds of dark-cloaked rants. Winter pulled her hood more closely around her head and entered, working her way along the back wall of the courtyard, keeping to the shadows cast by the torches.

Amazed by the vastness of the gathering, Winter began counting. She stopped at around four hundred, estimating that there must be at least two thousand rants packed into the hall. Each was standing still, as if awaiting something or someone.

Then those gathered began to chant rhythmically:

"Whole again once more."

"Whole again forever."

"Whole again with power."

"Whole again."

"Whole again."

Winter could feel the darkness in the words. Swaying in unison, the gathered beings chanted louder, the words taking form as they mixed with the torchlight. Winter could see letters and meanings rising above the chanting crowd.

"Whole again once more."

"Whole again forever."

"Whole again with power."

"Whole again!"

"Whole again!"

"Whole again!"

Winter put her hand to her heart and was surprised to find how fast it was racing. The words of the chant sizzled like drops of water in a hot pan—each word dancing on the surface and hissing into nothing but steam.

"Whole again!"

"Whole again!"

Suddenly the chanting stopped. As the words drifted downward, settling on the heads of those in attendance like ash, a tall, dark-robed figure ascended to a podium and raised his right hand.

It was Jamoon.

He stood at the front of the gathering. The bottom half of his robe billowed and swayed, filled with shadowy nihils. Every few seconds a couple of the dead birds would slip out, only to turn and work themselves back beneath his robe.

At his appearance, the crowd fell silent.

"The Sochemists have studied the Lore Coil," Jamoon declared. "They speak of bits of Sabine still in Reality—pieces that will work to create another gateway."

The crowd murmured.

"Shortly they will rebuild what was destroyed," Jamoon shouted, his voice ringing through the hall. "When the gateway

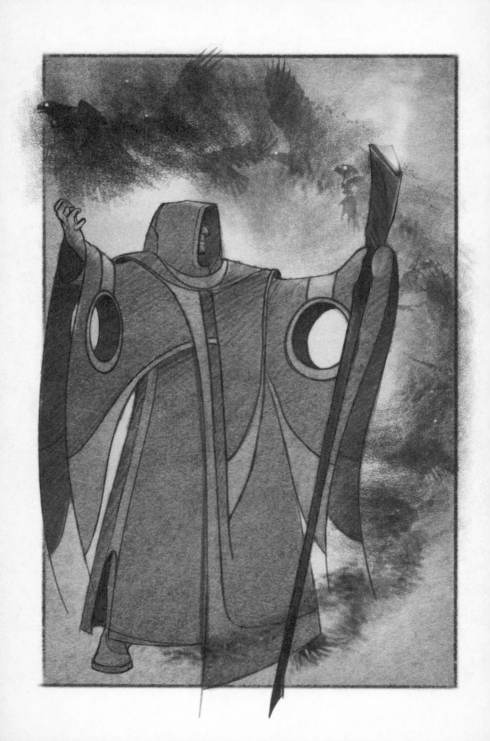

is reconstructed we will have complete access and will be made whole. Our armies gather at the Guarded Border waiting to spread the message of Morfit to all parts of Foo."

"What of Geth?" a short rant near the front yelled.

Jamoon's right eye burned.

"Geth will be found," Jamoon seethed. "That is why we are gathered. You are to search every bit of Foo, until you have recovered him and Leven. Dig up the gunt, tear down the trees, bury any who stand in your way, but find them—and when you do, kill them instantly. Their dead bodies are all the proof I need. They cannot be allowed to live."

Winter opened her mouth to gasp. Unfortunately, portions of the bickerwicks in her stomach were still fighting with each other, and their bickering could be heard.

"You digest!"

"No, you! I was here second."

A couple of rants in front of Winter turned to see what the fuss was.

"Who are you?" one asked.

"I . . ." Winter tried to answer.

It was no use. Half the crowd had now turned and was staring at her.

"It's the girl!" one yelled.

The hall erupted with angry cries. Even from where she was, Winter could see Jamoon begin to smile. Winter turned and ran toward the entryway. Three rants stepped in front of her, and she froze them. They fell against each other and became wedged in the opening. Winter quickly turned and bolted for another entrance.

"Seize her!" Jamoon yelled.

Winter looked back at the crowd of rants and froze them all—all of them half frozen, their other halves struggling and complaining about having to hold the frozen part up. The room was now full of a variety of half-dreams complaining. Even Jamoon was stiff, but as he stood there, Winter could see the dead, decaying nihils beginning to seep out from under his frozen robe. At first there were just a few, but in a couple of seconds there were whole flocks of them, out and racing toward her. She was not about to freeze them, fearing them more as ice than as simply dead.

Winter ran as fast as she could, slipping out of the archway and leaping up a stone stairwell. Behind her she could hear the shrill caw and hiss of the rank nihils overtaking her. Winter reached the top of the stairs to find a locked door. She pictured the wooden doorknob as ice and it froze. She then slammed the blunt end of the kilve into the knob, and it shattered into a million pieces.

"Thank you," the door sighed, happy about being set free.

The nihils were getting closer, their caws filling her head with fear.

Winter pushed the thankful wooden door open and stepped into the room behind it, then quickly closed it and leaned against it, breathing hard.

The nihils were in the stairwell outside the door.

Winter moved a large chair up against the door, but her

efforts were in vain. The black nihils began pulsing through the now-gaping knob hole like a geyser of oil. They flowed through the knob hole and under the small gap beneath the door, screaming and hissing like a cold, biting wind.

Winter did a little screaming of her own.

The nihils swarmed around her, biting and scratching her with their beaks and talons. Winter waved the kilve at them, but it was useless. As they closed about her, she had difficulty breathing and could see her vision fading. In a matter of moments she was unconscious and lying in a helpless heap on the floor.

The nihils turned and flew out of the room. They swept back down the stairs and over the half-frozen crowd. When they reached Jamoon they circled him tightly, warming him with their movements.

Jamoon soon thawed and headed up to Winter.

CHAPTER TWENTY-SEVEN

SNAPPED

The media had no idea what to make of it—a full-sized plane landing upside down in the middle of a busy freeway with no fatalities? Baffling. The only injuries reported were some scrapes and bruises and two broken arms, both belonging to the same person.

Some who witnessed the incredible episode claimed that fiery, demon clouds had softly set the plane down. Those who reported the story refused to even humor such a silly account. Regardless, traffic along Interstate 40 was backed up for hundreds of miles as everyone scratched their heads and wondered just how to move an *upside-down* 747.

Dennis sat on the edge of the freeway next to a number of other stunned passengers. He had a small, blue, airline blanket wrapped around his shoulders and was drinking some bottled water that a Red Cross volunteer had handed him. He really had no idea what had happened, but he was pretty sure he had something to do with it. He figured it would be best not to point that out to others.

After everyone had been evacuated from the plane, Dennis had noticed a small patch of black moving behind some foliage off to the side of the road. He watched it glide from one tree to another, almost as if it were stalking him. He could see it even now, lying beneath a large bush.

Dennis unzipped the fanny pack and looked down at Ezra.

"Did we do this?" Dennis whispered.

"We helped," Ezra said, jumping out of the fanny pack and up onto Dennis's shoulder.

"What is that blackness?" Dennis asked, motioning with his head to the bush at the bottom of the embankment.

"Not exactly sure," Ezra said. "But it's from Foo like me. It tried to talk to me—called me *Geth*," Ezra spat.

Dennis put his head in his hands and sighed. "I should never have ordered a sandwich."

The black shadow wriggled beneath the bush down below as trucks and cars drove by, people gawking and honking at the plane up above.

"Follow me," Ezra said to Dennis.

Ezra jumped from Dennis's shoulder and dropped down the side of the tree-lined embankment.

"I don't think we're supposed to . . ." Dennis slapped his forehead. "Ahhh," he gasped, stumbling over the guardrail and rolling awkwardly down the embankment after Ezra.

As usual, nobody noticed Dennis.

When he stopped rolling, Dennis scrambled to his feet and ducked behind some trees near the bush where the black spot was lying. The blackness fluttered away, moving deeper into the growth, with Ezra right on its tail. Dennis limped along after them, rubbing his sore knees and elbows. In a few minutes they had moved into a forest, far enough away from the freeway that they could barely hear the noise of the traffic. To Dennis it felt as if they were miles away from civilization.

The black shadow stopped, hovering above a decaying tree that lay sprawled out on the forest floor.

"Who *are* you?" Ezra yelled.

The blackness pulsated and whipped itself into a more ghost-like form. It had two small hands, tiny eyes, and an oozing mouth.

"Who are *you*?" it hissed. "You've been touched by Foo."

"'Touched,' my ankle," Ezra raged. "I've been cheated by Geth. He lives, complete and free, while I am nothing but anger."

"Geth," Sabine hissed.

"We are heading to the gateway to make things right," Ezra sneered. "If you wish, you can be my servant."

Sabine laughed wickedly. "You fool," he hissed. "The gateway is gone."

Dennis knew Ezra well enough to know that he was going to have to hold him back. He grabbed onto Ezra's legs and tiny tail as the furious toothpick swung with his arms and swore, trying to get at Sabine. Dennis could feel the anger raging through Ezra. It seemed to bleed out of the toothpick and into Dennis's blood. The sensation was almost overpowering.

"Fool?" Ezra seethed at Sabine. "I'll show you who the fool is."

Sabine withdrew a couple of feet.

"Listen," Dennis said, trying to calm things down and to understand the rage he himself was beginning to feel. "I think . . ." he stopped to soak in the rage. He opened and closed his eyes slowly. "I think . . ."

"Who are you?" Sabine hissed, drifting up to Dennis. "Who are you?"

"I'm Dennis," he answered, his body trembling with gathering anger.

"He's nobody!" Ezra yelled, his purple tassel writhing like a nest of snakes.

"Nobody?" Dennis whispered, his head beginning to pound.

"Nobody!" Ezra screamed. "I'm only using him to get me to the gateway."

Dennis couldn't remember feeling more agitated.

In the far distance the sound of sirens screamed. Dennis looked down at Ezra. He was holding the angry toothpick between his thumb and finger, and he studied the little monster's ugly face. It was contorted with rage and hatred. Dennis fed off the anger. He thought of all the times his father had been disappointed in him. He thought of how his mother had always wished he were taller or smarter. He thought about his employers and how they had always dismissed him as a nobody.

He knew they weren't even aware that he had left. And he thought of what he was doing. Sure, it was a ridiculous quest, but it was a purpose.

The anger Dennis felt was so strong he couldn't stop shaking. He looked down again at Ezra, who was still screaming.

"Nobody!" Ezra repeated. "Didn't you hear me? I said—"

Dennis couldn't help himself. He grabbed the top of Ezra and in one angry motion bent him in half. It was so sudden and unexpected that Ezra had no time to react.

Dennis stared at the bent toothpick. Ezra's upper half was connected to his lower half by only a thin splinter of wood. The top half of Ezra stared up at Dennis in total shock.

"You . . ." Ezra sputtered. "I . . ."

Dennis looked at Ezra in his palm and felt no pity. In the distance the sirens grew louder.

"I'll be making the decisions now," Dennis seethed, a look of determination on his face such as he had never had before.

Stunned into silence, Ezra blinked weakly, and Sabine withdrew a couple of inches.

Dennis looked up, his eyes red and wet, his blood filled with anger.

"Dennis," Sabine hissed.

Dennis reached out with such surety that Sabine didn't even flinch. He grabbed Sabine and twisted him around his forearm like a thick rope. Sabine responded by spreading up and around Dennis's shoulders, forming a ragged, black cloak. Sabine's eyes and mouth lay two-dimensionally at the neck of the cloak.

"I've never dreamed before," Dennis said angrily.

"I can fix that," Sabine hissed.

"I want to see this Foo," Dennis demanded.

"Of course," Sabine hissed. "Of course, Darrin."

Dennis turned and lowered his head so that Sabine's white eyes were directly in view of his. "My name is *Dennis,*" he spat angrily.

"Of course," Sabine hissed.

"Listen . . ." Ezra weakly begged.

Dennis wasn't in the mood to listen. He stuffed Ezra's broken body into the fanny pack, Ezra moaning the whole time. Then, straightening his wrinkle-proof pants and wearing Sabine as a tattered, open cloak, Dennis stood tall and puffed out his chest. He smoothed the sticker the bank teller had placed on his chest, viciously zipped up his fanny pack, and stomped farther into the woods, leaving behind the scene of the accident and the person he once was.

Dennis felt invincible.

ii

Tim Tuttle was slightly nervous about flying. Normally, he wouldn't have given it a second thought, but the strange story he had just heard about a plane landing upside down on a freeway was making him a bit uneasy.

Uneasy but determined.

People were also talking about the twenty-four-story office

building in North Carolina that had simply gotten up from the corner it was on and "walked" to the opposite side of the street. A plane landing upside down, a building changing location: nobody had a logical explanation for either event. Some thought it was the result of earthquakes and tornadoes, but the problem with that theory was that there was no other indication that any earthquake or tornado had actually occurred. One television network reported that these incidents were illusions staged by a clever magician who was trying to make a name for himself. They retracted their story a couple of hours later.

The world seemed like a crazy place. What made Tim most uneasy was that in the very back of his mind he couldn't help but think that all these things were somehow connected to what Winter was going through.

Before his flight, Tim had spent the day at the library, researching newspaper stories from around the world. If it was true, and Winter did have some way of freezing things or hypno-tizing people, there certainly had to be an article documenting something odd going on somewhere. And Tim figured that if that odd thing had something to do with ice, then he might be back on the trail.

Unfortunately, the newspapers were full of odd people and odd events. But nothing he had found had any obvious connec-tion to Winter or Leven or ice.

There was one brief article, buried in a London newspaper, describing a bizarre incident that had taken place in a Munich, Germany, train station a few days previous. According to the report, something had turned the station into a chaotic mess, with travelers being hurled around or lifted up by unidentified assailants. Blame was tentatively placed on a malfunctioning new heating system at the station, but nobody who had been there bought into that at all.

There were quotes from passengers who had lived through the ordeal. Tim would have thought it was simply another odd story, except for the last quote from a Frau Dent. She had said: "A young boy and girl started clapping, and for some reason that seemed to help settle things down."

There was no mention of ice, but the young boy and girl stood out. Tim had printed the article and stared at it for hours, thinking. When he called his wife, Wendy, to tell her what he had found, she encouraged him to do what he thought best.

"I've always wanted to go to Germany," Tim said, "and my passport's current from that convention of the International Waste and Litter Society last year in Nottingham."

"Then go find her," Wendy urged.

So, Tim was now on a plane crossing the Atlantic Ocean, wondering what in the world he would find when he landed in Germany. Winter had meant a lot to his family, but this quest was more than that. For the very first time he was truly beginning to understand just how important Winter was. The secret the old lady had whispered to him was finally beginning to make sense— sort of.

"She holds the seventh key, but does not know it. Watch her carefully."

Tim turned off his overhead light and pulled his ball cap down over his eyes. He needed sleep, and he had a feeling this might be his last chance to get some for a while.

"Seventh key," he whispered as he drifted off, wondering how he could *watch* Winter when he still had no idea where she was.

CHAPTER TWENTY-EIGHT

SIGNS O' THE TIME

By the time Leven and Clover and Janet reached the other side of Fissure Gorge, Janet had stopped crying, Leven's stomach hurt worse than ever, and Clover had tried more times than you can count to convince Leven to let him take care of the key. On the Niteon side there was a giant stone wall running along the entire length of the gorge, protecting Niteon from who knows what. Leven stepped off the bridge, through an opening in the wall, and onto solid ground.

"You're a beauty. I'll tell the world about you!" Leven yelled back to the bridge as he walked away.

The sentry bird on the Niteon side was less kind, ordering Leven to move on and stop talking to the bridge.

"They can sense insincerity," the big bird chirped, thinking Leven was being sarcastic.

Leven moved away from the gorge and into Niteon. He

could see nothing but a moonlit landscape. There were small hills and beautiful trees dotting and accentuating everything he could see. A broad stone path, with stone arches randomly stretching over it, ran far enough into the distance that Leven couldn't see the end of it. The only structure in sight was the giant bird's guardhouse.

"So, why do birds guard the bridge?" Leven asked Clover as they passed beneath two stone arches and onto the path leading to Cork.

"What else would birds do?" Clover asked, confused.

Leven shrugged. It didn't feel right to go farther without Geth. In Leven's mind there was no way Geth could have gotten in front of them, and it made sense to wait a bit for him.

He mentioned his concern to Clover.

"You're forgetting that Geth could have traveled in a number of ways," Clover said. "He could have found a sarus and ridden on top of it the whole way. Or he could be traveling on the back of a roven, or maybe he hitched a ride with a Sympathetic Twill and has taken one of the other bridges. You watch. When we get to the turrets, he'll be there."

"You're right," Leven said, knowing he needed to just focus on their goal of reaching the turrets and let fate do the rest.

Leven motioned for Janet to follow him and began walking quickly toward the turrets. In the distance there was a thick, lumpy patch of black horizon, darker than the night.

"What's that darkness over there?" Leven asked, pointing toward a gigantic, cystlike growth in the sky. Even in the darkness of the night it stood out, looking like a mushy black hole. It was in the opposite direction of the fire shooting up from the turrets. The blackness looked too substantive to actually be hovering in the air.

"It's not good," Clover said.

"Then what is it?"

"Bad," Clover suggested, sounding as though he wasn't all that impressed with Leven's level of knowledge.

"I understand opposites," Leven said, frustrated.

"We used to have the most spectacular sunrises," Clover said, leading into an explanation. "It's been many years, but we in Foo used to wake to find the marvelous dreams of mankind painting our world brilliant colors. Like a kaleidoscope. Sure, there were always spots and lines of black, and mornings of great darkness, but mankind was ultimately moving forward and dreamed of being better. There were some who were selfish, but now . . .

"That blackness is the result of sick dreams. The Children of the Sewn can't frame the dark dreams fast enough. And the museum expansion where they hang and store the dreams has been caught up in bureaucratic red tape for years. But, if they can frame a rotten dream, then it is less likely to spread and grow. Whereas the good dreams, when properly framed, are much easier to focus in on and achieve—their frames expand. But as I was saying, the Children of the Sewn are behind in both areas."

"Children of the Sewn?" Leven asked.

"They have the gift of framing the dreams of mankind."

"You can't frame dreams," Janet spoke up, making it obvious that she had been listening in. "Dreams are just your brain trying to sort out all the garbage life throws at you."

Clover made himself visible. "Excuse me?" he asked.

"I saw it on a TV special," Janet said with less enthusiasm. "It's just your brain trying to organize the junk you see during the day. I'm pretty sure that's what's happening to me now."

Clover shook his head.

"This can't be real," Janet said. "I can't even touch you."

"It wouldn't be appropriate anyhow," Clover pointed out.

"I can't eat. I can't even sit," Janet complained. "And I can feel I'm somewhere else. Somewhere, someone just needs to wake me up."

"Sorry," Clover said unsympathetically. "You are very much awake, both here and in Reality. The sooner you understand that, the better off you'll be."

Janet looked at Leven as if he might have something to add.

Leven shrugged. "I don't know much more than you," he said. "But I do know that despite things looking different here, I can feel it's real."

Janet didn't argue, but she did begin crying again.

"Women," Clover said, disappearing.

Leven and Clover and Janet picked up their pace, running along a narrower, worn stone path that bordered the brink of the gorge. Every few hundred feet the path in front of them would suddenly lift up, move to the right or to the left, and then drop down again, creating a new trail in a new direction. The fourth time the path did that, Leven began to question if they were going the right way.

"We are," Clover insisted. "Just stay on the path."

"But it keeps changing," Leven said, his breathing labored.

"It'll make up its mind eventually," Clover said. "No path wants to just lie there. It's trying to provide you the best journey."

"That's nice and all, but we need to get there."

"We will."

"Isn't there a normal path?"

Leven was going to argue the point further, but the path in front of them had heard Leven and was insulted by his ingratitude. It no longer wanted to go to the trouble of providing an interesting journey. So the path picked itself up, rose fifty feet into the air, and then slammed down, making a straight line through some trees and right to the turrets.

"Happy?" Clover asked.

"Thrilled," Leven answered, running even faster down the trail and toward the flame.

Leven's concern for Geth kept him going. But he was tiring. Gradually, his running turned to jogging and the jogging turned to walking and the walking led him eventually right up the front steps of a house that sat at the entrance to the turrets. The house was four stories tall with an ivy-covered porch that wrapped all the way around the ground floor. The roof was made of wood shingles that looked dry enough to spontaneously combust. There was a wide front door that was painted blue and had a fat wooden doorknob on it. On the wall next to the door was a sign that said:

HOURS: 8-8

In back of the house, a tall wooden fence ran for miles in either direction. Leven could see the high, distant flames of the turrets. They were still many miles off, beyond the fence.

"What is this place?" Leven asked, wiping sweat from his forehead and pointing to the old home.

"The gatehouse entrance to the turrets," Clover replied.

"Entrance?"

Clover read the sign. "Gates open at eight."

"We can't wait for the gates to open!" Leven insisted. "Geth needs our help!"

Leven stepped onto the porch with Clover and tried the handle of the front door. It was locked. He looked back at Janet, who was still standing on the path. Leven moved to a large window under the porch and pressed his face to the glass. Inside he could see shelf after shelf, each lined with books. A couple of the books slid off their shelves and began to approach the window. Two opened and pressed themselves up against the glass, showing off their pages. Leven jumped back.

"Books are so vain," Clover said. "Always wanting everyone to know their story. If they think for a second that you don't know what is inside of them, they'll strut around showing off their stuff forever."

Another book slammed up against the glass, trying to get Leven to look at it. It was opened up to a page with a painting of a boat on the Lime Sea.

Leven moved away from the window and back over to the door. He knocked and listened for any response. Something inside banged and rattled. A few seconds later the doorknob turned, and the door opened.

Leven recognized the man instantly. It was Albert, the same gentleman he had helped rescue from the forest. Albert gave no indication that he recognized Leven. Beyond Albert, inside the house, Leven could see a fat sycophant resting in a chair with its feet dangling in a bucket.

"Gates open at nine," Albert instructed.

"The sign says eight," Clover said.

"Well, what do signs know? Gates open at nine."

A couple of books had moved out of the library and were now trying to get out the front door to present themselves to Leven. Albert kicked them back with his foot.

"We have to get to the turrets," Leven begged. "We need to meet someone."

"Well, meet them in front of here," Albert insisted. "There is no one inside, and no one will be allowed inside until the gates open at ten."

"You said nine," Leven pointed out.

"That doesn't sound like something I would say," Albert claimed, kicking another book. "Gates open at ten."

Albert slammed the door.

Leven walked to the edge of the ivy-covered porch and looked around the house at the tall fence behind it, then stepped off the porch and walked toward it. He reached out to stick his hand through the slats, but as he reached, the fence shifted to block him. Leven scooted over and tried to reach again. Again the fence moved to keep him from even reaching through.

"Do you think we can climb over it?" Leven asked Clover.

"No way," Clover said. "This fence would swat you down every time you tried. We'll have to wait here."

Leven was going to argue the point a bit more, but he spotted a thick patch of soft-looking green grass growing beneath some tall trees.

"I don't know about both of you," Leven said, "but if we have to wait, I could really use some sleep and maybe some food. My stomach feels awful."

Clover materialized and handed Leven a filler crisp. "Just nibble it. It'll fill you right up."

"Thanks," Leven said.

"So what about me?" Clover asked.

"What *about* you?" Leven said, kneeling down on the soft turf.

"I'm not actually tired, and you know how much trouble I can get in with a couple of hours of unsupervised time. And in the dark, even."

"Janet will watch you," Leven mumbled, lying down on the soft green grass and closing his eyes. "Gates open at ten. Hopefully."

Clover looked at Leven and tisked. He looked up at Janet, who had begun crying again.

"Wanna play a game or something?" he asked.

She just stood there.

"Come on," Clover finally said, "follow me."

Janet followed Clover into the trees.

ii

The moonlight rested upon the secret's shoulders like a thick dusting of dandruff. A light wind caused the dandruff to swirl. The very tip of the secret's feet still burned orange from the heat of the soil; the rest of it had cooled nicely and was practically invisible to the naked eye. It swatted a few pesky decoy secrets away from its head.

It breathed.

It then exhaled a torrent of soft whispers and low murmurings. The secret stepped lightly across the ground. It had braved crossing the bridge and was now moving down the same path Leven had traveled earlier.

It sought the soul who had dug it up.

It had not gotten a complete look at who had set it free, but it had seen the eyes, and that should be enough. The secret shivered. It could still feel the hands of the nit who had buried it so many years before. It could also feel the fear and the anxiety the nit had placed deep in the soil along with it.

The secret expanded and then contracted. It wanted so deeply to let go of what it was holding inside. Even in its state, it knew it held a secret that many would kill to hear.

It reached the turret's gatehouse.

For some reason it was frightened of the sycophant and was relieved to see no sign of it. But there beneath the trees by the fence lay a tall boy sleeping.

The secret moved closer, making no more sound than a pair of bare feet walking in long grass.

The secret whispered, hoping the boy would stir and open his eyes slightly.

The boy moaned and rolled over, his closed eyes pressing into the grass.

The secret whispered louder.

It was no use; the boy was sound asleep.

The secret moved behind the trees. It would wait.

CHAPTER TWENTY-NINE

THROWING FEAR

W inter could feel her hands beneath her chin and her knees pushed up against her chest as she sat curled up in a ball on the dirt floor. She opened her eyes, but couldn't see much more than she had been able to with them closed. She straightened her back and moved into a kneeling position. The soil around her knees crunched and crackled. Her head felt thick and littered with streaks of darkness that the bite of the rotting nihils had left behind. Winter was covered in leftover bits from the decaying birds—a claw here, a beak there, and two eyeballs caught in the hem of her shirt.

As her green eyes adjusted to the dark, Winter looked around the room she was in, taking in every inch. The room was huge, with white, tile-covered walls and a domed ceiling. At the center of the dome was a small opening that created a skylight of sorts. A circle of moonlight was dripping in, and Winter could hear the sound of wind building.

Jamoon stood at the edge of the moonlight near a table filled with steaming food. Winter had forgotten how hungry she was. In the corner of the room was Jamoon's roven. The roven rocked sideways, clicking its lips. Jamoon ripped off a big piece of meat from a platter on the table and threw it to the roven.

Winter thought about diving toward the food, but instead she worked her way up onto her feet and dusted off her knees and palms. She touched her sore shoulder and winced. The last thing she could remember was running from Jamoon's nihils.

Jamoon smiled. Of course, it wasn't the kind of smile you would see on a four-year-old in a family portrait; it was more like the kind of smile a wicked darkness would smile after it had successfully destroyed everything good that had ever existed. Jamoon was still wearing his robe, and the dream he had stepped into Morfit with was of a body builder. His left side was ripped and strong. Most rants would never leave Morfit if they were lucky enough to get such a useful left half. The body-builder side matched some of the natural strength and size Jamoon's right side enjoyed. The bottom of Jamoon's robe billowed.

"Do you not recognize this room?" Jamoon asked tauntingly.

Before Winter could answer there was a knock on the door and a cog entered, carrying a small board with a dream film over it. The blue-handed cog showed the board to Jamoon.

Winter looked around again. The room *was* familiar to her. She tried to force her mind to remember.

Jamoon handed the board back to the cog.

"Well," Jamoon said, "there is still some uncertainty, but the Sochemists feel that your beloved Geth is dead."

Winter's stomach lurched.

"They are still debating it," Jamoon went on. "But in time, they will come to an agreement."

"He can't be dead," Winter insisted.

"I can bench-press my own weight," the body-building side of Jamoon bragged.

Winter stayed quiet.

"Send the locusts," Jamoon instructed the cog, ignoring his other half. "Transmit a message from the Sochemists. Let all of Foo know we have Winter. That should bring the boy here."

"As you wish," the cog said, backing out of the room and closing the door behind him.

"Geth is not dead," Winter asserted.

"Perhaps," Jamoon said. "The Sochemists will sort it out."

"Just because they say it doesn't make it so."

"You have no understanding of the politics of Morfit."

Winter pictured Geth in her mind. She thought she could feel he still lived. But her head was so full of dark and depressing thoughts she wasn't sure if it was a false hope.

"You helped create this room," Jamoon said, bringing the subject back to where it had been before the cog had entered. "You thought you were helping Foo, when in reality you were forwarding Sabine's plan. Now look at you: alone, and possessing the blessed ability to die."

Winter closed her green eyes. Her hands were trembling. She

let her fear race through the open ceiling and out into the night air, trying to picture Leven wherever he was.

"You really don't remember any of this, do you?" Jamoon laughed wickedly.

"I remember," Winter lied, not wanting to give Jamoon the satisfaction of being right.

"I don't believe you do."

Winter was silent.

"If you do, then where's the key?" he demanded.

Winter had absolutely no idea what Jamoon was talking about, but she decided to stick with lying.

"Wouldn't you like to know," she snapped, raising her green eyes to meet Jamoon's single exposed one.

"Toy with us and Leven dies," Jamoon said. "Of course, he will die anyway. The Lore Coil has made one thing perfectly clear: Leven is mortal. There are many who will smile at his death."

Winter couldn't allow such talk. She thought of Jamoon's right side as ice. Nothing happened. She focused her green eyes. Still nothing.

Jamoon laughed. "Surprised? Your gift is useless in this room. The Want himself has touched these walls. With his touch he took away the ability for any who stand in here to exercise their gifts. Crazy fool."

Winter could feel the panic rising in her throat like sour mush. Fear shot off her and into the air. All Winter could think of was Leven.

"No gift and the ability to die." Jamoon stepped closer. "You betrayed us once before. Now you will pay for it."

Jamoon seized Winter by the wrists.

"Somebody spot me," his left side demanded.

Jamoon twisted Winter and threw her to the ground like wet garbage. The nihils beneath his robe poured out. Winter screamed, and once again her fear shot off from her, through the window, and into the night air.

"I am only letting you live so in case Geth does still exist I can use you as a bargaining chip," Jamoon sneered. "But, I don't have to keep you alive *and well*—how about just *alive,* and how about *just barely?*"

The nihils fluttered and screamed, darting around the room like black pulses of light.

Winter, still on the ground, crawled to get away. She was too slow, and there was nowhere to go. The nihils flowed beneath her like water and lifted her into the air as Jamoon stepped closer. His right eye burned with rage.

Another bolt of fear shot off of Winter and out through the window. *Leven,* Winter pleaded, her heart trembling.

Leven.

CHAPTER THIRTY

EGYPTIAN SILK

Dennis looked at himself in the hotel mirror. He moved the disposable razor over his scalp, removing the last bit of hair from his head. He was ready to be someone else. He toweled off the remaining bits of shaving cream and took another good look at himself. He was surprised to see himself smiling. It made sense, seeing how he had never been happier. He had also never been more sinister. As a general rule, sinisterism is usually not that happy a thing, but Dennis was so new to it, he couldn't properly interpret his feelings. He dried off the top of his bald head and looked back at Sabine.

Sabine was sprawled out on the second bed in the hotel, looking like a ghostly black towel. All the lights were turned off, aside from the small one in the bathroom. Sabine preferred the dark. Dennis had worn him in as a robe, and now Sabine was trying to feel sinister despite the elegant, thousand-thread-count sheets he was lying on. Luckily for every wicked cause he was a part of, he was perfectly sinister, whether sleeping on satin or in soil.

Dennis had no answers as to what his future held, but he and Sabine felt that heading toward the spot where the gateway had been located was as good a move as any. With Dennis's help it might be possible to build a new and better gateway. Dennis picked up the fanny pack and pulled out the crippled body of Ezra. He looked at what he now saw as the pathetic little tyrant and wondered where he would be now if he had ordered a piece of pizza instead of the sandwich Ezra had been in.

"Need to look at what you did?" Ezra seethed, his speech weak and airy. "Broke a defenseless toothpick in half."

Dennis pinched Ezra tightly. There was still some feeling of anger and hatred in the sliver of wood, but Dennis knew that most of the passionate hatred the toothpick had once housed had been transferred to himself.

"You don't know what you're getting yourself into," Ezra coughed weakly. "You don't have the stomach. You gutless—"

Dennis didn't let him finish. He jammed Ezra back into the fanny pack and zipped it up.

"No stomach?" Dennis said to himself. "We'll see."

He splashed water on his face and approached Sabine, who was still sprawled out on the bed.

"I want to know what Foo is," Dennis said.

"Why?" Sabine hissed from his small mouth at his far corner.

"How can I build a gateway without knowing where it leads to?"

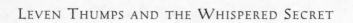

"Foo is paradise," Sabine seethed. "A paradise that is being withheld from people like you."

"That doesn't seem fair," Dennis said, trying to sound bold. "And this gateway?"

"It will be the hope of millions," Sabine lied. "You will be a hero to millions."

Dennis liked that.

"And what about this Geth that Ezra spoke about?"

Sabine hissed and then breathed in very slowly. "Don't think of Geth," he demanded. "He will be dead before you get there. My other half will see to that."

"And that's a good thing?" Dennis asked.

"That's a perfect thing," Sabine hissed. "One less wall to knock down before we can have it all."

Dennis liked that too.

Dennis flicked off the bathroom light and climbed into the other bed. They had an early flight to catch. Dennis slept soundly in his white shirt with the bank sticker and his wrinkle-proof pants—getting ready for whatever lay ahead.

ii

Tim didn't understand a word of German. People wearing felt hats and drab clothes just stared at him as he walked down the street, trying to figure out where he was. He had taken a taxi from the airport, but the cabbie had dropped him off at the wrong spot, insisting that he was where he had asked to be.

Tim was confused. He needed the train station, but all he could see were houses and a few small businesses. He stepped into a tiny delicatessen and bought a bit of cheese and bread with some of the money he had exchanged at the airport.

"Excuse me," Tim tried. "Train station?"

The owner of the shop looked at him as if he had just let a pack of monkeys loose in his store.

"Trains?" Tim said again.

The owner wiped his hands on his apron and pointed to the west. "You go," he insisted.

Tim couldn't tell if he was being instructed to leave or given directions.

"Thank you," Tim said, backing out. "Guten Tag," he added, trying to be gracious.

The German shopkeeper just shook his head.

Tim walked down the street in the direction he had been pointed. Germany was so green and beautiful, with honest-looking people. He couldn't believe he was here. If someone had asked him two weeks before where he would be today, he never would have guessed.

Tim was happy collecting trash. Now here he was halfway across the world, working off a hunch to find Winter and a boy named Leven. As with the trash he collected, he couldn't wait to figure out the story behind what remained.

After walking two miles, Tim found the train station. He walked in and looked around as if the answer might be right there.

It wasn't.

Instead, there were rows of wooden benches in the middle of the depot and people walking back and forth trying to catch trains that would take them someplace they would stay until they went someplace else.

Tim walked through the crowd and up to the ticket window. Behind the glass sat a skinny woman with braided hair and crooked white teeth. She smiled, which took Tim by surprise.

"Do you speak English?" Tim asked, smiling back.

"A bit," she said, still smiling.

"I read about the situation that happened here a couple of days ago," he tried. "People flying around." Tim waved his arms in the air as if to demonstrate.

Her smile left.

"Were you here?" he asked.

"No," she said solemnly. "But Herr Wondra." She pointed to a ticket window four glass panels down. "He was here."

"Thanks," Tim said.

He slipped four windows down and found himself facing a man with no smile.

"Do you speak English?" Tim asked.

"Of course," he answered curtly.

"You were here during the incident?" Tim asked. "When people were flying around?"

Again with the arms.

The German man sniffed. "I was," he said sharply. "This is a result," he added, lifting up his right arm to show off a cast. "I hurt it flying through the ice."

"Ice?" Tim asked, the hairs on the back of his neck dancing like a bunch of uncoordinated teenagers.

"Glass," the man corrected. "I flew through the glass."

"Not ice?" Tim questioned.

"Some of the glass may have . . . melted," he finally admitted, looking around as if concerned that others would overhear. "I flew through this glass," he said confidentially, pointing toward the pane of glass he was behind at the moment. "The glass, it . . . broke, and I fell on my arm. I was scared to be getting up. That I might get cut . . ." He paused to see if Tim understood.

Tim nodded, "Of course."

"But it wasn't glass," he continued. "There was water everywhere and the glass was melting. I took one day off," he said shamefacedly.

"Only one?" Tim said sympathetically.

The ticket master liked that. "I've never missed another day in my life," he declared proudly.

"So it was the heater that caused all the mess?" Tim asked.

"Certainly not," the man said, sticking out his strong German chin. "No heater could do that."

"So what happened?"

The ticket agent looked as though he were thinking, but he

obviously already had the story down. "It began while I was in pursuit of a young American."

"Girl or boy?" Tim asked.

"Girl," he said, as if proud of his memory. "She was in tears and wanting to travel to Berchtesgaden. I remember, because I have spent many weeks there."

"What did she look like?" Tim asked, trying to stay calm.

"Wild, blonde hair," he sniffed. "Young. Stubborn, of course."

"Of course," Tim said, his pulse racing. "And this Berchtesgaden . . . ?" he prompted.

"Proof that God prefers Germany," the ticket agent said proudly.

"Did she go there?" Tim asked.

"How should I know?" the agent said suspiciously. Suddenly he was far less friendly than he had been. "Why all the questions?" he asked.

"No reason."

"Are you traveling somewhere?" the agent asked, switching to a professional tone. "If not, please step aside."

"Actually," Tim said, "I would like a ticket to this Berchtesgaden place."

The ticket agent didn't smile. It was apparent from his eyes that he was suspicious and concerned about all he had said. He straightened himself and brushed back the sides of his hair, as if physically regaining his composure.

"Your papers, please," he finally said.

Tim handed the man his passport, happy to oblige.

CHAPTER THIRTY-ONE

CHOOSING A PATH

Leven wasn't dreaming—which wasn't too surprising, seeing as how he was in Foo and dreams there are more common among those who are awake. But, even though he was not dreaming, he was most definitely sleeping. The soft bed of grass he was lying on in front of the turrets' gatehouse was enjoying his company, and it swayed gently, rocking him as he slumbered. A couple of large mushrooms wandered over to give his head a decent place to rest. A little-known fact of Foo is that all fungi are incredibly friendly and love to be of service when they can.

If it had not been for the pain in his stomach, Leven couldn't have been more comfortable. At the moment, he was sleeping facedown on the grass, his forehead resting on the spongy mushrooms.

Small wits, tattered pieces of old dreams with a bit of life still left in them, watched over Leven. The wits liked to hide in trees, disguised as odd-looking leaves. They would pluck off the large fantrum leaves to make space for themselves in the trees. The plucked leaves from the nearby trees had drifted down and covered Leven in his sleep. He was so camouflaged that when Clover came back looking for him, he didn't spot him right off. Luckily, Leven gave himself away by his contented snoring.

Clover leaned over Leven and gently shook him.

"Leven," he said softly. "Leven, wake up."

Leven barely stirred.

"Leven," Clover said casually, "that whisp woman's in trouble."

Leven's eyes flew open, and he sat up. He looked at Clover, blinking. He shook his head and tried to pull his thoughts together.

"Janet's in trouble?" he asked, still confused by sleep.

"Oh, Janet. That's right," Clover laughed. "I keep wanting to call her Pam."

Leven rubbed his eyes and stood. "Is she in trouble?"

"Here's the thing," Clover said, clearing his throat. "Someone I know wanted to sleep, and so as to not bother you I decided to show Whispy a game I used to play. I never thought anyone would take her."

"She's been taken?" Leven said. "By who?"

"I don't know." Clover tried to cry. When he could see Leven wasn't buying it, he knocked it off. "They had horns and outdated hair. Oh, and they were dressed in fire."

"Fire?" Leven asked.

"Their skin was burning and they were wailing. Probably

because of their hair," Clover said. "They told Janet to follow them, and she did."

Leven was fully awake now. He looked about wildly. "We need to find her. Do you know where they were going?"

"My guess is to the gorge, or the Guarded Border, or the Lime Sea."

Leven put his head in his hands and sighed. "What game were you playing, anyway?" he asked.

Clover was quiet for a moment. "Rotscotch?" he finally said tentatively.

"Rotscotch? How do you play that?"

"I don't want to bore you with the details," Clover waved. "Let's just say it's really fun and involves decay and jumping."

Leven gave Clover a serious look.

"All right," Clover sighed. "It wasn't really so much a game as me wanting her to dig up something for me to eat."

"She can't dig," Leven pointed out.

"Tell me about it," he said. "She was a lousy player. I ended up having to do most of the work. But as I was digging around some trees, I accidentally dug up some things I shouldn't have— some bad thoughts," Clover whispered. "Judging by their hair, I'd say they'd been buried there since the early seventies."

Thanks to Terry, Leven's step-guardian, Clover had watched a lot of TV while in Reality. When Leven was sleeping or doing chores, Clover would slip up by Terry and watch whatever was on. Consequently, Clover knew quite a bit about American culture, popular history, and old hairstyles.

"We need to find her," Leven said.

"She'll be all right," Clover insisted. "She's a whisp. She can drift off whenever she wants, and they can't do a thing about it."

"So why did you wake me up?" Leven complained.

"Gates open in five minutes," Clover said casually.

Leven suddenly remembered why they were here. "Geth didn't come, did he?" he asked, glancing around.

"Not yet," Clover said, as though it were just a matter of time.

Leven's stomach lurched again. "Why is it still so dark?" he asked, turning to face the sun.

The sun was covered by a stippled black cloud.

"Maybe it's going to rain," Clover said.

"I don't think those are rain clouds," Leven said, watching the dark, grainy splotches move closer.

"Well, then what—" Clover stopped talking and his pointed ears began to twitch, to better listen to the distant buzzing in the air.

As the cloud drifted closer, it began breaking apart. Long ribbons of darkness hurtled down from the cloud like stringy, wet noodles. To avoid the approaching storm, Leven and Clover hurried up onto the porch of the gatehouse, taking cover under its roof.

The cloud moved overhead, showing off its belly. It was a cloud, but not in the normal sense. Leven could now see that the darkness was caused by a dense swarm of locusts. All at once thousands descended, flying wildly, filling the air with the buzz of their wings.

Leven leaped for the knob on the gatehouse door, but it was locked. Locusts in plaguelike proportions whipped and tore across the sky in a boiling mass.

"What are they?" Leven yelled above the din.

"Locusts!" Clover shouted. "They communicate news from Morfit."

The locusts began to settle, roosting on any rail or structure they could find. As soon as they landed, they dried up into small husks. Leven looked beyond the porch, and as far as he could see there was nothing but a blanket of light brown, dead locusts covering the ground. He took a step, and the husks beneath his feet disintegrated into a fine dust that drifted in the air, carrying in it the words of an unspoken message.

"There is little life left in Winter. She draws her last breath at the top of Morfit. When the morning arrives she will be no more. Neither the Waves of the Lime Sea nor the Want can prevent what will soon happen when the Ring returns."

For the first time in his life, Leven understood the adage, "No news is good news."

Winter was in trouble.

"What does it say?" Clover asked, refusing to touch any of the locusts.

"Winter's in trouble," Leven said. "We'll have to hope fate gets Geth here because we've got to get to Morfit, and fast. I've seen people fly here in Foo. How is that possible?"

"Only with the help of dreams, unless it's your gift," Clover said.

Leven shook his head, knowing those were not possibilities.

"There has to be another way besides simply running there," Leven said to himself, pacing the porch and rubbing his uneasy stomach. Desperate for a solution, Leven closed his eyes. When he opened them back up they were burning gold.

Leven looked around, light from his eyes sweeping the porch like a searchlight. He saw nothing but the images in his head. Stars streaked across his view. He saw strange, red-cloaked beings reading the locusts and hopping onto the backs of huge, lizard-looking creatures and racing across the ground. Leven shook his head and stared at Clover. His eyes were luminous.

"Wow," Clover said, "you must really see a clear view of fate."

"I saw some red-robed beings riding on giant lizards," Leven said. "They were heading our direction."

"The lizards are probably onicks," Clover said. "I don't—"

"Are onicks fast?" Leven interrupted.

"Not many things are faster," Clover said. "And they're loyal only to the rider on their back."

"Do you have any rope in your void?" Leven asked urgently.

Clover looked at Leven like he was crazy for even questioning.

"Get it out fast," Leven said. "And give it to me."

"All right!" Clover cheered, reaching into his void. "This should be fun."

Leven dashed off the porch and down the stairs, pulverizing thousands more of the dry locusts as he did so. He ran toward the edge of the locust-covered lawn. Clover was following behind him, yelling something about how real friends fill friends in.

"I'll tell you in a second," Leven shouted back, continuing to run. His stomach lurched and he stumbled a couple of steps before he could get his stride back.

The path they were on shifted, and Leven followed the new direction to the edge of a grove of trees. Beyond the trees was a broad, open valley. Leven could see for miles. The ground was covered in every direction with dried locusts, and in the far distance Leven could see the string of riders coming his way. Leven's chest now burned, and he stepped back, remaining hidden in the trees. His stomach bubbled.

"Is that what you saw?" Clover asked, handing Leven a coil of white rope.

Leven let the rope uncoil. On each end was a pink, plastic handle with pink tassels.

Leven rolled his eyes. "Is this the only rope you have?" He was having a difficult time breathing. "It's a jump rope, and it's pink."

Clover's face was its own special shade of red. "Um . . . it belonged to my sister," he tried. "And it's all I have. Are you okay?"

"I'm fine," said Leven, his face turning pale. He tightened his grasp on the end of the jump rope.

Leven peered out of the trees at the riders, who were still a long way off. Even so, the red-robed beings looked huge.

Another small decoy secret hopped out from behind a tree and flitted in front of Leven.

"Look out!" Clover yelled.

Leven saw it too late. The secret grabbed onto Leven's nose, looked him in the eyes, and spoke: "I took the last life jacket on the sinking boat."

The secret laughed and laughed and then floated away.

"It must have followed you across the gorge," Clover said. "We should get out of here before the big one finds you."

Leven held the jump rope in his hands and hoped what he had manipulated in his head a few minutes earlier would come to pass. He could see the red-cloaked beings more clearly now. There were eleven of them, each clinging to the back of a huge lizard. The lizards had flat, iguana-like heads and long, lean bodies, with thin, spiky tails. All the lizards' legs were a blur, and the scaly beasts were running single file, moving at an astonishing speed, on a path that led right past the grove where Leven was hiding.

"Who are they?" Leven asked, willing his stomach to settle.

"Like I said, they're onicks, and you don't—"

"Not the lizards. The riders. Who are they?" Leven pressed.

"They are members of one of Sabine's Rings of Plague," Clover answered. "They must have been searching for you and Geth. The locusts have probably asked for them to return."

"So they're bad?" Leven asked.

"The worst," Clover replied, turning invisible. "Listen, Leven, maybe we should give up on getting to Morfit."

"What?" Leven asked, shocked, putting his hand to his mouth to hold back a burp.

"The Ring is dangerous," Clover said. "We should get to Cork. We'll be safe there. That is the job of a sycophant, keeping his burn mentally stable and safe."

Leven didn't reply. He knew they were not too far from Cork. He also knew that Cork was paradise, untouched by the wickedness of Sabine's plan. Cork was supposedly the most peaceful place in Foo.

The onicks and their riders were getting closer.

Leven thought about eating real food in Cork and getting some real sleep. He thought about resting and feeling better away from fear and the secret that was stalking him. He thought of Geth and hoped that somehow fate would help him and Winter.

"What do you think?" Clover asked. "Let the riders go, and we'll get to Cork. It's too dangerous out here. Winter's tough, and Geth will be fine."

Leven looked at Clover with disappointed eyes. "No way," he said. "Cork would be nothing without Winter and Geth."

Clover smiled. "I was hoping you'd say that. I was just trying to be a real sycophant."

"I could never—" Leven's stomach cramped up. He bent over and reached for his throat, his face was as white as bleached cotton.

"Are you sure you're okay?" Clover asked.

"I . . ." Leven gagged. "My stomach . . . and my throat . . ."

Leven leaned over, holding his stomach with one hand and his throat with the other.

The onicks were getting closer.

"Seriously," Clover said, "are you all right?"

Leven answered by opening his mouth and projecting a stream of white foam. The foam ran from his mouth and puddled on the ground. Leven instantly felt better. He put his hands on his knees and breathed in deeply. His throat had quit burning, and his stomach no longer ached. He wiped his mouth and then his forehead.

"Did you eat too much filler crisp?" Clover asked.

"I guess so, but I only had—" Leven stopped talking because something in the white foam was wiggling.

"What's that?" Clover asked.

Leven looked at the foam on the ground. Clover leaned in close and smiled. He turned back to Leven.

"I told you Geth would find us," Clover said proudly, pulling Geth from the goo.

Geth was shuddering, spitting, and wiping foam off himself.

"How?" Leven asked, completely amazed. He took Geth from Clover. "You were in my stomach?"

"You swallowed me when that beast bit open the gaze," Geth sputtered. "I tried to climb out, but I couldn't do it. After you ate that filler crisp, I ran around for hours, working the contents of your stomach into a lather."

"I'm so sorry," Leven said.

"Fate's not always attractive," Geth admitted.

"Apparently, sometimes it's disgusting," Clover added.

The approaching onicks could now be heard, breathing hard, their scaly feet making a loud scratching sound on the stones of the path.

Geth looked out between the trees and saw the red-robed riders.

"The Ring of Plague," he whispered in awe. "The Ring is here, now?"

"Um, the turrets are back that way," Clover pointed out.

"But the Ring," Geth said excitedly, hope flowing back into him.

"We were going to hop on one of those lizards and try to save Winter," Leven explained. "But shouldn't we get you to the turrets first?"

Geth wiped the last bit of froth off of himself. He was still hardening and could feel himself growing closer to being nothing but a dead sliver of wood. But Geth understood fate. And it simply felt too fateful to have been thrown up just as the Ring of Plague was arriving. Geth had defeated the other Ring, and to die helping Leven knock off the last remaining one was just too significant to ignore. Plus, Geth cared for Winter too much to think only of himself.

"Leven," Geth said boldly, "this is your decision. You are an offing, and it's time you began trusting fate. It will be much harder to defeat the last Ring if we let them get to Morfit."

"But you're dying," Leven reasoned.

"What is death if not everyone's fate?" Geth said calmly. "I'm a lithen. I don't think now is the time to start making decisions based solely on my own understanding. And you, you are an offing who has made it through the Swollen Forest, escaped a gaze, survived a roven's rip, and traveled unharmed over Fissure Gorge."

The sound of the thundering onicks was growing louder.

"You are the grandson of Hector Thumps and essential to Foo and the dreams of all mankind," Geth continued. "And now fate has put you right here, right now, with the Ring approaching. Can you not feel the fate?"

Clover looked at Leven with anticipation, recognizing the importance of Geth's words.

"You are Leven Thumps," Geth said solemnly.

The onicks were almost there.

Leven closed his eyes. He could feel fate settling over him. He knew it would take some time to get Geth to the turrets despite how close they now were. He knew that Winter was in need and that the Ring of Plague had to be stopped. But he believed that fate had set him right where he was and that it was up to him to seal that fate and work on the Ring. He hoped time would stretch to accommodate everything.

"I've got a lizard to catch," Leven said, swinging the end of the jump rope and feeling much better with an empty stomach.

"Fantastic," Geth cheered, even as his body hardened further.

Leven smiled, happy just to have Geth back with them. Not that he had truly been gone, but it was nicer to have him out of his stomach and visibly along for the ride.

The onicks had arrived. They began racing by, just outside the trees Leven and Geth and Clover were hiding in. The onicks were amazing creatures. Their eyes were thin, blue slits, and their skin was green, streaked with red and pink that seemed to bleed backward in the wind as they hurtled along.

On the back of each thundering lizard rode a single being. All of the riders were wearing long, red robes with black rings around the cuffs.

" . . . eight, nine, ten," Leven counted to himself.

Leven leaped from behind the tree and whipped his rope toward the last rider and its onick.

Leven was one off.

The rope curled around the tenth rider, the pink handle whacking him in the face. Leven yanked as hard as he could, and the rider flew backward off his onick and into the eleventh and last rider behind him. Both riders came hurtling toward Leven. He dodged out of their way and ran toward the two riderless onicks, which had stopped, confused over losing their passengers. Leven jumped on one and whistled as loudly as he could.

It didn't move.

Clover materialized and slapped the confused lizard on the behind.

The onick took off racing down the path just as the two riders who had been knocked off staggered to their feet and began to compose themselves. Geth worked his way into the pocket on the front of Leven's T-shirt.

"This is much better," Geth shouted, feeling some life returning to him. It seemed as if Foo was suddenly filling up with hope.

Leven sped after those in the lead, who had not seen what had happened in the rear. He fit so perfectly on the lizard's back, it was almost as if it had been made for him. The huge beast had large shoulder blades that rose up, and Leven tucked his head

behind them to lessen any wind resistance. With its aerodynam-
ically shaped head, the onick whizzed along at a breathtaking
speed, drawing ever closer to the red-robed riders in front.

Leven was trying to decide what to do next when Clover
screamed, "Watch out behind you!"

Leven looked back and spotted the two riders he had pulled
off. They were riding double on the other onick and coming up
quickly behind him. They pulled next to Leven, and the one on
the back reached for him, his red robe flapping like flames. Leven
lashed out with his foot, but the rider grabbed it and wouldn't let
go. Leven kicked until he lost a shoe, and the assailant flew off
the onick and onto the ground.

"You have a hard time keeping your shoes on!" Clover yelled.

Leven would have said something in reply, but he was too
astonished. The fallen rider had dived into the soil and was
beginning to burrow after him. The mound of dirt was speeding
toward him. It was not a comfortable sight.

Leven dug his knees into his ride and pleaded with it to
speed up. The rider racing next to him tried to reach out and
finish the job that his now burrowing passenger had been unable
to accomplish. Leven leaned to his right, and the onick veered in
that direction, racing off the path and into a thick field of cork
and ivy.

Leven's mounted pursuer was still right on his tail, both
onicks thundering across the ground. The rider pulled close to
Leven and, grabbing Leven's shoulder, dragged himself onto
Leven's ride. As they wrestled for control of the racing lizard, the

rider's hood blew back and Leven could see the face of his
assailant. He looked quite normal, like a math teacher or a doc-
tor. His eyes, however, looked like they belonged to someone
who made a habit of harming others.

"You have no idea what you are tampering with!" the rider
yelled. "The Ring of Plague cannot be defeated!"

Leven's onick had reached a thick growth of trees and was
now wildly dodging through them. Leven's heart raced with fear.
He was having to fight to keep himself from pulling away and
riding off somewhere safe. Leven closed his eyes and let fate settle over him again. He opened his eyes back up and threw his
weight against the hooded foe, causing him to lose his balance
and teeter to one side of the speeding onick. The cloaked
assailant tried to right himself but suddenly disappeared when he
was clipped by a passing tree trunk and violently snatched away.

"Nice move!" Clover cheered.

Leven's right hand burned. It began to glow red and swell.

"My hand," Leven yelled. "It's glowing."

"Interesting," Geth said.

"Yeah, real interesting. But keep riding," Clover urged. "We
have to keep moving."

Leven steered with his knees, turning his onick in a wide
circle back through the trees and toward the path they had
detoured from. When they broke from the trees, the ground in
front of them suddenly erupted as the burrowing rider Leven
had kicked off earlier popped up right in front of the plunging
onick. Getting into the spirit of things, Leven's mount didn't

miss a beat. It lowered its head and ran directly into the hapless being. The impact sent the astonished rider spinning into the air and out of the way.

Then Leven's *left* hand began to burn, and a redness began to creep up his arms. Leven could feel the burning, but his mind was calm, as if it had been expecting this to happen.

"What's happening?" Leven hollered.

"You're changing," Geth shouted back. "Offings grow by experience, not time!"

Leven looked away from his hands and spotted the riders up ahead. They were kicking dirt up as they sped over the top of a tall hill and down toward the valley before the gorge. Leven didn't have time to trail behind them. Winter was in trouble.

"Come on," Leven yelled at his ride. "We can't let them beat you."

He found that onicks have a rather competitive spirit. His onick suddenly accelerated. He had picked one fast lizard.

Leven counted the riders in front of him.

There were nine.

Leven raced up alongside the last one in line and steered his ride into the side of the thundering beast. The unexpected bump unseated the rider, who went flying. The rider came down hard, bounced twice, then landed on his feet, sprinting after Leven.

"Looks like we've got a runner!" Clover screamed.

Leven looked back.

"He's huge," Leven said. "He's twice my size."

"Well, then you'll have to hit him twice as hard," Geth

observed. "Think of Winter and remember who you are!"

Leven's arms burned red.

The runner could barely match the speed of Leven's onick, but as he got close he reached out and grabbed a handful of Leven's shirt, trying to pull Leven off or pull himself up onto the racing onick. Before he could do either, Leven flexed, elbowing the runner in the jaw. The runner's teeth popped out like popcorn. He lost his grip and dropped to the ground, wounded and out of the chase.

Leven wiped his forehead as his chest and torso began to burn and swell like his arms. The swelling wasn't painful, and it seemed to give him strength. He thumped his heels against the sides of his ride.

"Come on!" he commanded.

His onick responded. Under Leven's urging, it raced in behind the next victim, and with a swing of its head it was able to send the rider tumbling off into the dirt.

Leven's right foot burned as images of his life in Reality began to crowd his head. He could see Addy and Terry and all the misery they had put him through. He could feel those experiences making him stronger now.

"Get 'em!" Leven shouted to his onick.

The beast surged ahead and easily toppled the next rider with its head.

Leven's onick would have gotten a third rider if the cloaked being hadn't turned and spotted them. This rider was big and had a square face with one terrific eyebrow and twice that many moles. He looked at Leven with an expression of surprise. Then he opened his mouth and blew out a terrific blast of flame.

Leven could feel the fire licking at his own eyebrows and part of his torn shirt. The heat also entered Leven's nose and throat, but it only stoked the burning in his chest and caused his body to grow stronger.

The fire-breathing rider leaned back and blew flame at Leven's onick. The speeding lizard veered to avoid the blast, and Leven lost hold for a moment but gripped the onick with his heels. He regained his seat and urged his ride forward. As it pulled ahead of the fire-breathing rider, Leven's onick flicked its tail, catching the fire-breather by surprise and causing him to do a rather spectacular flip into the air before slamming into the ground far behind them.

"Wow!" Clover said, impressed.

"I didn't expect the fire," Leven admitted.

"Tell me about it," Clover said, a small tuft of hair above his eyes smoldering.

"Are you okay?" Leven asked as his onick thundered closer to those still ahead of them.

"Fine," Clover lied, his leathery forehead dripping with sweat. "It's you I'm worried about."

"Me?"

"You're changing," Clover said with awe. "Look at your hands and your shoulders. I've never seen it happen so fast or so strong. Something big must be coming."

Leven tried to look at himself the best he could. He could see his hands and his feet; more important, he could feel the change.

"Worry about that later," Geth directed. "We have five more riders to take care of."

Leven dug his heels into the lizard, and the onick's tongue shot out. Leven jabbed with his heels again, and once more the beast's orange tongue leapt from its mouth and then recoiled. The onick's tongue was at least four feet long and moved with lightning speed. It was bumpy and coated with thick, sticky-looking mucus.

The tongue gave Leven an idea. He moved in behind the next rider and dug his heels into his ride. His onick's sticky tongue shot out and wrapped around the left wrist of the rider in front. As the tongue retracted, it pulled the rider off. Leven watched the poor nit land on the side of the path and tumble down a steep incline.

Leven rubbed his lizard behind the ear. It turned and tried to bite him. Apparently his ride wasn't doing this for him. As Leven was rubbing the onick he noticed that his hand, while not burning red any longer, now looked larger than it had only moments before.

"Yeah, yeah, nice hands—now stop admiring yourself and get those other riders," Clover yelled out from on top of Leven's head.

Leven's cheeks burned red for a different reason as he sped up to the next rider and watched his onick use his tongue to pull the rider off. The rider was momentarily suspended in the grip of the tongue, and he glared at Leven. He had a blue face with red lines running horizontally across it, like a bloody barcode. Leven blinked, and the rider was gone.

Leven looked around nervously. His head felt foggy, as if he were in a dream.

"Where did he go?" Leven yelled.

"He's still there," Geth hollered.

Leven looked and was surprised to see a miniature version of the same rider there on the tip of his onick's tongue. He looked like a small action figure. Before the onick could retract its tongue, the small rider ran along the bumpy surface and jumped onto the onick's head, where he stood glaring at Leven defiantly.

"Let me handle this one," Clover said, jumping onto the head of the onick and grabbing the miniature rider in his hands.

The rider returned to his normal size, and Clover found himself holding onto the rider's ankle. The rider kicked his leg, sending Clover into the air behind Leven just as the onick tossed its head, sending the rider careening to the corklike soil.

"Clover!" Leven yelled as his onick raced on.

"Right here," Clover responded, scrambling up the onick's tail as they continued to fly across the ground.

Leven's heart was racing as his entire body seemed to enlarge. He sped up alongside the next victim. The rider looked at Leven in shock; he had been blissfully unaware of anything going on behind him. He waved his hand, and Leven's body began to lift off the onick. Leven grasped the shoulder blades of his onick in a desperate attempt to stay on.

"What's happening?" Leven panicked.

"He's levitating you," Geth answered.

Leven's still-burning feet were pointing straight up in the air, making him look as if he were doing a handstand on the shoulder of the onick. The rider caused Leven to sway from side to side, trying to force him to release his grip on the onick. Leven's fingers were burning again as he dug into the skin of the beast. The onick didn't really appreciate that. It twisted and bucked, whipping Leven's legs into the rider who was levitating him.

Before the rider could react, Leven's onick followed up the kick by flicking out its tail, catching the rider just under his chin.

The levitator flew farther than any of the other victims Leven had knocked off previously, landing with a dull thud in a field thick with temperamental holes.

There were only two riders left in front of them, and they were rapidly nearing Fissure Gorge, still at breakneck speed.

Leven could feel his legs growing longer, not by inches and feet but by centimeters. The white strip in his hair glowed like a lit bulb. Once again he could see scenes and bits from his life in Reality. He could see Terry and Addy screaming at him and telling him that he would never be what he wanted to be because that was impossible. Resentment burned inside of Leven, like a gasoline-marinated lump of coal that had just touched a lighted match.

Leven also saw his neighbors who had ignored him and his peers who had made fun of him, and he felt nothing but pity for them. He wished they could see how their behavior had contributed to making him who he was. Leven's entire body burned as if on fire.

Leven let the feeling wash over him as he raced closer to the gorge. He began trying to think up compliments he could yell at the bridge.

Leven's onick moved up and bit the tail of the onick in front of him. It didn't do any damage, but it did cause the rider to turn and spot Leven. Instead of turning to fight, however, the riders ahead picked up speed, racing even faster toward the gorge. Leven was concerned: They seemed off course for meeting up with the bridge. In fact, they were heading straight for the wall that bordered the edge of the gorge.

Leven tried to turn the head of his onick, but the lizard wouldn't have it, going after the two in front of it with its tongue.

"Whoa!" Leven yelled. "Turn!"

The giant lizard wasn't listening, and the wall bordering the edge of the gorge was rapidly drawing near. The two onicks in front of Leven ran faster, showing no signs of slowing. Leven tried his best to concentrate to manipulate the outcome, but all he could get his eyes to do was burn gold while his soul rose up into his throat.

The riders in front of him reached the wall and, without slowing, their onicks leapt over it and out of sight.

"Stop!" Leven screamed at his own ride. He thought about jumping off, but it was too late.

His lizard reached the wall and sprang over it and out into the void above the gorge. Leven allowed himself to scream as he held tightly to his doomed ride. With his eyes closed, he heard the wind whistling against something. He opened his eyes to see wide, dark, leather wings extending out of each side of the onick. The beast had suddenly slowed and was drifting down, still following the two in front of it, which were also moving in what felt like slow motion.

Clover materialized. "Don't let go!" he screamed, his voice strangely loud in the sudden quiet. He was holding tightly onto Leven's arm and staring down into the depths of the gorge.

"I wasn't planning to!" Leven said, also speaking needlessly loudly in the now-quiet air.

The onick he was on was swimming slowly through the air toward the two in front of it, its giant wings acting as fins. The two onicks split, one drifting up and one gliding down. Leven's lizard aimed for the high one. It floated up and circled slowly, using its sticky tongue to send the other onick into a slow roll. It unseated the rider, who flailed about with his arms as he floated down.

Leven watched as the rider slowly descended through the air, down into the gorge. Halfway down, he hit hard air and began to drift in a different direction, becoming trapped in the maze of air. Leven held on even tighter to his ride, not wanting to experience the same fate.

Out of nowhere, lightning ripped through the air, illuminating the gorge like a violent bug zapper. The strike missed Leven by a few feet, but his onick screeched and used its wings to swim higher. The rider Leven had just unseated apparently had the gift of lightning, and though trapped in the maze of air, he began firing bolts as he drifted up, then down, then sideways.

The ribbon of lava at the bottom of Fissure Gorge belched, and a warm wind wafted up, lifting Leven's onick and its passengers even higher and scattering the new lightning that was now shimmering continuously. The uneven air in the gorge caused the jagged bolts to sizzle in all directions.

From below, the only remaining rider ascended toward Leven, urging his onick up. The two lizards screamed at each other as Leven tried to maneuver his out of the way.

He couldn't completely avoid the beast, and as it passed Leven's ride, there was a terrible ripping noise followed by a hideous scream—his onick had lost its tail. It turned in the air to face its assailant, crying like a wounded bird.

The last rider made a slow, wide turn and came back directly at Leven. As the two onicks collided, they thrust out their tongues and grabbed hold of one another, slowly twisting in the air, like two alligators wrestling.

Neither onick would let go of the other's tongue, and the struggle made it almost impossible for their wings to get the air they needed underneath them. They were all drifting down, surrounded by shimmering lightning.

Wide-eyed, and clinging desperately to the back of his enraged onick, Leven watched as Clover swam through the air and onto the head of the last rider. Clover pushed back the hood of the rider's cloak, grabbed a huge handful of his hair, and pulled on it as though he were a farmer trying to harvest the world's most stubborn beet. The rider's eyes watered as he frantically reached up, causing his onick to twist and lose more air.

The rider grabbed Clover by the throat and squeezed as hard as he could. Clover's eyes bulged as he tore at the rider's hands. Leven didn't think about how useless it was for the rider to try to kill Clover; he just reacted.

The rider was large, with a huge frame and thick, black hair. If it had been weeks before and Leven had been in Reality, he wouldn't even have dreamed of confronting someone like that. But it was not weeks before, and Leven was mounted on a winged lizard, floating miles above the ground, with burning fists, watching someone hurting Clover.

Leven drew back his right hand and swung. The air parted to allow his fist to travel the distance to the rider's jaw. A terrific crack sounded, and the rider twisted sideways and floated off his lizard. The poor beast released its tongue and descended belly up toward the bottom of the gorge, desperately struggling to get some air beneath its flailing wings.

"Not bad," Geth remarked.

Released from the rider's grip, Clover caught an updraft and drifted up. Leven pulled up on the head of his onick and urged him toward Clover. Leven's onick swam through the air beautifully, and Leven blinked, suddenly realizing that he could see the soft outline of the different layers of air. He navigated in and through them as he made his way steadily toward Clover. Lightning continued to lick at everything—at the walls of the gorge, the clouds, and at the air around Leven.

Leven dodged a thick bolt. He swooped gracefully beneath Clover and reached out his hand, surprised to see Clover smiling widely, his cheeks glowing. As the onick continued to rise, Clover took Leven's hand and swung onto the onick right behind him.

The ribbon of lava at the bottom of the gorge belched once more.

Leven and Clover were lifted up as a thick scratch of lightning flashed next to them.

"You're not done yet," Geth warned.

"What?"

"That last one may be onick-less, but he's flying after us."

Leven dug his knees into his lizard as the last member of the Ring flew through the void toward them. He grasped Leven and turned him, wrapping his arms around Leven's burning chest. The being was incredibly strong, and he was squeezing the air from Leven's lungs, forcing his life out.

"You fool," he hissed into Leven's ear. "You have damaged the Ring."

Leven couldn't respond due to his lack of breath and his impending doom.

The last rider gasped in sudden realization. He wrenched Leven's head around and stared fiercely into his eyes.

"You are Leven," he seethed. "I've found Leven."

Leven would have asked *his* name—but again, the dying thing.

"You can die," the hooded assailant hissed joyfully. He tightened his hold, bleeding every last drop of breath from Leven's lungs.

Leven willed his gift to kick in, but there was nothing, and his vision began to go black as lightning continued to flash everywhere.

"Not so fast," Geth ordered.

Geth was out of Leven's shirt pocket and standing on the rider's arm that was wrapped around Leven's neck.

"What?" the rider cursed. "What . . . who are you?"

"I can't believe you've forgotten me, Sam," Geth said boldly.

"Geth?" Sam said in disbelief. "Geth?"

Sam released his grip on Leven just a bit, and Leven gasped for air, realizing that he could now see the maze of air in the gorge almost perfectly. His offing eyes were completely adjusting to Foo. In fact, Leven's amazing eyes could read the air so well that he could see a solution to the brute holding him. Leven lightly nudged the onick he was on with his right heel. The beast drifted over and down as Sam turned his attention to the bold little toothpick.

"The great Geth," Sam laughed. "We've been searching everywhere for you, and now I see you are too insignificant to be a concern."

"The least bit of good can put a hole in a mountain of evil," Geth said wisely.

Sam laughed, having no idea how literally Geth was speaking. Geth leaped up and came down as hard as he could with his legs pointed. Geth pierced Sam's forearm, causing Sam to yell and momentarily release his hold on Leven. Geth pulled himself from out of Sam's arm and grabbed hold of the white in Leven's hair.

Leven knew it was now or never. He kicked his onick in the

ribs and it bucked, propelling Sam straight up into a strong current of air. Leven then navigated the onick through the clear
patches, swimming through air and crashing lightning toward
the top of the gorge.

"He can still fly," Clover pointed out as they were rising.

"If he can work his way out of the air," Leven replied.

Leven had propelled Sam into a thick, complicated maze of
air. Clover looked back to see Sam flailing about in slow motion,
desperately trying to find his way out of a maze he couldn't see.

"Brilliant," Geth said. "He could be stuck in that air for years."

"I couldn't have done it without you," Leven said.

Clover cleared his throat.

"And you, of course," Leven added.

"Could you see the air?" Geth asked in disbelief.

Leven nodded.

"Amazing."

A gigantic bolt of lightning flashed from below, just missing
Leven's feet.

"We should get out of here," Clover said needlessly.

Leven dug his heels into the onick, guiding the beast upward
through the maze of air.

Fissure Gorge belched again, helping to push Leven and
Clover into the open sky above the gorge.

The cool air felt wonderful on Leven's face.

"Back!" Leven commanded the onick.

The onick instantly agreed, flying them safely to the other
side of the gorge and one step closer to Winter.

"You were smart to follow fate," Geth said.

Leven only smiled.

Once above land, the tireless onick glided to the ground, retracted its wings, and began running again at its familiar astonishing speed. Leven couldn't resist patting the beast on its head. Once again it snapped at him.

"Some people never learn," Clover shouted, so as to be heard above the rush of air. "The onicks are loyal to the passengers on their backs, but they don't like to be reminded that they've helped someone out."

"What an amazing creature," Leven yelled back.

With that, Leven tucked his head behind the onick's shoulder blades as they raced toward Morfit.

The afternoon was deepening. Purple sky pushed against the yellow horizon, giving the world of Foo a thick green cast. A milky stream of whisps passed in front of the dipping sun and caused the entire scene to shimmer. Leven thought of Janet and hoped she was all right.

"How much farther?" Leven asked Geth, raising his voice above the swish of the passing air.

"We've got a bit of a ride still," Geth answered. "But we should be able to see the tip of Morfit soon."

"I hope Winter's all right," Leven yelled.

"You know, this all could be a trap," Clover pointed out.

"I'm sure it is," Leven said quickly. "But we'll let fate take care of that."

Geth smiled.

"Besides," Leven added, "we have—"

Leven was unable to finish what he was saying, due to a heavy jolt of energy ripping through the air and striking him squarely in the chest. The impact sizzled, sending pain to every inch of his body and causing the key hanging beneath his shirt to burn his skin. The shock went through Leven and into the onick. The beast's legs were knocked out from under it, and it began to roll, throwing Leven off and even farther down the road.

Dirt and pebbles rained down as they both skidded to a stop. Dazed, Leven coughed and spat as he pushed himself into a sitting position. The poor onick got to its feet, shaken and limping.

Clover tried to comfort Leven as he sat on the ground.

"What happened?" Clover asked.

"I don't . . ."

Again Leven was cut off, an invisible bolt of energy tearing through the air and slamming into his back. Leven was thrown forward ten feet and landed on his face on the ground.

"What's going on?" Geth yelled.

Before Leven could answer, he was struck again, this time directly in the heart. Leven clutched his chest, moaning and writhing in pain on his back on the ground. Clover came to him.

"I don't know what you—" the little sycophant began.

Leven opened his eyes, shutting Clover up. Never had Leven's eyes burned so gold. It looked as if fire were leaping from them.

Clover reared back.

"Wow," Geth whispered.

Although she was not there, all of a sudden Leven could see

Winter. Her face was pressed flat against a dirt floor. There was darkness all around, and she was screaming.

Leven got to his feet and looked in the direction of Morfit. With clenched fists and his eyes ablaze, he began to viciously manipulate fate.

Clover's knees were shaking from the intensity of Leven's actions. The sky pulsated, beating out the light for the day, while Leven's gaze stretched farther into the dusk. Leven raised his hands and closed his eyes.

"Winter," he whispered fiercely, seeing her in his mind. He could also see a tall, hooded, two-sided being standing over her.

Leven held out his arms and directed his energy toward Morfit.

CHAPTER THIRTY-TWO

STOLEN

Jamoon pushed Winter to the ground with his right arm, relishing the delight of being seemingly unbeatable—as long as Winter was without her gift.

"Give up," he hissed.

Winter reached out at Jamoon and scratched his arm until she drew blood. He screamed angrily and let her go. While Jamoon was looking at the scratch marks, the decaying nihils circled around him, waiting for their next order.

With Jamoon distracted, Winter glanced around the room. She spotted the kilve she had once carried. It was leaning up against the wall, and she dashed across the room and grabbed it. In one swift motion she turned and struck Jamoon on the right shoulder with the heavy staff. Jamoon dropped to one knee, and his dark nihils began to screech.

Winter wheeled toward the door. The roven in the corner

stretched its wings, blocking the exit, and the nihils swarmed around her, pecking at her skin with their beaks. The pain drove Winter to her knees.

Jamoon was back up. He parted the nihils and grabbed Winter by one of her pigtails. He pulled and his grip stretched every feature on Winter's face and made it hard for her to breathe.

Jamoon mocked her as she struggled. "Not much of a fighter without your gift," he sneered. "How wonderful it is that now you can die."

"What about the plan?" Winter gasped, hoping to catch Jamoon off guard by being honest.

"What plan?" Jamoon asked, glaring into her green eyes.

"The one you whispered about to me in the ice caves."

"You mean *your* plan?" he asked coolly.

"My plan?" Winter choked.

"You really can't remember, can you?" Jamoon laughed. "Look around you. Doesn't this room mean anything to you?"

Winter looked around, confused. "No."

Jamoon's grip tightened. "You were so different then. Young, but not as young, and so willing to help make Foo a better place. Fool."

"I don't understand," Winter gasped.

"Don't you remember what you did up here? The experiments, the use of metal? You walked right into it. So willing to break the rules in an effort to help the common cog—such an idealist. Those poor souls who have no gift," Jamoon taunted. "And you just wanted to find a way to give them one. That's when you dreamed up this room."

Winter winced as Jamoon pulled even harder on her hair. The nihils chirped sadistically as the candles on the wall increased their flame, brightly lighting the room. Winter looked closer at her surroundings. The walls were white and tiled. Along two of the walls were large ceramic hooks. Beneath the hooks were tables covered in sheets made from white feathers. Behind Jamoon, there was a mechanical-looking contraption.

The machine looked familiar.

"It's such a sad thing when a nit dies," Jamoon went on. "Such a sad, sad thing—a life and a gift gone for good. Fewer dreams can be enhanced in a powerful way. Yet, even when dying nits wish to transfer their gifts, they can't. Or should I say, they *couldn't.*"

"So you're extracting gifts?" Winter gasped.

"Unsuccessfully, until we found you," Jamoon laughed.

Winter began to cry as small bits and pieces of what had actually happened came back to her.

"You had just the right brain to solve such a complex and taboo problem," Jamoon exulted. "You wanted so desperately to help, and Sabine was happy to let you. You figured out how to do everything we needed. With the ability to possess multiple gifts, we could conquer Reality easily. Of course, we needed the gateway to get there, and its destruction was a depressing blow. But, thanks to your *fate* and what remains of Sabine, I believe we have hands working in Reality to rebuild the gateway. There is only one person who can ruin things now."

"The Want?" Winter guessed sadly, fear almost suffocating her.

"That fool," Jamoon hissed angrily. "What good is he to us, now that we can take and, soon, bestow gifts?"

"Then—" Winter stopped herself, suddenly realizing that the one they needed to stop was Leven.

"Who can rebuild the gateway?" Winter asked, sure that Jamoon was bluffing.

"With enough pain and persuasion we are confident Leven and you will show us everything," Jamoon spat. "Of course, you'll be much easier to work with once we've removed that bothersome gift of yours."

Jamoon moved closer to the odd metal machine, dragging Winter with him by her hair.

Winter's heart was thumping like a flat tire on a spinning rim. She looked down and was surprised to see it was still in her chest.

"Leven," she whispered.

"Leven," Jamoon scoffed. "He can't help you now."

Jamoon forced Winter to sit and strapped her right wrist to the machine. Fear was everywhere now, swirling around the room like a sticky twister and mixing with the flapping nihils. Ignoring her whimpering cries, Jamoon strapped down Winter's left wrist. While Winter thrashed and screamed, Jamoon secured her left leg.

But as he reached for her other leg, a thick bolt of blue shot down through the skylight and struck Jamoon in the right shoulder. Jamoon flew across the room and slammed into the wall. He hit it so hard, the wall cracked and broken tiles rained to the floor. Dazed, Jamoon shook his head and weakly tried to stand. With his nihils circling him, ready to inflict further pain on Winter, he looked wildly around the room.

"What was that?" Jamoon demanded.

Winter was silent.

"You'll pay for that," he said, figuring the attack to be a work of Winter. His eyes narrowed in anger. "What was that trick you just pulled?" he demanded.

Winter had no idea what had struck Jamoon, but as she looked fearfully at his angry face, another bolt of blue streaked in from the skylight—this one striking him squarely on the chin. Jamoon was lifted four feet into the air and then dropped to the ground in a heap. Dazed, he looked up from where he had fallen and growled.

The nihils swooped down and began to tear into Winter. As she screamed and thrashed, Jamoon staggered to his feet and lurched over to the machine.

"Let's end your tricks!" Jamoon raged, strapping down her remaining foot.

The birds lifted off of Winter as Jamoon reached over and hit the switch on the side of the machine.

Light flashed and Winter was out.

ii

After having fought with Jamoon from a distance, Leven turned to glance at Clover and Geth. Clover looked like a new bride who has just discovered she has married a monster. His blue eyes were wide with fear, and his leathery little mouth was hanging open.

"What?" Leven asked defensively.

"You were either fighting something," Clover said, "or you were doing some really awkward dance."

"I saw a large cloaked being," Leven explained. "Both halves of him didn't match."

"It was probably Jamoon," Geth deduced. "He's a rant. Rants can't just manipulate a dream and move on. Half of each rant remains in a dreamlike state."

"Jamoon," Leven whispered, looking down at his hands.

Clover shook his head in disbelief. "He had Winter?" he asked.

"Is she okay?" Geth asked.

"No," Leven said. "I couldn't completely control my thoughts. But I think I knocked Jamoon down a couple of times."

Clover's jaw dropped again. "You actually manipulated fate from a distance?"

"I don't know," Leven admitted. "It was more like my actions here affected what was happening there. What does that mean?"

"It means that I have one heck of a burn," Clover said proudly. "As an offing you shouldn't be able to do that. Isn't that right, Geth?"

Geth didn't answer.

"So what *am* I?" Leven asked, talking more to himself than to anyone else. He had felt so different ever since his fight against the Ring of Plague. He could see things more clearly, and it felt as though his heart had expanded to fill his entire body. His eyes were burning gold at the moment, but there was no vision behind them. When he shook his head, the gold remained.

It felt like the first day of summer, when school is finally out and days and days of freedom stretch out before you. It felt like he was somebody else—somebody stronger and unafraid. He couldn't remember ever having been scared or hurt, and he could see hope and possibility in things as insignificant and insecure as himself. He felt as if he were made of putty and someone had shoved their thumb under his ribcage and pushed him taller. Even the horizon looked to be at a different level. He looked at his feet to see if he was wearing platform shoes. He wasn't, but the high-water pants he was sporting were even higher on him.

"What's happened to me?" Leven asked, this time wanting an answer.

"We need to get you to the Want," Geth said, hopping onto Leven's shoulder. "You are definitely Hector's relative."

"First things first," Leven replied. "How are you doing, Geth? Can you hold on? If you're all right, I think we had better go help Winter."

"Don't worry about me," the battered little toothpick said. He could feel himself hardening even more, but he didn't want to admit it. "I think you're right. Winter is the one we need to concentrate on."

Leven tucked Geth behind his ear and jumped back onto the onick. He took his seat behind its shoulder blades and was surprised to find the fit different from before. The broad back felt somehow smaller.

After making sure Clover was also aboard, Leven dug his heels into the onick, and the quick beast took off, racing toward Morfit.

CHAPTER THIRTY-THREE

ECHOES OF THE BLAST

The world is full of people who like to bring people down. I know of at least two. You can probably think of more than that.

Then there are those people who are helpful and constructive and like to reach down and help others up. Those people are way better than the first kind and very much in the minority.

Tim Tuttle was that second kind of person. He had spent his entire life thinking well of others and helping where he could. He had a lovely family, and though his job was menial, he had the brain of a genius.

He also hadn't traveled much, and when he got off the train in Berchtesgaden, Germany, he was blown away by the spectacular scenery. "Who knew Mother Nature was so big on green?" he said in awe.

As the train pulled away, Tim began walking down toward

the Konigsee. It was early morning and there were very few tourists out. A couple of old men were working with brooms up and down the street, cleaning gutters and walkways, and a tiny car passed by, delivering firewood.

As Tim strolled toward the lake, he admired the clean shops and stores along the way. A woman with matted hair and short arms wheeled a case full of bread in front of him on her way to her shop.

"Excuse me," Tim shouted after her.

She turned.

"For sale?" Tim asked, pointing to the bread and holding out some money.

She looked bothered, but not bothered enough to pass up money. Tim bought two small loaves and thanked her in German.

She wasn't all that impressed.

Tim tore into the bread and was so involved in eating it as he arrived at the lake that he almost stepped off the dock and into the water.

He stopped himself just in time. He looked up, and his jaw dropped. His bread fell out of his mouth and onto the ground— instantly four ducks raced for it. The Konigsee was the most beautiful sight Tim had ever seen.

You may have read in books that one spot or another is the most beautiful place on earth. Well, those books are lying, *unless* they are talking about the Konigsee. Surrounded by tall, snow-capped mountains and forests of gorgeous pines, the valley where the Konigsee rests is breathtaking. The green water and the pristine setting would make even Zeus look into the price of real estate there.

"I'm not in Iowa anymore," Tim said honestly.

At the dock Tim purchased a ticket and climbed onto a boat going across the lake. There were only three other tourists on board, so Tim stretched his legs up onto the seats next to him. Halfway across the lake the boat stopped and shut off its engine. A stocky German man in leather shorts stood on the front of the boat and began to play a trumpet. The ring of majestic mountains surrounding the lake created a beautiful echo that accompanied the trumpeter.

Tim couldn't sit still. He stood and turned around, taking in the entire scene. A German boy with a thin mustache and white, freckled skin who helped run the boat noticed the look on Tim's face.

"Spectacular, isn't it?" he said in almost perfect English. There was obviously something about the outfit Tim was wearing that gave away the fact that he was an American.

"It feels like my eyes can't properly describe it to my brain," Tim smiled.

The German boy grinned.

"I'd never heard of this place before," Tim said.

"Most people are more aware that Hitler died nearby," the boy said, sticking his chin out. "Such a beautiful place to be marred by such evil. You are from the States?" he asked, changing the subject.

"Yes, Iowa."

The boy didn't know what Iowa was, but he nodded his head. "Here on business?"

"I think I'm here to see this," Tim said, motioning to the lake and its surroundings. "And, I'm looking for someone—a young boy and girl."

Again the boy smiled. "There are lots of boys and girls that come here."

"It would have been a couple of days ago," Tim clarified.

"I wasn't working," the boy apologized. "I wish I had been. I would not have missed the explosion."

"Explosion?" Tim asked anxiously.

"Booosh," he said with excitement. "It was after sunset, and an explosion went off under the water," he explained. "Some think it was an earthquake, but my mate was here, and said it was no earthquake."

"Was anyone hurt?"

"No," the boy waved. "A number of fish have died. But, I tell you, earthquakes don't usually kill fish."

"Did they investigate?" Tim asked, the hair on the back of his neck standing up again.

"I'm not sure I understand," the boy said.

"Did anyone search underwater, or try to find out what it was?"

"It's pretty hard to see anything under this water," the boy said, referring to the beautiful green color that hid everything below.

Tim looked over the side of the boat and down into the

water. The surface was a milky emerald green. There could have been anything hidden down there.

"The authorities thought it could have been a terrorist, or some trick," the boy went on. "But I know of no reason why someone would want to do that here. Maybe it was Hitler turning over in his grave," he tried to joke.

Tim laughed politely, since he was one of the nice kind of people previously mentioned. He looked down into the water again.

Tim needed to think. He also needed something else to eat.

The boat started back up and continued traveling to the distant side of the lake.

ii

The Munich Germany Airport was as busy as any place Dennis Wood had ever been. People pushed forward like determined mice with no maze and a straight shot to cheese, and the overhead speakers kept shouting instructions in German. The old Dennis would have been intimidated, but the new Dennis was not.

As Dennis walked through the airport, people moved out of his way. He stood tall, stone-faced, and dark. He wore Sabine like a robe over his shoulders, soaking in the blackness with each step he took.

He reached a small glass booth with a large, uniformed man sitting inside. The man's girth was almost more than the glass booth could accommodate, making it look as if the entire thing might burst at any moment. The uniformed man had a short forehead and a wide, moist nose with a sweaty little mustache beneath it.

"Your passport, please," he asked, his jowls jiggling.

Dennis handed him his driver's license. The man looked at it as if it were a joke. As he looked up, however, bits and pieces of Sabine floated like black lint off of Dennis and into the official's ears. Dennis could see the flecks actually moving around in the whites of the man's eyes.

"Business or pleasure, Mister Dennis?" the man asked, his voice sounding as if he were in a slight trance.

"Business," Dennis answered.

The guard looked Dennis up and down. He stared at his bald head. "Your hair color?" he asked, following his routine and not realizing he wasn't holding an actual passport.

"Blond . . . when I have any," Dennis answered.

"And your age?"

"Thirty-one," Dennis sniffed.

"And the business you are on?"

"I'm here to rebuild something," he said, frustrated. "Now can I go?"

"One moment," the guard waved uncomfortably, which was a struggle, seeing how he had so little extra room in his booth. "What is the company you are with?"

Dennis said the only thing he could think of: "Gateway."

"They make a fine computer," the guard sniffed, stamping

the front of Dennis's driver's license as if it were a passport. "Enjoy your stay, Mister Dennis. Next."

He handed Dennis the stamped card.

Dennis walked away fuming. He was tempted to correct the guard about his name, but he let it go—for now. Someday, however, the entire world would get it right and fear the presence and power of Dennis Wood.

iii

Wearing Sabine as a black, tattered robe with an ugly hood, Dennis stepped off the bus in Berchtesgaden. He pushed back the hood, and the October sun danced off his bald head.

"This is it?" Dennis asked, referring to their location.

"It is," his robe hissed.

"I want to see the spot."

Dennis walked with purpose toward the lake. Wearing Sabine had given him great confidence. It had also helped him understand what was happening. As a cloak, Sabine had seeped information into Dennis. The seepage had left dark, tattoolike marks all over Dennis's skin. Sabine had told him of Foo. He had told him of the gateway, and he had promised Dennis great power and endless dreams if he helped Sabine return.

Dennis had never dreamed before, and the mere thought drove him mad with ambition. He trusted Sabine. And he reveled in the blackness that had entered his life. He could see that there would be things to stop him or impede his progress, but none of those things overshadowed the fact that if he held on, Dennis would be able to escape his past and, for the first time in his life, dream powerful dreams.

"How'd he do it?" Dennis asked Sabine as he walked. "How did he build a gateway here? More importantly, how will we?"

"We will work at night," Sabine buzzed. "We must secure materials."

Dennis looked around as he got closer to the lake. He couldn't see anyplace nearby to get the kind of materials they would need. "We'll need a car to get the supplies," Dennis said. "It could take some time."

"We don't have time," Sabine seethed.

Dennis couldn't wait to dream, but he was also thirsty from traveling. He crossed the street and entered a dimly lit gasthaus where a few patrons were drinking and eating fish. The walls were lined with decorative china plates and beer steins. The floor-boards were wood and worn from years of thirsty people walking across them. Dennis walked past the tables and booths and took a seat on a stool at the long wooden bar. There was a lone man, wearing a blue baseball cap, sitting on the stool next to him. Dennis waved at the waiter and ordered a drink.

"We shouldn't delay," Sabine hissed silently and directly into Dennis's skin.

"I just need a drink," Dennis whispered aloud. "Don't worry. I'll work as fast as I can," he said irritably.

The man in the ball cap on the neighboring stool heard

Dennis talking and thought he was addressing him.

"Excuse me?" the ball-capped American said nicely. "Were you saying something?"

"No," Dennis snapped. He was about to follow that "No" with something along the lines of, "Mind your own business" or, "Why would I be talking to someone like you?" but Sabine burned into his neck, sending a signal to hold his tongue.

The bartender delivered Dennis's drink, and Dennis took a gigantic swallow and then belched. "Sorry," he said to his neighbor. "I was thirsty."

"No problem," the ball-capped patron said kindly. "Are you from America?"

"Yes," Dennis answered, getting signals from Sabine to play along.

"What state?"

"North Carolina, actually," Dennis answered.

Sabine fluttered and rolled. There was something about the American that made him burn. It was clear that this man had not been to Foo, but it was as if he had been in contact with someone who had. Weary of Dennis's poor communication skills, Sabine decided to take over the conversation.

"Where are *you* from?" Sabine hissed out of Dennis's mouth. Both the American and Dennis looked surprised. "I mean, where are you from?" Sabine said, in a lower and softer tone and with an almost comical voice.

"I'm from Iowa," the American said, looking at Dennis with confusion. "My name's Tim. Tim Tuttle."

Tim stuck out his hand, and Dennis shook it.

"Why are you here?" Sabine said, using Dennis's mouth again.

Tim smiled awkwardly. "I'm looking for a couple of kids," he said.

Tim was the kind of person who usually thought the best of others. Most anyone who sat next to Dennis would have thought him to be a creepy jerk at best. Tim, on the other hand, saw Dennis as just a dim-witted oddball, and felt compelled to talk to him.

"Kids?" Sabine hissed hungrily out of Dennis's mouth.

"Are you okay?" Tim asked, tilting his head to study Dennis's face.

"Fine, fine," Dennis lied. "I've just got a wicked cold," he recovered. Sabine burned through Dennis's skin, commanding him to let Sabine do the talking. "You're looking for kids, you say," Sabine prompted.

"A young girl and boy," Tim said seriously. "But this is the end of the trail at the moment."

"Are they in trouble?" Sabine asked.

"I think so," Tim answered. "But I'm not sure I even know that."

Sabine's pulse quickened. He loved to take advantage of fate when it was working in his favor, and an extra person like Tim would make the work of building a new gateway much easier. Fate was such a fool.

"Leven," Sabine said out of Dennis's lips.

Tim spat his drink out, getting the bartender wet.

"Excuse me?" he said, wiping his mouth. "What did you say?"

"You're looking for Leven and Winter," Sabine said matter-of-factly.

Tim's mouth dropped to the floor, and his eyes gave the decorative plates lining the wall some competition for saucer size. "You know them?" Tim asked.

"I believe we are working for the same thing," Sabine said through Dennis, trying to keep his voice light and as un-sinister-sounding as possible.

"How do you know them?" Tim asked, so excited that he didn't let his great brain take a moment to analyze the bad vibes coming from Dennis.

Dennis stood and motioned for Tim to follow him. "I've got a lot to tell you."

"I can't believe this," Tim said with excitement, following Dennis to a corner booth. "Are they okay?" he asked.

"I believe so," Sabine hissed out of Dennis.

"Thank goodness," Tim said, taking a seat, the smile on his face impossible to suppress. "I've been so worried."

"We've all been worried," Dennis hissed.

Tim was too excited to see the danger sitting right before him.

CHAPTER THIRTY-FOUR

DOOR NUMBER ONE

The onick slowed as the base of Morfit came into view. It was dark by now, but thousands of small, glowing lights twinkled from all over the mountain. Leven could see people and creatures trudging toward the base, carrying rocks of various sizes in their hands. Leven guided the onick behind a row of short, orange-colored trees and hopped off.

"Will it wait for us?" Leven asked Clover, referring to the onick.

"If no one else jumps on its back," Clover answered. "Onicks are loyal only to those who are on top."

"Maybe we should hide it or something," Leven suggested. "It could come in handy later."

Clover was already fishing around in his void. He pulled out a thin wooden jar with a small lever on the top. It looked a bit like an old-fashioned can of aerosol spray. Clover read the label and smiled. "Doesn't expire for another twenty-two years."

He sprayed a shot of air at the onick. The air created what looked like a hole in the poor creature.

"Wow!" Leven said. "What is that stuff?"

"An attempt by the citizens of Cusp to be more like the sycophants," Clover said haughtily. "It can make you invisible, but it's very sticky and uncomfortable. Plus, it takes hours to wash off. Not to mention the bugs that get stuck in it." Clover tisked. "Everyone wants to be us."

Clover began to spray the onick all over. The poor beast didn't mind because he didn't know what was happening. In a few moments nothing remained visible but a bit of rope tying him to the fantrum tree.

"Hurry," Leven said, as Clover was putting the finishing touches on his masterpiece. "We need to get in there."

"I'm almost done," Clover said, turning toward Leven. As he did so, he accidentally sprayed the lower half of Leven's left arm.

Leven just stared at his lack of limb. His arm looked as though it had been cut off just below the sleeve of his T-shirt.

"Oops," Clover said, just as the can sputtered out the last of its contents.

"Perfect," Leven complained.

"Sorry," Clover tried. "But don't worry. It'll wash off eventually."

Leven looked down. It was the oddest sensation not to see his arm and hand there. He brought his hand up to his face and touched his nose. As he pulled away he noticed a slight stickiness on his invisible fingertips.

"I'm sure this will help," Leven said sarcastically.

"Mister Sunshine," Clover beamed happily. "That's the attitude."

Leven was tempted to use his invisible hand in an unkind fashion. Instead, he said, "No 'Mister Sunshine.' Let's just find Winter so we can take care of Geth."

Leven stepped away from the fantrum tree and began moving toward Morfit. Clover followed close behind after leaving a vapor stick beneath the tree. He had cracked the vapor stick, and a horrible smell was now lofting through the air. The noxious fumes made Leven light-headed.

"That'll keep people away from our onick."

"I'm not sure I want to go back now," Leven said, pinching his nose with his visible hand. "That's awful."

Clover would have responded, but he was having a hard time breathing himself. Leaves on trees began to droop as small bushes and plants curled up or threw dirt on themselves to escape the stench. Leven and Clover could hear the poor, invisible onick gag, pass out, and fall against the ground. Due to the odor, however, neither ran back to help it. It wasn't until they were a good three hundred feet away that they could safely breathe again.

"I'm not going back there," Leven insisted. "I've never smelled anything that bad before."

"It was a strong stick," Clover agreed. "But the smell will fade."

"Wait a second," Leven said. "Where's Geth? I thought you had him."

"I did," Clover said ashamedly.

"Well, where is he?"

"He was riding on my back," Clover explained. "I was afraid he might blow away. Plus, he started lecturing me about some of the things I've been doing. I'm sorry, but I'm my own person, unless of course you want me not to be."

"Clover, where is Geth?"

"Don't worry, I just put him in my void."

Clover started fishing around in his void for Geth. He pulled out a sticky popsicle stick.

"Nope, that's not him," Clover said. "What if it was? That would be so weird."

Leven shook his head.

Clover put his hand back in the void and pulled out a post-card with the state of Oklahoma drawn on the front.

"Nope."

He pulled out a leaf shaped like a kitten, a plastic spoon whittled into a plastic knife, an apple core, a temporary tattoo of a butterfly, a dry spaghetti noodle, a live moth, and a dead fish before he finally found Geth. Clover pulled him out and held him in his palm.

"Here he is," Clover announced.

Leven had never seen Geth looking frightened before.

"Don't *ever* put me back in there," Geth whispered fiercely. "Ever. Please."

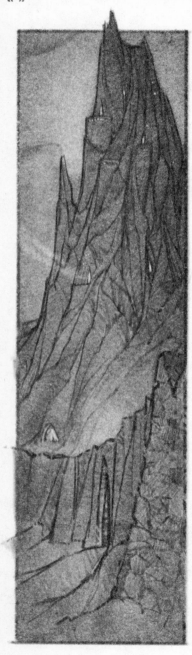

Leven picked up Geth and put him in his shirt pocket. "Sorry."

Geth clung to Leven.

Leven moved to the edge of the trees and near a wide dirt path. He could see a number of people shuffling toward Morfit. Most held stones in their hands and wore robes of some sort. Leven looked down at his pathetic outfit. The flood pants and his torn shirt he had bought in France were about as uncool as anything he had ever seen. Clover had fished another old sneaker out of his void, so Leven now was wearing two shoes, though they didn't match.

"Shouldn't I be wearing a robe or something?" Leven asked.

"We don't have one," Clover pointed out. "But you might want to pick up a rock and look sorry about it," the sycophant instructed.

"A rock?"

"Morfit is built by the stones of everyone's shortcomings," Geth said. "Bringing and leaving rocks frees you of your guilt. Toss a rock and it meshes with the mountain, growing up or out, depending on your throw. Morfit was once a sacred place that had something to do with the power Fissure Gorge produces. Now it's nothing but a huge, dark reminder of how far we've come."

Leven looked up at Morfit, towering high overhead. "So, any rock will do?"

"Any rock," Clover concurred.

Leven bent over and grabbed a large stone from the ground, holding it in his one visible and one invisible hand.

"Wow," Clover said dramatically. "You must have done something awful."

"You said 'any rock,'" Leven pointed out defensively.

"Still," Clover resounded.

Leven ignored Clover and tried to look distraught.

"Are you going to be okay?" Clover whispered.

"You said to act guilty," Leven reminded him.

"Well, you're pretty convincing," Clover said suspiciously. "Now we need to do something about your eyes."

"What about my eyes?" Leven said.

"They're still burning gold," Geth answered.

Scattered about the ground were small puddles of water. Leven leaned over one of the puddles and looked at his reflection. Leven's eyes *were* burning gold, despite the fact that there was no vision in his head. Leven, however, was more taken aback by how much older he looked. The white streak in his hair was brighter and more prominent, and his face looked less like a child's.

"I look—"

"Here," Clover interrupted, rummaging around in his void. "Take this."

Clover handed Leven a black gumball.

"I'm not eating anything you give me out of there, without some explanation."

"That takes some of the fun out of it," Clover said, "but if you must know, it's a Pigment-o."

"And?"

"It should help disguise your eyes."

"How?"

"It changes your eye color," Clover said briskly. "Now take it so we can go find Winter."

"It'll change my eye color?"

Clover crossed his heart.

Leven stuck the black ball into his mouth and chewed. Surprisingly, it tasted like real gum. Leven chewed quickly, stretching and pulling the gum in his mouth.

"So?" Leven asked, wondering when something would actually happen.

"Now blow a bubble," Clover instructed.

Leven blew a great big bubble. The gum pushed out beautifully, creating a perfect sphere. Leven kept blowing and the bubble grew even greater, dwarfing the size of his head.

Leven blew more, and the bubble popped.

Instinctively, Leven closed his eyes as it burst, and when he opened them back up he was surprised to find he wasn't covered in the remains of his popped bubble. Not only was there no trace of gum on his face, but it was no longer in his mouth. Leven looked around on the ground, but there was no sign of any chewed gum. It was as if it had disappeared completely.

"Where'd it go?" Leven asked Clover.

"It didn't go anywhere," Clover said. "As it popped outside it also popped in you."

"Popped in me? So my eyes are black?" Leven asked.

Clover looked closely at Leven. "Yes . . . yes they are."

Leven leaned over the puddle again.

He had thought he looked different *before*. There, staring back at him, was some person with light gray skin, black lips, completely black hair except for one gray streak, black eyes, and black freckles. Leven dropped his rock and lifted his one visible hand to his face, noticing that his fingernails were as black as night. He looked like a poster boy for Goth coal miners.

Geth tried to look sympathetic, but he was still too spooked about spending time in Clover's void. Leven felt his own face and grumbled.

"It wears off," Clover insisted.

"So when you crossed your heart and said it would change my eye color, you left out a few things," Leven accused.

"I was going to say more but, again, where's the fun in that?"

Leven shook his head.

"I could have given you pink," Clover said defensively.

"I suppose I should be happy then," Leven joked.

"See, Mister—"

Leven stopped Clover with his dark eyes.

"Right," Clover said. "Maybe we should just go."

Leven smiled weakly, retrieved his stone, and began walking forward. They soon joined others on the path who were carrying stones and making their way closer to the mountain of Morfit.

The wall surrounding Morfit was impressive in size but not in condition. Everything in Foo looked as if it had been built hundreds of years ago and had been crumbling ever since.

The gate Leven was moving toward was manned by four tall rants in orange robes. One was currently turned away from the travelers coming in. The way he was shaking and buzzing, it was obvious he was taking on the shape of a dream and trying to hide from the eyes of others looking on. Leven stared at all the rants in amazement.

"Business, or the result of pleasure?" one of the rants asked Leven.

"I've got a stone to place," Leven answered.

The rant grabbed Leven by the shoulder. "Where's your arm?" he growled, glancing at Leven's invisible limb.

"I lost it in Reality," Leven answered.

The rant looked at Leven's dark eyes and skin, then impatiently waved him through the gate.

Leven stayed silent until he was well within the walls.

"So, they *are* looking for you," Clover whispered from the top of Leven's head. "You're lucky I thought to spray your arm."

"I'm pretty fortunate," Leven joked, slipping close to the base of Morfit and moving cautiously around those souls who were dropping or throwing their stones. The air was filled with the click and scratch of clattering rocks.

Morfit was as imposing as any mountain, town, structure, or person Leven had ever seen. He would have felt less threatened with Terry standing over him, tearing into him as he had so many times before. Up close, Morfit was like a jigsaw puzzle that had been haphazardly put together—rocks and bricks and materials of all kinds had been fused into one massive maze and mountain.

Around its base was a fringe of thick, dry moss and steep trails leading upward that penitents could climb to deposit their stones. The sound of clicking rock was everywhere, along with harsh laughter and agonized screaming.

"I'm not sure I like this place," Leven whispered.

"The wise stay away," Geth whispered back.

The dark night sky seemed to mesh with Morfit, but the burning lights scattered across it gave its shape some definition. From where Leven stood he could see thousands of dimly lit holes and dwellings stacked upon each other. In the circle of each light there were people or beings, talking or fighting or eating.

"Why would anyone come here?" Leven whispered. "It feels horrible."

"Morfit has long been a place of deceit and blackness," Geth answered. "Since the early days of Foo, people have gathered here to argue about the fairness of such a place as Foo and how they can govern a world with so much instability and possibility.

Morfit is also a safe place to get away from dreams, seeing how they can't penetrate the mountain. Rants stay in their current form when they step in. Some rants stay here for years because they like the other half they are currently entertaining."

A stone door flew open near the base of Morfit, and a thick swarm of whisps streamed out, giving the appearance that Morfit was exhaling. The whisp swarm dipped and swooped into the dark night and disappeared.

The stone door snapped shut.

Leven could see a row of small shops, each offering to sell bags for carrying stones. Next to the shops were mounds and mounds of straw for sale, to feed the assorted beasts that transported so many to Morfit.

"The rest of Foo is so beautiful," Leven whispered. "This place even *feels* ugly."

"The dark dreams of men and those who controlled Sabine and probably now control Jamoon have great strength in Morfit," Geth said.

"Who controlled Sabine?" Leven asked.

Geth didn't answer, due to a large group of rants coming their way. The rants all wore robes and were holding kilves that glimmered under the moonlight.

"We have to get out of here," Geth whispered. "Don't let them see you."

Leven spotted a small door. Above the door was a stone head with stone wings behind it. The stone head had a glowing ring in its mouth. Leven stepped up to the door and pushed it open with his hands—his invisible one leaving a sticky residue on the door. Inside was a narrow, dark hallway that sloped upward. Lining the wall were yellow claws, each holding a blue-burning candle. The lights ran along both sides and stretched on for what looked like miles. Leven felt like a plane coming in for a landing.

"Where are we going?" Clover whispered.

"Go up," Geth said.

The lights on the wall seemed to draw them in. Leven looked down and could see bits of feather and bone littering the dirt floor. The walls of the chamber were constructed of uneven stone, with the claw-held candles protruding every ten feet. In each claw was a fat, blue, glowing candle that whispered in insecure fear as it burned.

"Look away."

"Let me burn."

"I'm trying."

Leven ignored them all, moving deeper into the belly of Morfit. There were no doors or windows or alternate chambers. Leven turned and realized that the candles gave the illusion of multiple directions. After he had gone a few feet, Leven had no idea where he had come from or where he was going. And, most distressingly, he could no longer feel the pull of Winter's fear.

"This isn't right," Leven whispered to Clover.

"That's true, we're going left."

"No, something is foul."

"Sorry," Clover apologized. "I may have held onto the vapor stick a little bit longer than I should have."

Leven wasn't listening. He turned and began to make his way in the other direction. The candles were singing a different tune now.

"Wrong way," they mocked.

"Turn around."

"Lost?"

Leven spun and looked behind him. It appeared to be one long tunnel, stretching endlessly in both directions. But he couldn't tell if he was heading out or in. Even the floor was confusing. It seemed to slant in both directions.

Clover sounded nervous. "Just pick a direction and go."

The candle flames had turned vicious now, calling out names so unpleasant it would be wrong to repeat them here.

"Run!" Clover yelled.

Leven took off running in the direction he had committed to, not knowing whether he was heading in or out.

As Leven ran past them, the candles began spitting small wads of blue flame at Leven. He felt one land in his hair. Clover yelped in alarm, appeared, and began violently slapping Leven's head in an effort to put out the flame. The candles were shooting so many little torches around, it looked as though Leven were running through a shower of fireworks. A ball of flame fell into his right front pocket and started his pants on fire. Leven beat on his pocket and put the flame out.

"We're not going to make it," Leven screamed.

"Make it *where*?" Clover asked, so confused by what was going on and where they were heading he couldn't think straight. "I think I'm going to be sick."

Leven thought that would add perfectly to the situation. The language coming out of the candles was now so vulgar that Clover was tempted to stop and ask them if their mothers knew they spoke like that. But seeing how candles don't have mothers, and Clover was scared for Leven's life and trying to hold his lunch down, he refrained.

"There's a door!" Leven yelled.

They reached a large, wooden door; it swung open upon Leven's touch. He ran through it, turned, and slammed it, pushing his back up against it, shutting out the candles and their taunting. A few sparks sputtered through the keyhole and then died down.

"What was that?" Leven asked, breathing hard.

"Some people's candles," Clover huffed disgustedly, trying to catch his own breath.

Leven looked around the room they were now in. It was hexagon-shaped with a high, domed ceiling. The walls were covered with large rugs that kept changing the patterns that were woven into them. In the center of the room was a huge, open fire pit. The flame was silent, but flickered gracefully in the warm air. Small furry balls that looked like circular mice rolled around on the floor, to and from the fire, stealing tiny bits of flame, which they carried out of the room through small holes at the base of the walls.

"Is this a good room or a bad room?" Leven asked Clover.

"I don't know, but the fire has better manners than the stuff we just left," Clover responded.

"Well, I'll tell you something I'm *not* doing," Leven breathed. "I'm not going back out that door."

Leven stepped away from the door and began to walk around the room, looking closely at the floor and walls. The small furry balls scattered from in front of him. He looked up and could see an opening where the smoke from the fire was able to rise and exit the room. He couldn't see another door, but the rugs were covering a fair portion of the walls of the six-sided room.

Clover jumped from off Leven's head and onto the floor.

"Who lives in Morfit?" Leven asked, as he examined the rugs.

"Anyone who has the stomach for it," Geth answered. "And a lot of children."

"Children?" Leven questioned.

"Of course," Geth said. "Children who step into Foo had better hope they enter in Niteon or near Cusp. If not, they are usually rounded up and brought here for education. Some of the highest levels of Morfit are used for keeping and teaching children."

"What are they taught?" Leven asked, the idea of children living in such a dark place feeling perverse and depressing.

"They are taught to manipulate dreams in a way that is pleasing to those in power."

"Like Sabine?" Leven asked.

"Exactly," Geth said.

"Do you think we could fit through that hole?" Leven asked, pointing toward the opening in the ceiling.

Clover smiled.

He climbed into Leven's hands and pulled his hairy ears

down over his head, making it look as though he were wearing a swim cap.

"What are you doing?" Leven smiled.

"Throw me," Clover said, nodding upward.

"I was thinking of tying these rugs together and climbing out," Leven explained.

"There isn't time," Clover insisted. "Besides, how would you tie them together? Now, throw me."

Leven shrugged and held Clover in his two hands that looked like one. Leven pumped his arms and threw Clover as hard as he could up toward the opening. Clover missed the hole by at least three feet, slamming his head against the ceiling and falling back to the floor with a thud.

Leven hurried to his side and kneeled down next to him. "I am so sorry," he said, picking Clover up.

"Don't worry about it, Winter," Clover slurred, calling Leven the wrong name while looking at him. "Hey, did you always have stars flying around your head?" he asked dizzily.

"Great," Leven said, shifting Clover in his hands. "Let's try to tie the rugs."

"No," Clover waved, shaking the cobwebs out of his head. "Maybe I'll see if the fire is strong enough to climb."

"Climb?"

Clover leapt up and jumped above the fire. Instead of falling, he hovered in mid-smoke. Then he grabbed onto the smoke and began to climb the warm air. There was barely enough smoke to hold Clover, but he eventually made it all the way to the hole.

"Why didn't you do that in the first place?" Leven yelled up.

"I didn't think the fire was strong enough to hold me," Clover yelled back.

"Should I try to climb it?" Leven asked.

"No, you're too heavy. Let me find something to throw down to you."

Leven waited a few minutes before he heard the sound of something loud scraping against the ceiling. A few moments later there was a large stick being lowered down. The wooden pole was long, with thick, twisted, bulging knots on it every two feet. It was cold and wet, but long enough to reach from the floor to the ceiling.

Leven wasted no time scaling the stick and climbing up through the hole. It reminded him of the stiff ropes he'd been forced to climb in gym class.

"Good job," Geth said as he reached the top.

"Where'd you find that stick?" Leven asked as he stood.

"It was over behind that rock partition," Clover explained. "I think they use it to push things through their pipes."

Leven wished he hadn't asked.

"Let's go," Leven said, reaching out for Clover.

Clover looked at Leven's hands and ewwed. "No offense," Clover said, hopping onto Leven's back.

"None taken," Leven replied, wiping his damp hands on his high-water pants.

"Where to now?" Clover asked.

"Up," Leven answered.

CHAPTER THIRTY-FIVE

THE FUEL OF FEELINGS

L even climbed the stairs three at a time. He could feel the pull of Winter again; she was somewhere up above them.

Leven climbed the stairs four at a time.

He reached another floor and ran down a hallway with open arches toward another flight of stairs.

"Do you know this place?" Leven asked Geth, the lighter streak in his hair glowing from the moonlight that seeped through the arched window.

"Yes," Geth said. "Behind that wall is a staircase. They must have Winter in the Want's room at the top. But walk softly—the council room for the Sochemists is at the head of the stairs."

"The Sochemists?" Leven asked.

"They do nothing but interpret and argue over information any Lore Coil might still be passing. They never agree on the warped and incomplete things they hear, but Foo takes their interpretations seriously."

Leven moved down the open hallway and toward the stairs. Soon he could hear voices coming from the room next to them.

"I'm telling you. He is alive and well," a voice yelled.

"Ridiculous," a different voice yelled back.

A third voice responded loudly, "The coil said nothing about him being well. Maybe you should open your ears next time, Fadium."

"Oh, you haven't heard a coil correctly in years!" he argued back.

Leven tiptoed past the door to the Sochemists' room and then began running up the stairs, taking them three at a time. After the equivalent of five floors the stairwell ended, opening into a small alcove off a long hall. The alcove was dimly lit with candles that hummed softly, and the walls were lined with large paintings depicting the first age of Foo. Leven looked at the pictures and could feel emotion over each scene.

"It was a dark time," Geth said, sensing his interest in a picture of a large group of men and beasts gathered on a field.

"I can see metal," Leven said, touching the picture. He withdrew his hand quickly, not liking the uneasy feelings the painting generated.

"Of course," Geth said, "before the great battles, metal was widely used. Now metal only exists in dreams or on the Thirteen Stones."

Leven moved farther down the hall and stopped at a gigantic

mural that depicted a great battle. All the combatants were depicted wearing blindfolds. Leven touched the mural and shuddered from the pain it produced. He pulled his hands away.

"They fought blindfolded so that the killing wasn't intentional and death could occur," Geth explained softly. "Those days were as dark as the ones we have yet to go through."

The candles began to weep.

There were paintings of the mangled bodies of Eggmen scattered along the shores of the Lime Sea. Next to that picture was one of the Waves of the Lime Sea retreating to guard Alder.

"Is there any hope?" Leven asked reverently.

"Of course," Geth insisted. "There must be for you and Winter—for all those around us, and for those in Reality. Few understand how connected we all are, or how our happiness comes as much from the experiences of others as it does from our own."

Leven continued to move down the hall. He wanted to run away, but the paintings seemed to draw him in.

"What is this place we are standing in now?" he asked.

"A forgotten arm of the school," Geth said with disgust. "For many years they taught history here. Now it is nothing but an unused museum of things we would like to forget, but will soon remember as we do them all over again. Winter was taught here."

"She was?"

"Sabine himself picked her to lead his noble cause," Geth said sarcastically. "I now believe that he tricked her into finding a way to steal gifts."

"Jamoon can steal gifts?"

"That's what Sabine was trying to do when I was put into a seed," Geth said. "From what I could make of the Lore Coil, they were successful."

Leven came to a stone staircase. The stairs were so infrequently used that they moaned beneath his weight as he climbed them.

Leven stopped and closed his eyes. He turned to Geth and shook his head. "I've been feeling Winter's fear pulling me closer," he said. "Now I can feel nothing."

"Let's hope we're not too late," was Geth's only reply.

Things didn't feel all that hopeful.

CHAPTER THIRTY-SIX

OPENING YOUR EYES

L even was spent. His short time in Foo had been exhausting. And now he had climbed so many stairs his legs were burning with pain. The path to the top of Morfit was winding, dark, and endless.

Outside, a strong wind had begun to howl in and around the mountain.

Morfit rumbled.

"What's that noise?" Leven asked.

"It's getting ready to rain," Clover answered.

Lightning flashed outside and tiny bits of white light glimmered, for an instant making the room look like a disco. Two seconds later, thunder boomed.

Thunder in Reality is pretty straightforward—it grumbles and fades. In Foo, however, the thunder roars awful and insulting words.

"Did it say something?" Leven asked.

"Just ignore it," Clover said.

Lightning flashed again, and thunder roared its vulgar response.

"That's harsh," Leven said, having heard something in relation to his IQ. "Is it talking to me?"

"Everyone hears something different," Clover said. "Keep going."

"What do you hear?" Leven asked.

"Oh, it loves to call me fat," Clover mocked. "It knows that bothers me."

More lightning and thunder.

"Hey, I'm the perfect weight for my height!" Clover yelled back.

"I thought you said to ignore it," Leven said, though the thunder was making him feel less than capable himself by commenting on his complexion.

Clover grunted.

"How much higher?" Leven asked. "And where is everyone? We haven't passed a soul."

"Nobody climbs this high," Clover shivered. "Bad things happen at the top of Morfit."

"Bad things?"

"Unspeakable things," Geth added.

Lightning struck again and thunder sounded.

"Oh, yeah?" Clover hollered, shaking his fist. "Say that to my face!"

"What kind of unspeakable things?" Leven asked, genuinely

concerned. "I mean, it might be a good idea to know what we're walking into."

"I've heard they've found a way to dispose of people," Clover said. "It's even rumored that they know the secret of sycophants."

"What secret?" Leven asked.

"How to get rid of us," Clover shivered.

"I thought nobody knew—" Leven stopped talking so as to better read what he was seeing. Up the stairs, a few feet from where he stood, was a closed door with weak, white light spilling out from underneath it.

"That's it," Geth whispered weakly. "The White Room."

Lightning flashed, followed by another wave of rude thunder.

"I'm not sure I can do this," Leven admitted, feeling tired and spent. "What if Winter's . . ."

"Don't even think it," Geth said. "You can do this. Foo needs you. You'll soon understand that the future belongs to those who believe in the beauty and power of their dreams. This is for so much more than you can now comprehend. Remember that feeling of fate."

Clover patted Leven on the shoulder.

Leven closed his eyes. He had changed, and he just needed his mind to believe it. Moving up the last couple of stairs, Leven reached out and took hold of the door handle. He held it in his hand for just a moment and then pulled it down.

Without a sound, the door slowly opened. Inside the room, a cylinder of bright light shone from the ceiling. Within it, lying on the floor, was a girl with red hair.

Leven blinked and looked more carefully. Then he leapt into the room and ran to her side. He knelt beside Winter and lifted her head into his lap with his invisible hand. She was covered in blood, and her clothes had been ripped to shreds.

"Winter," Leven whispered. "Winter."

She didn't respond.

"Is she alive?" Clover asked.

"She's breathing," Leven said, pushing her hair back from her face. "But just barely."

Leven glanced around the room. The walls and ceiling were lined with white tile. There were hooks along the walls and small, feather-covered tables beneath the hooks. In the middle of the room sat a machine. It was large, with a black leather seat and tall, thin metal handles that turned out like scythes. A thick chain lay near a footrest, and there were iron clamps where someone's hands would go. A blue splotch of light crawled up and down the handlebars like a fat caterpillar. Next to the machine stood a black-robed being Leven had never actually met, but one he had fought before.

Jamoon said nothing but simply stood there, using his lone right eye to glare at Leven. Next to Jamoon was the large roven that had helped destroy Amelia's house. The roven was still mostly hairless, although there were spots where new hair was beginning to grow in.

Leven wasn't happy to see either of them, but he was even less thrilled about what else was in the room.

Up near the ceiling, thousands of black nihils were circling.

Their beaks were silent, but their wings rustled ominously.

Leven's body began to burn with anger. He gently lowered Winter to the floor and stood tall. He no longer felt fourteen. He felt as though he had lived two lifetimes in the short while he had spent in Foo. He looked to be missing an arm, but he felt complete. He felt like he was back in school, confronting the bullies—only this time he faced something much more sinister.

"Look how ripped my abs are," Jamoon's body-building side bragged.

Jamoon sneered at his own left side and pulled his robe closed.

"What have you done to Winter?" Leven demanded.

Jamoon cackled. "It seems she was stronger than I had anticipated. She's alive—for the moment. Something I won't be able to say about you soon."

Jamoon gestured, and the nihils descended violently upon Leven. They pressed him to the ground, pecking at his closed eyes and body. Leven yelled, trying to swat them off, but there were too many to resist. Geth worked himself out of Leven's pocket and tried to skewer the nihils with his pointed head. But before he could do so, one of the nihils clamped its beak down on Geth. It shook him violently, then rose from the fluttering pile and flapped to Jamoon.

Jamoon smiled, reaching out to pinch Geth between his fingers.

"Enough!" Jamoon ordered his birds. "I have what I want."

The nihils stopped fluttering and pecking but continued to

hold Leven down with their tiny talons. Leven looked at Jamoon.

"The great Geth," Jamoon laughed, holding Geth in front of his face. "Your fate has certainly put you in a pathetic state."

"You know nothing of fate," Geth said calmly, feeling the final bits of his small body hardening. "You can't win."

"Can't I?" Jamoon seethed.

"Give him back," Leven demanded. "I'm the one you want."

Jamoon looked at Leven and dropped Geth to the floor. Before Leven could even register what was happening, Jamoon lifted his right leg and brought the heel of his boot down hard on Geth.

"No!" Leven screamed, willing his gift to come to him so he could do something. "Leave him alone!"

The nihils were still holding Leven down.

"How sweet," Jamoon hissed. "How touching. You care for a toothpick. We will find a way to merge Foo and we will take the gifts of every nit to use as we please in Reality. And there is nothing Geth"—Jamoon stomped his foot again—"or you can do about it. The dreams of mankind may die, but ours will be fulfilled."

Jamoon's birds closed around Leven's neck and squeezed.

Jamoon raised his foot and slammed it down again. Geth screamed out. Leven fought against the nihils' hold, but there were too many of them.

"Good-bye, Geth," Jamoon chortled. "As for you, Leven, you have no power in this room. Your gift is useless here. And soon, we will have it permanently. It appears that Winter was the perfect draw."

Thunder struck.

Leven's head felt full of tar, every thought sticking to the next. Leven had understood Jamoon's taunt about him having no gift in this room, but he could feel his abilities percolating beneath his skin and about to erupt.

Jamoon moved toward Leven. He waved the nihils out of the way and yanked Leven to his feet, then dragged him toward the machine in the middle of the room.

Winter stirred. Her eyes blinked as she lay on the floor and watched what was happening.

"No," she whispered. "Clover, are you here?"

Clover appeared on the floor by Winter. He tried to comfort her by petting her hair as she watched Leven being hauled away.

"Pull the switch," she whispered to Clover, "before Jamoon ties him in the seat."

Clover glanced at the machine and spotted the large blue switch on the side. He had no idea what it did, but he wasn't about to second-guess Winter. He jumped up and raced across the room. Jamoon was about to place Leven into the machine's seat when Clover reached the switch and hit it as hard as he could.

There was a loud pop, and a jolt of energy blew into the wall, cracking a large section of tile. Light rained down like confetti, swirling around the machine. In the unexpected flash, Jamoon let go of Leven and staggered back as wind began to push in through the broken tile.

Clover appeared, smiling as the air whipped past him. Jamoon spotted him and hit him with the backside of his right hand, sending Clover flying into the wall.

"No!" Leven yelled.

Leven closed his eyes and let fate settle over him. He then looked up, his eyes beginning to burn.

"It's about time," he said to himself.

His body shook and his muscles rolled, like a monstrous wave rising up from the sea to crash on a shore. Leven looked down at the one hand that wasn't invisible. His gray skin and black fingernails on his visible arm were trembling like coins on an active train track. Light shot from his fingertips and burst from his skin. The light in his eyes began to swirl like a tornado of fire, dispelling the black brought on by Clover's Pigment-o and shining across the room like spotlights.

Leven turned and moved toward Jamoon, and Jamoon gasped at Leven's glowing eyes.

"Your gift works?" he hissed. "Impossible!"

"Impossible is not a word," Leven said, echoing Geth's frequent saying.

Leven pointed his right hand at the cowering Jamoon, and light flashed from his fingers, striking Jamoon in his chest and hurling him across the room into the far wall.

Leven stared in disbelief at his own hands, surprised at what he could do. Then, remembering Amelia, he turned his attention to the roven. The great bird screeched and spread its mighty wings. It quickly shed the small amount of hair on its body, which fell to the floor and gathered itself into a dirty mass that surged through the air at Leven. Leven let his eyes burn, staring intensely at the hair as it rushed toward him. Every strand caught fire under his gaze, creating a fiery net that disintegrated in a shower of sparks.

Ashamed, the roven covered its naked body with its wings and turned away.

The nihils screamed and swooped wildly above everyone.

Leven closed his eyes and began to manipulate and draw in any existing wind he could envision. Air raced in through the hole in the ceiling and the crack in the wall, filling the room with noise and swirling currents, which suddenly reversed themselves, rushing back through the hole, creating a giant vacuum.

Leven opened his eyes to see Jamoon and his roven clinging desperately to anything that would hold them down. But the suction was too strong. It dragged Jamoon across the floor as the roven dug in with its claws and remained standing in shame in the shadows.

With a glance, Leven directed the wind away from Winter as she lay there nearly lifeless on the floor.

The vacuum gathered the nihils into the center of the room, sucking them into a swirling mass, suspended above the floor.

Satisfied that he had them under control, Leven stood in front of them as the terrible wind held them there.

Leven lifted his hands and stared at the decaying birds in awe. He had come a long way from the trailer park in Burnt Culvert. He was also a different person from the one who had stepped through the gateway with such doubt and lack of confidence. He finally understood Geth's insistence that "Impossible is not a word."

The wind tore in and out of the room, morphing and manipulating the nihils until their blackness took on a new form. The ragged form of Sabine stared at Leven with its tiny white eyes, the wind still holding it captive.

"Leven," the dead black mass hissed. "Foolish boy."

Leven's eyes burned.

The light was too great; the blackness that was Sabine seethed and writhed as the glory of Leven's stare caused him to wither and shrink. Leven closed his eyes and then opened them quickly. A fantastic flash of light shot out, exposing every inch of the room and rippling out into Foo.

There was one final, horrific scream, interrupted by a loud pop as the nihils and who they really were vanished for good.

On the far side of the room, Jamoon worked himself to his feet.

"You have ruined everything," he screamed. "You have stolen our chance to be whole."

"You're wrong," Leven said calmly, closing his eyes to suck the wind back out of the room.

Jamoon struggled to keep himself from being lifted off the floor. It was no use. Debris swirled around the room like a whirlwind, and like a black spaghetti noodle, Jamoon was suddenly sucked up through the opening.

"Leven . . ." he screamed one final time. "I've only got two percent body fat," his left side added.

The wind and lightning were beating against the tower. Leven could feel the walls vibrating and the floor swaying. It felt as though the top of Morfit wouldn't hold for much longer.

Leven hurried to Winter and lifted her up. She leaned against him, struggling for breath, but finally spoke. For some odd reason he envisioned her saying his name. Instead she whispered, "Geth."

Leven looked around frantically, worried that the poor toothpick had been swept up by the wind.

"Don't worry," Clover hollered, appearing on the left of Winter. "I picked up Toothpick as soon as I could." Clover opened his right hand to reveal Geth lying there. He wasn't moving, but Leven didn't have time to do more than grab Geth and stick him to the still-tacky skin of his invisible arm.

"Thank you, Clover," Winter whispered, smiling weakly. "I'm glad you're okay."

"Frozen," Clover smiled back, giving her another nickname. "I'm fine. Jamoon can't really harm me."

The tower groaned and rocked under the battering of the howling wind.

Leven cast a warning eye on Jamoon's roven and gestured for him to come. The shame-filled bird screeched, remaining right where it was.

"They're not like the onicks," Clover yelled above the noise of the storm. "He's loyal to Jamoon even though he's gone."

Leven looked around frantically as if there might be another solution to their dilemma.

"We have to get Geth to the turrets now!" Leven hollered. "If not, it will be too late for him!"

Clover shrugged his shoulders and strode across the room

toward the roven. The roven looked down at Clover and cocked its head in confusion. Clover swung his right foot and kicked the roven as hard as he could in the leg. The surprised beast opened its beak and screeched. It was just the reaction Clover was hoping for.

Clover leaped up and crammed himself into the giant beast's mouth. The roven choked and staggered around as Clover worked his way down its throat. In a few seconds Clover had taken some control of the roven's body. He walked awkwardly over to Leven.

"Are you sure about this?" Leven yelled.

The Cloven nodded.

Leven hoisted Winter onto the roven's back, then climbed up behind her. He wrapped his legs under the belly of the bird and held onto Winter.

"Fly!" Leven yelled.

The Cloven leaped from the floor and up through the sky-light, out into the dark and stormy sky.

Leven held Winter tight, and she turned her head to him. "Destroy the tower," she said weakly.

"What?" Leven screamed.

"Destroy the tower," she repeated, and fell unconscious again.

Leven looked back at the tower. Knowing that Winter probably wouldn't ask him to do something just for fun, he concentrated his thoughts, manipulating all the wind in the area to gather at this exact spot. He opened his eyes and the wind obeyed, hurtling like a giant wave toward Morfit. The tower swayed but didn't fall.

Still determined, Leven thought of his life in Reality and of the time he had chased two bullies away by manipulating lightning. Leven looked at all the light in the sky and closed his eyes to focus its force. When he opened his eyes, lightning converged from every direction, every bolt simultaneously striking the tower.

That did the trick.

The tower exploded, sending a shower of rocks and debris hundreds of feet into the air.

The Cloven screeched.

"Fly!" Leven hollered again.

The beast flapped its great wings, soaring ever higher.

Leven pulled Geth from off of his sticky arm and looked at his friend in his hand.

"Geth," Leven screamed.

Geth's mouth moved slightly, and Leven leaned in to hear what he was trying to say.

"You did it," Geth gasped.

"I'm not done yet," Leven said, tucking Geth into his pocket and commanding Clover to pick up his speed.

Clover threaded his way through the rain and lightning, his wings beating hard against the stormy air. Winter stirred, but remained out cold as Leven closed his eyes and attempted to see the future. He wanted to see if Geth would survive until they could get him to the flame. He wanted to know if Winter would be okay and where they would all be tomorrow and if they would be safe. But all he could see was confusion and rain playing to the sound of insulting thunder.

Clover made a sharp turn and sped up. As he did so, the key Leven had had tied on a leather string around his neck flew out of his shirt collar. Leven caught it and pushed it back into his shirt as quickly as he could.

Clover put the roven into a steep, diving turn. As he did so, the clouds opened up, and Leven caught a glimpse of Fissure Gorge far below them. The bottom of the gorge looked a million miles away.

In the distance Leven could also see the flames from the turrets.

"Faster!" Leven ordered.

The Cloven beat its mighty wings, then tucked them in, aiming for the pillar of flame.

As they drew closer, Leven could see that the fire was burning in the center of a formation of twelve stone turrets. Each turret was at least fifty feet high and covered with thick purple vines. Near the top of each tower was an opening big enough for a person to stand in, and the fire caused the inner side of each turret to glow orange. Surrounding the turrets was a large circular river. In the far distance, Leven could see the gatehouse and the fence he had slept near.

"Hold on, Geth," Leven said. "We're going down."

If there was a trace of life left in Geth, it didn't show. His features were as still as petrified wood. Leven wouldn't have it; clenching Geth in his palm, he hollered at Clover to fly into the flame.

Clover did as he was told.

The Cloven's giant wings glowed as he entered and hovered in the flame. Leven secured Winter under the braided harness and then he dropped off the beast, with Geth in his palm, down into the fire.

Clover flew off, leaving Leven hovering hundreds of feet above the ground, held up by the strength of the flame.

The fire licked at him, but it did not burn. Leven opened his palm just enough to see Geth.

"You can't die!" Leven yelled. "You are a lithen, and the last heir to Foo. You are Geth," Leven screamed. "You can't die. I need you!"

Leven let go of Geth and watched as he seemed to float in the flame. In a moment the fire caught onto him and ignited his whole body. Leven was tempted to reach out and grab Geth back, but he knew that this was the only chance.

In a few seconds Geth was gone, nothing but light ashes drifting down through the flame.

Leven closed his eyes and let the fire wrap around him and lower him closer to the ground. Leven was descending, as if in a fiery elevator. Remarkably, there was heat, but he didn't burn, and as he got closer to the heart of the flame, it seemed to thicken and absorb his fall. In a few moments Leven was low enough to jump from the flame to the ground.

He stood to the side and watched as the flame slowly diminished and was finally sucked with a swoosh back into the soil until another day. All that remained was a pile of white-hot coals.

There was no Geth.

Leven was pulled from his thoughts by the screams and cries of Clover in the form of a roven. He landed near Leven, and Winter weakly slid off his back and into Leven's arms. Leven held her, propping her up.

"Where's Geth?" she asked sadly, looking at Leven as if she had never seen him before.

"The fire consumed him," Leven said, confused. "Is that what's supposed to happen?"

Winter blinked, barely able to stand. Leven closed his glowing eyes and let the feeling of hope and possibility that Geth had always preached settle over him. Leven's mind was strangely calm. He somehow felt this was a beginning, not an end.

The Cloven screeched, and Leven opened his eyes.

A cluster of red, glowing embers was drifting down through the last wisps of rising smoke.

Leven and Winter stepped back and watched as the embers settled onto the coals, which began to stir and swirl. There was a flash of light, and as it dimmed, Leven could see shapes forming. There were feet and legs and suddenly there were arms. The light returned, shimmering around the body as it came into complete form.

There, standing in the coals, was a man.

"Geth?" Leven whispered, amazed that what he now saw had once been a toothpick.

Geth stepped from the coals and dusted himself off.

Geth was taller than Leven by a foot, and he was smiling

warmly. His blue eyes positively glowed with life. He was wearing a dark green robe over a black suit of leather, and his hair was dark blond and long.

Leven had never seen a more intimidating being. Though

Geth was a man, *beautiful* was the word that came to mind.

"Geth," Winter whispered.

"This feels a lot better," Geth smiled. "Much, much better."

He stepped closer and took both Leven and Winter in his arms.

"You did it," Geth said.

Winter was crying, Leven was trying not to, and Geth was lifting them both, his heart filled with hope again.

Clover tried to walk the roven closer, but he was losing control of the beast's body. Clover popped his head out of the roven's mouth and smiled at Geth.

"You're taller than I remembered," Clover said.

The roven coughed, propelling Clover out of its mouth and onto the ground. The angry beast shook its ugly head, screeched defiantly, and then flew away just as the ground below Leven, Geth, and Winter began to tremble and roll.

The sound of rushing water and splintering wood filled the air. In the darkness, buildings began to rise from the earth all around them. Small homes and shops popped up from the ground like structural mushrooms.

Leven took Winter's hand and steadied himself as the soil folded open and walls formed around them. A ceiling closed itself over all of them, and an old woman was there standing by an oven.

"What's happening?" Leven asked.

"The flame is restoring all that was lost," Geth said. "In a matter of minutes the fight for Foo will be closer to where it was before Sabine cursed me. What you see now is the City of Geth and all who occupied it at the time of Sabine's curse."

"The City of Geth?" Leven said proudly.

Geth just smiled, while through the windows Leven could see home after home popping back up. Leven's heart swelled so large he was afraid it was going to burst and mess up the whole scene. He looked at Winter and saw she was crying.

"Unbelievable," he said, smiling.

Winter could barely stand, but she leaned on Leven and smiled back. She couldn't believe how different Leven looked. He was taller, and looked at least a couple of years older.

Windows and walls continued to form around them as the City of Geth worked its way back to what it once was. People popped up from nowhere, unaware that they had been trapped in a static state. The old woman by the oven simply continued cooking, oblivious to any memory of having been anywhere but right there over the last while.

Geth led Leven, Winter, and Clover out of the house that had formed around them and down to the road. Legions of regal-looking soldiers marched in the streets.

"Amazing," Winter said. "Look, Lev, everything's so lovely."

A bright sun was just rising, illuminating trees and gardens of beautiful flowers, sparkling with morning dew. Cobblestone streets formed, lined with quaint cottages and impressive public buildings. Leven could see the silhouettes of a thousand homes and buildings rising from the ground.

Geth looked down at Leven and Winter. Clover appeared on Leven's shoulder. He had a big grin on his face.

"Remember when you were a toothpick?" Clover asked.

Geth laughed and rested his hand on Leven's shoulder.

Leven had never felt happier.

CHAPTER THIRTY-SEVEN

THE CONSTRUCTION BEGINS

Tim pulled the last of the lumber out of the rented truck.
Then, together, he and Dennis carried the building materials around the gasthaus and to a small abandoned barn not too far from the lake's shore. Tim was still trying to digest the story Dennis had told him earlier.

Foo?

Gateway?

Impossible!

Tim would have walked away from it all, simply thinking Dennis was crazy, but Dennis had known about Leven and seemed convinced a new gateway could be created. Plus, Dennis had shown Tim an angry, bent-in-half, talking toothpick. Tim now figured anything was possible.

Tim and Dennis had traveled to the nearest town and purchased a number of supplies to build a box that they would then place in the water to travel to an unknown destination hidden in everyone's brain. It was hard to believe, but Tim could think of no other explanation for some of the things he had seen and learned.

They stacked the wood up against the barn wall. Tim looked up at the night stars and then glanced down at Dennis, wondering why in the world he was putting so much trust in such an odd individual.

Dennis had on his tattered black robe and his wrinkle-proof pants. On the front of the robe he had placed his bank sticker. Dennis stood as if the entire ensemble made him invincible—his bald head shining under the light of the moon.

"So we build a box, fix it to the lake floor, and swim in?" Tim asked. "That's it?"

Dennis looked confused. Luckily for him, he was wearing Sabine. Sabine hissed up through Dennis's skin and out his mouth.

"We'll need a mismatched piece of ground," he breathed, trying hard to be civil, but sounding like an angry kitten.

Dennis began to writhe and scream. His black robe fluttered and whipped wildly about him. Dennis fell to the ground and lay there perfectly still. Sabine could feel that the last essence of him in Foo was no longer.

After a few moments, Dennis opened his eyes to find Tim hovering over him anxiously. "Are you okay?" he asked, reaching to help Dennis up.

"Fine," Sabine said out of Dennis. Dennis added a small hand wave to make it more convincing.

"So where do we find a mismatched piece of ground?" Tim asked.

Again Dennis looked confused.

Tim filled the silence himself.

"I guess we'll just build the box and worry about that when we get to it," he said enthusiastically.

"Excellent," Dennis hissed.

"I guess it's not too late to get started tonight," Tim added.

Dennis smiled and fought the urge to throw his head back and laugh wickedly. He won the battle with himself by placing his right hand over his mouth and pretending to cough.

Tim picked up a hammer.

CHAPTER THIRTY-EIGHT

THE CALM

L even had never seen so much food. The large table in the center of the room was covered with meat-filled platters and deep dishes of whipped roots and potatoes. Gravy boats drifted among the islands of bread, filled to the rim with dark, savory sauces. Carrots the size of small, closed umbrellas, sprinkled with parsley, lay stacked like wood in a large dish, butter melting slowly over them.

The aromas were delicious.

Leven looked around the table in the immense dining hall of Geth's magnificent castle. Next to him sat Winter. The red had faded from her blonde hair, and she had her green eyes open and on full display as she took in the delectable sights and delightful smells.

Leven took her hand and squeezed it. "You okay?" he asked.

Winter smiled, pushing her hair behind her ears.

It was miraculous that she was even alive. Sadly, her gift had been stolen. It was a terrible thing for a nit to lose her gift, and Leven knew it would take some time before Winter was truly healed. He had already promised her that he would do whatever he could to get her gift back.

Leven looked past Winter to Geth. Geth was busy making up for all the food he had been denied as a toothpick.

Leven laughed, watching him.

He thought of the feelings he had for the small toothpick and the joy he had experienced at being able to see Geth as he really was. Foo felt safer with Geth and his city restored.

Geth had promised Leven he could have a couple of days to rest, but after that they would be leaving Niteon and heading to Lith. Geth felt it was time for Leven to meet the Want.

"Are you getting enough?" Leven asked Geth.

"No," Geth answered, with a full mouth.

"You might want to use your old self to clean your teeth when you're done eating," Clover said from across the table.

In the last couple of days Clover had thought up, and used, every toothpick joke imaginable.

"Have I used that one before?" Clover asked.

"Yes," they all answered.

Next to Clover was an empty chair. It reminded Leven of Amelia. He had known her for such a short while, but he felt like less of a person with her now gone. He hoped wherever she was, she was with Hector and happy. He wanted her to know that as he fought for Foo he wouldn't let her down. She would always be in his heart.

Leven also thought of the whisp he and Clover had found in the woods. In a small way he could relate to her. She had been snatched from everything she knew and put down in a place she had never even dreamed of. He had already talked to Geth about trying to find her. It was another one of the things they had to accomplish.

Jamoon had not been found. He was assumed dead, since his falling had been an accident of sorts. Already the Sochemists had sent out two waves of locusts informing the residents of Foo that all was well and Morfit was still in control.

Geth had been monitoring incoming dreams and trying to figure out if there was any truth to the rumor that someone in Reality was constructing a new gateway. Geth felt the chances were slim, but knew it was possible, if the one constructing it had the right brain. Geth had also reported that so many of the dreams coming into Foo at the moment were showing signs of changes in Reality—buildings moving, planes landing upside down, and huge dirt avalands showing up all over. It seemed as if Reality was showing the first signs of the war it didn't yet know about.

Leven looked down at himself. He touched his new black shirt and could feel the key hanging beneath it. He had still not shown it to Geth or Winter, but he and Clover had studied it for hours. Clover had said over and over that it was probably just a useless key and that Leven should just give it to him to throw away. Leven wasn't falling for it. He didn't know exactly what it was, but he knew he'd be wise to hold on to it.

He had no idea just how right he was.

Leven looked at Geth and Winter and Clover and the empty chair. The sight and smell of food filled his senses to the point where he thought they might burst.

Leven stood and struck his glass with his wooden spoon. All eyes turned to him.

"Just a few weeks ago, I was in Oklahoma, wishing my life was more interesting," Leven said, smiling at each of his friends. "Thanks for making it so full."

Each raised his or her glass, and Geth smiled. "Hear, hear!" he shouted.

Outside of Geth's castle the purple night sky pulsated and the stars cheered.

THE WHISPERED SECRET

Moonlight flooded the room like a heavenly night-light. Leven had never been in a more comfortable bed. Outside his half-opened window the leaves of a cluster of fantrum trees rustled softly in the dark breeze. The trees closest to his window tapped against the top of the glass, as if summoning Leven to sneak out.

Leven wasn't going anywhere except to sleep.

Leven could smell the sweet air flowing in through the window and dancing around the room. The gold glow from his eyes made the black ribbons of breeze visible.

The night felt somehow different. Leven figured it was because Clover wasn't around. Clover had been begging for the last couple of days for Leven to let him return to untie the onick and to go to the tharms' cave and free all the captured sycophants. Clover had insisted that it would take no more than a day, and that if he went invisibly and alone he could be in and out with no problem. Leven had told Clover he could do whatever he wanted, but that wasn't good enough. So, Clover kept on begging. Finally, Leven had *insisted* that Clover go.

Now Leven wished he hadn't agreed.

Leven pulled his thick blanket up and closed his eyes. The breeze outside moaned softly. Leven fluffed up his pillows and repositioned his head. He looked down the length of the bed to where his feet were. He didn't remember ever sleeping in a really comfortable bed. The single bed on the porch where Terry and Addy had stuck him was lumpy and narrow, and the bridge Leven and Winter had slept under was even worse. Now, here he was, these last few days sleeping in a bed bigger than himself with a mattress that could give marshmallows pointers.

Leven sighed, and for a moment life seemed good.

It's funny how fleeting those moments can be.

Sleep settled over Leven like new snow as a soft whisper blew into the room through the half-opened window. The whisper moaned, swooping around the room like an undisciplined tornado.

Leven's tired eyes blinked open, and he looked toward the window as a thick patch of night sky began crawling in. It would have been impossible to see if not for the light color of the walls. The image reminded Leven of the air in Fissure Gorge.

Leven sat up.

Once through the window, the patch stood and slunk along the wall as if it were hiding. But the small amount of moonlight gave it definition.

"What are—"

Leven stopped talking because the whispered secret was tip-toeing closer, unaware that Leven could see it.

Leven was foolish not to act.

The secret stepped closer and stared Leven directly in the eyes. He had been recognized.

Any calm Leven had previously felt was now gone. The secret lunged at Leven, knocking him in the chest and sending him fly-ing backward off the bed. The secret banged in and out of his ears and through his brain like a metal stake.

Leven grabbed at his head and screamed in pain.

He tried to fight it, but there was nothing to grab. He knocked a water basin from a small table and sent it crashing to the floor. The once-buried secret moved off Leven and howled joyfully. Then it whipped around the room and began to slip out the window.

Leven sat there trembling.

Suddenly the door to his room opened, and there stood Geth. He looked around the room and spotted the secret slipping out. Without saying anything, Geth lunged for the window and grabbed hold of the secret's feet. The whispering secret hissed and kicked itself free, pushing all the way out of the house.

Empty-handed, Geth turned to Leven.

"Are you okay?"

"I think so," Leven replied, still shaken by the experience.

"You released a secret?" Geth demanded.

"By accident," Leven said. "I dug it up in the forest, days ago."

"Has it been following you?" Geth panicked.

"Clover had been keeping an eye on it," Leven said in a daze and feeling more frightened than he ever had before. "I didn't realize what it really was."

"What was it hiding?" Geth demanded. "What did it tell you?"

"I can't say," Leven said. He was trembling all over. "I can't tell you."

"Of course you can," Geth insisted. "The whole of Foo will know in a matter of days. Once a secret informs the soul who dug it up, it's under no obligation to keep it to itself. And a secret that strong will tell anyone who will listen."

Leven stood in a panic. "We have to find Clover," he insisted. "Now!"

"Why?" Geth asked.

"Because," Leven moaned, "in a few hours all of Foo is going to know how to get rid of sycophants."

"Sit," Geth insisted, pushing Leven's shoulders down. "You know how sycophants die?"

"I think so. We have to find Clover."

"You couldn't possibly know," Geth said. "That secret is untouchable. It can't get out. If sycophants could be killed, then their lands could be captured. And their lands hide some of the most important tools in Foo."

"Then what was that secret?" Leven asked, still shaking and pointing toward the window it had escaped through.

"It must have been a decoy," Geth said calmly.

"How can you tell?"

"The real secret is locked by key," Geth said. "There's no way it could get out unless you had used the key."

Leven's face went pale. He reached down his shirt and withdrew the key that had been hanging around his neck.

Not since Geth had been pulled from Clover's void had he looked so frightened. Geth touched the key carefully.

"How?"

"It was an accident," Leven said. "We were in the forest."

"The Want must be told," Geth declared. "Tonight."

"And we have to find Clover."

Geth looked down at Leven. "Of course," he said.

Leven stood and glanced at the soft bed he was leaving. It didn't matter; he could think of nothing but Clover. Leven threw on his dark robe and let his eyes burn gold.

He had a secret to stop.

WHO'S WHO IN FOO

LEVEN THUMPS

Leven is fourteen years old and is the grandson of Hector Thumps, the builder of the gateway. Leven originally knew nothing of Foo or of his heritage. He eventually discovered his true identity: He is an offing who can see and manipulate the future. Leven's brown eyes burn gold whenever his gift kicks in.

WINTER FRORE

Winter is thirteen, with white-blonde hair and deep evergreen eyes. Her pale skin and willowy clothes give her the appearance of a shy spirit. Like Sabine, she is a nit and has the ability to freeze whatever she wishes. She was born in Foo, but her thoughts and memories of her previous life are gone. Winter struggles just to figure out what her purpose is.

GETH

Geth has existed for hundreds of years. In Foo he was one of the strongest and most respected beings, a powerful lithen. Geth is the head token of the Council of Wonder and the heir to the throne of Foo. Eternally optimistic, Geth is also the most outspoken against the wishes of Sabine. To silence Geth, Sabine trapped Geth's soul in the seed of a fantrum tree and left him for the birds. Fate rescued Geth, and in the dying hands of his loyal friend Antsel he was taken through the gateway, out of Foo, and planted in Reality. He was brought back to Foo by Leven and Winter.

SABINE (SUH-BINE´)

Sabine is the darkest and most selfish being in Foo. Snatched from Reality at the age of nine, he is now a nit with the ability to freeze whatever he wishes. Sabine thirsts to rebuild the gateway because he believes if he can move freely between Foo and Reality he can rule them both. So evil and selfish are his desires that the very shadows he casts seek to flee him, giving him the ability to send his dark castoffs down through the dreams of men so he can view and mess with Reality.

ANTSEL

Antsel was an aged member of the Council of Wonder. He was fiercely devoted to the philosophy of Foo and to preserving the dreams of men. He was Geth's greatest supporter, and he was deeply loyal to the Council. Snatched from Reality many years ago, he was a nit who had the ability to see perfectly underground. He was a true Foo-fighter who perished for the cause.

CLOVER ERNEST

Clover is a sycophant from Foo assigned to look after Leven. He is about twelve inches tall and furry all over except for his face, knees, and elbows. He wears a shimmering robe that renders him completely invisible if the hood is up. He is incredibly curious and mischievous to a fault. His previous burn was Antsel.

JAMOON

Jamoon is Sabine's right-hand man as well as a rant. Because he is a rant, half of his body is unstable, transformed continually into the form of the dreams being entertained by humans. He is totally obedient to Sabine's wishes. Jamoon believes Sabine's promise that if he and his kind can get into Reality, the rants' unusual condition will be healed.

HECTOR THUMPS

Hector Thumps is Leven's grandfather and the creator of the gateway. When fate snatched him into Foo, he fought to find a way back to the girl he loved in Reality. His quest nearly drove him mad.

AMELIA THUMPS

Amelia is the woman Hector Thumps married after he returned to Foo a second time. She is Leven's grandmother and lives between Morfit and the Fundrals of Foo. She was the protector of the gateway to Foo.

TIM TUTTLE

Tim is a garbage man and a kindly neighbor of Winter. In Reality, Tim and his wife, Wendy, looked after Winter after being instructed to do so by Amelia. When Winter goes missing, Tim sets out to find her.

DENNIS WOOD

Dennis is a janitor whom fate has picked to carry out a great task. He leads a lonely life and has never dreamed.

JANET FRORE

Janet is a woman who believes she is Winter's mother but has no concern that Winter is missing. She has spent her life caring only for herself.

TERRY AND ADDY GRAPH

Terry and Addy were Leven's horrible-care givers in Reality.

THE ORDER OF THINGS

CHILDREN OF THE SEWN

The Children of the Sewn live beneath and amongst the roots of the Red Grove. They are patched together from dreams and imaginations. They are the only framers in Foo. Their task is to frame the strong dreams so that they can be focused on and achieved, and to frame the darkest dreams so that they are contained and stopped.

COGS

Cogs are the ungifted offspring of nits. They possess no great single talent, yet they can manipulate and enhance dreams.

EGGMEN

The Eggmen live beneath the Devil's Spiral and are master candy makers. They are egg-shaped and fragile, but dedicated believers in Foo.

FISSURE GORGE

Fissure Gorge is a terrific gorge that runs from the top of Foo to the Veil Sea. At its base is a burning, iridescent glow that creates a great mist when it meets with the sea. The heat also shifts and changes the hard, mazelike air that fills the gorge.

GIFTS

There are twelve gifts in Foo. Every nit can take on a single gift to help him or her enhance dreams. The gifts are:

See through soil
Run like the wind
Freeze things
Breathe fire
Levitate objects
Burrow
See through stone
Shrink
Throw lightning
Fade in and out
Push and bind dreams
Fly

LITHENS (LIE´-THUNS)

Lithens were the original dwellers of Foo, placed in the realm by fate. They are committed to the sacred task of preserving the true Foo. Lithens live and travel by fate, and they fear almost nothing. They are honest and are believed to be incorruptible. Geth is a lithen.

LORE COIL

Lore Coils are created when something of great passion or energy happens in Foo. The energy drifts out in a growing circle across Foo, giving information or showing static-like images to those it passes over. When the Lore Coil reaches the borders of Foo, it bounces back to where it came from. It can bounce back and forth for many years. Most do not hear it after the second pass.

NIHILS (NILLS)

Nihils are black scavenger birds that pick at the leaves and bark of trees, searching for and eating small bits of leftover dreams that have settled in the trees. They are aggressive and a nuisance.

NITS

Niteons—or nits, as they are referred to—are humans who were once on earth and were brought to Foo by fate. Nits are the working class of Foo. They are the most stable and the best dream enhancers. Each is given a powerful gift soon after he or she arrives in Foo. A number of nits can control fire or water or ice. Some can see in the pitch dark or walk through walls and rock. Some can levitate and change shape. Nits are usually loyal and honest. Both Winter Frore and Sabine are nits.

OFFINGS

Offings are rare and powerful. Unlike others who might be given only one gift, offings can see and manipulate the future as well as learn other gifts. Offings are the most trusted confidants of the Want. Leven Thumps is an offing.

PALEHI (PALE´-HIE)

The palehi are a group of beings who refuse to take sides.

They escort people through the Swollen Forest. They are pale from all the frightening things they have seen. Their arms are marked with stripes that keep count of how many trips through the forest they have made.

RANTS

Rants are nit offspring that are born with too little character to successfully manipulate dreams. They are constantly in a state of instability and chaos. As dreams catch them, half of their bodies become the image of what someone in Reality is dreaming at the moment. Rants are usually dressed in long robes to hide their odd, unstable forms. Jamoon is a rant.

RINGS OF PLAGUE

The Rings of Plague were created by Sabine. There were originally two, but Geth defeated one of them. The remaining Ring consists of eleven nits plus Sabine, each possessing one of the different gifts of Foo. Collectively having all the gifts, they are a threat to most.

ROVENS

Rovens are large, colorful, winged creatures that are raised in large farms in the dark caves beneath Morfit. They are used for transportation and are sought after because of their unbreakable talons. Unlike most in Foo, rovens can be killed. They are fierce diggers and can create rips in the very soil of Foo. When they shed their hair, it can live for a short while. They often shed their hair and let it do their dirty work.

SARUS

The sarus are thick, fuzzy bugs who can fly. They swarm their victims and carry them off by biting down and lifting as a group. They can communicate only through the vibration of water. They are in control of the gaze and in charge of creating gigantic trees.

SIIDS

There were originally seven siids—humongous, mountain-sized beasts whose weight helped balance the landscape of Foo. Siids have the gift of killing and in turn can be killed. Years ago some siids were hunted and killed off, and now many in Foo feel that the unbalance and darkening of Foo are somehow connected to their absence.

SOCHEMISTS

The Sochemists of Morfit are a group of twenty-four aged beings who listen for Lore Coils and explain what they hear. They are constantly fighting over what they believe they have heard. They communicate what they know to the rest of Foo by using locusts.

SYCOPHANTS (SICK´-O-FUNTS)

Sycophants are assigned to serve those who are snatched into

Foo. Their job is to help those new residents of Foo understand and adjust to a whole different existence. They spend their entire lives serving the people to whom they are assigned, called their "burns." There is only one way for sycophants to die, but nobody aside from the sycophants knows what that is.

THARMS

Tharms are short, smelly creatures who populate the Swollen Forest. They have a third arm where a tail would be. They are mysterious and love to capture and bury things in the forest. They also like to ransom those they have caught for favors.

THE TURRETS

The turrets of Foo are a large circle of stone turrets that surround a mile-high pillar of restoring flame. The turrets sit on a large area of Niteon and are surrounded by a high fence. The main way to the flame is through the gatehouse that sits miles away.

THE WANT

The Want is the virtually unseen but constantly felt sage of Foo. He lives on the island of Lith and can see every dream that comes in. He is prophetic and a bit mad from all the visions he has had.

THE WAVES OF THE LIME SEA

The Waves of the Lime Sea are a mysterious and misunderstood group of beings who guard the island of Alder. Their loyalty is to the oldest tree that grows on the island.

WHISPS

Whisps are the sad images of beings who were only partially snatched from Reality into Foo. They have no physical bodies, but they can think and reason. They are sought after for their ideas, but miserable because they can't feel or touch anything.

---◆---

THE ADVENTURE CONTINUES
IN BOOK THREE,
LEVEN THUMPS AND THE EYES OF WANT

---◆---

The stairs took Leven to a small room lit by two glowing candles. At the edge of the room was a large wooden pump with a bucket sitting at a tilt beneath it. Next to the pump was a short wall hiding a deep, rancid hole.

"I miss normal toilets," Leven sighed.

Before Leven left the washroom he ran water from the pump over his hands and looked in the mirror hanging unevenly on the wall above it. He pulled back the hood of his robe and was somewhat surprised at the reflection of himself.

Leven's face was a bit fuller than he expected, and his brown eyes glowed a subtle orange around the rim of the pupils. His hair was long, and the white streak above his right ear was as bright as if it were an active light source. His straight nose and teeth were familiar, but different.

Leven ran water over his hands and pushed them both back through his hair. The few freckles he had were fading. The uneven mirror made his skin look different shades of white.

"You brought us into this," Leven's reflection spoke.

Leven looked at himself in the mirror in surprise.

The image he projected sighed. "Don't act too surprised," it said. "You've seen stranger things in Foo."

Leven touched the mirror, and his reflection smiled a crooked smile. Leven pulled the mirror away from the wall and checked out the back of it.

"You always were slow to believe," his reflection said. "Of course, now that you are in Foo, you are forced to believe simply by being here."

"How are you speaking?" Leven asked, glancing intently at himself in the mirror. "Those aren't my thoughts."

"Why would they be?" his reflection snapped. "I might look like you, but I have a mind of my own."

Leven's reflection sighed another heavy sigh. "I have stared back at you for so many years," it said. "Never able to speak. Now you're standing before me and I finally have a voice."

"How is it possible?"

"This is a reflective mirror," the reflection said. "It allows me to reflect in more ways than just image. You're taller now."

"I guess I am," Leven answered, looking away from the mirror and down at himself.

"There's no guessing," his reflection said. "You are taller. Experience has made you grow. Normally we reflections have time to stretch ourselves out to keep up with your growth, but you are moving so fast."

"Sorry," Leven said.

"No matter." His reflection waved. "What's with your eyes?"

"What do you mean?"

"There's gold around them."

"I'm not sure what causes it."

"I like it. And the white in your hair seems more pronounced."

"It needs to be cut."

"So who's out there with you?" Leven's reflection said, trying to see around Leven and get a better look at the room behind him.

"No one."

"No Clover? No Winter?"

"I don't think Winter would be caught dead in here."

"Of course," the reflection said, sounding more proper than Leven would ever be. "How does Foo fit you?"

"I'm adjusting," Leven answered. "I hardly think about my life before it."

"What life?"

"Exactly," Leven said. "Sometimes I wake up here amazed to be in Foo. There have even been moments when I've longed to be back in Oklahoma and not having to go through what is happening here. But when I think of what my life was like, I know instantly that no matter how hard it gets here, fate has still dealt me a far better blow."

"Thanks for stating the obvious," Leven's reflection snipped. "I assume you're not traveling alone?"

"Geth and Winter are here."

"Sounds like a kind of gum," his reflection said smartly. "So, do you still have the key?"

"Of course," Leven said.

"Let me see," the reflection said with hushed excitement.

Without thinking Leven pulled the key up out of the top opening of his robe. It hung around his neck on a long string of leather. The key sparkled under the light of the torches. His reflection reached to touch it, but was stopped by the glass.

"Flip it over," Leven's reflection said.

Leven flipped it in his hand. "I wish I'd never found it," he said seriously. "I'd rather it were lost for good."

"Still," his reflection salivated, "it's a beautiful thing."

Leven squinted at his own reflection. "I'm not sure I like this. I feel like I'm talking to myself."

"Well, you have little choice in the matter," his reflection said, standing up straight. "I am who I am, and there is really no way for you to change me."

"Really?" Leven said skeptically. "No way?"

"Well, there's always a way, but it—"

Leven's reflection stopped speaking as an Eggman stepped into the washroom. The Eggman looked at Leven and grunted. A white, greasy substance leaked out around the rim of his yolk-colored lips.

"Hello," Leven said.

The Eggman looked at Leven. He then looked at Leven's reflection. "I've never really cared for mirrors," the Egg said. "I can't stand what I see looking back at me."

Leven looked at his reflection again.

The Eggman pulled what looked to be a splintered twig from his pocket and ran it through the three or four tangled pieces of thick hair on his head.

Leven stared.

The Eggman was amazing-looking, but not necessarily in a "pleasing-to-the-eye" way. The small bits of skin Leven could see were mushy and thin. His body looked like a white balloon that had been filled with oatmeal. His face was wide and spread out, with a pronounced curvature that kept his left eye from view.

Leven pumped some more water over his hands as the

Eggman moved into the washroom stall. As Leven stepped back from the pump, a small orange rag hanging from a hook near the mirror leapt over and wrapped itself around Leven's hands. It twisted around and up, drying both hands off quickly. It then sprang back and settled on its hook.

Leven smiled.

Leven turned, pushed through the door, and ascended the dark stairs. He pulled his hood back up over his head and stepped quickly. The stairs were poorly lit and cold; wind buffeted him from every direction. Each footstep Leven took created a brittle echo off the stone walls.

A thin voice drifted through the cold air.

"Leven."

Leven stopped to listen.

"Closer," the voice whispered. "Closer to me."

Leven turned to look back down the stairs. The door was shut, and there was nothing there. He could faintly hear the Eggman still in the washroom singing a song about a walrus.

Leven took another step up.

"Closer," the voice sounded again. "Closer to me."

"Who's there?" Leven called out.

A warm wind parted the cold. It wound up the stairs and brushed past Leven like a good memory in the midst of a bad event. The only light came from the faint glow of a single candle down by the washroom door and one up at the very top of the steps.

"Is anyone there?" Leven hollered.

There was nothing but darkness in the rafters above. Leven took another step.

"You're coming closer," the voice hissed. "That's good."

Every pore on Leven's body opened, and cold air rushed in to fill them. He shook and looked up toward where the voice had come from. He could see a blue blur shift in the air and thump down against the stone stairs. The blur raced past him and down to the washroom. Before Leven could turn around, the candle outside the washroom door was snuffed out, making the stairwell even darker. The wooden bolt slid into locking position, leaving the Eggman trapped in the washroom.

Something brushed against Leven's right leg. It circled up around his waist, spinning Leven as it moved.

"Geth! Winter!" Leven hollered.

"Geth! Winter!" the voice mocked. "Geth! Winter!"

Leven pulled his hood tighter and glanced up toward the ceiling. He motioned as if to move farther up the stairs.

"Don't move," the voice insisted. "There is nothing but you and me."

Leven wanted to stare directly at whatever it was, but the words of Geth to hide his eyes stuck in his mind. The cold bullied the single candle flame at the top of the stairs and pinched the light out.

There was nothing but darkness now.

Leven stood still. He could hear whatever it was breathing long and slow, almost directly above him. It lowered to the level of his right ear. Leven brushed at it as if it were a flea. "Who are you?" he demanded.

"I think you know," the voice whispered.

"The secret," Leven guessed.

"Of course. I've been waiting for you," the secret answered, its reply the sound of a long burp.

FOR FANS OF LEVEN THUMPS

I have met very few people I didn't like. There was that one fellow with the long, sharp knife, and that tall woman with the beyond-bad attitude, and of course all those who fight against Foo, but for the most part I find people agreeable.

That is not the case with Terry Graphs. He is despicable, mean, cruel, and—on the occasions when I have had the misfortune of being near him—smelly. So it was with some concern and yet great excitement that I contacted him after seeing what he had posted for sale on eBay. His ad read:

> Old dumb book—wife thinks it's worth something. Written by Foo, or a professor, or a sycophant, whoever that is. Found on the Oklahoma prairie not far from where our house was demolished. I personally discovered it while picking up the pieces of the single-wide I still owe on. You tell me what you'll pay for it and we might have a deal.

I flew to Oklahoma and happily bought the book from him for thirty dollars and the silver watch I was wearing. Terry had no idea what he had found or what he was selling. He also had very pungent breath.

I have studied the book for many months now. The best I can figure is that sometime during Clover's stay in Reality it fell from his void, or perhaps he was looking at it on the prairie and foolishly left it behind. Either way, we are lucky. There are many things about Foo and the sycophants that can be gleaned from it.

Read it carefully. It is a tremendous glimpse into the mind and life of Leven's faithful friend Clover.

Fate was kind to drop it in my lap. Of course, luckily for all of us, fate seems to favor Foo.

Obert Skye